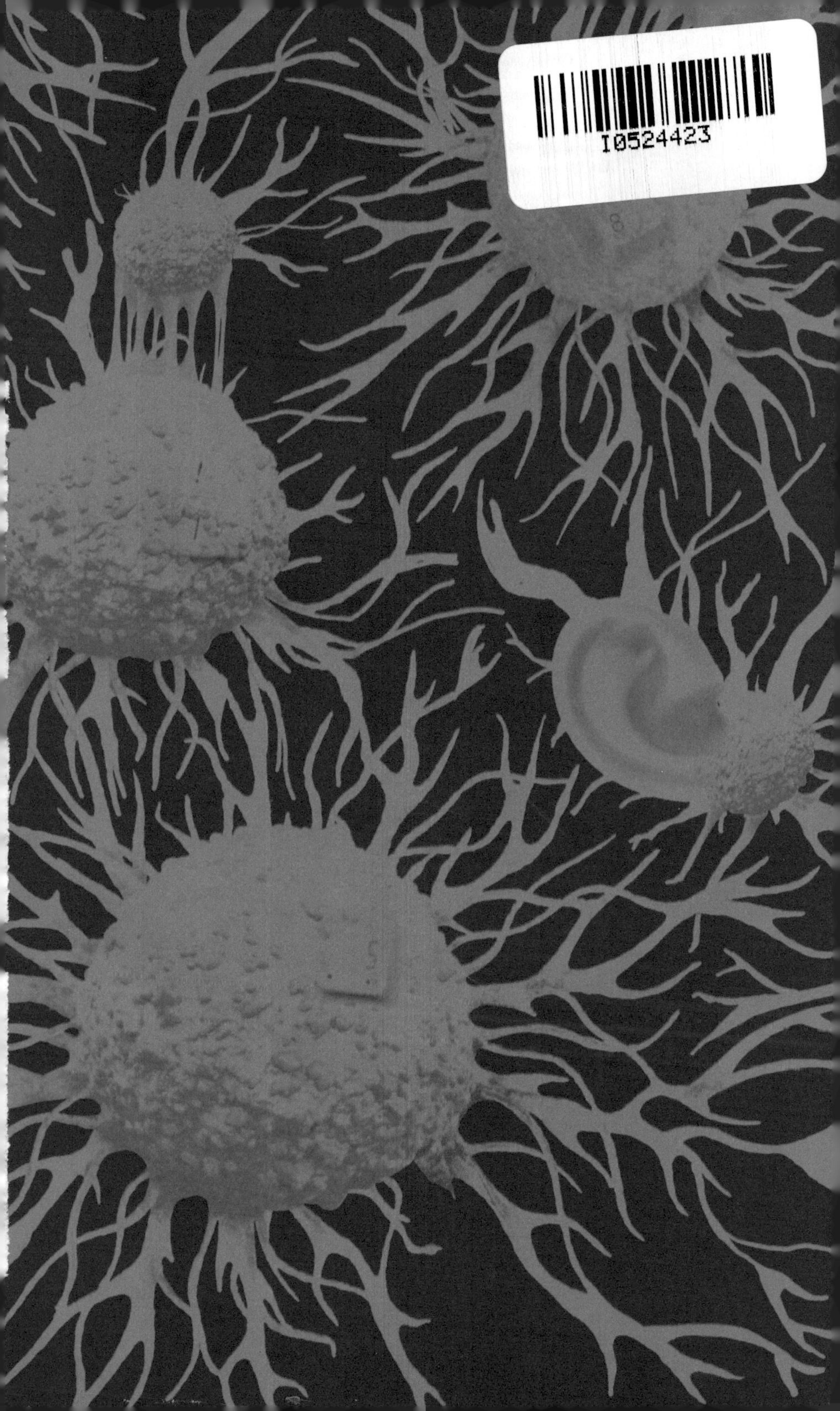
I0524423

# FICTIONAL REALITY: A NUCLEAR KID IN EMBRYO

## OR A PROCRASTINATORY APPROACH TO END A CONVERSATION

ELLIS KROSS PRESENTS . .

# FRANKIE

FICTIONAL REALITY: A NUCLEAR KID IN EMBRYO

OR A PROCRASTINATORY APPROACH TO END A CONVERSATION

First Edition, April 2017
Written by Ellis Kross
Edited by Sidonie Lailler



ISBN: 978-0-9976453-3-0
Kross, Ellis, 1983—
Fictional Reality: A Nuclear Kid In Embryo Or A Procrastinatory Approach To End A Conversation
I. Title. Fiction. Mystery/Thriller

**ISBN: 978-0-9976453-3-0 pbk.**

Story by Ellis Kross
Cover Design by Izzy
Cover Artwork by Dalivia Plaut

This is a work of fiction.
Names, characters, places, and incidents are the products of the author's imagination. Any resemblance to actual persons, living or dead, is entirely coincidental.

Printed in the United States of America



PUBLISHER'S NOTE
This is a work of fiction. Names, characters, places, and incidents either are the product of the author's imagination or are used fictitiously. Any resemblance to actual persons, living or dead, business establishments, events, or locales is entirely coincidental.

SHUT up and listen.

The only way we get out of this thing alive is if we follow the rules.

Remember Fahim's words: *don't let her in.*

Just wait here until help arrives.

Don't make a sound. Don't let her in.

I force myself to focus on the flicker of light, don't think, don't even carry a single thought in your head, don't speak.

See.

Even that, something as basic as seeing, seems like an impossible feat due to a heavy cloak of darkness inside the laboratories. Carnage is decorated everywhere like the remnants of a fever dream, coming in and out of a pulsating light during each violent flash outside the laboratory window; the flashes momentarily bring out puddles of dark blood in short bursts of horror; streaks of bloody handprints come forth below me.

I keep my attention pinned to an area in particular but can only make out a body or two, but even the bodies aren't "all" together; they're chewed up and contorted, unrecognizable. Is she responsible for their deaths?

I slap myself across the face—don't think!

I try to keep my thoughts from venturing into questions, but I end up breaking the second rule—which means I only have a couple of minutes to live before she tracks me down—even then, I'll already be a dead man.

How I go about it leaves me with no answers or solutions to my inquiries, only whether or not I choose to take the easy way out.

In these rare and untimely moments, the thought of picking up the jagged shard of glass overwhelms me; then, as the thoughts play out like a movie and I imagine the scene before my eyes, I end up breaking the third rule yet again.

What would that final moment feel like when all of the misery that I've inflicted, not only to myself but also to others, fades away—*the pain gone! You're dead!*

How easy it would be? To just close the book and say one last final goodnight and kiss this life goodbye.

I even go so far as to grab the shard of glass off the floor; and I nurse it in my hands as if it's something precious, as if it's a life form, fragile and significant.

One thought carries over into the next and as I grip the weapon of my choice in the palm of my hand, an idea—as remarkably dangerous as it might be—comes to me as quickly as the next excruciating breath. . .

It's the *only* way to stop her from reaching the outside.

I rise from my cowered position and stand to my feet. The cool darkness weighs heavily on my shoulders and chest and increases the tension between my broken ribs, now pinching at my every breath. I listen closely for any remaining survivors but all I hear in return is the disturbing calmness of footsteps stomping through the hallways and cutting through the loud, unbiased silence.

Suddenly, a sniffle or sob, I can't distinguish one from the other. Only one continuous stream of nasty rebellion, each thought trying to figure out what happened after the breech, what went wrong—Who are these people?

Mentally, I tell myself again and again.

Three times, it rings like the tiniest pin: *Don't speak. Don't think. Don't blink*

As I muzzle each groan by clenching my jaw, I climb onto another table and pull out a lighter from my pocket. I fumble the light in my hand. My eyes start to burn. My vision, now blurry from the blood and sweat dripping into my eyes.

"Please forgive me, Frankie," I say, wiping my eyes with the backside of my hand.

I locate the spark wheel and ignite the flame. An orange halo cast over the flickering darkness. My face drenched with blood, sweat, and shadows. I adjust the black-rimmed glasses slipping from my nose—my left lens cracked in half but I'm still able to see through the other one—and then I dangle the flame below the sprinkler until water shoots out with a furious spit.

As the water rains down, I ease from the table and stay low to the ground.

"Saul?"

A sudden *thud*, so distant yet so close.

"Jefferson?"

More *thuds*, closer.

On my hands and knees, I crawl along the slippery floors. Marble-sized shards of glass press into the palms of my hands. I ignore the broken glass, ignore whatever toothy things poke or prod at me, ignore each surge of pain—I practically ignore every little thing except for the sounds. My voice falls below a murmur from Frankie stomping through Corridor B.

"Saul? Jefferson? Talk to me. *Please. . .*"

Eventually—finally—a response slips from the darkness. I change direction and move toward the noises—and that's all they are, just noises being made by the mouth of what might be a human.

"Saul? Is that you?"

I make it to the source of the noise.

"Saul!"

I check on my partner. The only thing that remains of him is a torso, the bottom half of his body nowhere to be found; the noises, I conclude after brief examination, are coming from the death gurgle. Strings of frothy blood bubble from the corner of Saul's mouth. I check Saul's pulse. He's gone.

More *thuds* followed by screams acts like a wrench tightening around my gut.

I manage to sneak from the laboratory. I'm welcomed by a brighter strobe light of horror.

The hallway is covered with a messy painting of blood and body parts. Nothing living or dying. All that remains is the aftermath of something awful.

More noises, more cries, more disturbance coming from the other end of the hallway—this time, I know exactly what it is.

Too frightened to move forward, I rush back into the laboratory, grab a digital recorder from the table, and seek cover underneath a desk. I manage to gather myself despite the chaos. I press the record button on the digital recorder.

I embrace a deep, painful breath before speaking into the microphone: *Soon, you're going to want answers as to what's happening around the entire world, the phenomenon, the hysteria, the strangeness in the air. You may be frightened or even uncertain about your place in the world. These are only natural reactions, reminding you that you are still human; however, I must warn you not to fall . . .*

Screams pierce through the darkness!

More flashes of violence.

I pull the recorder away for a moment, grimacing from my injuries.

More cries, more shrieks, more growls.

More violence.

*Do not fall victim to the lies and deception either on TV, on the Internet, wherever it may be. The events that you are going to hear about in the next coming days are merely tactics meant to distract you from the truth. So, I ask you to not give in. Whatever you do—*

The recorder turns warmer in my hand.

*—Whatever you do, don't. . .*

I release the recorder before the buttons soften and melt along my fingertips!

The door to the laboratory suddenly crumbles like a piece of paper and gives way to the disfigured silhouette lurching in the flickering light!

"Frankie?" I say, peeking past the corner of the desk. "Is that you?"

As the strange creature approaches—ready to tear my body to shreds—I curl my body into a fetal position, close my eyes, and brace for impact. The desk is flung across the laboratory!

Now, I'm left vulnerable, ready.

In my final moments, I can't help but wonder how wrong I was about the water.

# PART ONE
## CLOSE TALK

# 1. BEFORE / JUDITH

IT'S starting to happen again, the sleepwalking.

It all starts with me fighting off sleep the night before—usually with a book in hand or something that involves reading or writing, as in me spilling my guts on the little sheep of Central Agatha. Somehow, though, with all the struggles, I drift away. From there, it's all up in the air really. Sometimes, I wake up, startled or scared. My eyes bolt open while I'm curled in bed. At times, I feel confused as to where I am, how I ended up in my bed, hours feeling like seconds. Strange how that works, how the mind perceives time when you're tired. Other times, I'm dumped in places like this, wondering if I'm still dreaming.

I trace the vines climbing along the holey ceiling. Morning sunrays splice through sheets of aluminum and bring to light the dusty emptiness around me.

Where am I?

Honestly, I don't know where I am or what's really going on with me as of lately, whether I'm dying or just fading away.

Whatever's going on, I can feel it starting to take hold, each day growing stronger, like something buried deep within me is trying to force its way out; and each day, it's clawing at whatever good still remains inside me, leaving me with only traces of good.

The air is different, not like the tang of fumes that constantly hovers over Agatha. It's tart like pinesap, and it even sticks to my skin like the forest mist. Nothing seems familiar. I mean absolutely nothing. Everything is ruined and rusty, forgotten like me. The entire building is choked with weeds and the musk of an old factory sits on my face like a spider web. Not sure what used to be here. Whatever it was, I'd say it was something all right. The only artifacts I find are flattened discards of potato chip bags and empty beer cans. Perhaps this used to be a potato chip factory. Even an old brewery. I inspect some more. I don't see any tanks or whatever you call them; though, I find it interesting. I'd like to think that this was a place where things were produced to the public and that people were once trying to make a living in this now desolate establishment. I can recall a lot of places—like this one—closing shop when I was around eight. I can't remember much of anything around that time, only that my dad told me things were getting really bad for some people, things were changing way, *way* too fast—his words—according to my dad, not the good kind of change. I think my dad is like all the others, though, the talkers. They talk about change as if it's a cancer. I don't think it's that bad. He once said in his annoying sarcastic voice that lots of businesses were pushed aside by more "eco-friendly" businesses and neglected by a rapidly moving society. Reminds me of myself, always moving, wondering, searching for something better than Agatha. Half the time, I wish I knew where I was going and what is waiting for me when I get there.

I walk around the inside of the building, putting together the pieces of last night. When did everything go so wrong? When did it all start: my decline.

It could be some kind of phantom illness that somehow skipped generations—last month when I started to get really concerned about the sleeping or the lack of, I decided to ask my grandma, who moved into the yellow room after Grandpa Lynch passed away, if anybody on her side of the family, distant cousin or whoever, was known for waking up in strange places without knowing how he or she got there, but she clearly thought I was on drugs or something—still does. I can see it in her eyes, the way she holds them on me without me knowing. She thinks I don't see her, but I do. I know the rules and how you're supposed to respect your elders even if they're totally full of shit, but how can I respect someone who thinks I'm something that I'm not. Once, I don't know when, but I think I looked forward to seeing my grandparents whenever we visited them in Greensboro. I don't know what happened. After Grandpa died, she changed drastically. She talks different. She even looks different. She hardly changes her outfit or takes showers. She doesn't even put her hair up anymore like she used to. Instead, she lets it hang over her shoulders, scraggly and uncombed like an old outdoor cat. Occasionally, my mother will make her B-effort attempt to take my grandma to the salon to get her hair done. Lately, though, she'll come up with an excuse not to go. So, basically, everything about Grandma Lynch is different. I guess it's like whenever someone loses a loved one they carry a new look, yet it's an old look, like the ones I see in history books. Grandma Lynch is all wrong about me, wrong in every single degree. Once, I smoked a joint with Mary-Kay, and I didn't care for the way it made me feel afterwards. Mary-Kay said she got the joint from some black kid in Creekside who tried to convince her to play spin the gun with him but, knowing Mary-Kay, she was scared to death from even the thought of playing the game, let alone playing it with some kid who lived in Creekside. I think it might've been laced. Mary-Kay said she felt weird, too, like that pre-surgery feeling when you feel mellow at first, then, after about an hour, you can't wait for the drugs to leave your system. Whatever the case may be, that was the last time I ever smoked. I mean, seriously, you can point a gun to my head and I still wouldn't smoke—but Grandma Lynch would never believe me if I told her.

The only other reason I could be sleepwalking is the environment—maybe something our shady power company, Hornet Energy, is putting in the water and emitting into the air. I've never trusted them—still don't—especially after they started burying lines around Agatha. What are they really up to?

I even tried to google what was wrong with me on the Internet, first by typing in what it meant to wake up in strange places and not remember how I got there (What's my diagnosis, Mister MD?), but the search sent me on a holy quest of nothing, dragging me from one forum to another, me scrolling through a maze of columns filled with a bunch of hypochondriacs who spend all day looking for problems with their bodies, as if looking for things like a rash or ache had become a new hobby. I don't consider myself falling into the category of the extremely paranoid, even though I can't help but wonder if something is really wrong with me. Does that make me paranoid? I've given serious thought about seeing a doctor, but I don't trust them, even though everybody I've talked to on forums recommended that I see a doctor after telling them about my condition. One guy, Bob from Wisconsin, thinks something might be wrong with my head, something "neurological." My body is telling me I should seek help as soon as possible; but if I can't trust a doctor, then who can I turn to? Just last week I've found myself waking up in a strange place three times in one week—I actually woke up one time next to a dumpster behind a Food Lion clear across town. A couple of weeks before that, it was twice in one week. All strange places and me not knowing how I got there. I don't know what to do. I feel lost. I feel trapped. I feel like I don't belong here anymore, like I *never* have belonged here. I don't know if I even want to belong here. I'm pretty sure that's what everybody wants in life, to belong, to feel as if they belong to someone or something, like a cause or an organization.

I don't belong to any group at my school. I like some of the girls on my team—Akea or Monica, the only ones who talk to me—but that's about it. Whenever they're not playing lacrosse, they go back to their certain groups, except me. I have no group. It's just me. There's Stew, my coach, who's way cooler than some of the kids at my school. I've never had a coach before, but Stew's not like the other coaches, especially the stereotypical ones on TV. Stew's extremely nice to me, not in an overly sentimental kind of way but more like a father-daughter relationship; in fact, he's the only person who I think understands me. He doesn't judge me or talk down to me, like my dad. He's okay. I don't belong with the Skaters, either, even though there's Kevin, who takes time out of skateboarding to say "hi" to me. I like Kevin, although he's somewhat of a close talker, meaning he gets really close to my face when he talks to me and I can smell whatever food he ate that day. He's like the only boy I know who's actually gone out of his way to make me feel comfortable, despite his funky breath—if I could see myself from the outside, I can't imagine how terrified I must look when I'm around a group of boys. Whenever he's hanging around his skater friends, he acts completely different. He acts like I don't exist, like I'm somehow carrying a deadly contagious disease. It happens all the time with me. When people start to ball up, they start to cling and they do everything they can in order to survive, even if it means pushing other less significant people who aren't a part of their little clique aside. Like me, for instance, finding someone who I might consider being a future friend, then, when they crawl back to the safety of their clique, they change into some other creature. Kevin's not my friend, though. He could be. What qualifies someone to be your friend? Is it as simple as saying hi? I don't belong with the Gamers or Athletes. I've never cared much about video games or sports—surprising, I know, for someone who plays lacrosse. The only reason I'm playing this year is so I don't have to spend another god-awful summer at Camp David. After days of begging, I wore down my mother and came to a compromise with her. She told me if I played a sport or joined a club, I'd be granted a rain check at Camp David this summer. We ended up striking a deal. Besides soccer, lacrosse seemed like the one sport that didn't require much skill or participation. It's not bad, though, even though I don't understand what throwing around a ball accomplishes, except for getting my ass out of yet another summer wasted with plastic friends and lame activities. I mean, really? What's the freaking point? I don't belong with the Blacks, even though there's Rhea and Ebony, who are both on my team. Rhea eats her lunch with me from time to time but it's only because she's trying to impress her insecure friends who walk around with a chip on their shoulders. She can drive me crazy sometimes but she's on my team. I've never confessed to Rhea how much she gets on my nerves, especially when she goes on one of her weekly rants about how white boys touch her hair when, in fact, nobody gives a shit about her hair. The local idiot, Seth Mires, touched Rhea's hair from behind one time when she wasn't looking; it was totally uncalled for but she still can't get over it; and now, every time someone who's not black compliments her hair or even looks at it, she shows an attitude. I don't belong with the Geeks or Cyberpunk kids. I don't belong with the Techies. I don't belong with the Goths. I don't belong with the Emo or String Cheese kids who act as if they don't even know what's going on half the time. Then, there's the Dead Heads who live in their own world. The Thrashers or Gangstas. The Bubblegum kids. I don't even belong with the Writers, even though I like to write and all. Ever since I was twelve, I've been recording every conversation and daily activity that I have done. I guess it's sort of my way of expressing myself without having to actually speak to anybody else. My brother calls it a diary. If he really knew what I've been writing about him in my so-called "diary," then he'd cease to call it a diary. So, with that said, it would be fitting that I belong with Writers or Journalists or even our school's Newspaper Club, but even they carry a waft of pretentiousness that stinks worse than dog shit. It's so sickening sometimes to watch how overly pretentious they can be. How they impose their way of life onto you. Every single thing they do has become political! Give me a break! If you look up the definition of whom they claim to be, the first word you'll see is *open.* But they're not open to anything. I mean, they claim to be so open-minded about everything but mostly the trending topics—the kind of stuff the people of power and money want us "lesser" people to fight over so they get more powerful and rich—yet when other people share a view or opinion that's different from their own, they ignore them; even worse, they make an example out of them by publicly shaming them in front of a mass audience. It's so barbaric it's unreal. Not only that, they'll tell others what to do or what to believe in—practically shove it down their throats only to please their own emotional-driven, self-centered views, as if their way is the only way. Tolerant, my ass! What pigs they are!

The way I look at it: society is no different than school. It tells you who you are, where you belong or where you *should* belong. I find it so freaking hilarious how people try to put other people in certain groups.

If only they knew how dumb they sound.

I wish there were others like me, people who don't belong, people who just want answers. But if there were more people like me, wouldn't that make me a part of a group? Probably. I wonder what group they would put me in: maybe the Outsiders. I'd like that, being on the outside, part of the ones always looking in.

Not like I care or anything but when people look at me, I sometimes wonder what they think of me: quiet, elusive, *creative*—so my mother says (I once heard her whisper that word to one of her wino friends when she was showing off my room during a tour of the house, but I really think my mother was just saying that because that's what all parents say about their kid, right? That their kid is the best at what he or she does. Either that, or she had already gone over her daily wine regimen and was starting to talk from the other places of her body. Whenever her wino friends aren't around, she's always on my back for whatever reason, and it's as if she spends her entire day trying to find a subject to argue with me about, like not doing my choirs or whatever. She gets even worse when she's plastered. Lately, she's been hovering between that fine line of buzzed and drunk. It's like she has to have two drinks before she can act normal. I swear it's like living with Doctor Jekyll and Mr. Hyde. The worse is when she talks about me whenever I enter a room. She'll act as if I'm not even standing in the same room as her. To her, it's like I'm invisible. She really gets me going, but what kid my age doesn't have disagreements with their parents. I mean, weren't we put on this earth to drive our parents mad? What do they know? My mother doesn't know how to use her own phone. She's always bugging me about how to check her email on her phone or how to change her password or how to access her preferences. I'm supposed to take advice from her? No thanks. I can't take advice from someone who doesn't even know how to make a post on MyCircle). I've also been called *creepy*—even psychotic. I once heard someone call me that when I was leaving a smoky room full of strangers. One guy called me an uppity bitch because I wouldn't talk to him when seconds earlier he was demonizing this girl with crutches.

When you're quiet—and when I mean quiet, I mean when you don't talk to anyone not because you're stuck up or "uppity" and you think you're better than others, but because you don't like talking to people because sometimes people can be real assholes—they always fill in the gaps that you can't quite fill in. Sometimes, it's like the words flow right in your head yet when they reach your lips they come out different and not like you intended or even wrote down the night before. For instance, the year before Grandpa passed, we celebrated his eighty-third birthday. I wanted to tell him how much I loved him—I even wrote down the words in my notebook—but when it came down to actually telling him face to face, I didn't have the courage to tell him. So, I ended up buying a *Hallmark* card that was mostly everything I wanted to tell him in person, but I could never tell him in my own words. My words. My grandpa was a man of style. Everyday he dressed as if it was the day he was going to die. When it came down to it, he was a good person who didn't have a mean bone in his body. I'm not saying all people are cruel, but after people like my grandpa have passed, it's just hard to justify that there are still good people out there when everybody is so ugly to each other. They may even make up a story about you that isn't true at all. Trust me. It happens *all* the time.

The one downside about being quiet—well, I mean there are several—but if I really have to tell you the number one downside about being quite is the ridiculous rumors. People say a lot of things about me and none of them are true—at least, not all of them. Once, some freshman kid asked me if I was related to the infamous Bill Ilderton—and if you don't know who Bill Ilderton is, then you've been living under a rock for the past four years. For those of you who don't know Bill Ilderton, he was convicted of the robberies that recently happened across the entire country. Not to mention, the dozen of innocent people who were murdered during his robbing spree. The news branded him as the new age "Billy the Kid" because he was so young—I think like in his twenties or something, but whatever. People actually created a parody account on Chatterz, and he—as in the real-life Bill Ilderton—was trending for two weeks straight on Chatterz. As someone who reads true crime, I followed Bill Ilderton's story, his beginning as well as his ending. I never expected him to continue what he was doing for long. People like Bill Ilderton have an expiration date. For two weeks, he might've been famous and all or the talk of the town, but once his story was over, you never heard his name spoken ever again—at least, whenever kids heard my last name being called out in front of class. It starts with the turning of the head, then the long stares, then the whispering. Sometimes, whenever I'm feeling in the mood, I poke fun at these people—I can't help myself—and I have a little fun with them and act as if it's all true—every word, every rumor. It always blows their mind. Either way, it always keeps them guessing, keeps them wondering: Why is she so quiet? Maybe she's going through depression. Or maybe she lost someone close to her. Maybe she's like, you know, one of those sleepwalkers, which is true, I guess, although I can't really explain what's going on with me.

Sometimes, I wonder if Abe is right about me, about my so-called condition or "lack" of condition or, in his words, my excuse. He thinks I'm doing all of this to get attention. He also thinks I'm using it as a way to get by with everything. I didn't make my bed yesterday: Because my condition. Didn't do my homework: Because my condition. Abe could be right. I don't get enough attention, as I should. He practically owns my parents, tells them what to do, bosses them around. Because he can. He's the older child. The first one. Somehow, the first ones always squeeze in the final word. But whoever said I wanted the attention, though? I just don't like the way I've been treated as of lately. I especially don't like the way Abe treats me, how he's always watching me, waiting for me to screw up, so he can feel tall by telling me how much better of a person he is. People like Abe need people like me, so they can feel good about themselves. I swear I'm starting to feel more like the spare child—actually, you know what? Ever since I could remember I've always felt like a spare—the one that's not as good as the original. Isn't that why parents have two? Just in case the first one slips or falls ass-backwards into drugs or depression, they have this backup child just in case, right? Someone to continue their so-called "legacy."

What a joke?

Abe's what I call the good son, yet he feels like the bad brother whenever he tells me what's good for me, or whenever he does everything right; he eats right; behaves right; he never complains about anything because he doesn't have anything to complain about because everything goes Abe's way. If they could only spend a day in my shoes.

I finally sit upright and try to recognize my surroundings, but, honestly, I have no idea where I am.

As I do whenever I wake up in a strange place, I search for clues. Give me an image—something, anything!

The last thing that I can remember is reading more than my assigned chapters from *Siddhartha.* I've been known to do this from time to time. I've always been good at school, not great, but good enough to get by—at least this was before waking up in strange places, but I'm trying to get to that place I was a year ago where I had a tendency to get ahead and read more than was required; but the only downfall about getting ahead is that sometimes you have to stop and wait for others to catch up. School aside, it feels as if lately I'm getting ahead of myself, waiting for my memory to catch up. I can't remember a freaking thing about last night! I was in my bed reading and then I must've dozed off and here am I, again not knowing how in the world I got here, like my body has time-traveled into another dimension.

I leave the business park and pass a yellow PRIVATE PROPERTY sign stapled on one of the many skeletal trees ripped of bark and ripened with decay. I check my pj's before entering the woods and find hard mud-clumps caked along the bottom of my feet. Another clue.

I walk for about two and a half miles. I've always been pretty good at tracking distances, like whenever I'm walking the track during gym class I always make notes. So I'm a little over two miles in—give or take—until I reach a creek snaking its way through a bed of moss-covered rocks.

This is Benjamin Creek!

That's at least six miles from home.

Six miles!

Last time, I remember, it was three miles.

Yes!

I woke up on the side of the street, again my memory riddled with holes. Mr. Shirley, who runs the local bakery with his wife, Katrina, passed me while I was wandering home and asked me if I was OK. I told him I was fine and that I was just going for a walk, but I know he didn't believe a word I said.

What should I have said?

Just sleepwalking again—if that's what this really is. The last thing I wanted to do was start a conversation about time-travel—or whatever ludicrous idea—with a man who spent his days beating dough. Not to judge and all or jump to any conclusions, but what does Mr. Shirley know about time-travel?

Still somewhat exhausted from the sleep-workout, I trek through the thinning woods until I come across an open road.

I spot a road sign: Knoll Street.

I don't know any street of that name.

A creaky station wagon passes by. I check out the back of the vehicle, hoping to find any clue as to where I actually am. I spot one of those cheesy bumper stickers—you know, the "Proud" parent stickers of an elementary school.

PIEDMONT ACADEMY.

I know a Piedmont Academy in Benjamin Creek. Has to be the same one.

As I continue my journey back home, I come across a red barrette on the side of the road. I pick up the hair clip and look it over and realize after a thorough study that it belongs to me.

Finally, after several miles of walking, I reach Marvin Gates, a road speckled with potholes and unkept single-story houses that—as far back as I can remember—have looked the exact same. This is what most of the people around here call the "black side" of town. Even the blacks know it's the black side of town and they don't take any offense to it, which is something I never quite understood. If I take Marvin Gates and head east for roughly a mile and a half, I'll hit Nimble Valley, which will take me directly into my spit of a town, good ole Agatha. *Good* and *ole*: two words from the commonly used phrases that you hear throughout Agatha, a town that act's as if it's on one never ending smoke break. Population twelve thousand, seven hundred, thirty-seven, and might I say, viciously growing by the hour. Most of the locals of Agatha like it just the way it is—or was, depending on the age. Everybody mostly keeps to himself or herself. Some people stay. Some people move onto better things.

As I'm walking down Marvin Gates, I pass different roads along the way, and it's like reliving history all over again. I haven't been down this road in what feels like ages—I'd say about five good years, back when things made sense even if they didn't, which was fine by me. Make my way down King Boulevard and I'll find myself at April's. She was a friend of mine whom I've known ever since the first grade; but when seventh grade came around, she was bused clear across town to West Davidson. She got a new set of friends. I didn't see her much after middle school. Take that road, 5th Street, and I'll end up at the Promenades, a new shopping center that has a Chili's, Panera Bread, and a Starbucks; and from what I heard, they're about to put in a new Vapor store, which is the last thing Agatha needs. Not too far away from the Promenade, they opened a state of the art brewery, which has drawn in a lot of new people—or transplants.

I make it to my street. My house. Abe has already started to warm up his car.

During the walk home, I tried to come up with a story as to why I've been out all night, but I have nothing.

I'm not much of a liar.

What do I even say?

Do they really want to hear my excuses?

I'll use one that I've used before.

I bump into my dad as he's throwing out the trash.

He's clueless. Half the time, he doesn't even know what's going on with me.

"Hey, honey," he says, unaware that I'm now just getting home.

"Hey," I say and go inside.

He does a double-take as I walk through the garage.

"Are you going to school like that?"

"Haven't you heard?" I reply. "It's the new look."

It's the new look all right: The "I Don't Give a Darn What People Think of Me" look. Hey! It could be trending. If it is, I don't care. I've seen some girls go to school in pj's before. I know. It's absurd, but whatever.

"To each his own," that's what Grandpa Lynch used to tell me before he passed. He was always filled with euphemisms. My grandma once told me a lot people around town wanted him to run for Mayor. He was a good man, personable, which made him unfit to have a career in politics—you know, since all of them are a bunch of lousy crooks.

My dad does his typical "whatever" shrug and keeps moving along as if the last thing he wants to do before he heads out to work is start talking about fashion trends among high school students with his sixteen-year-old daughter.

I dodge Abe and sneak into my room and as I'm washing up for school, I see this grinning face in the reflection of the mirror.

Abe, my brother.

"What do you want?"

"Long night, hey?" Abe says. "Lemme guess. Another case of sleepwalking?"

"Aren't you going to be late for school?"

"You know, if Mom and Dad find out that you were out all night, they're going to put you in a mental hospital."

"Why don't you die already?"

"You first."

"Shut up."

I splash my face and ignore Abe.

"So, when they do find out, can I turn your room into a study?"

"You wouldn't!"

I spin around, my face still covered with soap and water.

Abe finds amusement in my appearance.

"If you say a word to them, I'll shave your eyebrows while you sleep!"

"All right," Abe says, backing off. "Geez!"

I slam the door in Abe's dumb face. I can hear him deliberately stomping away, like he always does when things don't go his way.

I face the sink and finish washing my face.

I dry my face with a towel and can't help but look at my face in the mirror.

What am I turning into?

What if I reach a point where I can't control myself anymore?

What am I going to do?

## 13. AFTER / JUDITH

I'M back in the same stuffy room as before. I've answered all of their questions about what happened, but they continue to ask the same questions, as if they're trying to catch me in a lie. What if I give them the same answers but worded differently. Will I catch them in a lie? I mean, if what the Roger guy said did happen to those people during our first conversation, did something happen to me—I mean, physically, is something seriously wrong with me? Am I in a coma and now trapped inside my own head?

The slam of the door shakes my bones!

Another middle-aged man enters, not Roger. His face is browner, model-thin with a dark, spotty beard, which looks as if it he shaves with a sharp rock. He tells me that his name is Doctor Fahim Ahmad, and I can tell from the look on his colleague's face that they've recently had a disagreement. I don't know how exactly I know these things. Perhaps I have a keen observance to thank for that. The other one—Sy is what he calls himself—is acting more differently than he did the first time around. He's nervous but definitely not as uptight as this Fahim guy—even the way he speaks underneath a tremble in his voice suggests a lot about his character.

Sy asks me how I'm doing, asks me if I'm experiencing any headaches or blurry vision or any lightheadedness. I'm sure it has something to do with the episode I had after the whole shootout.

I shake my head "no" to each question.

Fahim interrupts Sy and asks me to look directly into the camera and state my name for the record?

"But you already know my name—"

"—For the record."

"Judith Ilderton," I finally tell him.

I get the feeling Fahim doesn't know what to think of me. It's the way he keeps staring at me, yet not staring at me. He wears the expression someone would wear when he or she is looking at an orphan. It's not a look of sadness, I don't think, instead a look of uncertainty but more so curiosity. Hard to believe, I know, especially coming from someone who doesn't know a single person whom she can genuinely call a friend. I don't know what to think of it, this feeling I'm having. Is it the sickness that they were talking about earlier? This unknown virus? Or, have I woken up from one long nap and now I'm starting to see things more clearly? It has all the ingredients of a post sleepwalking occurrence, but at the same time, I feel as if there's a chance I'm still dreaming.

And if this isn't a dream and I've been seriously kidnapped by a couple of these so-called "doctors," I can't help but laugh at it all—I mean, it's all I can do to hold it all inside.

A sixteen-year-old kidnapped by a group of black market doctors. I'm only saying this because they don't seem like the typical family doctor. Plus, I know it was them who were following me before I was abducted.

I stare at the machine next to me.

"It's only a polygraph."

I don't remember the polygraph the first time around. I don't remember entirely answering their questions with a *yes* or *no*, either.

"A polygraph?" I say.

Interesting.

"You're not in trouble, Ms. Ilderton," he says. "The polygraph is for 'our' protection. That's all."

"Your protection—"

Fahim interrupts, "—What Doctor Bloch means: we want this conversation to be transparent."

"Shall we begin?"

"Whatever."

"Okay, Ms. Ilderton, I'm just going to ask you some questions about what happened on your way to—"

He looks over some notes.

"—Middleton High School."

"Right," he says. "Middleton. Lacrosse game. Am I correct?"

"Is this part of the polygraph?"

He's not sure of my question.

"Not yet. I'm just going over some preliminary questions before we start."

"Sure. Whatever. Yes," I tell them. "We were scheduled to play the Middleton Bobcats."

"And who is *we*?"

"Central Agatha Black Bears."

"Junior Varsity. Correct?"

"Yeah—yes. JV."

"For the record, state your position on the team."

"I'm a defensemen."

"Okay. Good," he says. "Now, some other questions."

The doctor looks over a sheet on a clipboard and takes in a deep breath and lets out a heavy sigh as if he doesn't want to be here as much as I do.

"First and foremost, can you please state the current year, Mr. Ilderton?"

"The year is two-thousand sixteen."

"Very good."

"Where were you seated on the bus?"

That's a strange question.

"I was seated in the back with Emily."

"Emily Nyquist?" he says. "Is that correct?"

"Yes. That's her."

This Fahim guy wants to know everything about me, and that's what I find funny about him. He acts as if he's in control, yet he's *not* in control.

Who's the white rabbit now?

In a way, it's kind of amusing in a troubling kind of way because I can visualize Fahim's mind working like a clock behind his earthy brown eyes, each gear like a thought, moving from one to another. I have an idea of what he may be thinking: *Who the hell is this girl sitting in front of me? Where does she get the audacity to talk to me like that?*

I'm not one to predict what exactly goes through the mind of another person, but I'm getting pretty good at it. And this man right here, he's got a million thoughts running through his mind. An entire catalog of uncertainty and curiosity. I'd be lying if I said I wasn't curious in him. Why is he so interested in me? Why is he so determined to find the truth?

He asks me yet another question, but I remain silent. Normally, I'd be totally freaking out right now. I think a lot of it has to do with the conversation I had with the two FBI agents the other day—and that's all it was really, just a conversation, an awkward one at best. I don't remember much about the conversation, only me being a complete mess inside. I mean, who wouldn't? I think all of the girls were in a whole state of things: shocked, petrified, traumatized. I've never seen a person die before. I've been around dead people, like at an open wake, but I've never actually seen how they get that way. The process of life leaving the body. I can't help but wonder what a person thinks about when they die: Where am I going? What will it be like when I get there?

Surprisingly, I remain calm and act like I've done this sort of thing before. He wants to know what happened on the bus during the "eleven minutes" of what he calls *the silence.* His colleague calls it other things, too, like the "blackout" or the "strange event."

I don't know how to answer him because, like I told the FBI agents, I honestly don't remember what happened during this so-called "silence," only that something *did* happen and it was unlike anything I've ever experienced. Even now, thinking about it, this silence, this blackout, this strange event, it feels like the aftermath of a dream. When I was into true crime—that is, before I started to sleepwalk and lose interest in everything—I read this one story where the killer was mentally unstable, a deranged individual suffering from blackouts after heavy alcohol use. His name was William Backer and he was accused of murdering an entire family during one of his reoccurring blackouts; story goes that he woke up the next morning with his clothes stained with blood. According to several statements from bartenders, former friends or family members—I say "former" because they cut him off three years after he married the bottle—he'd literally drink until he passed out. One doctor, Clydesdale was his name—how could you not forget a name like that—was helping out investigators with the case. He explained what exactly goes on during a blackout: "nothing," his words. During a blackout, the individual doesn't create any memories. Parts of the brain shut down. Basically, the brain goes to bed while the body drifts around like a ghost. Sometimes, I wonder if that's what's happening to me, blackouts, *not* sleepwalking, although I'm still open to the notion. Personally, sleepwalking just sounds better. I wasn't a drinker—not a drinker—so, I clearly ruled out that theory. Nonetheless, it has me thinking about what happened during the "eleven minutes of silence." I still have memories of what happened; so is it right for Sy to use such a word as *blackout*? The more I try to think about what happened, the more it becomes blurry and harder to access and it feels as if I'm drifting away, like my mind's venturing somewhere else and if it ever arrives at this strange destination, I have a feeling that it'll never come back.

I quickly shake away the thought and focus on his actions, his words.

Fahim wants to know what I'm thinking right now, but I don't give him the satisfaction.

I tell him I'm thinking about why I'm here but I know that not to be true. I glance at the needle of the polygraph and it's not skipping around like it was at the beginning of our conversation.

"You're here to help us," he says.

He's speaking in half-truths.

"Help you?"

"Yes," Fahim says as he clears his throat. "We're looking for someone."

The doctor looks to his colleague. I can see his nervousness rubbing off his body and clinging itself to Sy.

"Looking for who—"

"—What Doctor Ahmad means to say is that we're on your side, *Judith*."

"I want to go home."

"I'm afraid it's not that simple."

"If you're on my side, then you'll let me go."

"I'm sorry, Judith. That's not an option."

I feel a tingling sensation all over from the sound of the name.

I remind myself to get it together.

Just answer his questions and they'll eventually let me go.

"Tell us," the other doctor, Sy, says. "What do you like to do for fun?"

What does he mean by that?

The needle starts to bounce a little.

"You're serious?"

He doesn't answer.

"You want to know what I like to do for fun?"

"That's right."

"I'm still having a tough time trying to digest what's been happening these past couple of days."

"And what's been happening?" he asks me. He's persistent. "You can tell us anything."

"I don't know," I tell them.

"Sure, you do," he says with a typical dad-shrug. His voice has changed. He's hiding something from me. "Talk to us, Judith." He says that name again. "You must have some interests, hobbies, something that you enjoy doing to pass the time. Movies? Books? Video games?"

Fahim's staring at me with much wider eyes.

"—Stay with us, Ms. Ilderton?"

"Yes."

"Any interests?"

The lights suddenly flicker overhead.

Everyone in the room tilts their heads upright. The two doctors look at one another with concern.

"Interests?" I say, as the lights stop flickering.

Fahim asks, "What's the first thing that comes to mind?"

"I don't know."

"You don't know?"

"I don't know," I say.

"What are you thinking about?"

I hear a voice pushing through my left ear, startling me. I look over my left shoulder, only to find the grayish vague blur of a slender woman answering the question for me.

The only word I can make out in her rambling is the word *death.*

## 2. BEFORE / RHEA

I seriously think my auntie's a witch.

Not like dem kind u read bout in dem old fairy tales written by dem lonely ole white dudes. I ain't talkin bout dem wretched-lookin hoodrats, either, wit the green skin, Pinocchio noses, dem fingers as crooked as tree branches, dressed up in raggedy black shawls, bodies so frail and all dat my lil' couz, T-Rock, could break dem skinny ass bitches in half over his knee. I'm talkin bout dem "new age" kinds of witches, the ones who be looking all normal on the outside but on the inside, they be bout as nasty as a tumor. Sum times, I jus be thinkin if my auntie, Genie, evin got a soul at all. For reals. If she had one—evin like a shade of one—it ain't like I seen it befo. She always be sayin things to me, like what my friend, Jill, be tellin me jus the otha day after English class, bout dem "double entrendres," u no, like words with double meanings or whatevah. Genie's got me thinkin and all bout shortcomings of my own self. And I got plenty! Believe me. Like the otha day, she bought me this cute lil' blouse with this rose-pattern thingy on it and all. A pretty-lookin number, if u ax me. The only thing was dat it was one size too small. I swear, took me like an hour puttin the thing on—can u believe dat? Me flounderin round my room like a fish caught in a net—and win I finally got the thing on, I couldn't breathe to save my life. I thought I was gonna die. The thing bout it: Genie *clearly* no's my size. And, not only dat, I make sure to take my old clothes dat don't fit me no more to the Goodwill, so I no dat, if she was rummagin through all my stuff, which Genie's been nown to do sum times, she'd find my current size. I no it was dat witch's "way" of tellin me dat I needed to drop a size, as if, all of sudden, I've turned into this hideous, gluttonous swamp creature. W-T-F! But dat's jus the beginnin, u see. There be plenty otha times she'd be puttin me down without actually puttin me down—if dat makes any sense. Evin facial expressions she be makin winevah I say sumtin or disagree with her, which, lately, be happenin all the damn time. She's somewhat right, dough, to a degree—I mean, I have put on a few pounds, but still, it ain't Genie's problem. I've been watchin' what I be eating and all, like the otha day, I had me this thing called kale—which I swear look like seaweed, if u ask me. I put sum strawberries in it and sum otha stuff that I ain't evah seen befo. I ain't evin heard of kale befo in my life but it was a'ight, I guess. I could git used to it. Plus, I don't feel as out of shape as I did the last year. Then, this morning, while I was eatin a cereal bar dat, if u close ur eyes, tastes like a flip-flop—like I'd no what a flip-flop'd taste like, but if I had to guess, I'm pretty sure dat it taste like a Totally-Grain Bar, but they say it's healthy and all—Genie be droppin sum otha witchy bully-bull on my ass. She ax me if I want sum pancakes, but I tell her nah, u no, cuz I'm watchin my fig, u no, but she clearly no's dat I'm watchin my fig. But she goes head and starts makin sum pancakes anywayz, like she's gonna eat dem all by herself. I no Genie ain't makin dem jus for herself cuz dat lil' skinny witch can only eat like two or three befo she says she full—yeah, she full a'ight, full of u no what! Anywayz, it's dat smell of maple syrup dat what really do me in. Like u no how win a cokehead hear dat tappin sound of a razor hitting a glass surface it'd be triggerin an urge to do a line? Or, like win them alcoholics see beer commercials on dem TVs, and then all of a sudden, they be cravin a drink? Wit me, it'd be the smell of my girl, Aunt Jemima. Talk bout a real witch. I swear dat woman definitely got a spell on me. So it's dat, and then what Genie says to me win she places dem great tower of pancakes on the table. It always starts with a comment, don't it? Well, anywayz, it wasn't like any otha comment dat Genie be cleverly slippin into conversations from time to time. This here comment was extremely personal, and it felt like a needle injectin me with a poison dat u don't think nuttin of it at first, then it slowly starts to work its magic well after its orientation.

Next thing I no, I be stormin straight up to my room with dat Wicked Witch of the West close on my heels.

I slam the door jus befo the witch can grab me by the arm.

I run to the corner of the room while Genie be bangin on the door, really loud too!

The bangin evintually stops.

Then, twenty minutes pass in what feels like seconds.

The witch is back at my door again, but this time she ain't nockin as hard as she was the first time round.

She's axin me if I'm ready to talk, but I sure ain't.

I check the time and realize dat, if I don't get dressed, I'm gonna be late for school. I can't be late. Twice this week I've been late, and the very last thing I want is a parent conference with dat Ms. Ratchet-like bitch, Mrs. Bennett, and Genie the Witch. Talk bout a real two-headed monster.

In the back of my mind, I wanna tell Genie dat I'm ready to talk. It wouldn't be dat hard. Would it? I'm ready to tell her how I truly feels bout her, all dem things she be sayin to me all the time, the way she be treatin' me lately. I wanna tell Genie everything—I mean, everything—but, instead, I tell her what she expects to hear.

Rhea Johnson, she shouts out behind the door. The door be shakin', like it ready burst from its hinges.

Genie only uses my full name win she's red-hot.

I can jus see dem steam oozing from dem pointy elf ears, raven-black eyes, and dat lil' wooden knob of a mouth.

She keeps demandin' dat I open the door or else.

"Or else" usually mean dat she's gonna get my stepfather, Rico, who ain't gonna do a damn thing but try and sweet talk me like he always be doin. Don't let the appearance fool u. Evin dough he's bout as swoll as a linebacker, Rico's a real softie.

I tell Genie to go away.

I don't talk to witches.

She a witch. For sure.

I leave out the witch-part.

She's sayin dat she's sorry bout earlier but I no she ain't the least sorry. She never sorry for anything she be doin.

She keeps nockin, keeps calling out my name, listen here, Rhea Johnson, keeps actin all witchy with all of her double-whatevah, but I ain't listenin no more. I'm tired of listenin to everybody all the time, telling me what I can and can't do. Sum times, I wish she'd jus vanish like smoke and jus leave me the hell alone.

After bout five minutes, she gives up and goes back to the kitchen where she takes out all of her red anger on the dishes like they was the ones who showed her an attitude.

I get dressed for school cuz jus imaginin Genie sittin down with my teacher, Mrs. Bennett, and humiliatin me is probably bout as worse as dat one dream where I be standin naked in a locker room full of a bunch of sweaty-ass fools from the varsity basketball team. In the dream, they all be starin at me wit these big and black demonic eyes like they gonna attack me or eat me or sumtin. I wake up sweatin all the time from it.

I check my phone again.

Ebony sent me this pic of what she be wearin: a black skirt wit this red and black-checkered sweater—which reminds me, I totally forgot bout the game today!

I hurry to my closet and grab all my things, my stick and my headgear. Then, once I got what I need for today's game, I slip on my game day skirt. Then, my sweater. It's a lil' too warm outside for a sweater, but I got to admit it does look good on me. See, Pam has this thing bout all of us lookin all professional befo the game. She thinks if we all dress like a team, then we'll learn how to play like a team. Dat be the day! She's into yoga or whatevah, and she always be talkin bout findin ur inner peace or sumtin like dat. I can't remember what she be sayin. The thing is we haven't won a single game this year and we ain't gonna win a game either cuz the fact is we ain't any good. We bad news. Like the sheep say, we baaaad! We actually worst in our division, which ain't sayin much cuz they ain't many teams dat good anywayz.

I make final adjustments to my swag: a red barrette to help keep my hair back.

Finally, I check my hand-me-down outfit in the mirror.

I take a couple of selfies till I find the right one for Corey. The fabulous one. Then, as I'm bout to send this fabulous pic to Corey, I change my mind at the last second and decide not to send it to him. I already no what he gonna say. Corey thinks I should play sumtin "less" aggressive, like basketball or softball, evin tennis, sumtin dat don't involve any physical contact. Evah since the Queen of Women's Tennis, Mercury, won the French Open last year, young black girls be comin out of the woodwork to give a shot at tennis. To me, it seems too intimidatin with everybody watchin u and all. Just u on dat court. All alone. I really admire dat. But talk bout pressure!

With lacrosse, there be otha girls to take the attention off me.

But Corey ain't the only one who hates dat I play lacrosse.

Genie thinks dat I'm gonna get hurt, like break an arm or leg. What does Genie no?

Maybe she's the one who needs to live a lil'.

Bitch.

Why can't she jus die already?

## 14. AFTER / RHEA

THESE fools be axin me the same questions ova and ova and it's startin to get on my nerves. They be talkin to me like I ain't worth shit, like I ain't listenin but I sure is. They keep axin me bout my barrette dat I be wearin on the bus, especially this here doctor man who's startin to give me the heebie-jeebies. I jus don't get why he be so interested in a lil' ole hairclip, but whatevah. I go head and tell dem, like I be tellin dem countless times, dat it once belonged to my mama and I found it in her jewelry box dat she left behind.

Accordin to this here lie detector, I ain't tellin the truth, which ain't a surprise. The fact: it don't matter where I got the barrette. They be tellin me Judith was carryin a barrette identical to the one I got, so I tell dem I liked the way the barrette looked on me so much dat I bought Judith one cuz the girl always be brushin the hair from her eyes out on the field and sum times, it be costin us the game. Plus, it's less distractin win she got her hair back winevah she plays. Not only dat, she looks a lot better. After all, dat girl's in desperate need for a confidence boost.

The doctor ax me why I felt as if this 'terrorist' was starin at me win she entered the bus.

So, I tell him as calmly as I can dat I don't exactly no what she be doin—it ain't my place—but she be startin at me a'ight.

He ax me if she be doin anything out of the normal. Lotta 'out of the normal' things happened on the bus. Dat's fo sure. He wants me to retrace my thoughts and tell these otha fools exactly what happened after she entered the bus. He ax me if she made any contact with me, like if she touched me or whatevah, but I don't remember her layin a finger on me, but the needle on the lie detector be jumpin round and gettin all excited again. I got this image in my head of her touchin me on the arm, like she dun with Mr. Stewart, but I dunno if it was real or not. Maybe I told dem Feds bout it. I slip my arm from the hospital gown and look down at my wrist but I don't find any of dem red markings or bruises like I had befo. The word *grabbed* be comin to mind but I don't remember much of anything, really, except for the fact dat this lady 'terrorist' wasn't like any terrorist I've evah seen befo.

Lemme ask u again, the white dude says, did she *grab* u?

I dunno, I tell them, tryin to hold myself together in front of all dem cameras pointed at me. Sumtin like happened to the air, u see. It got all wavy in parts. U no, like win u pressed the side of ur face against a hot road and if u look down the road, u can see dat heat in the air. Then, I remember the sky changin and gowine all dark.

This otha doctor be actin all old fashion like he time traveled from a different era and start takin notes with a pencil—who be usin pencils anymo? I don't no why they be writin wit pencils win they could be jus recordin my conversation with a recorder like dem Feds did. It don't make any sense.

He ax dark like how?

I tell him dark like night.

He says it could've jus been a cloud passin in front of the sun.

And I'm the one who ain't listenin?

Nah, I tell him, tryin to keep my shit together. This here was different. I remember lookin out the window during dat time and I couldn't see nuttin cuz it was dark outside. It went from day to night in the matter of seconds. Everybody be too scared to do anything bout it. What could we do bout it? So, we jus sat there in our seats, waitin for help—and dat's all we could do, was jus wait there—while this lady, who u be callin a terrorist but I ain't see no terrorist like dat befo, be standin at the front end of the bus, not sayin a damn word, jus starin at us like we foreigners win, in fact, she be actin like a foreigner herself.

Did she say anything to you?

Nah, I say. I remember Coach sayin sumtin to her—

The otha doctor fool asks me what Mr. Stewart said to her. I tell him he be axin what she want? Money? Whatevah!

He asks me if she answered, if she spoke, this terrorist, so I tell him nah. She turned toward Coach, then he got all quiet and scared, too. I ain't evah seen Mr. Stewart like dat before. We talkin bout Mr. Stewart! Dude scared of nuttin! This one time a snake got loose on the field and he grab the thing by its tail and carried it back to dem woods like it was a stick.

What happened after she made contact wit Coach Tabby?

Well, then she started starin at me with these strange, almost like—

Like what?

—Like these reptilian-like eyes. Like a snake's eyes. It all be weird, like she ain't evah seen a black girl before—

Then, he ax me if the story I said bout Mr. Stewart and the loose snake jus came to my mind win thinkin about this terrorist or if I thought bout it earlier. I dunno what he mean by dat. I jus tell him dat it was the first thing dat came to my mind win I thought bout Mr. Stewart bein scared. Dat's all.

He ax me once more where I got the barrette and I almost lose it.

I told u, I tell him like I mean it, the barrette belonged to my mama.

He ax me where my mama is. I can't believe this fool here went there win I no dat he no's what happened to my mama but now he's jus messin with me. I mean, after everything I've been through, I got to answer to this shady white asshole. He says I be lyin bout the barrette, sayin he got a feelin dat I ain't bein completely honest with him.

So, I tell him I stole it—if dat's what he wants to hear.

Fool!

I can't help it. I start cryin, like cartoon bawlin, waterfalls rainin from my poor eyes. I've been holdin it in for the past few days and I jus let go.

What u people want from me?

He says he no's how hard this must be for me, but I have to trust them.

I git super red hot.

Trust u! How the hell can I trust u fools? What the hell do u want?

They tell me that I need to calm me down but ain't nuttin I need but for dem to keep tellin me to calm down. Clearly, it ain't workin one bit. They jus wanna no what happened on the day of November Eighth, which, by far, gots to be one of the worst days of my life. Dat's all they want to no but I no they be lyin to me, like they be from the very git go. I no dat's not all they want. I dunno what they really want from me, but it ain't jus information. They say dat, after they get what they want, I can go back to my family, to my life, to my aunt, Genie.

The otha doctor, Mr. Seymour, starts talkin bout the terrorist attacks on 9/11. He don't seem as much of an asshole as the otha fool, but I no he means well. I ain't evah seen it happened in my lifetime, I tell him, but I heard bout it befo.

He ax me where I was win it *all* happened, as in 9/11, but I don't think he be wantin me to answer, like Mr. Forte be doin all the time in science class, axin questions dat be makin us think and all. It don't really matter cuz I wasn't evin born win it all happened, and I think dat there is a good thing—not bein alive durin all dat tragedy. Dat's always the first question people be axin him winevah sumtin tragic or 'big' happens dat completely shocks the entire world.

Like 9/11, Mr. Seymour be sayin, he remembers dat day as if it was yesterday. He was gettin ready for class win it all happened—he studyin his doctorate, a PhD in medicine. He received this phone call from one of his colleagues. Named Monte. This Monte guy then told him to turn on the TV. So, he dun dropped whatevah he was doin and turned on the TV. He be sayin those horrific images of the World Trade Center fallin to the ground after the second airplane crashed into the side of the buildin, then dat massive cloud of smoke billowin up in the air, coverin everything in darkness, then all of dat chaos down below, people runnin to safety or searchin for dem loved ones, all of it came at him at once and it nocked the wind outta him, like a punch to the gut. He hung round his apartment for a good while and his eyes never left dat screen—I don't blame em. I can't possibly imagine gowine through sumtin as awful as dat, watchin all dem people die on the TV. Evintually, Mr. Seymour pulled himself together and drove to the university. He mentioned sumtin about a haze, like walkin round all ghost-like, dazed, too, like everybody else, and he be sayin he felt like he was trapped in a horrible nightmare. Scared, *shocked*, slightly paranoid, wonderin if there was gonna be another attack. Then he started to think bout all of dem people who was killed win the World Trade Center came down. He tried puttin himself in their shoes, tried to imagine what they was thinkin at the time. So much was racin through his mind. So much violence and misery. 'Course, he new he ain't the only one out there who felt the same way as him. He be talkin bout how 9/11 was the start of sumtin darker and much sinister. Like it was the beginnin of the end. I no how sum times certain tragedies bring people togetha, u now dem clichés, like dat one bout makin us stronger as a nation—u no, like what dem politicians be sayin all the time to get votes—but dat ain't what he be talkin bout. To be honest, I don't quite no what he mean by dat, but it sure do mean sumtin.

Winevah a tragedy happens, Mr. Seymour tells me, u journey inward and u always think of yourself: What if I was there, in dat situation? How would I fight? How would I die?

He turns to me and ax me the same question as he did befo. I already no where he's gowine with the subject. If he no's how I ended up wit the barrette—I mean, it ain't like a robbed a bank or anything—he must no bout what happened win I was thirteen years old. It ain't none of their bizness, but I feel like if I tell dem what they wanna hear then they'll lemme go.

So, where was I win my mama died?

At home, I tell em.

Doin what?

It don't matter. She dead.

How she die?

Car wreck, but u already no; otherwise, u wouldn't be axin, right? They don't say nuttin. So, I tell em dat it's like every time I look at my auntie, Genie, I see my mama.

The otha man ax me how dat makes me feel, to look at my auntie, Genie.

All of a sudden, I git this itch on the side of my head, jus below my ear. I start to scratchin it and the more I scratch the worse it gits. Then, before I no it, my hole head be itchin like crazy. For sum reason I can't seem to stop.

He ax me again.

I pull my hands away from my head befo I start to look like sum junkie and tell him it makes me angry.

He ax why? Why it makes me angry.

She all I got, I tell him, but not anymo. Win she left me, I dunno, it felt like I was alone again, like I ain't got anybody to look after me. I wasn't close to my mama but she was good people and she really cared for me. Genie ain't my mama and she ain't gonna be my mama. Nevah! She may look like my mama but she ain't her. But I don't no. I jus wish we could get along but I think deep in my mind dat there ain't a chance of dat happenin.

He ax me what I was gowine through my mind win I laid eyes on the terrorist. What emotions?

I tell him dat the first time in a long time I felt like I can let it all go, the pain, the sadness, dat anger. Like it opened up a door inside me and revealed this scream I got buried miles deep inside. The closer I looked through this dark hallway, the more it tried to reveal itself to me. Like everyday it's tryin to make it to the door, mile by mile, but it's as shy as a stray, u see, it likes dem shadows, and for sum reason this scream is afraid of what people may think of it, it's power. I wanna step aside and jus let it out and let it go. Forever. Live my life without it. But it acts like it needs me as much as I need it. Once I saw it there, wantin to escape, it's like it opened up all of this hate inside me. Sum times, I don't no. I jus feel like my heart's gonna cave in from this scream I got livin inside me; and these past couple of days, it overwhelms me so much dat I can't evin catch my breath. I'm so tired of people walkin all over me, watchin me all the damn time and tellin me what to do or how to act. I'm tired of these people gittin all up in my bizness win they got dem problems of they own, yet all of these fools are too chickenshit to deal wit they problems themselves. So, they point dem fingers at me, jus tryin to look for sumtin to make dem feel all better bout dem sorry selves. You wanna no what I'm really tired of? I'm tired of bein treated like a second-rate citizen. What makes another person's life more important than mine? I swear, sum times, I wish I had the courage to unleash this scream I got buried inside me. Sum times, I jus wanna explode. Dat's how I felt. Dat's how I feel right bout now. Anything else, Doctor Man?

## 3. BEFORE / YADIRA

MY papi has what Jonathan calls flatfeet. When he walks, the earth literally shakes. Having hardwood floors throughout the entire house doesn't help; however, it has its advantages. I've also heard Jonathan call them "penguin feet," but Jonathan knows not to mention a single word—not even a peep—about my papi's feet outside the solitary confines of my bedroom. Being one of the hottest boys at Central Agatha, Jonathan is much more intelligent than he looks. He's what I like to call a lady whisperer. He knows how to please a young lady. I like to think that Jonathan knows exactly what I'm thinking, how I want it, where I want it at any moment's notice. It's almost like he's in my head, living there, all snug and sound in the tight nooks of my brain, hitting all my right notes with those electric fingers of his.

What can I say?

I'm a lucky girl; however, at the end of the day, with all lucky girls, their luck soon runs out.

I can hear Papi coming from a mile away, or in my current predicament, from the top of the landing to my bedroom at the end of the hallway, the low rumble often mistaken by the sound of a racing heartbeat or, in Jonathan's case, the sound of Zeus, ready to strike him down with a bolt of lightning.

Normally, Papi warns me whenever he's about to enter my bedroom with a couple of knocks at the door and shortly after, a pause for me to answer.

This time, I think he's onto us.

He knocks only once and as soon as Jonathan rolls from my bed, sweeps up his clothes as if his two arms are lassoes, hurdles out the window, and leaps onto the roof outside, all in what appears to be one motion, Papi swings open the door!

He finds no Jonathan, just me sitting on my bed with only a comforter separating every bare inch of me from his innocent eyes.

If it weren't for Papi's incredibly enormous Hobbit-feet, then my boyfriend, Jonathan, would've been tragically murdered. No question. I honestly don't know how he would've committed the heinous act (since it definitely would've been a spur of the moment—Papi was known to have a short temper—he more than likely would've resorted to strangling my poor Jonnie Boy until his eyes rolled over white; and when the police showed up at the scene of the crime tracing my belatedly deceased boyfriend with chalk on my bedroom floor, they'd most certainly call it a crime of passion; as a matter of fact, they'd even start a college course based around the infamous murder to educate horny lover boys about the consequences of sleeping with daughters of excessively protective fathers who struggle with the fact that their little *hija* is not a baby anymore).

"Papi," I cry out, shielding every inch of my body, "what are you doing?"

Papi doesn't exactly know that I'm naked, but what Papi doesn't know won't kill Papi.

I follow his eyes carefully moving around the room like a judge surveying his court, his nostrils twitching with each breath, as if he can smell a familiar scent in the air. I wonder if he smells Jonathan, who doesn't have much of a scent; he doesn't even wear cologne or deodorant, which is disgusting, I know, but it's not like he really needs it. I asked him one time why he didn't wear any deodorant and he told me that he likes to smell natural. Whatever works for him. Papi, on the other hand, won't leave the house without it. I've walked in on him one time before he heading out to work and I could see a misty cloud of all sorts of aerosol can fumes from deodorant and hair spray seeping from the bathroom like a jungle mist. He is like every other man; however, what makes Papi so special is that he is a man of many strengths and wonders. He could very well have the ability to detect boys who are up to no good, as if somehow these boys carry a distinct smell to them. Maybe Papi has other superpowers that I'm not aware of.

"Breakfast is ready," he says in his fatherly voice, as he stands at the edge of the doorway.

"Okay," I say, the facial expression on my face urges him to leave.

As he's about to walk away, he notices that the window is open. I'm cold by nature, like an amphibian. And Papi's well aware of my coldness.

He asks me if anything's wrong.

"It got a little warm last night," I say and mentally tell myself as soon as the comment leaves my lips that I won't have to go to church on Sunday because it did get warm last night—I mean, really, really warm and I was soaking wet (wink, wink).

I snatch the smile from my lips before it spreads across my face. I widen my eyes at Papi, indicating for him to leave the room without me having to tell him. Are you just going to stand there while I get ready?

He leaves. Finally. Thankfully.

As I throw on a pair of underwear, I step on Jonathan's boxers on the floor.

Oh Dios mío!

Did Papi see Jonathan's boxers? Is that why he was acting so weird?

If Papi did see them, he could've thought they belonged to me. Papi doesn't know what I wear underneath my clothes. Or, does he? Yuck!

I grab the boxers from the floor and lean out the window, only to witness Jonathan waddling away with his blue jeans around his ankles in the front lawn.

"Hey, Jonnie Boy," I whisper loudly, doing everything I can to hold in my laughter. I ball up the boxers and place it in the net of my lacrosse stick and fling the boxers down to him.

He quickly pulls up his jeans before he attempts to catch the boxers.

At the last moment, he fumbles the boxers and rightfully secures them.

"Nice shot, Yadi," he says.

"Nice catch, Jonnie Boy," I say and laugh at Jonathan as he scurries away.

Before I can get settled for breakfast, Alfredo is doing a pre-warm up as he always does before he's about to relieve himself: eyes bulging, looking around frantically, then digging his front two paws into the rug, as if he's mining for gold. I grab Alfredo before he does his business all over the new Persian rug Mamá bought at Carpet World last weekend. Lord knows how long she took picking out the right one. Literally took her two full weekends.

I rush Alfredo outside where he relieves himself in the lawn.

As I always do, I clean up after him; dispose the bag in the trashcan.

What a morning!

As I'm about to head out for school, I hear a strange noise coming from the garage. I check out the noise. Sure enough, my suspicions are true. Inside the garage a hummingbird is violently beating itself against the ceiling. By now, most—if not all—hummingbirds have already started their long journey back out West, which makes me wonder if this one has been left behind. The last time I saw one was about a month ago, and that was around the time the hummingbirds leave, when fall hits at the end of September and the weather starts to cool down. Mamá still has a feeder out back for the scraggliers, even refills it with homemade nectar everyday. So, I wonder if it was trying to stock up on some food before the trip.

Above the box for the garage door is a bloody imprint of what looks like the perfect shape of the hummingbird.

Next to the imprint are several other stains of blood from where it had banged itself against the ceiling.

I grab whatever I can find, a broom first, but I realize a broom would be too rough on the hummingbird. I don't have much longer, I realize. The hummingbird is weakening and loosing a lot of blood. I rush back inside and grab a bed sheet from my bed and race back outside.

By the time I make it back to the garage, the hummingbird is nowhere to be found.

Relief washes over me at first, thinking maybe the hummingbird mustered enough strength to fly through the opening in the garage. Wrong. I hear a squeak coming from the top of a cabinet. I follow the trail of blood to the cabinet. I grab a ladder and check out the squeaking noise. The hummingbird is lying on top of cabinet, motionless, possibly dead. I gently pick up the hummingbird and hold it in my hands. Its beak is caked with blood. It looks fragile and broken, but I don't want to make matters worse by touching it. So, I take the hummingbird to the feeder out back and try to nurse it into drinking the nectar. The hummingbird is too weak to sip the nectar, and I realize it doesn't have long. The hummingbird is going to die, and there's nothing I can do to save it. And that's what really troubles me the most, not having the power to save its life.

## 15. AFTER / YADIRA

IF this is supposed to be a kidnapping, it certainly doesn't feel like one, nor is it anything remotely like how I pictured one from what I've seen in the movies, which—now that I think about it—makes me wonder if all the movies that I've watched either didn't do their homework on kidnappers and got it all wrong or they were just whetting their own farfetched agendas by "stretching" the truth. Where I come from, we have a name for this. We call it *loco*, and there's nothing loco about what's going on here. Usually—I take that back, "stereotypically"—aren't kidnappers supposed to treat the captives as if they're objects? I remember I saw that once in the movie, *The Silence of the Lambs.* Jonathan says that I watch way too many movies, especially the ones that tend to lean toward the darker side of human nature. I think Jonathan's only saying those things because Jonathan's a scaredy-cat even though he would never admit it. Not all horror movies are intended to scare. Some can be used for educational purposes. In *The Silence of the Lambs*, the kidnapper, Buffalo Bill, never saw his victims as humans; instead, he saw them merely as objects to lotion up before he them cut up and wore them to satisfy his own personal fetish. So far, I've been treated well. Nobody's handing me a basket with lotion and told me to put the lotion on its skin. They've given me food to eat—as a matter of fact, more than enough. They're not cannibals, either. I know this because whoever's been magically placing the tray of food at my door looks way too thin to be a meat eater. I know there are more on the other side of the door—must be at least three of them—because I can hear a couple of them talking outside the room. I can't pick up what they're saying to each other from underneath the crack of the door for their voices are as light as whispers. I remember getting really faint and lightheaded. So, I decided to shut my eyes for a couple of minutes. Then, I caught a glimpse of the side of my kidnapper's face. He wears thin glasses, has the posture of a writer, shoulders slumped over. The one thing that I found was odd: a jacket made of corduroy. Papi used to wear corduroy back in the day, as in long before I was conceived. I've seen ancient pictures of Papi wearing chocolate brown corduroy. A handsome man who never placed his hands on his hips. I think he still has the jacket locked in a closet somewhere, collecting years of dust. They've also given me a bed to sleep in. It's not as comfortable as my bed, but it's not bad enough to voice a complaint on Yelp. Now, I'm staying in another room, ten times the size of the previous room—which isn't really a room at all but more or less the size of a prison cell. I have an entire library full of books at my disposal. I don't recognize any of the books, except for one or two, which were part of our required summer reading. A lot of the furniture is old as well: leather sofas and chairs with as many cracks as chapped lips; burgundy drapery around the tall windows, which, by the way, are covered with sheets of steel that are as thick as the walls.

How did I end up in a place like this?

How did I not see it coming?

I think it all started on Thursday, two days after the shootout, the morning I woke up with a serious hangover.

The night before, I snuck out and met up with Jonathan at Turtle Pond behind Beatty Park. He brought a six-pack of beer. He said one of his brother's friends bought the beer for him and he didn't want to drink it alone. We got drunk. I drank a lot more than I should have—three is my limit but I ended up downing four. Not like Jonathan made it his mission in life to take advantage of me, but he offered his last beer to me and I couldn't resist.

By the time I worked through the fourth beer, I was feeling loose. Jonathan didn't want to do anything that I didn't want to, but I was very emotional and I wanted Jonathan to console me.

We made out on top of the picnic tables and did other things underneath the stars; and when morning suddenly came faster than I expected, I was left wishing the night would never end. That following morning was when things started to turn into my own horror movie, which made me wonder if something happened after Jonathan and I left Beatty Park—Was someone watching us?

Were we being followed?

Since my parents allowed me to take a week off from school, I slept in most of the day. I was desperate to stay asleep for at least a couple of hours but the daily noises of routine kept jerking me in and out of sleep, like the viciously gruff engine of the mailman making his daily stops or the mumblings of my jobless neighbors walking their rat-sized dogs past the house—I couldn't hear what they were gossiping about but I had an idea—or the carpenter sawing through slabs of wood next to Mr. Borger's damaged front porch. I urged myself to sleep, but it was like the day would *not* allow me to sleep. I heard that some of the girls ended up mustering just enough willpower to go to school. I commend their efforts. I heard Donna went to school after spending most of the week in bed with a stomach bug. I can't believe I'm saying this but for once in my life I wish I was in Donna's shoes. I wasn't ready to face all of the questions that I'm sure so many students were going to ask me. Jonathan was worried about me, as he ought to be. He ended up skipping last period to visit me. I fixed him a ham sandwich. After he ate, we went for a walk. That's when that movie-thing happened. Jonathan was actually the one who pointed him out to me. He said that he saw the guy earlier last night, following him and his crew around. He thought maybe it was either some perv or an undercover cop staking him out. Typical Jonathan, always thinking of himself, like the cops care about underage drinking. At the time, I didn't think much of it.

When Jonathan and I parted ways, I went back home and Papi had gotten off work earlier to check on me. That wasn't really why he came home. He didn't admit to going through my belongings, but I know that was the most obvious reason why he came home early. I don't know what he was searching for, drugs possibly, condoms; I don't know what it was. All I know: my papi isn't a good liar.

* * *

"She let every single one of us off the bus," I say to Doctor Bloch. "She closed the doors behind us. She drove off."

"That's it?"

"Yes," I say, wiping the sweat of my palms onto my hospital gown. "That's it."

"Did you notice anything *strange* about her when you exited the bus?"

"Strange?"

"Did she seem different than before she entered the bus?"

"Not that I can remember," I say. "I remember she looked frail."

"Frail like sick or frail like weak."

"A little bit of both, I guess. To be honest," I glance at the polygraph and the needle remains steady, "she looked like a lot older than she looked when she entered the bus."

"Older? Please explain more."

"I know it sounds—I don't know—ridiculous, but it's like she dramatically aged before we left the bus. It was all blurry. I was very dizzy, as well."

"Dizzy from what?"

"I guess from all of the commotion outside, the gunshots, the screaming; there was so much going on."

"Can you remember anything else?"

I retrace my thoughts to that exact moment I stepped off the bus, my eyes connecting with her as she replaced Coach Tabby's position in the driver's seat.

"I remember getting a closer look at her as I was leaving the bus," I say, "and for a moment, she looked like she knew she was going to die. She didn't look desperate or anything. She looked like she was at peace with all the chaos and the violence surrounding us, like she had already accepted that she was going to die. She almost looked like she was. . . like she was at home."

"What to do you mean 'at home'?"

"I heard that somewhere before a person passes away they get really calm. She had a very calm demeanor."

"Ms. Santiago, did she say anything to you as you we're exiting the bus?"

"No," I say. "Not that I can remember. I remember the images pretty clearly, her face, but as far as the sounds, not so much. I was so frightened at the time and like I said, there was so much commotion outside. I was just trying to block it all out. I just wanted it to end already."

"Very good," Doctor Bloch says, sorting through his notes. "Can you tell us more about your papi? What kind of relationship do you have with him?"

"What does this have to do with what happened the other day?"

"Just answer the question, Ms. Santiago?"

"Good," I say. "We have a good relationship."

The needle starts moving faster than it was moving when I was describing the terrorist, and somewhere, I can hear Father Samuel calling my name.

"He's what I call very 'old fashioned.'"

"'Old fashioned?' What do you mean by that?"

I don't want to talk about Papi; as a matter of fact, he'd ground me for an entire week without any phone or television if he knew I was talking about him to strangers, who claimed to be doctors, although the other man with fiery red hair behind the table doesn't look like a doctor at all.

"You mean traditional?"

"Yes," I tell him. "Very much so."

"And how does that make you feel?"

Nobody's asked me that question before. I've always been raised in a household where we respect our elders even if they may be completely off their rocker or even out of touch with the modern world.

"It's none of your business how I feel about my papi."

"Just answer the question," Roger says.

I stare into the camera, but I don't answer his question. I don't give him anything.

"So be it," he says as he pulls out a piece of paper from a manila folder.

He walks toward me and hands me a picture of Jonathan.

I turn away once I see Jonathan's face. For some reason, I already know why they're showing me the picture. I know because I've seen it before in the movies. It's Blackmail 101.

"Look at it," he says.

I look at it.

The picture was obviously taken yesterday afternoon when Jonathan was leaving my house. Jonathan's hanging out with his loser friends at their normal hangout spot near the skate shop. The picture appears as if it was taken from a distance.

"Where did you get this?" I ask him, the anger starting to choke my words.

"Don't worry about how we acquired the photo, Ms. Santiago," Roger says, as he looms over me. "So, would your father approve of your boyfriend?"

"Who are you people? Really?"

He doesn't answer.

So, I answer his question.

"No," I tell him.

He sits back down across from me and remains silent.

"So, you're going to tell my father about Jonathan. Is that right? While you're at it, are you going to tell him what exactly you're doing to me? Because I don't think he would be too pleased to hear that you have abducted his daughter."

"Are you through?" Roger asks.

I don't answer.

Finally, after a few minutes of unbearable silence, I answer his original question: "He doesn't understand me."

"Your father doesn't like change. Does he?"

"No," I say as I clear my throat. "He thinks that all young people have become entitled and they have no respect for their elders anymore and that we don't have conversations or that nobody looks at each other in the eyes anymore."

"And he blames—what exactly?"

"Phones," I answer. "The Internet—"

"—Well, for some, the Internet's whatever you make it."

"Don't get me wrong," I say. "Papi doesn't mind the Internet. He doesn't like what it has done to people, especially younger people."

"For example?"

"Like social media."

"What about it?"

"He thinks social media has made people more cynical," I say. "He thinks they have no shame anymore. Nobody's held accountable for what they say over the Internet."

"And how do *you* feel about the Internet?"

"I don't mind it, I guess."

"And this fight you spoke about earlier, between you and your father, can you tell us exactly what the fight was about?"

I catch the words before they roll off my tongue and look down at the black and white picture of Jonathan—my Jonnie Boy. I can't even imagine my life without Jonathan; all of the ups and down we've been through together have only made us stronger. Jonathan's *always* been there when I needed him and I for him. I was there by his side when he lost his mother to a massive stroke, the "big one." His mother suffered from a disease called rheumatoid arthritis and she basically lived off pain relievers and anti-inflammatory drugs to help ease the daily pain caused by the disease. I remember visiting Jonathan's mother one time when she took a turn for the worse. She looked like something you'd see in a freak show—not to be so blunt, but it was true. Her fingers were deformed, like the bones in her hands had been shattered like glass, then, it was like someone had tried to glue all of the bones back together. Her joints hurt so badly that she could hardly move. After the first stroke, she didn't even recognize her son and the memories they shared together. It was the hardest thing to watch, a mother who could no longer recognize the life that she had brought into the world. Jonathan would never admit it but he was extremely close to his mother. When she passed away, we became even closer. We both understood how precious life was and how, at any second, it could be taken away from us if we weren't paying attention or looking out for one another. Ever since her death, Jonathan has never mentioned his mother to me, even though I know he wanted to at times. I can see it behind his eyes sometimes, the pain that he has tucked away like packed luggage in the back of the closet. I share everything with Jonathan. I think what makes our relationship that much more special is that we're nothing alike—I mean, seriously like night and day.

I turn my attention away from the picture.

"I was upset at him Wednesday when he came home from work."

"Why were you upset?"

"I was upset because he *wasn't* upset."

"You think your father should've shown more sensitivity to you, especially after everything you witnessed Tuesday afternoon on the way to your game?"

"Yes," I answer. "He does this all of the time. Even whenever I'm sick. Last year, when I caught the flu, he got mad at me. I think he gets mad, but really, deep down, he's mad at himself for not being a better father. Then, early Thursday night, I found him snooping through my bedroom—I didn't actually catch him in the act, but I know it was him—"

"—Why was he 'snooping' through your room?"

"I don't know," I say, "but he denied doing it."

"You don't believe your father was telling the truth?"

"Right now," I say and stare into the camera, "it's hard to believe anything."

## 4. BEFORE / AKEA

APPARENTLY, this month is Drunk Driving Awareness Month—or for those who tend to hang onto every word, the minions in charge of Central Agatha, Don't Drink and Drive Month. Of all the months to choose from, why choose November? Why not December or any of the other eleven months out of the year? I'm sure Thanksgiving has something to do with it, since, for most normal people, it can be a stressful time of the year. The holidays don't bring me that much stress or the need to drink, although drinking doesn't hurt. Like these awareness months really help? Just last week one of the seniors was killed in a drinking and driving accident: Andrew Wexler. From what I heard, he swerved off the road and hit a telephone pole head-on. Andrew—or Andy, as most of his friends called him—was in the Key Club. Apparently, an important kid who wanted to work with computers or something involving technology. Despite having done what he did, I'd say Andrew was one of the smart ones—not like his mom telling everybody she meets how smart her son is, but like really smart, like 4.0 smart, going to Harvard-smart. He wasn't much of a partier, either. I think one kid said he wanted to create apps when he grew up, but I'm not sure. I never knew Andrew in real life or on social media—over a hundred and twenty people started following Andrew's Chatterz page after he died. The number of followers is still growing. He stills makes chirps, too. Not the real Andrew. I've heard his baby sister, Janet, who's a freshman, a mousy girl who keeps a lot to herself, took over Andrew's Chatterz page and makes sure Andrew's page stays preserved by posting fresh articles on the newest technology or scientific research studies or news on upcoming software. It seemed like Andrew had good intentions, even if he was imposing his radical—dare I say, laughable—ideas onto others, as if technology was the "only" way to live. I mean, come on! An app that can literally drive for you? Even though I may disagree with Andrew, I admire the fact that he stood by a cause, like technology, especially during a time when so many people aren't who they say they are, especially on the Internet (there's this one girl in a couple of my classes, name's Megan, a hundred percent hypocrite, and she's always talking about all of the crap she does with charities and whatnot and she acts like she's the mother Teresa of social media, calls herself an activist when she doesn't do shit around Agatha to help out our increasingly growing homeless population, and she's also always using big words to make herself sound more important, words like *illustrious* to describe her week in Haiti, making posts about how much time she spends helping out the disabled or teaching children with attention deficit disorders how to read—seriously, she posted one photo of her reading to a Haitian kid in the middle of the slums—I can picture Megan tossing the kid to the ground once she was done taking the photo. It's totally a front because that's not who she is in "real life." For instance, one time I saw Megan making fun of Yasmin, a girl who has cerebral palsy, and if my phone was charged I would've caught that bitch in the act and exposed her for who she truly is). People, like Megan, only post what they want you to see or read; but I really think Andrew was one of those rare individuals who actually practiced what he preached. In a way, I wish I had gotten to know him. I only saw him occasionally during lunch. He ate with the other PC kids, but they weren't the type of kids who didn't talk to you if you had an iPhone. I mean, there are only two types of people at Central Agatha: You're either Apple or PC. Andrew was an Android, and not too many Androids associated with Apples, who can be stuck up and act like they got a stick up their butt—me, I'm guilty as charged. I've heard it's like forbidden in some schools outside Agatha. Whenever I passed Andrew either at lunch or in the hallway, I didn't know who he was at the time—Apple or PC. It really didn't matter. If Andrew didn't die, more than likely I would've never talked to him. I know it's messed up, but Andrew would've been just another face trying to change the world.

Most of social media has started calling it Stop Underage Drinking Month, but I'm sticking with Drunk Driving Awareness Month.

I arrive around twenty minutes early before the bell, plenty enough time to not only check out the school rock, but also have a convo with my friends. Seriously, I've been so dying to find out what happened between Omar and Demeter on Sunday night. The last time we talked she said she'd save all of the juicy details for the morning.

So, I'm pulling into the student parking lot, ready to admire my handiwork from last night, and I notice someone—probably a senior, if I had to guess, probably the two drama queens of Central Agatha, Sebastian and Julia, who run Central Agatha's Morning News, and basically, get away with anything —parked a smashed Corolla next to the rock, which is tagged in purple spray paint with Cat's seventeenth birthday. The car reminds me what the major cigarette companies did a couple of years back: sticking graphic images on the back of packs, like people missing their jaws from smokeless tobacco or holes in their throats from smoking; being way dramatic. The car job totally looks like something that frog-faced slut, Julia, would do—last year, I know Julia was the mastermind behind the whole "Dick in the Sky" prank to raise awareness of women's rights. She never came forward and confessed to the faculty she was the one who suspended the red inflatable above the school building but everyone knows it was Julia. Students were shouting out from below, "It's a bird! It's a plane! It's. . . wait a second. It's just a giant floating penis covered in blood?" I admit. It was so political it was borderline disturbing. The prank definitely broke waves for a good two weeks; then, after that, Julia was onto bigger and better things. As for

Sebastian being involved in the wannabe art in front of Central Agatha, I'm not too sure. Honestly, I mean I wouldn't be surprised if Julia ran Andrew Wexler off the road, only to exploit Andrew's death during Drunk Driving Awareness Month and receive praise and high-fives from the faculty. I mean, really, it's not like it doesn't happen. You see musicians and other people in the entertainment business do it all the time. Any publicity—good or bad—is great publicity. Is it not? Just a couple of weeks ago, days before Sneezy dropped his latest album, he checked himself into rehab for severe depression—even wrote a note on his MyCircle page saying he didn't want to live anymore and that he was going to kill himself. It was totally a publicity stunt, but people bought it, and he ended up at number one on the charts. Good for him—I mean, whatever works. So, Julia killing Andrew is a wild theory, but I would *never* put anything past her. She's a clingy wannabe who likes to capitalize on every moment, even if it gets her a moment to bask in the fake spotlight that constantly shines over Central Agatha.

As far as Sebastian, I'd say he's more of the artsy-type, the "brains" of the two, more sensitive on the outside but equally as devilish, the puppeteer secretly towering above the puppet who is Julia.

The wrecked car clearly upstages what Nellie and I spent so long spray-painting last night in the middle of a downpour—my hands are still sore and I've picked up a sinus cold that may or may not turn into an infection. The thought of staying home today never crossed my mind. Game day has a way of sweating out a good cold. Plus, I'm dying to see Cat's reaction. She's not really the social media type. Clearly. She doesn't even have a social media page. She says she uses the Internet from time to time, only for research and school stuff. I'll be honest. Cat totally despises social media and what it's done to people, how it's "driven humanity into an inescapable hole," and blah, blah, blah. I don't know what I'd do without my Chatterz. I'm addicted. I'm also extremely transparent when it comes to making a post. The only downfall: people get to know *too* much about you, like Brandon and his goon squad. Cat especially despises the whole Hashtag Generation. Only being a grade above me and hating social media is strange in my opinion. I mean Catherine doesn't even have a MyCircle page! But whatever. Cat's not really the whistleblower type or one to put down others. She's "traditional," she would say. She's probably the coolest junior I've ever met—not because most of the juniors act like God's greatest creation, but because I've never met a person with so much grace and charisma. Sometimes it seems like she was plucked off one of those old black and white movies. So, it's an honor that Cat's been playing with us for the past couple of weeks. She's extremely talented. I've once read about talent, how it's about as cheap as salt—or someone was echoing that on Chatterz, not sure—but Cat is next level. When Cat hits the field, she's Full Metal Bitch. I wish she'd stay on the team but soon she's going to be fully recovered and she'll move back up to Varsity. So the girls and I wanted to do something special for Cat and this was our—I take that back—this was like the only way of spreading the word about her big seventeen. I know it's a little "old school,"—what am I saying? 'Course, it's old school, but I wanted to stay between the lines of tradition. Cat deserves to be treated like royalty today.

I manage to find a spot close to the trailer where I have Fourth Period Sociology. Usually, I don't mind parking in the back with all of the other sophomores, but I have to run home after school and pick up my equipment, which I forgot. It happens almost all the time, especially during game day. I get so worked up about the game that I completely forget to prepare for the game.

As I make my way into school, I pass Brandon and I can feel my stomach tightening from the sight of him. An overwhelming wave of emotions surfaces. It's become an immediate reaction whenever I see him now. It's like he's a trigger for me to throw up. I put my mind on something else besides finding a quick route to the restroom but all I can think about is what Brandon did to me. Brandon and all of his dickwad crew are huddled near the trashcan. Fitting, in a way, why they always hang out in that one spot every morning, next to the trash. I do my best to ignore them by looking away, but I see Jamal sticking out like a shit stain in the corner of my eye.

It's now been sixteen humiliating days since Brandon went behind my back and shared the photo, even after I told him countless times the photo was meant for him and only him—his "eyes only" were the words I used. But did that stop him? What was I even thinking? It sucks, too, because I really liked Brandon. I thought he was one of the good ones. But I was wrong. Man! I was so wrong!

I glance over at Jamal, and he's still looking at me as if he wants to tear into me.

Sixteen days. Sixty days.

Does it even matter?

Every time Brandon's friends look at me, especially Jamal, it's as if the only thing they think about when they look at me is a photo. At first, I kind of liked the way they looked at me, the attention—I mean, what girl doesn't like attention? After a while, though, it became too much: the constant staring, the name-calling—Perky tits, Silver Dollar, Briar Patch, Red Eye, Corn Hole. The insults are greater whenever they're traveling in numbers. Sometimes, I overhear them talking about me, bantering back and forth with their friends, telling each other what they'd like to do to me, to my body. I often pray they'd go away for good, go crawl in a ditch so I could finally be left alone. On the flip side, I know it's just guys talking, and really, that's all it is, guy talk, but it's not just the guys. Like many girls who have put themselves out there, I went through a full week of slut-shaming. Wasn't nearly as awful as what the guys did—and still continue to do—but I'm a female and we females can't do anything without being picked apart with every little thing we do or wear. I'm guilty of doing it myself. It's what we do from time to time. Get over it!

Either way, the whole ordeal has me thinking more often than I should. That's all I've been thinking about lately—even my mom wonders why a girl my age has so much on her mind—but there's no denying it, I've been thinking whether Brandon made me this way or I've always been this way all along and now I'm turning into the person who I'm supposed to be; or I wonder if I've always been this way and I needed a gutterboy like Brandon to help with my transition. Brandon could've been my scapegoat. What bothers me: When will all the talking Brandon and his friends do turn into action? Will they hurt me? When will they finally cross that line? Will it happen whenever I'm not looking or leaving class? I might need to change my route from algebra class to world history. Will one of them sneak up behind me near one of the trailers and grab me? Many times, I've thought about going to Principal Acorn about them, but I don't want to be that girl, the tattletale. Girls hate that girl. Everybody hates that girl. I, myself, hate that girl. I can't be her. I can't be a victim. I'm better than that! Sure, I could be like that conniving whore, Shauna Egger, who recently dyed her nappy hair blonde, and let Brandon and his pencil dick butt buddies walk all over me as if I was a red carpet. Her last name speaks for itself. Egger. Say it three times fast. I'd like to egg her while she's on stage. She's this wannabe who thinks she's the next Beyoncé, yet she can't sing if her life depended on it. The other day she had this AMA on Read'em. She's done like only a handful of gigs, has something like three thousand followers on Chatterz, which clearly went straight to her head. I haven't met somebody so pretentious in my life. She can thank her mom for that. When you have a grownup constantly telling you you're the best musician in the world or how "creative" you are or praising you in front of all your friends, I guess after a while all of that approval changes you. In a way, I feel bad for Shauna for how pathetic she is. I got a couple of girlfriends to go on Read'em and screw up the sesh. Simple questions about music, like what kind of microphone does she use or what sound effect does she use on her voice—because clearly, she can't carry a pitch—turn into a shit-throwing contest. It first started with Brianna asking Shauna if she preferred a brown shower or a yellow shower and then from there, things got way out of hand. Seriously, talk about shitting in a blender without a lid. Bring your umbrella and your poncho. She's got what I call the musician's disease. She puts out a song. Okay. Big deal, right? Anybody can do it. Check it. Here's me making a beat, singing the words: *Little Miss Blonde, Little Fucking Bitch, Acts like a snitch, whenever she gets an itch. Look at her now. Too proud to be a clown. Get up out of my face, Little Miss Bitch.* Okay. Someone out there likes it. Wants to hear another song. Let's see what you got. She puts out another one. Starts a band with a bunch of basement musicians who dress like wannabe bank robbers. They call themselves "The Bandits," but they clearly haven't stolen a thing in their pampered lives. The only thing they've stolen was people's valuable time—I actually know the guitar player. Name's Tucker Carelton. He's this total wuss who spends his Saturday afternoons playing magic cards in the back of Journey with all of the rest of his virgin friends. Back to Little Miss Egg That Bitch, so all of the attention goes straight to her pretty head. Next thing you know, she thinks she's God's greatest creation. The One. Look at me. I'm the "Chosen" One. She actually feels as if she can change the world with her music (one time, she traveled with Megan on a missionary trip in the slums of Jamaica to help out the starving kids you'd see in TV commercials every year around the Holidays. The whole trip was basically a selfie fest; Shauna acting like Shauna but it was all for show. A weeklong photo op. It wasn't just a coincidence that she had a new album—which she was offering on cassette tape—coming out the week after she came back from Jamaica. I mean, seriously, cassette tape? Who still listens to cassette tape? What? Is she trying to bring back the Eighties?) She even ran a fundraiser—you know, what these pretentious musicians do in order to gain exposure—on the same people she made fun of in class. 'Course, it was to get attention. Anybody who does these things does it all for the attention—or, if they're the religious type, they think it might score them points with their God or Karma. It wasn't about community, like she was "supposedly" supporting. It was all about her, Shauna Egger. Talk about Queen Phony. I want to strangle these people who pretend to draw awareness to a serious issue when they're only drawing it to themselves. People are so dumb that they gobble up this crap like it's Reeces Pieces. I mean, the only thing famous about Shauna is her pussy. Seriously, it has its own private fan club; and every single day, her groupie fans follow her around like flies to a stench, hoping to get a whiff. Brandon doesn't think I know, but I saw Brandon flirting with her the other day. She's trying to make a statement. She's trying to rub it in my face. Before Shauna was a cool girl, she was the girl who used to wear yellow and bright colors, like a 1960's Stepford Housewife, in order to stand out. Any girl who wears that much yellow is only trying to draw attention to herself. For all I care, she can choke on whatever he gives her. Not like it's that big anyway. Just saying.

The only thought that keeps me going is that I only have two more years, then I'm free.

Hang in there, Akea.

Two more years.

I'm counting the days.

Before I turn away, I see Jamal grabbing the bulge in his pants and mouthing something to me.

Vintage Jamal.

I can just see him trying to undress me with his eyes. It happened so long ago, yet I still feel so humiliated.

I never quite pick up what Jamal's trying to tell me, as I make my way through the lobby. I don't care, but I do care.

Relief washes over me once I meet up with Demeter and the rest of my friends.

Before she can explain to me everything that went down with her and Omar, I tell her Jamal was checking me out yet again. She's mortified.

"Again?"

"Yeah," I say. "*Again*, again. I'm getting so sick and tired of trying to avoid them."

"You should really say something to them."

"Like that's going to keep them from looking at me."

"You can't keep people from looking at you, Akea."

"It's creepy."

"I'll say something," Veronica says.

"This is my mess," I tell her. "I need to handle it on my own."

## 16. AFTER / AKEA

THIS isn't real—none of this is real.

It *can't* be real, can it?

I know I'm just stuck in a horrible nightmare and soon I will wake up. Or, maybe I've been caught on one of those reality TV shows where I've fallen witness to something morally indecent and soon some suave TV host with a fifty-dollar haircut is going to pop out from nowhere and surprise me like in those hidden camera shows. A film crew tagging along with him as he greets me with his TV smile and says in his TV voice, "You're on TV!"

I grip my left hand with my right hand and squeeze it so tightly a jolt of pain radiates up my wrist. Not sure if someone can feel pain in his or her dreams. I once read that pain is only in the mind, same goes with fear, another artificial reality. I'm so infuriated by my left hand, what it's created, what it's done to me, all of the pain it's causing me, that I want to tear my hand away from my forearm, all of the ligaments and nerves and tissue and muscle stretching out like rubber until all of it finally snaps off.

"—Ms. Woods?"

They're staring at me, again. Why do they keep staring at me? Have I changed?

"Akea Woods?"

My hands appear the same, my left still intact. They're dry and crusty from the lack of lotion, but they're still a part of me.

I look back up at these doctors and the third man sitting among them and they're not staring at my hands, though, or any other part of my body. They're staring at my face.

I wonder if the drugs they said were being pumped into the room are having an adverse side effect on me. One minute I was searching for a way out of the room, then the next I wake up in here, not knowing how I ended up here, wherever here may be, answering questions on what happened Tuesday afternoon. I've never seen a person die before—that is, in real life. They also want to know how I felt about the terrorist—and still do, they want to know how I *feel* about her. For the past couple of days, I've tried to hold the image of her in my mind. Not once did I feel the least threatened by her, especially after everything she did to those soldiers as well as the FBI agents—not sure if they were FBI, but whoever they were, they're dead. She was much different than any woman I have ever known. Being grilled and forced to answers questions about myself is hard enough, let alone trying to express my feelings about another women to a group of men. I don't know how they know these things about me, personal things I would only share with my closest friends, Demeter or Veronica. How long have they been stalking me?

"Please, just answer the question and then you can retire back to your cell."

"Sorry," I say. "What was the question?"

"Why do you think your boyfriend, Brandon—"

"—Ex-boyfriend," I cut him off before he can say another word.

"Does your ex-boyfriend, *Brandon*," he makes sure to clarify that name for me even though the name is branded in the back of my mind, "make you feel some sort of resentment against men?"

"I don't see what this has to do with what happened on Tuesday. I told the FBI agents everything. What more do you want—"

"—Consider this off the record, Ms. Woods," the stranger says. "We just want to get to know a little about you."

"So, you wanna know why I hate men? That's your question?"

"Well, did you like Brandon or was it all a front?"

"*Front*? What do you mean by that?"

Suddenly, a feeling comes over me—not like that initial feeling of fear like the one I experienced when the bullets started flying overhead, but a squeezing feeling, like an invisible hand has wringed my insides like a wet beach towel—and I find myself holding back tears.

"Why are you so upset, Akea?"

"I'm scared about what people will think of me?"

"And what will they think of you?"

I think about Andrew Wexler and what everybody will be saying about me after I'm dead. Will all of the rotten truth come out about me? Will my name be painted on the school rock? Or, will they hang my photo in front of the school, like loved ones do at an open wake? They won't have to look far for a photo of me on the Internet. Will that be the last image of me that they'll think of, a photo of my tits? Is that all they will see when they look at me? My tits?

I wonder how many people will place flowers or carnations next to my naked photo.

I can't be that person, the one who gets pitied even by the pitiless, the one who was holding onto something dark inside her, yet she was too afraid to be herself because, at the end of the day, society would always find a way to condemn me—call me names like *faggot, queer, homo, lesbo,* and even worse, that one word, *dike.* Just the sound of it stabs me in the chest.

"They won't accept me because I'm different."

"Different how?"

One man suddenly looks around the bland room as if I've said something that caught him off guard and he's checking to see if the others heard the same thing.

"You know," I say, "like different."

"You need to be a little more specific—"

"—Please, Roger," the okay man says and turns to me. He asks, "What's her name?"

My heart is banging against my chest. A flash of heat runs through my skin. I'm taking in deeper breaths.

"Catherine. . . " I say weakly. ". . . Cat."

It feels so good to say her name, to tell another person.

"Are you afraid that Cat may not like you more than a friend?"

"Yes."

"Have you told her how you feel about her?"

"No," I say, feeling a weight slip from my chest. "I thought about telling her, but I don't even know where to begin. I just *don't* want the attention."

"Why don't you want the attention, Ms. Woods? Everybody likes attention, even the ones who say they don't."

"I know how people can be—I just wanna go about my life without having my 'sexuality' be turned into a bumper sticker someone bought at Wal-Mart for five dollars or turned into a political 'talking' point," I say, the beating is back, stronger, faster now. "I-just-want-to-be. I mean, is that so hard to ask? What the hell is wrong with that, just *being* without the labels, without politics, without the bullshit?"

"When did you start to have feelings for Cat?"

I take in a deep breath and try to calm myself by breathing through my nose.

"About a year ago," I say. "Well before she joined JV."

"Is she the first person whom you've had feelings about? Or, are there others?"

"Just her, really," I say, watching the device scribble next to me. "I mean, I thought my fifth grade teacher was attractive. She was young for a teacher. Probably in her early thirties. Maybe. I don't know. But she was—I don't know—just something about her. Maybe the way she carried herself. Her name was Ms. Rabb. I didn't think much of it at the time. I thought they were just feelings—that's all—and like all feelings they come and go. They certainly didn't define me, but they *were* feelings all right."

"Do you think you've always been this way?"

"Maybe it had something to do with my dad and the way he treated my mom."

"How did your dad treat your mom?"

"Like a doormat," I say without giving the question any thought. "That's how."

"Did your dad and your mom ever get through their issues?"

"They got through them all right," I say, thinking whether or not I should tell them the story about how my mom threatened my dad.

I haven't shared the story with anybody, not even with Demeter. Maybe me being here has something to do with everything that's happening to me and why I'm starting to be more open, whereas, in the past, I would never share my personal issues—if that's what you want to call them—with people, let alone strange men.

"One night, my dad came home drunk as always," I say, feeling the night creep back into my thoughts, the fear, the insecurity, the apprehension, the uncertainty, the bitter realization of the future. "Then, he started to get aggressive with my mom. I could hear them arguing downstairs from the top of the stairs. I don't know what they were arguing about, but I'm pretty sure it was about his drinking or coming home late. There's nothing to be proud of when your dad's an alcoholic. I've heard someone call him a 'functioning alcoholic.' Regardless, nobody likes an alcoholic. They're predictable and lame. I don't think my dad was cheating on my mom, either. So, it had to be the drinking because he didn't strike me as a man who would cheat. Then, again, I really didn't know who he was until I heard that loud *thud* in the kitchen. I remember hearing the blade sliding from the holder. I'll never forget that sound, that *zip* of steel. I ran to my room and hid in my closet. Counted to ten. He actually gave me that advice after one day I got into a fight at elementary school, he said to count to ten whenever I'm feeling upset or bothered or bullied. It's weird because I was using the same advice my dad gave to block out what he was doing to my mom downstairs. She ran into my room, hunkered down next to my bed. She called out my name, but I didn't answer. Too scared. Too everything, really. She had blood on her clothes. I realized, after I got a closer look through the closet door, that she wasn't hurt. She was out of breath, I figured, but she didn't appear to be hurt. I didn't see any wounds on her or whatever. So, I knew the blood wasn't hers. It was his." The anxiety fades away from my body and I feel light, as if I can float from this very room. "You know," I say, embracing the light of the stage, "the only *real* fond memory I have of him was the morning after it happened. My mom cut him good, too, and he had bandages all over his arms. He told me he got the cuts while he was trying to put these brand new blades onto the lawnmower. His hand slipped. What ah. . . " I clench my teeth, ". . . what a liar. He even walked me outside into the garage—even messed up the lawnmower to help cover up his story. My dad staged it all. He even dropped some of his own blood onto the ground. Showed me the bicycle I didn't get for Christmas. He said he finally got enough money to buy it. The man thought he could just buy me stuff to take my mind off all the crap he constantly threw at us. There was one thing he couldn't buy. He couldn't buy my feelings. My mom never left him—she should—but she didn't. Couldn't. I guess when a person has that much control over you, it's tough to make decisions on your own." My head suddenly starts to bob back and forth, my eyes struggling to focus on the pencil in the man's hand. "I don't know. . . what. . . I guess. . . "

The floating sensation intensifies and I find myself getting dizzy. I see streaks of light in the corner of my eyes, as if my body is ripping itself apart from the world before my eyes. I do my best to focus on an object—anything—so I pin my eyes on the lens of the camera in front of me, but my vision starts to blur and then the lens suddenly turns into two lenses, then three, four, five.

Am I dying?

Suddenly, one of the guards' phones *rings* directly behind me. The guard quickly shuts off the phone before it can ring a second time.

"I'm sorry," he says to the doctors. "I forgot. . . "

One of the men—I can't tell which one—rushes over to the guard and escorts him from the room in a hurried manner. He's whispering something in the guard's ear, but I can't tell what it is. The man is pissed off, so much that I think he's going to physically harm the guard.

Before I can make sense as to what's happening, my eyes are veiled in blackness.

* * *

A beam of sunlight washes away my black thoughts and I find myself waking up in the same cell I woke up in before.

How did I get here?

Everything about me is heavy, that familiar druggy feeling I had during the interrogation. I slowly stand up to my feet. The world spins a bit, but once I get the blood going, everything balances out. I come across a new glass of what looks like water on the floor. I pick up the glass and smell it. It doesn't smell like anything. I set the glass back down. Another thing catches my eye: a book next to the door.

Before I passed out in the other room, I was reading another book called *The Children's Hour* by Lillian Hellman.

I pick up the new book.

Mary Shelley's *Frankenstein.*

## 5. BEFORE / MONICA

WHERE do I even begin?

My grandfather, the great Luke Phelps, a man who has been so prevalent in my life for these past three years, is now spending the remainder of his days wilting away in a hospital bed. Stage four brain cancer. A couple of months ago Luke went in for a routine checkup at the doctor's office. Mother said he had been complaining about a headache that wouldn't go away. Which is unusual. As long as I've known Luke, he's never complained about anything. He'd always say whenever I used to get upset that life was too short to complain—"life is absurd," he'd say, "so enjoy it the best you can!" The doctor examined his head, ordered a whole bunch of imaging tests, and whatnot. When the tests came back, the doctor saw an abnormality. Mother wanted Luke to be the one to tell me. So, he sat me down after school and told me about the cancer. It was as if the world around me started to collapse. The doctor found a tumor about the size of a kidney bean in his brain. Doctors gave him options: remove the tumor, which seemed imperative; then do the chemo. There was also a new drug on the market, recently approved by the FDA, which had shown significant results in many patients. Luke was a man of dignity, a man who demanded respect. He wasn't too keen on titles. Didn't even like to be called Grandpa or Papa. He had already been so many other things in his lifetime. So many "titles." He was a man of many names. I think he had like seven different names, but I only know of three: Lu-Lu, Captain Phelps, and Bearclaw—apparently Luke was once a recluse who lived in a cabin in the Appalachian Mountains; he spent two years in silence, no contact or communication with the outside world. So immediately I understood why he didn't want to be known as a victim of cancer.

"A man only has one title," he used to say, "and that's his given name. The others are either names given to you by your ex or merely reflections of what you do."

Ever since I was a little girl, Luke was a total enigma. He'd show up in my life every couple of years, a Christmas or a birthday. Every time I saw Luke, he carried an aura about him, as if he was indestructible, traveling from one time period to the next, yet he appeared as if he never aged a day.

Now, Luke looks like the feeble stranger I always imagined him to really be whenever I heard Mother talk about him and his many problems. He reminds me of the raggedy men who linger around downtown Agatha, begging for something, *always* begging either verbally or through their body language. I don't exactly know what happened to Luke, when he started his steep decline, but it's like something evil or dangerous had taken over his body—I can't quite tell which one is yet, but I'm leaning toward evil.

Lately, I've gotten to know more about my grandfather and I'm glad.

After these past few years, I consider myself to be closer to Luke than my actual parents. Unlike Luke, my parents don't get me, and I don't think they ever will. My father and I used to be somewhat close, but now, it's like we're enemies keeping a close eye on one another. I like to think that it's entirely my fault, but he's changed. He's not the same person. I think Mother had something to do with it. Now, he walks around like a body snatcher; and whenever he acts interested in what I'm doing and starts asking questions, it's as if he's handing me a megaphone and he puts me on the spot in front of everybody. I don't know whether he's disappointed in me or he wants me to prove to people, even strangers, that he raised a decent kid. He used to speak for me all the time, and it annoyed me so much. Whenever we would go out in public, he treated me as if I was a foreign student and he was my translator. I loved my father, I think. But whenever he'd embarrass me in front of people, I despised him. I know his intentions were good. Now, I don't know what's going on inside that head of his. Sometimes, I think he's thinking the same thing about me: What's going on in your head, Money? I want to tell him, but I just don't know how. Luke is easy. There were times when I could sit with him and just listen to him talk for hours—anywhere, the park, a shopping mall. Hell! Even the beauty salon! Wherever, it didn't matter because it felt as if nobody around us existed, and it was just me and him sharing our thoughts. Most of the time, he'd talk about what was going on in his life; he'd talk about the different places he'd been, the places where he traveled; he'd tell me all about life outside Agatha, the people, the faces. No matter what, he always wanted to hear what I had to say first. He was so interested in what I had to say, or what little I had to say. He had an entire chest full of stories, waiting to be shared, stories that may never see the light of day, stories like fossils buried deep in the earth, waiting to be discovered. He used to tell me stories about the time he spent chopping down trees in Mammoth, a mountain town which sat in the shadow of the Blue Ridge Mountains, to meeting his third wife, Camilla, the one whom I called grandmother—God rest her soul—in a local library (she was a librarian, he a lumberjack) to fighting in the Vietnam War, those long days in the darkness of enemy territory, longer nights underneath the stars. He was older than I was at the time, around his early twenties. He used to tell me about the jungle and how it would speak to him. There were times I thought he was out of his mind—he said that he never told people he fought in the war because 1) people thought you were messed up in the head—imagine your thoughts being shoved through in a meat grinder, then, afterwards, trying to put them back together—or 2) people thought you were a beggar. Regardless of what Luke said, I've always been curious about what was going on during that time period, the Sixties and Seventies. Two decades filled with smoking pot and making love and dancing to music, while at the same time protesting the war. I've heard about all of the uprise that went on during those days. It seems like there was so much going on, so much division. I've seen grainy black and white videos with people protesting against soldiers, like Luke, who were fighting in Vietnam. He said he felt as if his country had betrayed him, like in that one movie, Rambo; he came back from fighting in a war, only to be greeted by protesters who spat on him and called him murderer—I think that's why Rambo was so popular during that time. Everyday people were desperate for this strong, masculine figure to stand up and fight against the evils of the world, despite all of his flaws. I can't possibly imagine what it must've been like for Luke, for his own people to publicly betray him when he needed their support the most. I may disagree with Luke on so many things, but I have so much gratitude knowing there were people out there like Luke, but I'm starting to lose faith. I never hear about them. Ever. All you hear is one side. The false narratives. I never agreed with the war in Vietnam—but what am I saying? I can't speak about it because I never lived during that time. I want to believe Luke was doing a good thing, even if it wasn't the right thing—or wrong, depending on the person. Even if Luke did something that another person believed in, it didn't give that person a right to disgrace him for what he had done. He was just doing his job. And that job required a sacrifice to his country while at the same time it expected nothing in return but only respect and freedom he so rightfully deserved. As with Rambo, when he came home from war, he received neither of those things that sometimes I take for granted. I can't even put into words the way I feel about my grandfather, how he took a bullet for the country he was the most proud of. Who would even do that? March into battle, surrounded by the enemy, knowing there is a chance they wouldn't make it out alive, fighting for a greater cause. Just the thought of Luke risking everything—it feels like my heart is going to explode from all of the appreciation I have not only for him but also the others like him, who have fought in wars—pointless or not—taken bullets, lost limbs for our freedom, yet when they come home—even today—it's like all of that appreciation turns into this anger for the way I see others treat people like Luke. He humbled me. He showed me, in his own actions, not his words, the model of a human being.

How could anyone not respect a person like that?

Here's a prime example: Slick Rick is acting up again.

Tourette's Syndrome on full blast. He's been known to do this thing where he'll blurt out noises and blame it on other kids in the classroom. Classic. He doesn't really have a disorder—that is, if being a jerk is considered a disorder.

Ms. Young threatens to send him to Principal Acorn, but she's afraid to tell him how she really feels. I can see myself in Ms. Young's shoes, trying to deal with some disruptive kid who's just trying to get a rise out of other kids. She wants to tell him how she really feels about his behavior, but she can't and she won't, otherwise she may lose her job. Parents will hold protests, demand for her resignation. It'll go on like this a couple of more times, random outbursts, and then soon, I know because Slick Rick is about as predictable as an election, he'll start throwing things at the other kids, like balls of crumpled paper or anything he can get his hands on until Ms. Young calls another faculty member, or if it gets really out of hand, she'll call one of the resource officers, which is her last option. It happens like two times a week. It's become a normal routine.

While Ms. Young proceeds to write down our math problems on the chalkboard, I stare at a blank piece of notebook paper on my desk.

The only two words I've managed to scribble down are the words *Dear* and *Luke.*

I have so much to tell him, so much to write.

When I was younger—even now, with Andrew's death last week, then a couple of months before him, Springer found hanging in his closet by a noose—I saw and heard about other people, some friends, some not, some strangers, all of these people experiencing tragedies. I've known people who passed away, people who I was somewhat close with for a while before they were replaced with shittier friends or better yet, kids who were just there. One kid named "Shady," lived down the street from us. We used to go to his house whenever we were skipping school and smoke pot on his back porch. I wasn't close with Shady. I never knew his last name. He'd hook me up with pot and that's about it. I didn't know how it happened, but from what I heard from his sister, Paula, he was discovered sprawled out on the bathroom floor with blood and foam streaming from his nose and mouth. The investigators ruled Shady's death as an overdose. He was on a whole mixture of pills, mainly oxys—oxycontin, I remember that was his drug of choice; he'd eat them as if they were Skittles—and he was drinking hard liquor on top of all that. There was another kid who was probably more close to my neighbor than me. The kids called him Chafe—I honestly don't know where he got that name. During spring break, Chafe fell off a two-story deck and broke his spine. Paralyzed from the waist down. Just a year later he died from pneumonia. Then, Ashley Moore, a girl whom I've practically known since kindergarten. She lived in the midnight blue house at the end of my street. Neighbors rolled their eyes whenever the Moores were brought up in a conversation. Ashley's parents were divorced and they never kept up the house or lawn. She was a couple of years older than me; but after we finally met each other, we'd hang out from time to time. Actually, I used to frequently pass her at Shady's house. She'd be stopping by for a bag of weed, but I didn't know that at the time. At first, I thought she was just with Shady. But I never quite understood why she would leave every time I showed up at Shady's. I didn't even know she smoked until one day she showed at Shady's with a couple of other seniors. We smoked a couple of times after that, once at the infamous abandoned house in Hawk's Ridge. She'd never hang out for long, though. She'd smoke; then she'd be on her way. Last year, she died in a car accident. Hit head-on by a drunk driver. It was Ashley's first year at State—and last. Then, not long ago, Felix Vasquez, whom I've hooked up with at a few parties (somehow, Felix and I were always the last two left standing while everybody was passed out. We'd always say, "Why the hell not?" At least we have one thing in common). Felix was the type of kid who could've gone all the way. A soccer player with a golden leg. I've never been into soccer players but his girlfriend was way prettier than me—and more "together" than me. They made a great couple—I'd give them that. I miss Felix's humor every now and then. I remember whenever we did shots of Captain Morgan, his silky Spanish tongue would make an appearance. I found it extremely sexy. Last Christmas, Felix was reported missing while visiting his relatives in Lima, Peru. Days later, his body washed up on shore. Stabbed thirty-eight times. I was heartbroken for months after I heard the news. Thirty-eight times. I couldn't even bring myself to go to his funeral. Even though we hooked up several times, I wasn't really that close to Felix but still, it stung for a while. I felt bad for his family. I think he had a brother, but I think he dropped out after Felix's death. You hear about all of these tragedies happening to people you know or don't know, the accidents, the murders, overdoses, but not once do you *ever* imagine your own family going through one. Your flesh and blood. When you're faced with a death, you're no longer an onlooker or a sympathizer, for now the death belongs to you and only you. It's your to bear. And it covers every inch of you like an old wool blanket, scratching at your skin every time you attempt to change position. You're all the way in this thing. Neck deep. And there's no escaping it. And you certainly can't run from it. Can't hide from it. It's as if you've entered the world you've always feared, the one underneath all the normal, and that one normal world you once loved has been flipped upside down and everything has become cold and dark, like the worms under a rock, as well as all sorts of slimy, putrid creatures squirming around, fighting for air and light. After you spend enough time in this world, you stop squirming and do all you can to cover up the grief. Whenever you do hear about other tragedies, like Andrew Wexler just recently, then Todd Springer, your heart just aches for their families and you do everything you possibly can to lessen that burden of grief. Everyday, you practice your smile in front of a mirror. You practice how to act or behave normal, how to speak normal. No matter what, though, words roll off your tongue with a different tone and rhythm. This new, dark world has an uncanny ability to smother words, and grief is its greatest ambassador. It'll always be there, *that ache*, in your gut, in your bones, in your thoughts.

Like a tapeworm absorbing all of the valuable nutrients inside you.

No matter what, it will always take more than half of what you put in.

In a way, you need the parasite as much as it needs you.

It's a sad world and it can be even sadder if you carry all your problems out into the other world.

If only I could reverse time; instead of each day dying, each day I could start living.

I don't know what I'm going to do with myself after he's gone. I'm worried about my sister, Lucile. She's only twelve years old and she's about as cynical as someone five times her age. She cried for like two days when her favorite character from *The Walking Dead* died, yet when Grandma passed away from cervical cancer, she couldn't even squeeze out one teardrop. Luke told me that she's probably going through one of those phases. I don't know what's going to happen to Lucile when she's older, what person she's going to become. After Grandma passed, I couldn't even be around my parents for like a year. I tried to avoid them every chance I got because one minute Grandma's name would slip out in a conversation and every time Mother spoke her name, it felt like she was stabbing me with a knife. She was fully aware of how close I was to her parents—I talked to them more than I did to her. Sometimes, I felt as if she'd deliberately talk about Grandma, like she got some kind of pleasure out of watching me squirm or wiggle. It was obvious to everyone; whenever she brought up grandma's name, I'd immediately leave the room. I'm not sure what's going to happen after Luke dies. I'm not sure if I'm going to make it on my own. One day, I'll be forgotten or replaced or left on the side of the road, like one of those beggars, begging, always begging even when they're not.

I know Luke wouldn't want me to mourn him or to mope around all day after he dies. He'd want me on that field, playing, win or lose, nonetheless, trying.

Ever since Luke ended up in the hospital, most—if not all—of my friends have faded into the background and now, they're just "there," like the others, like these objects, faces with names. The only friends who've had my back are my teammates. We may not hang out at parties or socialize outside lacrosse, but we share a special bond that cannot be forged anywhere else. Some players have been bringing by food, like casseroles and whatnot, for my family. Just the other day Ebony's mother brought over these boneless barbeque ribs that were to die for. I wouldn't consider myself much of a carnivore—I try to stay away from red meat as much as I can—but they could convert any vegan. All of my teammates have been good to me—great, actually.

Slick Rick is acting up yet again.

When I think about Luke, who represented the stoic men of class, I can't help but think about how much I hate kids like Rick Winston.

Another side of me admires Slick Rick—fully and unconditionally—in fact, wishes I could be more like him, more outspoken, more upfront, more everything. I like how he doesn't care about what people think of him.

Maybe the world needs more kids like Slick Rick, kids trying to shake up the world and turn it on its head.

I focus on the letter while Ms. Young calls a resource officer.

Where do I even begin?

## 17. AFTER / MONICA

SOMETHING'S up with this living room. The room appears as if it's part of movie set. Even the jewelry box on the chest is hollowed out. A fake like everything else.

Why would anyone have a jewelry box with no jewelry?

So far, the only real things I've come across are the books and board games that I used to play with when I was younger. There are so many books, ones that I've never read before. Some, I've read when I was younger.

As far as movie sets, I know a little bit about them. Two years ago, Luke took me on a tour at Warner Brothers Studios. He knew a guy, a hotshot producer in Hollywood, who served with him in the army. It was probably the best birthday present ever. We visited the sets of some of my favorite TV shows. Amazing how some of the scenes filmed in bedrooms are part of sets. They said it's much easier to build a bedroom on set because there's more room for the cameras and lighting. Ever since I was younger, I've always been fascinated with the movies and how they're made, the process—I can't believe how many people are involved with making one. One day, I'd like to write a movie of my own—that is, if I make it out of here alive, wherever here might be. The last thing I can remember was grabbing some water from the vending machine.

Luke just passed away.

He went at exactly five minutes till midnight on a Friday night. I was still trying to wrap my head around what he said before he passed.

Who was watching me?

He never referred them to a man or woman; instead, he said, "They are watching you."

They?

Who are they?

I looked like a train wreck. My entire face was swollen and red from wiping away tears. So many things happened before he passed, so many things left in the air. Most importantly, I was still trying to figure out if the dream I had was real or not. I remember dozing off while I was sitting by Luke's bedside. Then, I remember Luke getting out of bed. He removed the IV from his arm, then the catheter. The alarm would've gone off. The nurse would've checked on Luke. I know I was in a dream because none of those scenarios happened. I followed Luke into an empty hallway. No nurses were at their station. No doctors. No patients. At first, I thought maybe they were on a break. Slow day maybe. I continued to follow Luke and I remember I couldn't keep up because my legs were heavy. He turned around and looked at me when he reached an intersection in the hallway. I couldn't recognize his face; both of his cheeks were sunken in; skin as gray as newspaper; and his eyes were dark and beady and lost inside each socket of his skull. Part of his gown peeled open, revealing the skeletal body hiding underneath. I was scared of Luke, scared of his appearance, but he kept moving. I kept following him into the unknown. He ended up taking me to the hospital's chapel where a black priest was reading scripture to young children. He stopped at one of the pews in the front row opposite of the children. He sat down and he stared at the crucifix hanging above. I remember it wasn't like any crucifix I have seen before. The Jesus on the cross wasn't made of wood. The Jesus was real flesh and blood. Strings of blood were pouring down his arms and legs. He was whispering to Luke, but I couldn't make out the words. I approached Luke. He snapped from his daze and looked up at me. I sat down next to him on the pew. He wasn't talking to me, nor was he responding to any of the questions I was asking him.

Then, all of a sudden, Luke grabbed me by the wrist and spoke those four words to me—Now that I remember it wasn't the word *they*. It was *He*.

His grip kept tightening over my arm. He was hurting me. I tried to let go, but his grip kept getting tighter and tighter.

The dream ended.

I woke to the sound of nurses rushing into the room, unaware of what was going on.

I honestly didn't know what had happened. Nurses were trying to revive Luke. They told me he must've slipped away while he was sleeping.

After Luke passed, I went to the main lobby and grabbed a bottle of water. I went outside, then, from there, nothing. I have nothing. No memories. Only a stream of blackness. I remember I was staring at the stars. A bright light suddenly shined over my shoulder. I believe it was the headlights of a car maybe, but I'm not sure. Something happened. Then, I woke up in a prison cell with a hospital gown and a fresh pair of white socks lying on the bed.

I come across a vent. I place my hand underneath and feel a cool draft.

Whoever these people are, they must be pumping something into the room. Some kind of sleeping gas or something. I need to find something to block the vents or else.

I rip off the drapery from the window and tear away pieces of cloth and place them over the vent.

I do the same with the other vents.

Place pieces of curtains over the vents.

I wait for something to happen.

Then, it happens.

A voice from behind: "*Let's have a talk, Ms. Phelps*."

I turn around, only to find a strange man standing at the doorway.

I don't answer the man. I don't know him nor do I like the way he looks at me. My father used to look at me like that, like he was waiting for me to speak.

He reaches in his pocket and pulls out a folded piece of notebook paper.

My letter—or, my lack of letter.

I must've forgotten it. I don't remember taking the letter when they made us dress into these hospital gowns. He unfolds the letter. Reads the two words on the piece of paper.

I already know the two words, obviously.

What does he want to know about my grandfather?

## 6. BEFORE / CATHERINE

TWO periods down so far, and I'm still left picking up the highlights from last night's dream.

Over my shoulder, Mrs. Hoffman makes her morning laps through the classroom aisles as if she's sniffing out who didn't read their assigned reading for last night's homework.

I find myself sinking in my seat because I didn't read Act Four of *The Crucible.*

She stops at my desk and looks down at me, her eyes cutting right through me.

We share a glance for a moment before she continues to stalk from one aisle to the next.

Mrs. Hoffman doesn't play around. She's boss. When you step into her classroom, shut up, speak when spoken to, and no matter what, be prepared to learn. Of all the teachers I have this year, Mrs. Hoffman is, by far, one whom I respect the most. She doesn't tolerate any nonsense. She only expects cooperation from her students as well as an unapologetic willingness to learn. My last teacher, Ms. Cramer, was average. It was her first year teaching English and at times, she'd let the students walk all over her and dictate what went on. I didn't learn a thing last year.

So far this year, we've read *Jane Eyre* by Charlotte Bronte, which, to my surprise, I enjoyed more than I'd expected—I can't believe Mr. Rochester was hiding his "crazy" wife on the third floor of the house!

Mrs. Hoffman stops at the front of the classroom and asks us to pull out our *Crucible* books.

She starts writing some Paideia questions on the board.

With her back facing the classroom, my mind starts to drift and I'm left trying to piece together the dream last night. The dream always starts the same, with me in the most epic bike race—which is always strange to me because I'm a runner and as I runner, and I think I speak for all runners, I can't stand bikers. I hate bikers when they zip by you without giving you a verbal heads up. Once I got clipped by one dick while I was running the trails. Some of them can be assholes and act as if they own the trail.

Bikers aside, the bike race dream has become my "go-to" dream. I don't know why I would dream about something I don't like. Even when I'm stuck in a boring dream or even a nightmare, I always end up in that one dream. Each time the theme of the dream may change; instead of bikes, I may be riding like a motorcycle—I've had a dream where I'm riding a bike and then, all of sudden, the bike turns into a car; either way, the dream is always the same: I'm in a race. It's an intense race, most of the race is held on the desolate streets of a small downtown, like Agatha, but way more roads; most of the participants are bundled together in a pack. I'm in first place, just by nose-lengths, and if I slow down for a second or break speed, I know I'll be left in the dust. I'm approaching an intersection. I ignore these massive barricades and somehow, my eyes catch this one little red flag. It's the first lap, so I'm not sure where to go. So, I decide to follow the little flag in the top left corner of the facade of a building. I hook a sharp left and the path turns bumpy and dark and stretches out into an ominous-looking desert. I can only see so far, only a backdrop of jagged, geometrical-shaped mountaintops, before the path trails off into a stormy darkness. I turn my shoulder and see the other bikers going the opposite way. I realize I've gone the wrong way. I quickly change direction and catch up to the others. As I'm about to reach my spot among the pack, the path suddenly drops at a dangerously close ninety-degree angle. The path is windy and steep and I'm racing out of control. All I can see is sky around me and a pathway splitting through a wash of dark blue. The front end of my bike digs deeper into the ground and I can feel my body weight shifting forward, ready to fall and tumble. I realize if I fall, I'm dead. I learn how to embrace the steepness by turning my bike sideways and riding the hill on its side like a skier, my fingers raking through crumbly asphalt, which helps slow me down. We reach the bottom and just when I think I'm about to level out, we go down another steep hill; and the race keeps going on like this, over and over, one hill after another.

As any dream that brings forth the inner clues of the self, I know this one dream in particular is telling me two things. It couldn't be more obvious. I'm out of control with my life and if I don't slow down, I'll keep falling. The dream's also telling me I need to stop following others and travel the "road less traveled," as Akea's mother told me when I told her about the dream. I haven't told my father about the dream, and I don't plan to, either. I can't speak to him because every time I try, it feels as if I'm speaking through him. I want to tell him how I truly feel about him, how he tries to control me. I know he means well. He wants me to continue playing lacrosse because he feels lacrosse can get me a scholarship and pay for college. I've spent the last two years of my life religiously playing lacrosse. I'm beginning to feel spent. My day is surrounded by lacrosse. My entire summer was wasted at Lacrosse Camp when I could've been hanging out with my friends.

I glance down at the glossy magazines in my bookbag. My father believes that I have no future in fashion design. I think he's afraid of me being so far away from him. He doesn't want me to live in a place like New York City. He thinks it will eat me up and spit me out. I'm aware the competition is fierce, but I'm up for the challenge. Lately, it seems like my father doesn't approve of anything I do.

The truth: my heart is not into lacrosse anymore.

If I tell him the truth about how I feel, I'll let him down—I can just hear my father now, "I'm disappointed in you." The last person on earth who I would want to disappoint is my father, especially after everything he's experienced.

*But*, on the other hand, if I don't tell him the truth, I'll be letting myself down.

Mrs. Hoffman finishes writing down the questions on the board.

She faces me and it's like she can see right through me.

"Ms. McDonald," she says, my own name startling me.

"Yes, Mrs. Hoffman?"

"John Proctor makes a stirring speech about the madness that has gripped Salem. He says, quoting, 'I'll tell you what's walking Salem—vengeance is walking Salem.' Do you agree or disagree? And explain why?"

"Agree."

"Why?"

"I'll tell you why. . . "

## 18. AFTER / CATHERINE

SHE showed me a life without the ones I love. These are the exact words I use to describe the terrorist to these doctors and there's no question that they get some kind of arousal from my response. That's the most reaction

I've received in the past hour I've spent going over the minutia of details on the bus. I don't know where the words came from, but they were words that I assumed they needed to hear. They want me to explain more about her, as if I hadn't done enough explaining as it is. I just want to go home. They tell me I can't go home. Not now. It's not safe, according to Roger.

Doctor Bloch urges me to relax after I explain to him my situation but he obviously doesn't understand how vital it is for me get back home to tend to my father.

He keeps asking me questions about my father even after I plea with them to let me go.

"Help us understand, Catherine," he says, lowering his voice. "Why do you need to get back to your father?"

"He's disabled," I say, even though it's none of their damn business.

"Does he have anyone else to take care of him?"

"My aunt," I say, "but she can't take care of him on her own."

They're curious about my father. They act like they want to help me. The doctor sends one of his colleagues to give my aunt a call and ask her if she needs any assistance. I'm not sure if they're trying to prove me wrong, but they're acting as if they care. I don't know what to think of them.

As one of the doctors exits the room, Doctor Bloch tells me to talk about my father.

I've never talked about my father with another person before.

I ignore the theatrics around me, the cameras, the strange men, the eyes, and speak my mind: I remember the days before my father would leave for tour; the way I felt, it's like it'll always be there, reminding me. All the preparation. Mostly mental stuff, like visualizing his return, seeing his face again. In the back of my mind, way deep behind all of the pleasant images—the fantasies—there was always that one image of my father being brought home in a casket just like the others, wrapped in the flag. You can try to prepare yourself for the worse.

It always helps me. Giving myself options: Will he come home? If so, how? Every time he said goodbye, I knew it was possibly going to be the last time I'd see him. I'm the daughter of a decorated Marine. We don't rest. We don't have the luxury of resting. It's who we are, not what we've become. It's our job to be strong, no matter what happens. I wanted there to be a time when I didn't have to prepare anymore or worry about anything anymore. Now that he's back home for good, it's like he's fighting a war he cannot win. He just can't do it on his own. Sometimes, I get sick of worrying what will happen tomorrow or the next day. Will my father return back to normal? Normal? I don't even know what that word means anymore. Sometimes, I can 'see' him going about his daily life, running errands or whatever, just 'being there' with us, knowing that he was going to be okay. We were going to be okay.

Doctor Bloch asks, "What happened when your father returned home?"

My father was only back for three days until it happened. Those were probably the best three days of my life. I felt like this was going to be it. This was going to be that time I always dreamt about, not having to worry anymore. We were going to be okay. He spent years fighting, surviving, only to come home and have this happen to him. My father was a good man—a great man. He would've given that man every dollar in his wallet, every penny in his pocket. He would've bought that man a nice suit for a job interview to help him get a job. He would've helped that man. That's the kind of man he was.

"Was?" he says. "You said 'was.'"

I don't understand the remark at first. I pull myself from my thoughts and retrace what I had just said—*was a good man.* I like to think those words to be true. Still. Sometimes, I can see 'old' him in there—a glimmer of good—but it's like the bad is preventing the good from coming out. He acts as if he's a dead man, an object to be moved around. I don't know where everything went wrong for him. At times, I tried to take myself back to a time when things were *normal*, long before war, and wonder if all of the bad which had now taken over him was there inside him, like the good now, hiding like an elusive creature afraid to crawl out from all that dark slime. I'd say it was after he came back home from his third tour when he started to change a bit, the nubs around his soul had started to wear down. I'd like to think Dwayne Louis Mayweather was responsible for ruining my father's life, but a part of me would only be lying to myself. He began his slow descent well before he left. He looked like a man trapped or cornered. Mr. Mayweather brought out all that was hiding inside him and eventually it got to the point where the bad had finally won. I know there's a part of my father that wants it all to end—just to walk away from life—but I think there's also another part of my father that would never let that side of him do that to me.

My eyes start to burn, my jaw trembling.

I wipe the tears from my face and try to hide the emotions from the camera.

"I know there's still some good left in him," I say to myself, "but I just don't know. I feel—he feels like his country betrayed him. Everything that he fought for, it meant nothing anymore. My father did his time. He fought to protect us, to make the country a stronger nation. He put in the hours. He deserved to live the rest of his life in peace. Like Monica said, it's like the world doesn't want men like our fathers or grandfathers anymore. So, what do they do? They cast them aside like old, rotten meat and then they feed them to the wolves. And now, with my father, it's like he doesn't want anything to do with the world anymore. I'm hoping one day he'll come around, but I just don't know anymore. . . "

"What's his condition, if you don't mind saying?"

"Paralyzed from the waist down," I say over a wet sniffle. "The bullet hit his spine."

"Did they catch whoever shot your father?"

"Yes," I say. "They did. And he went to prison. His sentence was reduced after he took a plea bargain. Go figure. He even had priors. He was a convicted felon. The year before he shot my father, he was released from jail after doing a ten-year stretch for armed robbery. Before that, he did time for stabbing his wife with a steak knife."

"You think people like Dwayne Mayweather can't be rehabilitated?"

"I think people like Dwayne Mayweather don't deserve a third or fourth chance. You should only be allowed two. But I guess that's what our country has turned into. *Soft.* Weak. A country overrun by spoiled brats who go and cry whenever they don't get want they want," I say, the tears flowing down my face. Angry tears. The kind of tears that hurt. "There is no class or no middle ground. You're either hypersensitive or desensitized to everything. How did we get this way?"

"You don't think we've always been this way?" he asks.

"It feels like it's only getting worse."

Doctor Bloch leans forward over the table and unfolds his hands.

"What are you going to do about it?" he asks.

"What can I do about it?"

"Do you—or will you—forgive this Dwayne Mayweather for shooting your father?"

"By the time that son of a bitch gets out of jail, I'll probably have children." I shrug. "Hopefully."

The anger dissolves from the thought of children. You can have all the pessimism in the world, but when it comes to children, it's like all those negative feelings vanish, like they were never there to begin with.

"Would you like to have children?" he asks.

"Yes," I say. "Very much."

"How many?"

"I've always wanted to have two of them," I say clearly. "A boy and a girl. I'm sure, if I have children by the time he's released, I'll have a much different answer to that question. Right now," I look into the camera, sharpen my eyes, and give him a clear answer, "No. I don't forgive him. I'll *never* forgive a man like that. He can die in jail for all I care."

My tears become hotter and when they roll down my face, they sting.

I don't bother wiping them away. Yet, I let them coat my cheeks.

I embrace the fire.

"What's on your mind, Catherine?" the doctor asks me, as if he knows there's way more to my answer. "Do you wish you could've taken the law into your own hands?"

"Does it matter? He's where he should be."

"Surely, you must *fantasize* about avenging your father."

"I've given some thought to it but that's all it is really, just thoughts."

"Say, if you were given a chance to face the man who shot your father: What would you say? What would you do?"

"I'll tell you what I would do—"

The door suddenly opens behind me.

The same doctor from before, Doctor Ahmad, enters the room. I can hear commotion outside the room, but a loud humming noise is drowning out the incoherent chatter.

Doctor Ahmad rushes toward Roger and whispers something in his ear.

The first thing that races through my mind: *something bad has happened to my father.* They're not telling me anything.

Both of the doctors turn toward me and they're carrying a look of concern on their faces. They nod at one of the guards standing behind me.

The guard approaches me with a needle in his hand. He sticks me in the neck with the needle, then a couple of tense seconds pass before I'm knocked out cold.

## 7. BEFORE / HALEY

SO far, everything is going just as planned.

Without Ms. Walters looking, I unplug my trusty heating pad from the electrical socket next to the desk and slip it back inside my bookbag. Now that all I'm hot and feverish like the sick penguin I am, I put on my super-duper dopey I'm-so-sick face and waddle my way up to Ms. Walters like the sick penguin I am and tell her in the feeblest I'm-so-sick voice that I'm not feeling well and that I seriously need to visit the school's nurse. The smile on her face drops and she almost instantly looks concerned. She places her hand along the top of my warm forehead all thanks to my trusty heating pad.

She writes a note for the hall monitor.

Too easy.

1. Get the sick note: ✓

2. Leave Third Period: ✓

It should take me around five minutes to arrive at the nurse's office, but I can give myself at least an extra ten minutes. Since I'm "not feeling too well," I can just tell the nurse I made a pit stop at the girls restroom—that is, if any questions are asked as to why it took me so long, but I seriously doubt it. Nobody ever questions a sick person.

At the end of the hallway, my ever-so wicked partner in crime, Marie Shaffernak, flashes the glow of her phone at me while she's "supposedly" grabbing her school things from her locker.

Three flashes means go.

Two stop.

Three flashes.

It's on.

3. Receive the signal from Marie: ✓

I meet up with Jessie outside Mr. Hathaway's classroom. Jessie's got one heck of a "stomach bug." I'm talking about one of those twenty-four ones that hit him right in the middle of Latin class. Poor Jessie even forced himself to puke. He jammed his finger down his throat and then, Old Faithful all over the floor. What a champ! He's a dedicated individual. The janitor, Mr. Malone, who just came from Room 112 where he had to clean up poor Patrick's mess as well, is in there mopping up Jessie's partially digested blueberry English muffin while other students remain at a safe distance.

"Nice sell," I tell Jessie.

Jessie, pale faced, gives me an innocent shrug.

"Years of practice." Jessie reanimates himself by suddenly widening his droopy eyes. "Speaking of practice," he blurts out. I know where he's going with this but I let him continue anyway. "I've been doing a lot of practice on my own. I think this is what *it* should look like," he says as he can hardly contain himself and his youthful excitement. He pulls out a piece of folded notebook paper from his pocket, unfolds it as fast as his fingers can work, and shows me this sketch of the Herbert Booth statue—or what used to be Herbert Booth. Ole Herbie here is wearing the head of the black bear mascot. Strapped along his waist is what looks like a big black dildo; a giant yellow number one hand sign over his hand; thick gold chains wrapped around neck like a rapper from the Nineties. Written across his chest are the words *#WeAreBlackBears.*

"Oh my God, Jess!"

"What do you think?"

"Really with the hashtag?"

"We want it to go viral, right?"

"Yeah, but it kind of ruins everything else. Makes it more topical, you know. Loses its shelf value."

"What are you talking about? No it doesn't!"

"It just limits it to the Internet," I try to spell it out to my young apprentice. "The goal's to go beyond the Internet, remember?"

I point at the penis-shaped contraption on the statue.

"Is that what I think it is?"

"Yep."

"Is it really necessary?"

"Don't bears have big dicks?"

"Not that I'm aware of. I think you might be thinking of horses."

"I kind of like it. Gives it a certain charm."

"Charm?"

Jessie gives me another shrug, but this time more lively.

"What?"

I hear a voice from behind: "What are you cool kids up to?"

I pocket the sketch and spin around. Pam is approaching us. She's making a silly face from the sight of the crime scene inside the classroom. I don't really have to pretend or put on my sick face in front of Pam. She's not like any other teachers I know. She's one of us, but like an older one of us. Pam's beautiful in a sporty kind of way—if I were a guy, I'd definitely give her a shout, but I've also seen some of the girls look at her in a way that may suggest some extra thought. I don't know any teachers who would prefer to be called by their first name than their last, but like I've said, Pam's not like other teachers. Her body is as toned as one of those sports models in tennis shoe commercials; decent face, the kind of face most women her age wish they could have.

When I had Pam last year for health, I wondered what it felt like to be with an older woman—I mean, in a sexual way. It might have been a phase or something, but there was no denying the feeling I had for her. Pam used to wear these u-neck shirts that ran above her cleavage—sometimes, I thought she wore them to mess with the boys. She would often lean over students' desk while helping them with questions, then if you looked close enough from the right angle, you were likely promised a surprise. Most boys looked—I take that back—all of the boys looked. Some girls, too. The boys were the worst, especially afterwards when they'd cover up their boners with a textbook or try crossing their legs or even tucking it underneath their belt buckles. She put the *boo* in boobs. I remember one time she strutted into class wearing a plaid skirt that was considered too short according to the school regulations. Principal Acorn—who kids called Beavis because he looked like the dude from *Beavis and Butthead*—didn't do anything about it. Actually, I remember Beavis walking into our class to check on how our class was doing. Total bullshit. He was waiting for Pam to give him a "little" surprise. One time, he did the whole "drop the pen" move in front of her. Seriously, who does that anymore? I don't know if Acorn's hands were sweaty from being all nervous in front of Pam, but it worked. She kneeled down and picked up his pen—*Boo!* Then, boing! Run for cover! I was never that pathetic as the boys. I had a crush on Pam for a semester. But who didn't? I think Pam felt something for me too. I was never one who'd peep down her blouse whenever she wasn't looking. I mean, I did once. And Pam caught me in the act, too. She smiled, I remember. Forget shoe commercials! Pam would make a great spokesperson for yogurt. I can even see her in a commercial, marketing yogurt as if it's the best thing since sliced bread. Pam's the kind of woman who knows she's pretty and clearly, she's well aware that all of the boys—and girls—think she's pretty. Sometimes, she uses it to her advantage. I would.

Pam passes us, not really expecting an answer. The only involvement in the conversation—or lack thereof—from Jessie or me comes in the display of awkward reactions: a scratch of the head, a falling of our eyes, a shrug of our shoulders.

I know it's Pam's way of telling us that she's watching us, she knows what we're doing or what we're about to do. I don't know how she knows, but she does; and if I know Pam like I think I do, we're totally in the clear.

While Mr. Remington's at lunch, Jessie and I go into the auditorium. Jessie keeps lookout while I sneak into the dressing room backstage and grab the head of our school's mascot. I place the head on top of a stack of chairs, then place a black sheet over the chairs. It doesn't exactly cover up all the chairs but it covers up the head.

That's the whole point: when I roll the chairs into the storage room, the cameras will only pick up me pushing a stack of chairs. The sheet over the chairs will come across as being suspicious. Nonetheless, the head will be covered up and nobody will think a thing of it. If they do, all we have to do is deny, deny, deny. "The sheet was already on the chairs," I could say. "I put the sheet on top of the chairs because I didn't want them to get dirty." There are a million reasons as to why there's a sheet covering the chairs.

Now, the real kicker: What am I doing taking chairs to the storage room when I should be in the nurse's office?

Aren't you sick?

Let's rewind.

Right before I met up with Jessie, I "bumped" into Johnny the Body. Johnny the Body's a freshman. You're probably wondering why we call him the Body. He actually picked up the name for the certain "acts" that he could do with his body. He was born with strange abilities. Johnny the Mutant would be more fitting, but one day, he was doing his act and a junior came up behind him and gave him a high-five and said, "Way to go, Johnny with the Amazing Body!" After much debate, we decided to shorten it to just the Body and take out Amazing. You have to at least win like a World Series or like parachute from the tip of the CN Tower in Toronto before you can earn a word like *amazing* in front of your name. The name followed him around ever since. He can pop certain areas of his body out of joint, like a wrist or shoulder or elbow. He and Emily would make quite a cute pair. They could probably open up their own freak show together. He also does this gross thing where he turns both of his eyelids inside out. He once made a kid puke—that's got to count for something, I guess. Talent aside, he's a puppet. Not just any puppet, but our little puppet. He'll basically do anything we tell him to do; otherwise I'll expose him for the perv he really is. A couple of weeks ago I caught Johnny the Body filming underneath a freshman's dress with a selfie-sticks—the freak's got balls—he practically made the video while walking to class, then, anonymously posted the video online. Nobody knows Johnny the Body was the person behind it all, except for me and Marie. We saw the whole thing go down while we were at to our lockers. Not only are we black bears, we're blackmailers. Now, we own Johnny the Body. He may be one of our fall guys, but he's willing to do anything to get a rise out of people. Johnny the Body tells me he needs a little help with some "chairs" that need to be taken out of drama class and transferred to Ms. Ramirez's classroom—now, Jessie or myself included didn't exactly question why Ms. Ramirez needed the chairs; instead, we took Johnny the Body's word. This was the crucial part. Transferring these chairs from one location to the other is based around a lie—or miscommunication, if the school calls in the big guns. Do they even have detectives for schools? Anyway, we could just say the whole thing was lost in translation. Ms. Ramirez, our Spanish teacher who is from Venezuela, has a thick accent, and at times, her words can easily be mistaken for other words.

I told Johnny the Body that we would be glad to help. I told him to meet us at the storage room outside the auditorium. I couldn't help but notice the distraction in his breast pocket and I'm so amazed that the kid managed to carry it around on him all morning. It was so adorable. I wanted to pet the little thing. It was a shame that more than likely it was going to die. I almost felt bad. Almost. Either way, the exercise wouldn't hurt. After all, Jessie and me were both "sick as dogs" and I read once in an article on the Internet that exercise helps when you're sick—that's total bull. But that's our story and we black bears are sticking to it.

Now that you're all caught up, I place the chairs in the storage room. Johnny the Body meets up with me and before he grabs a handful of chairs, he places the distraction in the corner of the room. He says he only needs four chairs. So, he grabs two chairs for each arm and leaves. You see, at Central Agatha it's all about helping out your fellow man.

Jessie and I have done our good deeds for the day.

The minor workout was enough to get a temperature rising again, but the nurse doesn't need to know about our detour.

As we make our way to the nurse's office, we pass Marie. She's pushing a cart with an "inoperable" projector. It's an easy fix; however, most of the projectors are outdated. I've heard next year they're going to replace them with computers and tablets—that's the rumor. Computers are much trickier to sabotage, opposed to projectors. All you have to do is move some things around inside them or remove the bulb. Marie's chemistry teacher, Ms. Abernacky, isn't the least tech-savvy. She's basically retarded when it comes to technology. The extent of her knowledge when it comes to technology is flipping the ON/OFF switch.

Marie's right on time. She doesn't have the bug; instead, she was the first one who volunteered to grab a new projector from the library. The storage room happens to be on the way to the library. It couldn't have worked out better.

If it weren't for the weed brownies I gobbled down in First Period, then I'd be jumping out of my skin right about now.

The brownies help take off the edge.

So, while riding a nice buzz, I continue my way toward the nurse's office and from behind I hear the deafening *screech* coming from Marie!

She completely sold it.

I can imagine she's passing the storage room right about now. She's already gone inside the storage room to grab the mascot's head. She's already concealed the head by placing it on the bottom shelf of the cart.

But the real question that may initially come forward during the schools' investigation: What was Marie doing in the storage room when she should've been going directly to the library?

That brings me to our "little" distraction.

Johnny the Body calls him Lenny. He got the name from the book, *Of Mice and Men.* Lenny is an ordinary field mouse Johnny the Body found in his backyard while doing whatever it is Johnny the Body does in his backyard. Johnny the Body was close to Lenny, but, like I said earlier, we own Johnny the Body and we needed a cult sacrifice for our project and just as Marie passes the storage room, she spots the little furball in the corner of her eye. She's curious, as any other person would be. She pushes the cart inside, checks out the movement in the corner of the room. . . Slasher-film horror! Marie totally freaks. Oh my God! Oh my God! What is that?

After Marie's freak out, she grabs the nearest resource officer. Now, I'm not sure who she's going to grab—more than likely, Mr. Kellogg, who's normally patrolling hallways around this time. Mr. Kellogg or whoever checks out the commotion. Reluctant of his presence, Marie shows Mr. Kellogg or whoever the movement inside the storage room. "It's just a little ole mouse," he'd say.

Then, either two things: one, Little Lenny gets the boot. Literally. Squash soup. Or two, if I know Mr. Kellogg like I think I do—the gentle giant who was there for me when I lost my phone last year and he spent all afternoon helping me track it down—Little Lenny gets set free outside the school. Either way, Marie now has the head and she goes about her business while Mr. Kellogg takes care of the school's rodent problem.

Marie takes the "inoperable" projector to the library where Marie's older brother, Evan, is currently taking Library Science. She leaves the head with Evan and returns to the classroom with a new cart and now operable projector.

Here's where everything can fall flat: Johnny the Body's good friend, Brain—real name Brian. I don't know why they call him Brain. I met him once, and I swear he's missing a brain. But anyway, if he doesn't screw up the projector before Fourth Period, then all of the hard work will be for nothing. The only thing we will really gain from all of this is that Central Agatha's equipment is crappy, like a decade-outdated, and that we really do need those new fancy computers as rumored.

For now, let's say Brain does come through. He tweaks the projector, causing Ms. Hawkins, a first year teacher who can be easily manipulated, to call Evan, who, in return, will gladly bring by a new and operable projector for her.

While Evan brings the new projector to Ms. Hawkins Social Studies class, which happens to be in the trailer where there are no cameras, he'll carefully place the head underneath the second trailer; and then, from there, Patrick, who's caught something ugly and has already received a note from Nurse Blair for early dismissal, will gladly grab the head and load it in the back of his car. All we have to do now is wait until it gets dark outside and then that's where all of the fun begins.

By this time tomorrow everybody at Central Agatha will be talking about what happened to Herbert Booth, the founder of Central Agatha—and from all of the stories I've heard, a wealthy man who once rewarded his students for good behavior with cash. That's right! Cash! Can you believe it? What an individual! The story goes that he used to pay his students to read, then, at the end of the week, he'd require the students to tell them what they learned. It sounds strange to pay students to learn—sure nowadays you'd probably get thrown in jail—but most of the students from what I've heard turned out to be best selling authors or Nobel and Pulitzer Prize winners. It makes me wonder if Herbie was alive today, could he get away with it without the parents ratting him out. Would he pay students like me? Doubt it. No offense to Herbie, but I can care less about money. So eat that, Stereotype! Soon, my hashtag will not only be trending all over the social media websites, but it also will be talked about around campfires for decades to come.

I'll soon be famous.

I can see the headlines now: IS CENTRAL AGATHA "BEAR"-ING THE BLAME?

You can't make this stuff up.

Seriously.

## 19. AFTER / HALEY

THE door has a child safety lock on it. I can't catch a break! Obviously, there's no way to unlock the door from the inside. What now? I search for another way out. The room is much different than the cell I was staying in before. I wonder if my parents are to blame for all of this. Did they really stick me in a nuthouse? The secrecy is mind-boggling. So far, I haven't seen the doctor. One minute, I was at home. The next, *poof*, I'm in a cell without any windows. Speaking of windows, this room doesn't have any either. I already tried to break my way through but I had no luck. It doesn't look like any hospital I've stayed at before. I've been inside a hospital only like a handful of times, including several times when I visited past relatives before they rolled over and died. I remember hearing horror stories, one with my cousin, Amy, who went in for minor surgery. Like the *Overlook Hotel*, you check in, but you don't check out. Amy never turned all psycho and chased around the nurses with an ax, but she did catch this nasty bacterial thingy from dirty instruments. Spent months in the hospital recovering; then she got a blood clot in her leg from being immobile and it took a couple of weeks to get her on the right blood thinners. My own personal experiences: once, when I had an appendicectomy (like my cousin, "routine" surgery—that's what they told me—wasn't as horrible as I imagined it to be, like the doctor giving his best slapdash performance by cutting me open, digging around inside me, then scooping out all of my organs and throwing me in a giant salad bowl, but once I was riding the anesthesia like a lightning bolt, all of the anxiety melted away), my body was on a fluffy white cloud minutes leading up to the big slice, then, somehow, I was wandering through a golden wheat field. When I woke, the pain sat like an obese man on the side of my belly. I guess, the one perk about post surgery were the pills. Man did they give me some good pills! Usually, the pain goes away after a couple of days—usually, as in you can "stretch" it out for a little bit longer. There was this other time when I broke my wrist while trying to impress the strikingly handsome yet incredibly awkward Joseph Martin—Awkward Joe is what the kids called him. I was hanging upside down on the monkey bars; then my legs slipped and splat, like a bug hitting a windshield! My wrist caught the fall. The break was even more painful than having my appendix removed. Breaking my wrist was really the first time I experienced pain, as in I discovered the certain buttons of pain scattered on my body. Ever since my first break, I think I've pressed every single one of them. Your first pain is the worst, especially when bones are involved. The break only paid me a visit to the emergency room; got myself a pretty white cast—which, the next day, was bleeding with signatures. In a way, I'd like to think my cast was like a trophy, reminding me of how easily the body can break. I've heard when you break something, like a bone, or you get hurt, your body becomes stronger and it learns from experience, then your body adapts to breaks and molds itself around each flaw. As of now, I've broken eleven bones.

While I continue to search for exits, I feel a draft coming from the baseboard of the wall!

I get down on my hands and knees and press my ear to the floor.

I suddenly hear a tiny *thud* against the floor, sounding like something has dropped in the room next door. I can't see anyone. The crack underneath the baseboard is too narrow to see through, although I see shadows dancing along the floor. There must be a trapdoor or hidden door in the wall!

What am I even saying? Trapdoor, really? What do I have to lose?

I search frantically for anything—something!—a door handle or switch to access the next room. Maybe the lighting fixture along the wall is like a lever or something.

I pull down on the bronze piece and it tugs right back and for a moment, I feel like the biggest idiot on the planet. Only in the movies, Haley.

I continue to search for ways out. I spot this out-of-place Teddy bear sitting on the top shelf of a bookcase. It's worth a try. I climb my way up the shelves, trying not to slip or fall. I get a much closer look at the stuffed animal when I reach the third shelf. Both of its eyes are different from one another.

Two more shelves to go.

I cling to the last shelf, my fingers start to slip!

I grab the stuffed animal and as I pull it away from the shelf, I feel a slight resistance.

I climb back down and realize, after I finally reach the floor, I've yanked a cord from the back of the Teddy bear.

I follow the cord to a black electrical device inside. I turn the stuffed animal around, carefully study its face, its glossy eyes especially. One of the eyes is a button, whereas the other one is the lens of a camera!

I dig out the lens and conclude that it is, in fact, a camera.

Panic creeps in and I feel an overwhelming uneasiness about where I am.

I put the bear inside and scurry around the room. I don't know what I'm looking for or what the hell I'm doing. Utter confusion.

I force myself to stop pacing and I take a couple of deep breaths.

I find a vent on the floor.

It's open. . .

That's it!

I remember now.

I'm back at my house, inside my bedroom, sitting on my bed, staring at the vent on my ceiling while the cool air blows over my face. All of a sudden I hear this noise coming from the hallway. I decide to check it out. My parents *never* get up in the middle of night. Sometimes Elan does whenever he's had a nightcap. I'll hear the flush of the toilet, often mistaking the noise for a nightly catfight between Schmuckers and Alfonzo, the one-eyed catbeast outside my bedroom window. This noise is strange, like a windbreaker rubbing together. I crack open my bedroom door and get about halfway down the hallway when I hear a *hiss* of a snake in my left ear. A mist of some kind of synthetic substance is suddenly sprayed in my face! I jerk away, turn to my left, only to find a shadowy man standing next to me.

The smell in the air, I remember, stinging every inch of my sinuses.

I suddenly get lightheaded, too disoriented to scream for help.

I fall to my knees.

The shadowy man stands over my body, holding a device in his right hand. He begins to double, then triple. Now four men tower over my body, all looking the exact same. The last things I remember are the silver braces along their wrists. Not a device. Some kind of contraption. . .

I remember Monica telling me she was concerned—more so, on the "alarmed" side. She said someone had been following her after the shooting, but I didn't think anything of it at the time. She was going through a lot. She said her grandfather wasn't doing so well. The last time I talked to her, she wasn't doing so well either. With everything that happened a few days ago, witnessing all those people die, then having a loved one about to die, I don't blame her for the way she was handling the whole situation. I'd be flipping out.

But—and this is a *big* but—what if Monica was right?

What if someone was following her?

I rush toward the boarded-up windows and tear the curtains off the wall. I start ripping. I take a handful of curtain and stuff it against the vent. I find another vent hidden behind a table and do the same.

Next, I grab a wooden chair and break off one of the legs. In the process, a jagged piece of debris cuts my leg and draws a lot of blood. The cut is deep, too, and the blood is starting to puddle over the floor—I get an idea!

I rush to the bookcase and grab the first book I find from the shelf—*Moby Dick,* fancy that.

I tear the last blank page from the inside.

Next, I peel off a large splinter from the chair leg and dip the very point of the splinter in the puddle of blood along the floor. I start writing a message in my own blood on the blank piece of paper; then I blow on the blood until it's dry; and I manage to slip the note underneath a crack in the baseboard. It's worth a shot.

A *creak* in the floor!

I take a piece of the curtain and wrap it around my leg good and tight.

Someone's standing outside, unlocking the door, now entering the room!

I rush toward the door and just as a lanky man steps forward, I take the chair leg and hit him in the back of the head, knocking him unconscious.

Another man—shorter—slips in behind him, a gun drawn. He aims the gun at me, but I grab both of his hands, including the gun, and ram them into the center of his face. His head jerks back. His eyes swim in his head, he falls to his knees, then night-night.

I ease from the room and step into a dimly lit hallway. Old and dilapidated. Not a hospital—definitely not a hospital! It looks more like a dungeon, yet the room I was just in was as clean and tidy as a room one would find in Wayne Manor.

All of the doors are locked, except two. I check out the first door and find an office with metal filing cabinets lining the walls.

I start opening drawers, randomly starting with one filing cabinet that reads, "Project Day."

I search through manila folders, files on a young Japanese girl named "Frankie Day."

Cool name.

I come across another manila folder filled with photos of different people of all ages and backgrounds, men, women, children, some sickly-looking, cancerous, some bed-ridden, thin and gauntly, there's this one photo of a skeletal man—or at least I think is a man—others who'd make Johnny the Body look like a normal human being.

I find a folder on a man named "Sam Lieber." A photo of this Sam guy in the newspapers. Lying on a hospital bed with his arm and leg in a cast. His leg left in an elevated position. The headline reads: A LOCAL MAN MIRACULOUSLY SURVIVES DEADLY CAR CRASH. Another photo, the same man, now talking to reporters as he's being pushed in a wheelchair outside a hospital. Headline reads: LIEBER WAKES FROM COMA. More photos of this mysterious man, this Sam Lieber dude, sitting in the same room that I was just in, the one with the library, another mysterious man with his back turned to the camera, teaching Sam Lieber how to read?

I finger through more photos—much older, I can tell, from the shape and discoloration and deterioration of the photos—that same Japanese girl with the cool name, some taken inside the same room. Reading books and playing what looks like board games and doing other educational activities. Some—if not, a lot—of the photos include this brawny fellow dressed in black with this young girl who I presumed is Frankie. The man looks similar to the other man in the previous photo, the one with Sam, but not the same. The two men could possibly be related. Not sure.

I get a closer look at the girl and realize the books and the shelves around her are much different. A crucifix is hanging on the wall next to the bookshelf. Below are the words *Order of Our Lady.* I find more photos of this strange girl, some of them taken with these stern-faced nuns in front of what looks like a convent. There's one frontal photo of the girl. Her hair is dark and greasy and her skin as pale as a ghost.

Other pages contain statistics, diagrams of bodies, mutations, mathematical equations, composition notebooks filled with handwritten notes, all on a subject called "Frankie."

More recent photos of a woman in her late twenties, maybe older than that. I can't tell because she looks very weak in a lot of the photos. She has a shaved head, nearly scalped. She looks nothing like the girl from the earlier photos. She has a longer nose, higher cheekbones; her facial structure is similar to a European model. And she's white, not Japanese.

I keep flipping until I come across a portfolio on a Doctor June Lugosi.

I find a photo of her taken with a group of doctors. One of the doctors looks almost identical to the man who was parked outside my house!

I look closer at Doctor Lugosi.

The woman on the bus—it's her!

Why would it take an entire army to kill a woman?

She's just a woman.

What the hell is going on here—

Another folder: THE MANHATTAN PROJECT.

Inside are photos of square men dressed in white lab coats standing next to a massive clock that reads midnight.

Underneath the clock reads: *The Doomsday Clock.*

What?

Before I can dig deeper, I hear something coming from the other room. So, I check out the noise.

I sneak into the next room. I come across a chair in the middle of the room.

Behind the chair is a projector.

I turn on the projector.

On the wall in front of the chair are images of diseases flashing at lightning fast speed. Graphic images of death and sickness. Skin infections. Warts. Little Lennys being infected. Caged monkeys. Rabbits. Aquatic creatures. Frogs. Snakes. Emaciated patients bed ridden by debilitating diseases. Death.

I can't turn away. Lots of blood and sickness and death.

I start to get nauseous from the images.

Suddenly, I feel a gloved hand pressing against my mouth!

I jerk away; and as I start kicking the scumbag behind me, I feel a prick in the side of my neck.

The world starts to spin.

All I see is death.

Then the blackest of black.

## 8. BEFORE / BRITTANY

THE minute hand on the clock above Mr. Tabby appears to be stuck on eleven and for the past fifty-nine seconds I've been mentally forcing it to move but, of course, it don't budge an inch. I wish I had telekinetic powers like that one girl in that one movie, *Carrie.* I would rearrange my entire day based off my powers, especially right now, when Mr. Tabby strays off topic and goes on one of his blathering fits about Civil War. The man is so obsessed with history! He once said to me that we don't have to go far to find history. All we have to do is look down at the ground below our feet. It's fair to say I enjoy Mr. Tabby as a teacher and a coach—I most definitely prefer Mr. Tabby over Mr. Rockwell who Mr. Tabby filled in for after he took sick leave to help with his wife who had breast cancer. Even though Mr. Tabby is basically a sub, not a lot of people take him that seriously, especially students. The class is more laidback since Mr. Rockwell left; however, that can be a problem whenever it feels like a teacher don't have control over a classroom. Another perk to telekinesis: I'd like to know what Mr. Tabby's thinking whenever he looks at me or whenever he's sitting at his desk whenever we're taking a test. At times, he's so absorbed in thought. The only downside about telekinesis—I can only imagine—is not being able to turn it off.

Sometimes, I'd like to get away from myself, to turn myself off.

I turn my attention back to the clock. Hasn't moved at all. Which makes me wonder if the clock's not working. I will be forever stuck in history class, listening to Mr. Tabby ramble on about Robert E. Lee.

My body gets tingly, and I find myself getting restless in my chair. We only have a couple of minutes to go, but I can't sit still. It's a habit I picked up in Holly Springs. It all started with a bastard named Randy.

I imagine if Christie and I didn't leave when we did, then Randy probably would've gotten the best of us. I came pretty close to shooting him after the first time he hit Christie. She has a .44 Magnum she keeps on the top shelf of her closet. If you're wondering, yes, that's the gun Clint Eastwood used in the movie, *Dirty Harry*. Christie may look like a girl from the valley, but, like she would say in her own words, she ain't one to mess with. Trust me. Besides Christie, I'm the only one who has the combination to the safe. I can see why she never gave the combination to Randy. I still think about him from time to time though, especially whenever I get caught thinking about time, doing all I can to wield it to my advantage. That'd be pretty cool, wouldn't it? To be able to control time. If I had to do it all over again, I would've told Christie the truth about Randy when I first met the lousy bastard. I think that would've at least persuaded her not to keep seeing him, if I kept pushing and bad mouthing him and exposing him as the dickless bastard he was. One date turned into two dates, then three dates. The only reason I lied was because I knew how lonely she was. I'd catch her on the computer late at night, scrolling through her online dating page with a glass of Chardonnay. She didn't know that I was paying attention, but I sure was. You'd never know Christie was that desperate of a woman by looking at her. Next thing I knew they were going out of town on weekends. They went to Bushy Gardens one weekend. I knew it was real serious because I think if any couple can handle a vacation alone together, especially Bushy Gardens, then they can handle anything together. Randy was a'ight during the first few months after we moved in with him. He'd buy me clothes and earrings every now and then. After a year, I started to see him as the creature he really was. Randy couldn't buy my affection. I think he started to change after he found a stuffed unicorn he bought me for my birthday in the trash. All that stuffing ripped out and strewn over the floor like white guts. Stuffed animals make great therapy. You don't want to know what I did with the horn. After that, he started to change, or better yet, he removed the hideous mask from his face and showed us the snake inside him. The liar. The crook. The manipulator. A goddamn monster. A lot of nights I dreamt about running far away. I imagine Christie was having the same dreams as I was. We were stuck—again. It felt like the time after Poppa died, when both Christie and I had that empty look in our eyes, both of us unsure about our future. Poppa was about as good as it gets. He was the balance in our lives—that rock. He kept us grounded and safe. When Randy came into our lives, Christie was looking for someone opposite of Poppa. She wasn't the kind of woman who'd hide her feelings but she sure did know when to put down her foot and say, "Enough is enough." I knew Christie was searching for a man like Poppa, someone who'd respect her, admire her, adore her, love her, all those good things you get out of a relationship, but I knew that man didn't exist, especially in places she'd hang out at. Stevie's Dive ain't really a hot spot for decent men, if you know what I mean. I'm sure that man may be out there somewhere, in another place far away from here. Perhaps they all got fed up with women and moved to Mars or somewhere cold. Either way, Randy Remington Bosworth was what we got.

I guess there comes a time in everybody's life when you have to follow your momma's words. Take a stand for something. Or fall for nothing. The relationship between not only Randy and Christie, but also Randy and myself was like a pot of boiling water. If we didn't leave, the water would've kept boiling until it was evaporated and all that remained would have been smoke. Eventually, the smoke would completely cover everything it touched. We would've never recovered. I didn't exactly know how serious the situation had gotten until Christie showed up at my classroom. She always respected my space, dropped me off blocks away from school, not once did she act all snoopy around my room. She was a'ight like that. When I saw her that day standing outside the classroom door and I saw the fear in her eyes—and trust me, such a thing like fear do exist—right then and there I knew things would never be the same *ever* again. This was her stand. It was our stand.

When we I were together, we were stronger. Christie and I. When she came home after spending the weekend with Randy in Palm Springs, it was like she had turned back into that same person weeks before she met Randy. A lonely, insecure insect. Nobody like anybody like that. I think Randy made her happy for a while, but only for a while. Her sadness had taken hold of her. Not only did her strength start to deteriorate, but also mine. Randy was pulling us down in the gutter with him. Christie was looking for someone to pull us out. I was the one.

When we left Holly Springs we kept driving north. I honestly didn't know where I was going, neither did Christie. Just anywhere away from him. They say the hardest part of about leaving is saying goodbye. I wish that were true. People, especially ones like Randy, them control freaks who act as if they're entitled to whatever they want whenever they please, people like that don't deserve goodbyes. They deserve everything that's coming their way. Karma is a bitch, ain't it? The police never caught the arsonist who set his house on fire. I can only imagine the look on that smug face of his when he came home from work. People can be real sensitive and in a way, they have every right to be sensitive. It's only natural for people to look after one another. If only he knew the harm he was doing to not only to Christie but also myself. He created something beyond my control. I had no other choice, really. He forced my hand. I couldn't just let him get away with him treating us the way he did and then that bastard going about his normal life like everything was okay. Everybody needs to be accountable for his or her actions, including Randy. I know what I did will come back to haunt me. I know I'll have to answer for the crime I committed either in this life or the next. Right now, I just don't care. I can't tell what goes on inside the head of someone else—it sure would be pretty cool if I did—but, in my defense, Randy knew exactly what he was doing to us and I think he got off on the way he treated us. If we continued to let him control us the way he did, with all the abuse—the verbal stuff and the physical—he would've ultimately destroyed us.

In a way, though, Randy has forever changed us, me especially, the way I think about people. We've moved three times in the past four years. Every year or so, Christie and I would move somewhere else. It got to the point where I didn't unpack anymore. There was no point, really.

When we arrived in Agatha, we knew that maybe we didn't have to keep running. Maybe, we could settle down in a place like this. Only two types of people who live in Agatha: people who were born and raised here and people who moved here because they were either looking for something else or running away from something far worse. I still haven't yet made that initial step to unpack the boxes in my room, but I'm seriously considering this might be the last place we move.

The other day, Christie told me she thought she was done moving, like for good. I'm so done with moving, so done with looking over my shoulder all the time, even though I've gotten so used to it.

I keep staring at the clock above Mr. Tabby, waiting for the last period of the day to come all ready. I even will the minute hand to move like a Jedi. But nothing.

The more I keep staring, the slower the hand moves.

Time has turned on me.

I tell myself I need to put my mind on something else, besides the time, of course, as well as Mr. Tabby going on and on about the Civil War. I like Mr. Tabby and all, considering he's my coach, but sometimes I'd like to wrap my hands around his throat and strangle him until his eyeballs pop out of their sockets.

The class bell finally rings!

Thank God!

As I'm about to leave, Mr. Tabby balls up a piece of paper and tosses it at me.

"Brittany, catch!" he yells out.

At the very last second, I grab the paper in midair.

Mr. Tabby's impressed by the grab—why wouldn't he be? Over the past month, I've really gotten good at lacrosse. I'm not great, but I'm good enough to keep up.

"Very nice," I hear a silky voice from behind.

Then, Mr. Tabby's: "Well, hello, Ms. Van Buren."

I turn toward the doorway of the trailer and Pam's shouldering her way into the classroom, one of the students checking her out as he walks away, snickering as all them other immature boys do.

Pam reminds me a lot of Christie, mainly in the way she carries herself. I'm talking about Christie 1.0. Christie without Randy. Christie when Poppa was still alive. Christie who saw so much of her in me when she was younger even though she'd never admit it—whenever some of Christie's old girlfriends stopped by when Wreck-it Randy was around, they'd call me a younger and more improved version of herself, more everything—like I was Christie's Mini-Me. I could definitely see the two of them getting together over a glass of wine, Pam and Christie, chatting about men while going through carpet catalogues. I'd say her confidence is fringing on arrogance—it's magnetic in its appeal, though. She's settled, yet unsettled. Pam knows exactly who she is. Sometimes, I feel as if she's invincible. That's the way I felt about Christie before Poppa died. She was the strongest woman I've ever known. I miss that woman. For real, she'd kick Wonder Woman's ass. No lie. When you surround yourself around a woman just like Christie 1.0, her strength wears off onto you and you feel as strong as her. Christie's not that woman anymore, but I'm starting to see shades of it. Regardless, I've learned to appreciate Christie over these past few years, more so than ever! She handled everything with grace, poise, and dignity. She knew she couldn't win the battle between her and Randy. Instead, she decided to win the war. That alone is worth anybody's respect.

Pam's here to drop off the roster for today's game. I overhear them say that both Donna and Elle are not coming to the game. Sick. Some bug thingy that's starting to go around.

I think Mr. Tabby is gaga over Pam. It's the way he acts whenever she's around. I see the way he looks at her, the way he tries so hard for her to see him—to actually "see" him—for who he is, for what he could be. I know Mr. Tabby has a girlfriend he never talks about. I've prodded at him many times, but he always changes the subject. Emily said she once saw this stuck up girl with him after the undefeated Trendon Lions gave us one serious butt whooping. Emily said she was treating him like dog shit. She was even pushing him around, which I can't imagine. Maybe she was a one-night stand who wanted more than just a hookup. Honestly, Mr. Tabby might be lying about the girlfriend part because I've never seen her at any of the games. He don't even have any picture of her on his desk like most of them teachers do with their loved ones. I don't know. Maybe she's one of them type of girls who he's ashamed to be with in public. Who knows? It's not really my business.

Pam slips by me, eyeing me over her shoulder.

"Hope you play like that in the game."

"We'll see, I guess."

Pam faces me.

"What kind of attitude is that, Ms. Smart?"

I don't answer.

"You're going to do great," she points her finger at me and holds it there like a blade. "I have a really good feeling about today." She rotates around toward Mr. Tabby with a queer smile on her face. "The Bobcats are going to be trembling in their boots once they set their eyes on us 'Black' Bears."

She rebelliously emphasizes the word *black*, and it can't be more obvious that she's poking fun on how our ridiculously politically correct school board is trying to get rid of the word *black* from our team's mascot. It's not a black and white issue, no pun intended. You either for the name or against it; and so far, the word has surprisingly created a lot of division among the school. It's just the name of a color, people. Even some of the black students, like Rhea and Ebony, totally support keeping the word—why wouldn't they? Akea, however, is on the fence, but if you know Akea like I do, then it's no surprise that she don't see eye to eye with most people.

From what I've heard, Haley's cooping up a scheme of her own that will send a direct message to not only the school board, but also the school's newspaper, *Central Agatha Times.* People get so offended it's stupid. Like Poppa used to say: No matter where you spit, you're always going to hit something. In other words: No matter what you say, you're always going to offend somebody. So, I guess it's best not to get so freaking caught up in what people say about you. People who talk crap to you obviously have a problem with themselves; otherwise they wouldn't be going out of their way to call you a name or whatever. Life is way too short to deal with people like that! Thas what I always say. If people say bad things about you, then that's their problem. Not yours.

"Okay." It's pretty much the only thing Pam and I can agree on.

"I'll see you later, Brit," Mr. Tabby says as he waves me goodbye.

"See ya, Mr. Tabby."

I leave the classroom.

Pam walks up to Mr. Tabby.

Like a switch, Mr. Tabby turns into someone he's not.

## 20. AFTER/BRITTANY

My bones are shaking from this terrible dream about being chased by a dog inside our old house. This ain't any normal dog that'd make a great pet. I'm talking about a dog on roids, an out-to-kill dog, like if *Cugo* had a nasty brother-in-law, only it was way larger and meaner. Every where I went or hid either it be lying under a bed or tucking myself away inside the back of a closet, piling myself with all sorts of junk like jackets and vacuum cleaners and boots and scarves and old luggage, the dog was always there, creeping around, sniffing me out as strings of drool hung from the corners of its mouth as if he was chewing on a tennis shoe, and he had these eyes glowing like fiery red dots at the far end of a dark hallway. I haven't been so frightened in a dream. I've had nightmares before, ones I can easily get rid of, but this one is much different. I try to gather my surroundings, first by clearing away the beads of sweat dripping into the corners of my eyes. Even the gown I'm wearing is drenched with sweat. I feel feverish and I have this headache, not like a piercing one that cuts like a knife but a dull, almost heavy kind of headache, like the one time I experimented with coffee, drank it for a couple of weeks, then stopped cold turkey, and it felt as if I had an adjustable wrench squeezing tighter and tighter over my brain as the day went on.

I sit upright on the brown leather couch—*ouch!*

A cold flash of panic suddenly radiates through my body and for a second, I feel as if I'm still in the dream.

I manage to stand up.

I walk around the room. Still dazed. I bump into a table, causing a vase to wobble.

I reach for the vase before it falls but the sweat all over my palms makes it hard to grab. The vase skips over the edge of the table and slips from my fingertips—

—The vase shatters on the floor!

Shoot!

I search the room for a broom to clean up the mess, but I can't find a damn thing. I give up on my search and grab the first book I can find from the bookshelf.

While I'm at it, I see if they have any Stephen King but I don't find anything by him. Most of the books are old hardbacks that I've seen on our reading list.

I quit my search and sweep the broken pieces of vase into a pile.

As I'm placing the rest of the vase in a nearby trash-can, an old rock song suddenly comes on inside the room!

Startled, I try to find the source of the music. I can't find anything. No speaker. No player. Nothing. The music seems to be coming from the walls.

As I sit back down on the couch and try to block out the guy in the song singing about some "Reaper," I notice a piece of paper on the floor. I don't recall seeing a piece of paper there before. So, I go and check it out. I get only a couple of feet away before I notice the red writing on the paper. I get a closer look. What is that?

The paper reads: *They're watching us.*

My stomach gets twisted in these knots. The blaring song don't help much either; instead, it makes matters much worse than they are.

Discreetly as I can, I kneel down over the paper, keep my legs close together, slide it underneath my pant leg, and slip it into my sock.

Who's watching me?

Who is *us*?

As I make my way back to the couch, I suddenly get faint. I decide to lie back down on the couch and close my eyes. I listen to the guy singing about a Reaper. The singer's words slowly start to fade.

I crack open my eyes once more but I end up struggling to keep them on one thing.

I become really dizzy. I close my eyes again.

The song stops.

* * *

I wake up in a wider, much staler room with a low ceiling, which reminds me of the DMV they got in Henderson, only without all the furniture or the slow-ass employees who act as if they'd rather be kicking back in their recliners. My head is still heavy, too, and the ache is now tender behind my eyes. I rub my eyes, hoping to relieve the pain.

As I pull away my hand, I look down at my hand and find wires wrapped around my torso. A clip on my fingers. A cuff wrapped around my left arm, similar to the one nurses use to take blood pressure.

I follow the wires to a machine next to me. . .

"Welcome," the voice says.

Two men sitting at a table come to before me.

Next to the men is a row of cameras on tripods. I see a tiny red light below each camera. I think it means it's recording.

"What did you do to me?"

"You passed out," one of them says.

"Passed out?"

"I'm afraid it's one of the side effects."

"Side effects?" I say, trying to keep my eyes off the camera. "What you talking about? Side effects to what?"

Before the stranger can open his mouth to speak, my mind starts racing; and every time a thought passes in a crazy loop, I get faint again. I can't stop thinking about the note, about those words on it, how they were written down—*Was it someone's blood?* I fire one question after another at him: "Where am I? Who are you people? Why you filming me?"

And what was up with the song?

Then, the most important one of them all: "What did you people do with my friends?"

I turn to my right and notice a piece of paper sliding through a machine. The machine is all out of whack. I see these large black zigzags being scribbled down on the paper.

"Please," he says patiently, "I need you to relax, Brittany." He says my name. The sound of my name pulls my attention closer to his words. His voice is soft, calming, like Poppa's. He tells me everything is going to be okay; tells me my friends are okay, and for some reason, I believe him. He don't look like a psychotic serial killer or perverted kidnapper. He looks like a man who's trying to help.

But help with what?

*What happened?*

I don't even know what I said until I hear his voice again, and he's telling me something happened during the terrorist attack. Terrorist attack? When?

The word slips out like a spit bubble: "Infected?"

The stranger tells me they're working around the clock on a cure. They're asking for my cooperation.

So, I agree and like a good girl, I decide to behave.

Why fight?

I tell them I will cooperate for them. *She* tells me it's all what they wanna hear from me.

About an hour into what they're calling a close talk—not an interrogation, even though it sure does feel like one—Doctor Bloch gives me a glass of water. I take a couple of sips, which helps with my dry throat.

Again, this Roger Sonnenberg says, "another" side effect.

They want to know about my poppa. They clarify stepfather, who ain't even close to Poppa. Those two ain't even in the same league.

"I've answered all of your questions," I tell them. "I don't want to talk about him."

"I take it you don't get along with him—"

"—Why do you want to know about him?"

They tell me whatever I say about him will not leave this room, which is BS.

"Yet, you filming me," I say, pointing at all the cameras. "What you planning on doing with the video? Are you gonna post it on the Internet? You got to have my permission, don't you?"

One of them holds in a laugh.

"And why would we post this on the Internet, Brittany?"

I got no response for them, only a measly flick of my lip.

"Enlighten us?"

"I don't know," I say. "Isn't that what people do?"

"The videos are for research purposes only because—"

"—Because of this 'unknown' virus, right?"

"Yes."

"How come I haven't shown any symptoms?"

"Well, that's why you're here, Brittany. We want to get down to the bottom of it."

The doctor pauses.

"Tell us," he says after a long pause, "why did you do it?"

"Do what?"

"You know."

"No," I say. "I don't. You gotta be more specific."

I said I don't but I do. I know exactly what he's talking about. How'd he find out? Nobody knows what happened, except for Christie. I never actually told her what happened; but when it did happen and she found out, she knew it was me who done it. I remember that day like it was yesterday. I was out and about, killing time at the mall, and when I came back home, she was talking with some rookie cop.

"Why did you burn down his house?" he asks.

Keep it together.

I've gone this long without talking about it.

Why break now?

"I don't know what you talking about?"

I find myself returning back to an old habit I do whenever I'm nervous.

I don't even realize I'm doing it until I feel the streaks of heat burning along the side of my neck and chest. I'm really going to town on my neck.

When I'm extremely nervous, I itch parts of my body like a junkie desperate for a fix. The nerves fire up like thousands of angry mites crawling over my skin.

"Yes," he says. "You do. You can't lie to us, Brittany." He nods at the machine, holds his nod there, waiting for me to acknowledge it. "If you're as good as I think you are, you may be able to fool the machine, but you're *not* fooling me. Like I said, nothing you say will leave this room. This conversation is strictly confidential. Now, you tell me. Why did you do it? Was it because the way he treated your mother? Did he harm you in any physical way? Did he touch you inappropriately? Why, Brittany? Why did you do it?"

"You don't know what it was like living with him," I tell him directly. "What he did to her, what he did to us. . ."

"Did you feel relieved after you did it?"

I think about the answer to the question, how I felt after I did it, me not feeling a shred of remorse while standing on the street watching those flames rise into the black sky.

I reach down inside and tell him the first word that comes to mind: "Free," I say. "I felt free."

## 9. BEFORE / EMILY

My last period of the day happens to be aquatics with instructor Mrs. Raleigh, whom I've grown to appreciate over these past couple of weeks, despite the many derogatory names students call her behind her back: Sourpuss, Octopussy, *Creature from the Black Lagoon*, Deli-meat, which had spawned other names like The Club, Sandwich Club, Subway. How she ended up with these absurd names came from one incident last semester when Mrs. Raleigh jumped into the pool to save a freshman who couldn't swim. Her swimming trunks fell off as she was pulling the kid from the water and she nearly flashed half the class—but mainly a bunch of immature boys who probably hadn't even seen a close up of a vagina, let alone the vagina of a fifty-four year old mother who had given birth to five offspring—giving them the ultimate money shot. The names still follow Mrs. Raleigh around, even a semester later; the kids whispering names, then came giggling. If I were Mrs. Raleigh, I wouldn't put up with their nonsense. But she's handled it all very nicely.

After I received my schedule, I so desperately wanted to change classes—mainly because of the rumors spreading about Mrs. Raleigh, despite how an act of bravery had turned into a public humiliation—but I ended up missing the deadline by just a day because I had a family emergency and I missed the first week of school. Turns out Mrs. Raleigh is a former Olympic medalist and coached for the Central Agatha swimming team. Her team won States last year. She can be super intimidating at times and incredibly hard on students. Like most of the instructors, all they care about is giving the student an opportunity to put forth the effort. Me, I'm not much of a swimmer, more of the dog-paddler type. I usually play goalie whenever we play water polo every other Thursday. I figure it's the only thing I'm good at when it comes to a physical sport, putting my body in front of the goal, stopping the opponent from scoring. I don't mind the physical contact; however, I've actually been dreading this day in particular all month.

When I first started class, Mrs. Raleigh listed the major agendas from the curriculum and one of them happened to be diving, which had these several subcategories. There was diving head first into water from the diving board. That, we did last week. It took me a couple of times, but I ended up perfecting my dive the way Mrs. Raleigh taught us.

Now, Mrs. Raleigh wants us to retrieve bricks from the bottom of the pool, which means we *all* have to go under, which means we all have to hold our breaths, which means I'm dead.

Mrs. Raleigh doesn't waste any time by chucking rubber bricks into the deepest end of the pool. That's when I know there's no other way of getting out of this.

She asks who wants to volunteer first. I know going first will strategically work to my advantage because I can get it over with.

Immediately, I raise my hand and just as I'm about to yell out me first, Kelly jumps up from the bleachers and says casually, "I'll go."

Kelly doesn't waste any time and fetches the bricks at the bottom of the pool. No problem.

I end up watching every single student go before me. I don't even attempt to raise my hand anymore—the thought of going doesn't even pop in my mind. Instead, I cower in the back of the bleachers, wishing for Mrs. Raleigh not to call my name.

After every one has received the bricks, Mrs. Raleigh looks directly at me.

I turn away, hoping that if I don't make eye contact with her she won't call on me.

"All right, *Emily*," she says. "We've saved the best for last. You're up." She waves me in. "Come on. Let's go."

"I think I'm coming down with a cold," I say weakly.

"No excuses," she says, waving me closer to the pool.

Eventually, I gather the nerve to stand. My legs are trembling. My knees even buckle. I use the students' shoulders to help me down from the bleachers. Eventually, I make it.

I walk to the edge of the pool while next to me stands Mrs. Raleigh with her arms crossed over her chest. A couple of the students are cheering me on, which doesn't help at all.

Mrs. Raleigh reassures me our volunteer lifeguard, Conor, who hasn't volunteered for anything in his life, will be ready to grab me if anything goes wrong. I have to put my life in the hands of a kid who flunked out last year. I can't trust a kid who's repeating his sophomore year.

I tell myself that the only way to conquer our fear is to face it head on.

I nod my head.

"I'm ready."

Kelly, who happened to receive four bricks, is in the lead so far. All I have to do is swim down and grab one brick, but I really want that fifty dollar gift card to Books N' Things and I know that I have to earn it. A new MANGA called *The Gifted Child*, volume two of the series, *V.I.G.I.L.A.N.T.E.*, just recently came out and I really, *really* want it. I'm not going to sugar coat it. I'm completely obsessed with the series. Even dressed up as Spiderhawk at last year's Cosplay in San Diego. I've heard from one of the writers that the series was inspired by the graphic novel, *Watchmen*, which is probably one of my favorites books of all time—and I'm not even talking about comic books! I mean literature. Alan Moore's *Watchmen* can easily stand next to any book written by the greats like Orwell, Welles, or Wells.

The thought alone of earning *The Gifted Child* by retrieving the most bricks gives me that needed push.

Five bricks, I tell myself. Piece of cake.

"All right, Emily," Mrs. Raleigh rallies.

I dive into the pool and swim twelve feet below.

I grab the first brick, secure it in my hand, and then spring myself upward by pushing my feet against the pool's floor.

As I swim to the surface, I can hear the muffled sounds of students cheering my name. Their faces are wavy; all of them are staring down at me, waiting.

There's this one student, Jalen, who's filming me behind Mrs. Raleigh's back, which makes me even more nervous than I ought to be. Why is he filming me? Does he see something that I don't? What if I were to stay down here? Underneath the water? Eyes stinging cherry red from the chlorinated water, trapped like an attraction, forever gazed upon by curious eyes. People always talk about how they would do the big "it" but they never go through with it. The only reason why people talk about it is because they're too afraid to actually do it. I'm passed the point of talking about it—I did once, all the time. I wouldn't shut up about it. But now, I'm done talking about it. Now, I just think about it all the time—when, how, where? Of all the thoughts, it's probably one of the scariest things: where?

Maybe right here.

Why not?

In the blue.

Would they even jump in to rescue me? To save me from all of the anger I have inside me? Or, would they just stand there and watch me slip away into a blur? Even worse, would they film me drowning on their smartphones? Share it with a friend or post it online? What if I became a viral sensation? Look at this 'GIRL CAUGHT DROWNING' video on the Lube Tube. What if I started trending on Chatterz? Hashtag that people of the world: #GirlDrowning. Even so, it would only be for like a minute or two of a person's attention before I was scrolled aside, like any other post.

Onto the next.

Deleted.

Unfollowed.

Dead.

What would the comments be like?

A side of me doesn't want to know, yet another side wants to know what they'll say about me, a side that feeds off other people's sickness, watching or listening to others shame others on the Internet, a place where the goal is to gain in popularity, like followers, when you put someone down or make fun of them, only to make them feel tall; but in the end, they sound like another echo lost in a dark cave. I'm totally aware kids can be cruel in real life, even crueler over the Internet. It's become an issue, constant hazing, name-calling. I've gone on pages where grown men—adults, thirty-plus year olds—are calling other people names or insulting people for expressing the

Fifth Amendment, like they're obligated to express themselves or vent to a glass screen. Has the Internet become our Digital Therapist? Have we become stuck in the triviality, all thanks to the dumb Internet kids, these cyber kids who are all into nonconformity, yet they copy what everybody else does on the Internet. They're not so smart as they claim to be, coming up with new words or terminology to fit our new digi-savy lifestyle. It's all pretend, really, insecure kids hiding behind masks, afraid to reveal to the world who they really are. Yet, they stay hidden among the tall weeds, cowardly finger-warriors, a million plus strong. Thirty/forty-year-old manboys stuck in a time period who share pictures of their children on the Internet. Completely contradict everything that they follow, a struggle to detach far from the machine and become integrated with the machine.

Is this what we have turned into?

Most importantly, is this what I've turned into?

Why can't I cut myself free?

Jalen kneels down for a better angle.

Smile, Emily, I can hear him say behind the smartphone. You're going to be famous!

I once saw a video of a woman being burned alive and even to this day, the images make me cry: a crowd was standing on the street while her overturned car caught on fire; the woman crawled out of the car, engulfed in flames, kicking and waving on the street, screaming for help. Nobody would help her—eventually two people out of a crowd of a dozen or so people decided to step in and save her, but it was already too late; the burns were too severe and the woman's lungs were scarred beyond repair. She died after spending two days attached to a ventilator. The video doesn't speak for all people, but it sure does speak for how low we have become. Primordial. Infatuated by violence. So preoccupied with ourselves and impressions we leave behind on the Internet—our digital footprint—or whether people "like" or "not like" what we post that we've turned our backs on humanity? Have we become as hollow as the machine itself? Or have we always been this way? Me, I don't know if I want to live in a world so cold and gray, a plugged-in world where you're constantly looking over your shoulder, wondering if you're being watched or filmed or recorded, all for the sake of a "like." I don't want to live in a world where every little thing has become political; everything you do is frowned upon and questioned, or whatever it is you do or whatever opinion you share, you're immediately pegged or placed in certain groups. What makes one person's life more worthy than another's?

So, yeah, I think it'd be kind of nice if I could stay down here forever, underneath the water with all of the other tiny monsters.

Laugh it up, Jalen. Will see who has the last laugh?

Maybe I expect too much from people, kids like Jalen. I expect them to show common sense or respect to other people—isn't that something we learn when we're children?

Now, it feels like the world's gone wrong. I wonder if it's been like this from the start or if it goes through these phases every three decades or so. I wonder if the world's not changing. I wonder if I'm changing.

My eyes are open and for the first time I'm seeing how awful this world has become. Nobody has respect for anything anymore and all of the great wonders of the world have been pushed aside and we've all settled for less because that's what we've all been reduced to, lesser than nothing.

But do I stand by and let the world eat itself?

Or, do I fight?

And how about all of the hypocrites out there, polluting the world, preaching about the environment while stuffing their faces with cheeseburgers and driving cars that run off gasoline.

How does one breathe with all of the bullshit coming out of people's mouths?

I'm specifically talking to my dad, the walking chimney. I have ideas—I think they're interesting ideas—and sometimes, I guess that's all they are, just ideas. Like for example: I have an idea where someone decides to put an end to cancer infecting our society by destroying all of the tobacco companies and basically, wiping them off the face of the earth. I hate cigarettes! I hate the smell. I hate the way cigarette smoke stains everything it touches. I hate what it's doing to me. My dad calls me "Chicken Little." I didn't know what the name meant until after I looked it up on the Internet. I think it had to do with a documentary, *Infest/Pollution*, that I showed him. The documentary focused on fossil fuels and others hazardous factors resulting in significant change in the climate. He thought it was *propaganda*. His words. I thought it would encourage him to quit smoking; but, of course, the following morning, I saw him on the back porch, lighting one up—and I think he did it deliberately, as if he was telling me nobody was going to tell him how to live his life. My dad has absolutely no consideration for my health. I've read statistics showing that second-hand smoke is worse than smoking itself. According to the CDC, tobacco smoke contains over seven thousand chemicals and hundreds of them are toxic. Seventy of those certain chemicals cause cancer. So, each time my dad lights one up, I have to think about whether or not I'm going to get cancer. Am I going to wake up one morning, wilting away from cancer? Suffering to my last breath all because my dad wanted to be a rebel and smoke a cigarette because he was stressed out? Is my dad slowly murdering me? I once pitched an idea to my dad about coming up with a device that is placed over the exhausts of big trucks—like the ones you see spewing out smoke all over the interstates—and the device would filter out all of the pollutants. I got the idea from my friend, Blair, who once used an empty toilet paper roll with a sheet of fabric softener stuffed inside while we were getting stoned in her bedroom. She didn't want to smell up the room, so, by blowing the smoke through the fabric softener, it got rid of the potent smell of marijuana. When I told my dad about the idea, he said I was cuckoo.

He acts as if he knows what's good for me when he has problems of his own. Sometimes, I wonder if he smokes out of spite. I wish I had the courage to carry out my idea, to destroy what's destroying us, kind of like the ending of *Fight Club*, destroying banks, erasing everything back to zero, giving us an opportunity to start over with a clean slate.

Maybe one day I'll turn into something political who people can waste their breath talking about over coffee breaks—water cooler talk. The Girl Who Was Angry At The World.

What keeps me up at night: What if the person I'm changing into is the person who I'll be forever?

I can't even remember the last time I was happy, especially in front of my parents. It's gotten to the point where I'm so used to being unhappy that if I was happy, it would be hard to show it in front of them, like I do with Cosplay. If I met someone who made me happy or made me feel good about myself, I know they would reject me because they're so used to that unhappy girl. It's like they want me to be unhappy with my life. The unhappier I am, the more control they have over me. I'm so unknown and irrelevant that I can't even have my own stalker. The only stalkers I have are my parents. Seriously! How pathetic is that? Do they realize the psychological effect they're having on me? I can't see myself living past thirty. If I do, it will be a miracle. Everywhere I go, they're always watching me—my mom especially. She's a real hawk. She wants to know everything I'm doing. She wants to tell me what to do or what *not* to do. It makes me so sick, just thinking about what they're doing. I think the only time I'm happy is whenever I'm not around my parents.

Another side to me is not ready to die. I just want to fight. It would be so easy to die—would it not? To flip that ultimate OFF switch. People said it's a cowardly thing to do. I think it's one of the most noblest acts there is, to flip that switch.

I'm not ready yet.

So many things I haven't experienced, so many wonders, so many dreams that can only take you so far. I know it'll take me an entire lifetime to experience these things I've always wanted to do. I can start my own world, a world that can be anything it wants to be.

If something's not broken, there'd be no reason to fix it or update it.

If something's broken, then I can keep it broken.

Why?

Because that's what I choose to do in my world. Broken things don't care if they're broken. In this world of mine, I can do whatever I want.

In this world, I can be whoever I damn well please.

With the brick secured in my hand, I swim to the surface and toss the brick at Jalen's feet.

Jerk!

He backpedals and slips, which causes him to drop his smartphone. The screen shatters! He's annoyed—feels good. Doesn't it, Jalen?

Mrs. Raleigh yells something at him but I can't make out what it is. Other students are laughing at him. He's making all kinds of excuses about the rules about not having a phone in class but I tune out everybody, except for Mrs. Raleigh, who's reaching out her hand as if she's ready to pull me out of the water.

"Good job, Emily," she says and attempts to lend me a hand.

I ignore her and dive under for another brick.

I bring the brick up to the surface.

Mrs. Raleigh doesn't help me this time. She seems surprised.

Another brick.

Take that.

I grab the fourth brick and bring it up to the surface. The students are no longer cheering me on. Yet, they appear in a state of shock.

My limbs go tired and I force myself back under one more time.

As I go to retrieve the fifth and final brick, I witness the floor suddenly billow outward, as if an air bubble has gotten trapped underneath the lining of the pool.

I reach for the brick. . .

A hand, as black as ink, stretches out from the bubble and grabs me by the wrist!

The hand tries to pull me into the floor but my elbow pops out of place. I drop the brick and rocket myself upward with a kick against the floor.

The hand slips from my wrist. I don't know how much longer I hold my breath.

Panic floods over my body, and I find myself desperately swimming to the wavy figures above me with one arm and all. My other arm limp like a wet noodle.

Conor's image fades before me. His body is getting blurrier and blurrier.

I finally surface, gasping for air.

Conor jumps in and helps me to the ladder.

"Are you okay, Emily?"

Mrs. Raleigh seems concerned. The class looks mortified from the sight of my arm.

I pop my elbow back into place, causing a couple of kids to shriek with utter disgust.

Mrs. Raleigh tells me I made a good effort in trying to retrieve all of the bricks but, unfortunately, Kelly wins the challenge.

Kelly's happy.

Good for her.

Right now, I don't care.

I'm still wrapping my head around what it is that I brought into my new world.

## 21. AFTER / EMILY

HOW much longer can I rot away while I miss out on life outside these walls?

I have to get out of here wherever here may be.

I lie down on the stiff bed of the cell, stare at the gray ceiling above me, and reflect on the days after the explosion.

* * *

I prune easily. It's not by choice. It's the way my body reacts to water. I can go exactly ten minutes in water without pruning, then, another minute after that, science happens, then my body takes on the form of a California raisin.

I remove my hand from the tepid water and hold it close to my face. I've only been in the bathtub for five minutes, give or take—just a quick soak was what I told my mom, then it was lights out. My hand looks as if I've been in the water for much longer.

How long have I've been sitting here?

I study each green-purplish vein in my hand weaving around each bone and ligament like its own vast network of communication. I don't know why I'm so interested in my hand, but it's the little things, like details of my hand, that seem so much more interesting than anything I've witnessed before.

I glance at Nyquil sitting on the edge of the sink. My mom said that it would help me go and stay asleep tonight. Honestly, I don't know if I want to sleep anymore because every time I close my eyes, I see her and the awful things she did to those people.

I look down at my pasty reflection rippling through the bubbly water, and I still can't believe what happened. I don't think police knew exactly what happened either. I think they were as baffled as I was. Those two agents kept referring to her as a suspect, but to me, there was nothing suspect about her. To me, it appeared as if they were attacking her, not the other way around. I mean, really, if she was a suspect in whatever terrible crime she committed (the two agents didn't exactly tell me what she did—whatever it was that she did, it was serious enough for them to activate the National Guard—and she wanted to destroy other people for whatever reason, political, religious, whatever), then why do I keep questioning what I saw this afternoon: Why didn't *you* kill us?

What made us so special?

Most important: What was going through your mind when you came onto the bus? Did you see something we couldn't see?

I start to drift.

I snap myself from the daze by shaking my head. A surge of energy rushes through my body, a voice screaming at me not to sleep. I carefully step out of the bathtub and leave behind the day in the bathwater.

* * *

I have a dream about what went down earlier that day. The dream is, more or less, a memory. Me and my cloudy mind piecing together each image: the wreck followed by a shootout between the National Guard and a mysterious woman who, by the way, didn't even have a weapon on her, yet she was owning each one of the soldiers as if they were nothing more than fleas to her, then, finally, me winding up in a roomful of Federal agents. They kept pressing me about what happened before the suspect entered the bus. Did she touch us, did she speak to us and if so, what did she say to us, what did she do, her actions? She didn't say anything. Not that I recall. She didn't do anything. Why? Who was she? I had a feeling they *knew* the identity of the woman.

How much did they know?

I'm not sure.

They probably knew little to nothing about this woman; otherwise, they wouldn't have asked me so many questions about her.

Or, they knew everything about her and they were testing me, keeping me in the dark.

About what that might be, I don't know.

Flashes of memory replay in my thoughts: Soldiers shooting at the suspect, yet the bullets had absolutely no effect on her. She stands behind an overturned trunk on the side of the highway, predatorily staring down each solider, then something happens, something bizarre. . . The soldier's arm bends behind his back, then he turns robotic and fidgety, then he starts randomly shooting at other fellow soldiers. Other bizarre things happen to the soldiers, and it's like something is controlling them, telling them to turn on one another. Meanwhile, the suspect doesn't even budge an inch. She stands there, frozen. Almost dead-like.

More soldiers come by the truckload.

The suspect starts moving again, through fire and chaos.

She approaches the bus, more soldiers firing at her. The bullets hit the side of the bus, yet they don't strike the bus like any other bullet would strike a surface.

That's the first thing that stands out the most: the sound of bullets hitting the bus sounded like pellets of rain.

Bullets strike the bus, yet they don't cause any damage.

How can anyone do such a thing?

If it's her, why?

To protect us?

Criminals, especially terrorists, don't care about civilians. All they care about is themselves or their cause.

She isn't a criminal—can't be!

She isn't a terrorist.

What is she?

The sky is overcast when I wake up and the ground is still saturated from a late night shower. I only caught a couple of hours of sleep and most of it was spent reliving memories that could've passed as dreams. I get out of bed. I'm already up and there's no point trying to sleep any longer. I head downstairs where my dad is outside on the porch doing his morning ritual: a coffee and a ciga-

cigarette, two things that go hand-in-hand before he starts his magnificent day. My dad runs a marketing agency called Stride. People come to him with ideas and he makes those ideas sell. He can market the hell out of a new product, like organic dog food, yet he can't give my exhaust filter a whirl. He doesn't have a creative bone in his body, yet he's like Gandalf when it comes to shoving new products down people's throats. My mom is the total opposite. She's a full-time accountant, part-time Nazi. She's works at a local bank in Roseboro during the day; then, at night, when she comes home from work she makes it her number one priority to get on me for whatever I did—or didn't do. I can never win! Her mom was the same way from what I was told. I've heard my friends call her by different names—Tiger Mom seems to be a popular one—but I tell them she eats tiger for breakfast. Ask the people who ask for loans.

I grab a juice and a granola bar and head back to my room.

My mom stops me while I'm halfway upstairs and asks if I'm ready for school. Like I have a choice!

I come this close to losing it in Second Period English class. Blake is reading a chapter from *Siddhartha* when all of a sudden his voice sounds amplified. I become extremely nauseous. I ask Mrs. Dolby if I can be excused from the classroom. She hands me a hallway pass. I exit the classroom as the granola bar starts to stir in my belly.

Before I reach the girls' bathroom, the vomit projects from my mouth and splatters over the wall. I ignore the mess, rush to the sink, and finish vomiting in the sink.

Flashes of memory: Soldiers killing one another; the suspect kicking the back of an abandoned van, sending it across the highway as if it's a happy meal toy, then, finally, the van striking the military hummer.

As I splash my face with water, flashes of violence sting my eyes.

*—Emily?*

I turn my shoulder, only to find Mrs. Dolby standing at the edge of the bathroom.

"Are you okay, sweetie?" she asks me as she steps forward.

"Yeah," I say. "Breakfast wasn't sitting right."

"Emily, you've been through so much these past twenty-four hours. Why don't you go home? You don't even have to worry about making up—"

"—No," I say, as Mrs. Dolby rubs my back.

"Emily, you're sick."

"I can't. I'll stay. I'm fine."

"Is this about you getting behind—"

"—I'm fine, really."

"You sure?"

"Yes."

She looks at my leftover breakfast on the side of the wall.

"And don't worry about this," she says. "I'll get Mr. Bradshaw to clean it all up. Okay?"

I nod my head.

"Everything's going to be okay," she says.

I'd like to think everything will be okay, but I get the feeling it's not.

* * *

I stop by Coach Tabby's trailer after lunch and ask him how Pam's doing. He's only one of the few who showed up at school today. The side of his head is bruised from where he hit the steering wheel. He had thirteen stitches put in, but he's a warrior. Come on! We're talking about Coach Tabby! The guy is the epitome of tough. He says he talked to Pam on the phone during the break between First and Second Period. She's still at the hospital, resting in bed, watching reruns of *Saved By The Bell*, which—now that I think about it—is something I should probably be doing. It'd be nice, being a couch potato all day long, getting caught up on episodes from my favorite show on my favorite witch, *Cleo's Proxy.* Coach Tabby says Pam suffered a mild concussion. She's fine, according to Coach Tabby. She can't wait to sleep in her own bed, but the doctor wanted to keep her there overnight for observation. Coach Tabby says he's going to leave around lunchtime and pay a visit to the hospital before Pam's release. So far, I haven't gotten anything done. It's been a waste of time.

"How are you doing?" he asks.

"I'm hanging in there. You?"

He points at the side of his head.

"It's not the first time I've been beaten up," he says. "I guess I'll just have to add it to my collection."

I nearly break down in front of Coach Tabby.

Like Mrs. Dolby, he reassures me by telling me everything is going to be okay even though I know it's not. He gives me a hug, and it feels good to know there are people out there who still care about me.

* * *

The story is all over social media. Normally, I don't go on the Internet for my news—you know, since ninety-nine percent of the news on the Internet is total BS—but I'm curious about what everybody's talking about. Somehow, one of the witnesses, Florence Brown, managed to post a live stream of the event. The video was immediately taken down after it was posted on MyCircle; however, it was up long enough for someone to make a copy of the video. I don't know whether or not the video's authentic—after all, it's the Internet. From what I can tell, the images look similar to what I saw yesterday.

A woman whom I assume is Florence is screaming in the background. She's praying to "Sweet Jesus" and asking the Lord for His help while the suspect acrobatically leaps over two heavily-armed WWE-sized soldiers, breaks off one of their legs with a sweeping kick to his knee—I mean, *off* off. The force of the kick literally breaks off everything from the knee down. The video goes shaky and is hard to make out before Florence runs for cover in a ditch along the side of the highway. From there, she doesn't get a good shot of the fight, only the feet of several soldiers being lifted and tossed through the air by the suspect. Somehow, she gets a shot of a side view mirror lying on the side of the road. The mirror must've broken off in a crash or the shootout.

As I'm about to close the window, I see a white flash in the video. I rewind the video to the moment the flash rips across the screen. I slow down the video, watch it frame by frame. What I think is the flash of an assault rifle is a glare coming from the mirror. I slow it down even more; watch one frame at a time. In the reflection, I witness a ghostly figure—some kind of white apparition—moving through the bodies of each soldier. Each soldier reacts differently whenever it comes in contact with this strange entity: a flinch, a jerk of the head, a gaping mouth, a tremble. They start acting different, stiff and mechanical. The white flash slices through a soldier; then he turns his weapon on another soldier. It's as if they're being controlled.

I read the comments below the video. Most of the rhetoric on the Internet consists of baseless rants or recycled phrases turned into arguments. Name-calling. Trolling. Desperate hacks peddling outdated ideas.

People have already started to come up with their own stories and conspiracy theories, like she used to be a "super soldier" protected by the government or an inmate who escaped from prison or an "alien" from outer space—I admit, that's a good one. Most people think the video is a bogus, doctored or photoshopped. No single person out there in this strange world has the strength to do such things—let alone a woman! More comments: mostly vicious attacks on women and their physical appearances, which then opens the door to a stream of Internet trolls ready to capitalize on the moment. Comments like "She's hot" and "I'd bang her" and so forth.

Stupid boys.

* * *

Akea calls when I'm finishing up the last bit of homework. It's taken me a lot longer to close my books, but my mind's been occupied these past twenty-four hours.

She's still freaked out about what happened yesterday.

"Demeter told me she saw you at school today."

"Yeah," I say. "I wanted to go."

"I don't see how you can go back there," Akea says. "I couldn't."

We share a couple of awkward pauses—Akea and I don't really talk that much during school. She has her friends and I have my little group of friends, who aren't really my friends, but I guess I have to call them friends because I hang out with them from time to time.

Akea wants to know if somebody's been following me.

"Following me? What do you mean? Like a stalker?"

"Yeah, but no," she says. "I mean like, I don't know, like those agents we talked to yesterday."

"Why would they be following you?"

"I don't know," she says, sounding worried. "I was walking to Demeter's house when I saw this. . . this guy parked on the street. I didn't recognize him at first but I think he looked like the same guy who was parked outside my house."

"You're just being paranoid."

"I don't know," she says. "Maybe."

It's been two days since the world felt like it was going to end. Two very, very long days. Now, the memories are starting to piece together much better. New details become clearer, colors, faces, cries. Like the one time I woke up from one killer hangover after Billie Barnes' birthday party. I'm not much of a partier, mainly because of the fact I don't think people actually want me there. I've known Billie since preschool, though, and he invited me. So, I went. It was the first time I drank alcohol and it was definitely the last—isn't that what everybody says after a heavy night of drinking? I'm never drinking ever again. I haven't touched a drink ever since Billie's party, not even a sip. Swishing mouthwash is the closest I'll get to alcohol. The memory is similar to the hangover, except for all the horror, like when my friend, Mia, vomited all over Billie's new shoes. I remember Billie was talking about the shoes all night long. He wouldn't shut up about them. Even random people were complementing him on his shoes whenever they ran into him or bumped into him: *Hey, Billie! Nice kicks!* Now, that the shock has worn off and details fill in the memory gaps, I'm starting to feel a little bit different about what the agents said about the suspects. It's strange saying this, especially with everything I've witnessed. I even feel strange saying it, but I believe she wasn't what the agents claimed her to be. I believe the both of them were lying to me. I believe she wasn't a suspect. Instead, she was a victim.

My friend, Stephanie Cronin, thinks going to the movies is exactly what I need after everything that's gone on this week. Seriously, what a week it's been! My parents don't approve of me going to the movies—lately, it's like they don't approve of anything I do. They feel more at ease since I'm going with Stephanie. They like Stephanie, I think. Who doesn't like Stephanie? I've heard them say one time behind my back that she's one of the good ones. Whatever that means. We end up going to see the movie, *Doctor Strange.* What a strange week it's been. Now, it's about to get even stranger. It was either *Arrival* or *Doctor Strange.* Stephanie wasn't in the mood for another alien movie. So, we went with a superhero.

After the movie, Stephanie and I drive around and listen to music. Stephanie brought a joint with her. I've smoked before—pot, that is. I'm no angel. I really don't mind getting stoned every now and then. Besides, it's way better than alcohol and it's much cheaper. Plus, not only that, smoking pot won't ruin my life or make me dependent like the whole heroin epidemic that's been happening at all of the schools around here. My parents would most definitely not approve, but what they don't know won't kill them. Like my dad has any room to talk. But that's another debate. Stephanie came prepared with Visine and perfume.

Halfway through the joint, I have to pee really bad. We're out in the middle of nowhere—somewhere near Benjamin Creek and Missette.

"Hurry up, Stephanie!" I cry out. "I'm about to pee my pants!"

"Okay already," she says and stops after we pass a bridge.

Ahead are railroad tracks. There are no cars around either.

So, I get out of the car and pop a squat along an embankment.

Suddenly, I hear a *thud* coming from the street. I finish up, climb back up to the street, and find Stephanie's car door open but no Stephanie. I call out her name, but I can't see her anywhere. Not too far away a car with no headlights is parked along the street. I call out her name once more.

I suddenly feel a tug on my arm!

I turn and find a man shooting smoke in my face from a device on his arm. I kick the man away and start running into the woods. Not once do I ever look back. I can even feel the pulse in the corner of my eyes, my vision throbbing.

I keep running.

The horn of a train is screaming next to me, the ground is vibrating with energy.

For the first time in a very long time, I feel alive. I take in the energy around me.

Absorb it.

It makes me stronger, faster.

I never knew I had such a talent.

Even when my chest starts to burn, I keep running, keep moving. I hear a yearning like a whisper inside me, telling me to stop, to catch my breath, but my legs are moving like a train; and if I do stop, then there is a chance I won't be able to get going again. A part of me doesn't want to stop. A part of me thrives in the thrill of the chase.

Don't look back, it tells me. I don't look back.

Don't wayward. I don't wayward.

I keep moving forward, one breath at a time, one stride at a time.

I can't even begin to describe what I'm feeling right now. Something is starting to come over me, my body, my hands, my feet. Something completely out of my control.

Something dangerous.

## 10. BEFORE / EBONY

IT'S been twenty minutes and Doctor Patel is a no show.

"What's taken him so long, Daddy?"

"I don't know, Sweetie."

Daddy grabs my hand while we wait forever on the doctor. Daddy's hands are warm and sweaty but I don't say anything about them. He looks way more nervous than me when it's me who should be the one climbing out of my skin right now. Momma doesn't do too well in these situations. Hence why I dragged Daddy with me. I'm surprisingly calm, though, despite being trapped in a cramped room that these nurses stick you in after you've been waiting in the waiting room with a whole bunch of people who are waiting for their names to be called. When your name does get called, they usher you to yet another waiting room, a much smaller room that's filled with more magazines and posters of how the digestive system works, the inner making of your stomach, displaying what an ulcer looks like—just looking at the poster makes me feel like I got an ulcer. Maybe that's the whole idea. Going to a doctor's office is like going through this whole series of waiting rooms, each one getting smaller and smaller. Then, you get to your final destination and what do you know, you got to wait some more—and not only that, they seat you on an exam table with that uncomfortable roll of paper underneath. I hate doctor's appointments! Hate the whole process. I wonder if the whole reason you go to the doctor is to get sick, then you got to go back to the doctor and buy medicine. I don't trust doctors. Never have. Neither does Daddy. Every time he gets a cold or whatever, he never goes to a doctor. He's the strongest man I know, and yet, right now, he looks as if he's about to melt into a pile of goo.

Concerned, I turn to Daddy and I know there's a war going on inside him. Any amount of emotion for Daddy is like this big ole world of emotion. He's not the emotional type, if you know whatta mean. The last—actually, the only—time I've seen him cry was after her death. I remember walking in on him while he was in the bathroom and he was sitting on the toilet, alone, crying. When he saw I was watching him, he wiped the tears and acted like he got caught doing something he wasn't supposed to be doing. I liked to think Daddy used to smile or even laughed before her death. I can't remember how he was before her death, if he showed more emotion or if he's always been this way. Even if he did, I wouldn't know anything about it. Last time I've seen him so worked up was when he got laid off. I'll never forget that look on his face. It was like a lot of emotion, all wrapped in one package: shock, fear, anger, guilt, sadness. I don't know what you would call such a look. If I had to pick one, I'd call it the same look I see whenever I look into the mirror before a game. I call it my "game day" face.

Like a lot of Dads, he had to change careers after the IT company he had been working for for over twelve years decided to lay off over half their employees due to downsizing. He enrolled at Plymouth and took these online courses while he got a new job at COMP N' US. For a while, it became this routine for Daddy: coming home really frustrated by people—customers—I think a lot of the frustration was self-inflicted, if you ask me. He was angry with himself for getting canned at the one job I think he liked—because that's what happened. He had been so loyal to his job; and he'd come home, like a Hindu monk, and ask me all sorts of questions about my day, what I learned in class. He'd never talk about his job because it was totally over my head, but I know he liked doing what he did and he was proud to do it for a living. Getting "laid off" was a more polite term and the thought of him not being good enough was what I think made him angry. Daddy wasn't exactly a people's person, so, of course, being in retail wasn't for him. He was too intelligent for retail—and I know he hated dealing with rude, dumbass people all day long. Even though the job may have been beneath him, he did it for me. He did it for us. At night, I see him on the computer for hours, doing homework while putting together these complex spreadsheets to keep track of bill payments and expenditures. After he received a degree in Engineering, he spent months doing interviews. Finally, Daddy found a decent job that paid better than the one at COMP N' US. Then, all of sudden, it happened. The bombshell.

It's been one week since the news.

If I knew a routine visit to the doctor would result in me staying the night in a hospital, I never would've gone to the doctor's office in the first place!

On the flip side, I probably never would've experienced the miracle—that's what I'm calling it and I don't plan on changing it because I know what I saw. I've only told Trinity about what happened. She believes me, so she says, but I can't tell with her most the time because most the time she totally exaggerates every detail that comes out of her mouth. Once, I overheard her talking to Momma about it, and she said that I saw it because I was looking for it. That there is a bunch of baloney. I want to say something to Momma, but if I do, then she'll know

I was spying on her. I mean, not too many girls my age get the news that they're gonna die at any minute from a blockage in their main coronary artery, according to multiple EKGs they done me. This young doctor, who was looking like he was straight out of college, gave me no more than two days to live. Two days!

What do you even say to something like that?

Sorry, Ms. Acres, but you're going to die in two days. Two days! Just the other day I dropped two goals on those conceited Mammoths. They ran me through all these tests, like X-rays of my chest; they ran stress tests; they did this chest MRI where they inject colored dye into my veins—they said that the dye makes it easier to see what's going on inside my body—and finally, the last test, a heart catheter, which would show everything that's going on with my heart. When they first told me how it was going to be done, I remember trying to visualize them going through my groin with a needle. They were telling me it was a common procedure. Even one of the radiologists said she had one done, which had given me a little bit of reassurance. She told me it was no big thing. I was *not* looking forward to the procedure at all. After I spent that night in the hospital, constantly being woken up by the nurse (she had me walk around the cold and lonely hallways of the hospital to get my heart moving faster but she was unaware that I was a runner and I swear I got the heart rate of a blue whale—then after a while, laying in an uncomfortable bed all night long, flipping through one channel after another and waiting for daylight while nurses took samples of my blood every six hours—which reason why: they said they were looking for these certain enzymes in the blood; apparently, when you have a heart attack, your body releases these enzymes and it's supposed to show up in your blood), I felt as if I had become this faulty product ready to be discarded. Like a piece of refurbished machinery about to be sent to the junkyard.

I felt worse, knowing how much hospitalization was going to cost Daddy. Even when they'd scan a wristband that they gave me when I was first admitted and I could metaphorically hear that *ring* of a cash register going chi-ching! We're going to have to keep you in the hospital overnight for observation and monitor your heart in case you don't die in the middle of the night. Another chi-ching! We have to take your blood three different times throughout the night where we look for certain "enzymes" that are released into the blood whenever someone experiences a heart attack. You guessed it. Another chi-ching! Here's a baby Aspirin. Chi-ching! Oh yeah! We need to do your blood pressure once more, like they didn't get it right the first time around. Chi-ching! We need to run some more tests. Chi-ching! A heart catheter. A whopping chi-ching!

I know all about hospitals because Nana once stayed in one for a week after her first heart attack. I remember she showed me the bill after she was released from the hospital and it was enough to buy a house.

So, the miracle, right?

I'm sticking by it because I know what I saw in that operation room. I wasn't just "looking" for some kind of sign, like people do whenever they think all hope is lost or whenever they think as if their time is up, like Trinity and Momma said about me—like those two know everything about me when they just don't. I know she was up there, somewhere, helping me out. Crystal. Putting in a good word for me. I know it. I felt it. I feel her. *Still* do.

When they put me on the table, I felt Crystal in my bones.

She was there.

Moments before the procedure that I clearly wasn't looking forward to at all—this was right before they shaved the area where they were going to poke me, the heart doctor walked in like a man in charge (after all, it was his show) and he numbed that area where he was going in—I was anxiously waiting there as one of the nurses tried to keep me calm. I remember lying on that table—still sleepy from a night of constantly being woken up by the nurse whenever my heart rate dropped below fifty—looking up at the lights, the ceiling, all the medical instruments surrounding me, waiting for those drugs to finally kick in. I don't know what it is they gave me, but it sure did calm my nerves. I noticed this one light bulb in the ceiling. The bulb was clearly dead because all the others were working perfectly and it wasn't like the nurse turned off the lights after the last surgery. Those lights had been on for a while, perhaps all day and night, yet that one light remained black and dead for a couple of minutes until I set my eyes on it. All of a sudden, a surge of energy moved through my body and I could feel it rising above me. I drew my attention toward that one light bulb, focused my eyes on it. I don't know why I was so drawn to that bulb. Then, the light suddenly flickered four times, then stopped, went back to being dead and black, then, it flickered again, but this time only one time, then stopped, then again, one more time, then two more times, then stopped, then, lastly, one time. An incredible calmness washed over my body, not like that druggy kind of calmness that tames them nerves. All of the worry that I had before the procedure went away and I knew that I was going to be okay. Even if I didn't make it out of this thing alive, I knew, in my gut, in my bones, I was going to be okay. When I set my eyes on the light bulb, it was as if it was blinking at me, trying to tell me something. I didn't know what it was trying to tell me, but it was something all right.

After the procedure was said and done, the results came back.

No blockage—*hurray!*

The heart doctor told my parents my heart looked like any other healthy heart of young, active women. Which meant I didn't need a stint. Which meant any notion of having some artificial thing being implanted in my body for the rest of my life was put to rest. Which meant I was good to go. Here's your bill. Thanks for your stay. See ya later!

Afterwards, my parents talked some more to the heart doctor—one of those well-groomed doctors from Duke who you'd think only existed in TV shows, handsome and resolute, the kind of man you'd love to marry but know you can't marry because they're just too perfect. They said that he told them he didn't know how to explain what happened. He's treated young people my age with heart problems before—even athletic people who showed no warnings of having heart conditions. I've heard the stories before. It's rare, but it happens. Young athletes, just like myself, dropping dead while playing sports. In my case, there was a possibility the EKG experienced a "technical" error—or human error, but they'd never ever, ever own up to that. Nana passed from a massive heart attack when I was around nine—the big one they always warn you about—so I knew that one day it might come for me when I least expected it. The first thing they asked me when they received the results of the EKG was if I had any family members or past relatives with heart conditions.

Total and irrevocable relief as soon as I got back home—however, still sore from where they poked me (the heart doctor plugged the hole, gave me a brochure educating me about the procedure, told me to limit any activity for at least three to four days. So, basically, plant yourself on the couch, which wasn't that hard to do, until the wound finally seals shut by this pasty stuff that looks like liquid concrete. Plus, I needed to catch up on some of my favorites shows on Stream. Plus, I missed a couple days of school. So, I didn't have to worry about homework or getting behind and I swear, despite the whole ordeal, it was almost like I was on a mini-vacation for those couple of days after the hospitalization. That time off from school gave me enough time to think about what happened. I thought about the light.

The blinking.

What was it trying to tell me?

I asked myself so many questions, but I had not one answer. The thing that got me thinking was that there would be no answers.

Four blinks, one blink, three blinks with a space between the first blink and the next two blinks, then one more blink, resulting in nine blinks.

Nine lives?

Nine what?

Morse code.

I rushed to my computer—more like hobbled but I remember I moved pretty fast, despite the soreness.

I researched Morse code.

Four blinks: H

One blink: E

Three blinks with a space after the first blink: R

One blink: E

HERE.

She was there.

She is "here."

My primary care doctor, Doctor Patel, finally enters and he checks my bandage. He asks me if I have been experiencing any pain or bleeding.

"Just a little soreness; there was a little discharge but that's it. It don't seem—"

Daddy taps me on the shoulder.

"—It doesn't seem as bad as the other day," I correct myself.

The doctor has good news for me.

"You've been cleared to play today."

"Really?"

"Really. Everything looks good down there."

Doctor Patel asks me how I feel about playing, asks me if I'm ready to play, and I tell him that I feel good.

"I can't wait to get back on the field."

"I bet."

Before I leave, Doctor Patel writes me a note for both Mr. Keifer and Mrs. Anzola, my Third and Fourth Period teachers.

Central Agatha has this new policy that if you don't have a note, then you can't get through the gates—even after school is over. It's like a prison. But if that's what it takes, then so be it.

Today is the first day of my life and the last thing I want to do is start off the day in a bad mood.

## 22. AFTER / EBONY

SHE isn't dangerous.

She is balance.

Her breath is fire.

Ancient like desire.

She is the final equation, the question, the answer.

Images come at me in random spikes of pain: my hand catching the table as I fall to the floor and everything on the table coming down with it; a group of white pant legs entering the library; two cold fingers pressing against my neck; then, a black bag being placed over my head.

The drugs they give me have little to no effect on me, and I can't make out anything around me except for my own feet being dragged below.

* * *

When the black bag is removed from my head, a strange man dressed in tactical gear is placing wires around my chest. I follow the wires to this machine with needles next to me. But what strikes me as really odd are the gloves the man is wearing. And, not only that, he's acting as if I have bubonic plague, like if he were to touch me, then he'd keel over and die. Two men are sitting at a desk and asking me questions about the year and other things, like history questions, and I answer them with automatic responses. The one man, tall and attractive, calls himself Roger Sonnenberg—I don't really know who the man is because he's got this way about him that doesn't seem as if he's in the business of handing out diagnosis. He's not like the others. He walks among them but he is not one of them. He asks me about what happened on the bus moments leading up to the crash. It's been several days, and I've reached that point where I've started to erase what happened on the way to the game. Unlike most of the girls, I went back to school and went about my daily life. Even the doctors appear stunned as to why I went back to school after such a traumatic event.

I start questioning myself, traveling through each cluttered thought inside my head, trying to figure out if something is seriously wrong with me.

The more I think about the incident, the more my head spins. The thought of that woman presses against my chest like a weight and I'm having trouble breathing. The room is spinning—what's happening?

***

I wake up next to this woman sitting next to me on a hospital bed. She's holding a tall glass of orange juice and she's telling me to take a sip.

"What happened?" I ask her.

"You lost consciousness."

"I did?"

"Here," the woman extends the glass of orange juice to me, "your blood sugar was very low. This will help."

I take a sip of the orange juice.

"I need you to drink a little more," she says.

I take a couple of more sips, then hand her back the glass. I turn to my left and notice a curtain wrapped around the entire bed in a perfect circle. Above, a bright domed light shines down on us. All that remains behind the light is darkness. I can't make out a ceiling either. This place doesn't look like any hospital I've been inside. The air is stale like a hospital; however, there's something weird behind the curtain. It feels as if I'm being watched.

"Where am I?" I ask the woman.

"No need to worry. You're in a safe place," she says, as she places the glass on a tray next to the bed. Isn't that what people say when you should be worrying? I don't know what to think of her. Her hand is shaking, as if she knows something about me that I don't know. Why is her hand shaking? She takes in a deep breath through her nose, then faces me. "My name is Doctor Kipling, but you may call me Deborah—"

"—Where's my daddy?" I say. "I want to see my daddy."

"You need to relax, Ebony—"

"—How do you know my name?"

"I know a lot of things about you—"

"—Who are you people?"

"All you need to know is that we're here to help—"

"—Help? Help with what?"

"Please, Ebony," she attempts to hand me the glass of orange juice.

I push the glass away, causing the glass to shatter over the floor!

I stumble out of the bed.

Deborah reaches for me, but I push her away.

As I stand to my feet, the room starts to spin again. I stagger around the tight space and grab hold of the curtain. Part of the curtain peels open and reveals the masked face of a solider dressed in black. There are dozens of these men standing like statues behind the curtain, all armed with guns.

Streaks of light race across my vision and my limbs turn numb and icy and I feel as if I'm about to pass out again.

Deborah helps me to the bed.

"What's. . . what's going on—"

"—Just relax, Ebony," she says. "I know this is a lot to take in."

I lay back down. Deborah sits in a chair next to the bed.

"Ebony, I need you to explain to me what happened on the way to Middleton High School. Every piece of detail is vital. Can you do that for me? Just start from the beginning. After you left Central Agatha. . . "

Once the dizzy spell wears off, I tell her everything that I remember. Brittany and I were talking about Justin right before the bus swerved. When I mention

Justin's name, Deborah becomes more intrigued. She wants to know more about Justin. I tell her that Brittany thinks I should ask Justin out.

To be honest, I don't really know why she's so interested in wanting to know about Justin.

I tell her that he's a boy.

"Is this boy in your class?" she asks.

"No," I tell her. "I pass him everyday when I leave First Period."

She wants to know why I'm so interested in Justin.

So, I tell her.

"You like Justin?" she asks.

"Yes," I tell her.

"Why?"

I can't tell her why.

I try to make sense of the situation, the machine that they had hooked up to me.

What are they not telling me?

I turn my eyes to Deborah's leg. Her right leg is rapidly bobbing up and down—a nervous tick perhaps. I can't keep my eyes off her leg. Daddy does the same thing whenever he gets anxious. But why would a skilled doctor be so anxious around me? Maybe she's not a doctor at all. Maybe she's got like social anxiety disorder. I admit that I get the same way, especially around Justin.

So, I tell her, hoping that it will bring some answers as to why I'm really here.

"There's just something about him," I say just as she's about to open her mouth to speak.

"Justin, you mean?"

"Yeah," I tell her.

Yeah is like a universal language. It can be either a yes or a no, depending on the way you look at it.

Yes, I'm agreeing to whatever it is you're asking.

No, I'm agreeing to whatever it is you're asking but I'm not really agreeing. I just want you to stop asking me the same question.

She wants to know more about Justin.

"It's the way he carries himself," I tell her. "Like he knows who he is, like he's carrying around something special inside him, like a glow, and nobody can touch that. He's so confident, yet he walks around with this pain, like he's got this terrible burden over his shoulders. He doesn't care what people think about him, yet he does."

"What does this Justin kid do?" she asks. "Is Justin into sports? Video games—"

"—Drawing," I say. "He likes to draw."

"So, he's an artist?"

She becomes even more intrigued.

"I guess you can say that," I tell her. "I used to be into drawing myself, but I'm not really good at it. I've wanted to design my own clothes. One time when Justin dropped his pencil during lunch—he always eats lunch in the courtyard by himself—I was passing by and I caught a glimpse of the notebook he always carries around with him. He was drawing this sketch of this alien-type creature sinking its fangs into a body. It was like something you see in movies. It was so real and it had so much detail in it. He caught me looking at the sketch and he noticed how interested I was in it. The next morning, when I was going to my locker, I found a sketch of me sitting with other students who were all grayed out. It was so different than the other sketch I saw in his notebook."

"Did you ask him about this sketch?"

"No," I tell her. "I didn't."

"Are you afraid of Justin?"

"I'm afraid that, if I finally gather the nerve to carry on a conversation—I mean, like more than two words—something awful might happen to me."

"Something awful? Like what?"

"I'll be judged."

"Judged? Nobody is going to judge you. Ebony, what are you really trying to say?"

"I'm afraid my heart will beat so fast that it will explode."

"Why would you say that?"

"I don't know," I say and shrug as if it's my only defense mechanism for blocking away the awkwardness between us. "Every single time I'm around Justin, my heart beats really fast around him."

"Are you afraid that he might reject you?"

"Yeah."

"Ebony," she says, leaning closer, "what I'm about to tell you next is extremely important and it may come as a shock to you but I need you to understand that we're doing everything we can to figure out what's wrong."

"What are you saying?" I ask her.

She grabs my hand and tells me the bad news first.

There is no good news.

Only the bad.

## 11. BEFORE/STEWART

THE ambulance arrives a few minutes after she drives away. I am little banged up; the girls are fine, mostly frightened; but I must stay strong in front of my team. Ebony is hyperventilating. Brittany's helping her with her breathing, telling her to inhale through her nose and exhale through her mouth. The scene is chaotic; people are screaming and crying while others remain in shock from the sight of carnage. I've never seen anything like this before; bodies are completely dismembered. I check myself for any other injuries. My head is not doing so well. I might need several stitches, but, overall, I'll live. Most of the girls appear unharmed, except for Rhea, who's having trouble standing. She appears to be having a panic attack. I rush over to Rhea and reassure her by telling her to concentrate on something else. The more I talk to her, the sooner she starts to settle down. I do a headcount, making sure everyone is accounted for. I spot Pam among the chaos. She has a couple of lacerations on the side of her face. She says she's okay, just a little dizzy. I think she may have suffered a concussion, but she'll live.

Once I do the tally, I check on the other survivors. There doesn't appear to be any life-threatening injuries. Nothing much remains of the soldiers, only limbs and body parts scattered around the bloodstained highway.

I look around, thinking about what just happened. I can't even put into words what happened. It all happened so fast. I was making a left turn onto Church Street when she came out of the blue. The way she moved, it wasn't real.

I tend to my team, more sirens getting closer. More ambulances and fire trucks.

A team of paramedics checks on the girls, each one asking them if they've suffered any injuries. One paramedic is shining a flashlight in Pam's eyes and asking her questions like "What's the day?" or "What year is it?"

One of the paramedics finally tends to me and says that he needs to take care of the wound on my head. I tell him that I'm fine, but I know he's just doing his job. He treats me on the spot by clotting the wound with pressure and tells me the unavoidable news that I'm going to need stitches.

As I ride in the back of the ambulance, the paramedic continues to apply pressure to my head. He throws out the blood-drenched gauze, replaces it with a fresh gauze straight out of the pack, and then reapplies pressure. The bleeding seems to be somewhat under control—but it hasn't completely clotted, as the paramedic tells me. He asks me how I got the wound and to the best of my ability, I tell him, "I think I hit my head against the steering wheel when I ran into the guardrail—"

—My voice comes to a sudden halt by the screech of a radio!

The lights flicker throughout the ambulance!

A staticky sensation runs over the hairs on my skin.

"What in the world?" the driver trails off.

A barrage of scrambled, chaotic noises continues to play on the radio.

The driver switches off the radio, causing it to spark and smoke.

"Denise," the paramedic calls out to the driver, "what the heck is going on up there?"

"I have no clue," she says.

The lights inside the ambulance go black.

"Alan, the steering wheel is locking up!"

I hear a screech of tires!

The ambulance violently shakes before coming to a stop!

A deafening explosion rocks the entire ambulance!

The driver gets out of the ambulance.

"Alan!" the driver's yelling out. "Come out here and look at this!"

"What happened, Denise?"

"Come here! Hurry!"

The other paramedic turns to me, places my hand over the gauze, and says, "Keep pressure on it. . . "

He steps out of the ambulance.

I can't help myself.

I have to find out what's going on, so I hold the gauze over my head and step out of the ambulance.

"What was that?" I ask the paramedic.

"I don't know," he says. "It sounded like an explosion."

Not too far away, a massive black smoke cloud slowly rises into the sky. The trees are blocking most of the view. I wonder if what happened in the ambulance had something to do with the explosion. All I can do is wonder.

## 23. AFTER/STEWART

HERE we go again: Am I ready to talk?

They think silence is an admission of guilt when it's me sticking it to them. I've answered the same exact questions the FBI agents asked me. Halfway through our conversation, they switch subjects and bring up the answer to a question they asked earlier in the conversation, the part where I was talking about coming to after being knocked out on the bus. She touched me on the shoulder, and all of those emotions I had as a teenager came flooding back over me. Call it *nostalgia.* Call it whatever. I called it a nightmare. They start asking me questions about what's been happening in the world as of lately. They want to know what I think about the riots and protests and all of the hysteria.

Somewhere during the string of monotonous questions, I mention what I was seeing on television with all of the unrest and whatnot. They want me to share something personal that only *I* experienced, something that changed or redirected the course of my life.

A couple of weeks ago, during all of the unrest, the football team got in trouble for hazing other players. Nothing extreme, like suspension, but the players involved ended up sitting out three games. I don't exactly go into much detail what seniors of the football team were doing to the younger players. It gets a little R-rated and I'd rather leave out the details. All I can say is that objects were being placed in certain areas of their bodies. The players were busted after word had gotten out.

Coach Bluth—a one hundred percent asshole by the way—found out what his players were doing, the weird, social, male dominance, pecking order experiments.

Which makes me question if Coach Bluth knew what was going on and decided not to say anything.

"When I mean *trouble,*" I clarify, "I mean a slap on the wrist."

The incidents reminded me of what I went through, especially what happened on the television with that poor kid being beaten. It hit home for me. I couldn't help but think of what happened to me so many years ago. Years it took me to forget all about the incident. Hearing about the football team, the things on television, it really got me.

When I was fourteen, just a couple of years younger than the girls, me and some friends were hanging out in the courtyard, minding our business, when the football team showed up and started bullying people around. There was one kid who had it in for me—he had my number, if you will—I don't know what his deal was, but he didn't like me. Or, maybe he did like me or he was jealous. I don't see any reason why he would be jealous of me. I was an average kid from an average family. You can say that there were a whole bunch of maybes with this guy. We go about our business, we move; something comes over him. Next thing I know he's charging at me. He grabs me as I make a run for it, and I'm fighting and kicking and doing everything that I can to keep him off but all of a sudden I got half of the football team grabbing at me. I kick them off—pop one of them in the jaw with my foot—but I'm completely outnumbered. One of them manages to unbuckle my belt while another guy is ripping off my pants. I turn to my friends and they're standing there, watching. Other kids are laughing at me, what's being done to me. I know it's not their fight, but deep down inside, I wanted them to help me; they strip the clothes from my body. I'm doing all that I can to cover up myself with my hands; now, everybody's laughing at me. I was so humiliated that I wanted to die right then and there. From that point forward, I looked at the football team and anyone associated with football in a different way. Even if there was someone who was actually decent—I know they exist, the softies—if he played football, I still looked at him differently. Years pass. I saw a video on television, which has become what the kids call a viral sensation over the Internet. The video was of a young man, probably no older than one of the girls. He was at one of the many conflicting protests—which, even till now, I still don't know what they were protesting. I looked at me as kids letting off steam and directing it at the wrong place. There was nothing wrong with the protest—after all, it was protests in the past that help us move forward as a nation—but I felt as if agitators without a cause were capitalizing on the opportunity to wreak havoc. A group of college-age men, ambushed the kid in a parking lot, beat him up so badly that they broke his ribs and severed his spleen; they stripped the clothes from his body. Whenever something horrible happens to someone—a crime especially—it's natural to think about what was going through the victim's mind. It's human nature to look after one another, especially when things get out of hand. With this kid, I couldn't help but think of what was going through his mind when these angsty men were attacking him; and like most people do, you turn toward yourself and you start to see yourself in that person's shoes, what you would've done differently if you were in that position, or like me, I couldn't help but think of myself because that very same thing happened to me in the past, and just by seeing something that I tried to erase from my mind so long ago, all of that emotion flooded over me. I wanted to break down; then I thought about how he'll feel afterwards, the hatred not only for one individual. A couple of bad seeds don't ruin a whole bag; but now, I'm sure in the back of the kid's mind, he'll start to see it differently. Can a person actually have hatred for an entire demographic or age group of people? That's millions and millions of people out there, innocent people who, in this kid's mind, will be stained with an image that he'll want to try to erase from his mind. Forever. What chills me to my bones the most: *What if my girls encounter these types of men after they graduated?* More than likely, they will. If someone—say a man—did something awful to a woman—something that scared her for life—could she trust a man ever again? Same goes if the roles were reversed.

That video just got me thinking—that's all.

I don't tell these two doctors the entire story. Instead, I give them more of the *Cliff Notes* summary. I decide to spare them the sob story.

"I'm sorry to hear about that, Mr. Tabby," the doctor says.

I'm not sure if he's really sorry and just saying that to be polite.

"Do you have any children, Mr. Tabby?"

"Why are you asking me these questions? Seriously! According to the questions you've been asking me, it seems as if you would know whether or not I have children."

"Just answer the question, Mr. Tabby?"

"Tell me what's really going on here? What do you want from me?"

"We're asking you these questions, Mr. Tabby, because we want to know if you're who you say you are."

"And exactly who in the hell would I be?"

## 12. BEFORE / PAMELA

THE nurse escorts two FBI agents into the hospital room. She asks me if I can talk, but I can only bring myself to a nod of my head. One of the agents is already pulling out his ballpoint pen and leather-covered memo book, as if he's ready to catalog my entire life story.

I'm still a little foggy from the blow to my head, but I tell the agents that I'm glad to help them in any way that I can.

The first question that the gentleman asks me: Did you get a good look at the suspect's face?

I zone out for a moment, sift my way through the thick fog, and find myself back on the bus, moments before the events, starting from the very moment I was violently launched from the front window of the bus.

Since the imagery is so vivid and chaotic, I have to take a moment to catch my breath. The agents wait on me to gather myself before going back in. I let the images inside. The violence. It feels as if I'm reliving the horror right before my eyes: A child screaming in the station wagon next to me; bullets whizzing overhead, pelting the passenger side of the car, chewing through the metal; each *pop* of a gunshot sending me to take cover on the ground.

I stay low and bring my arms and legs close to my body.

One bullet skips off the concrete and strikes the tread of a tire inches behind my head, causing me to curl my body into a fetal position. The first thing that runs through my mind, except for trying to survive, is a terrorist attack. We've been attacked again. I search for the terrorist, but I can't see any in sight.

Underneath the car, I witness armed soldiers and startled police officers being torn apart, each one of their limbs being ripped from their bodies by an unknown force. They appear to be firing in random directions. Confused.

I spot a camouflaged figure leaping from one squad car to another, like a gust of wind. I hone my eyes on the creature, trying to keep up with it but I become woozy. I close my eyes and rest my head against the hubcap.

I'm having yet another flashback: I'm in a heated argument with Primo, and we're having one of our weekly fights about money.

It's been three years since Primo proposed to me during a Sabertooth's game, hundreds and thousands of people surrounding us, Primo and I shoulder to shoulder with strangers, our faces blown up on a jumbotron. I hear a woman in a pink ball cap whispering to what looks like her husband behind us that we look so adorable. What if I said, "No?"

What happened to us?

We used to be so open with our affection. Primo used to hold my hand whenever we would take nightly walks through the city. Times I felt like he would never let go of my hand. The thought had given me great comfort, knowing that I was his and he was mine. We'd stop at this diner called Sophie's, which reminded me of Hopper's famous *Nighthawks* painting, for hot chocolate and sit by the window and get lost between night and morning.

Primo would give me a foot massage underneath the table while I played and curled his raven-black hair. Every now and then, Primo would sneak in a kiss whenever I wasn't looking. And we'd make comments about each person passing by, guessing his or her life story based on the way he or she dressed. You know a lot about a person based on what he or she decides to cover their skin with. As the night grew brighter and people started to taper off, Primo and I would talk for hours until Jib kicked us out. We used to talk so openly about things we wanted out of life. We didn't care what others thought about us. We were undeniably crazy for one another. Primo and I were in love, and love was something I couldn't buy. I had to earn it and continue to earn it. Love is a full-time job. The house, I remember, was everything. I envisioned a house somewhere near the lake. Primo had other plans. He wanted the same American dream that was shoved in his face ever since he was a child: Victorian-style house with this white picket fence that screamed cliché, a lawn to mow every Saturday morning, and two Labradors to keep us entertained. One black. One white. Primo came in a package with all those things attached, the dreams, the house, the dogs. And I couldn't have one without the other. I had to make a compromise.

The argument is about me buying wrong dish soap. It's always me. *Me* not paying attention. *Me* not listening. *Me* not saying the all right things. So much has happened in those three short years. Primo and I tied the knot at Dunlin-McGuire Castle in the small dusty town of Grinnage. That was the day I officially became Mrs. Pamela Van Buren Levi—maiden names never really sound all that great. It's like splicing two films together. Names aside, the location of the wedding couldn't be any better. The castle was most notable for holding extremely extravagant weddings. The year before the wedding Primo and I went to a Halloween party at the castle. Every year, they opened up the castle to the public and had these insanely epic Halloween parties. Primo went as Dexter from that one TV show, *Dexter*, and I went as one of his victims. I wrapped my entire upper body in cellophane, splattered my chest with gobs of fake blood—I had ended up piecing the costume at the very last minute, so the blood I bought at the closest Party City—covered my face with white powder and shaded dark circles under my eyes to make myself look dead—some people thought I was a mummy. The things you do for love. Later that night, Primo and I had the best sex. I kept on the cellophane. Maybe it was all the Rum and Coke. Or me being around the many costumes and all that gore and violence rubbed off on me. For some reason that night, I felt like being constrained. Primo and I had fallen in love with the location so much that we decided to have the wedding at Dunlin-McGuire. Primo's parents were cleanly rich, as in his parents had fought for every single penny they earned. During the time I spent around Antonio and Jeanette, I never saw them *not* working, as in they were always occupied with developing a new addition to their mansion in Escargo or investing their money into old houses to flip. Primo was strangely close to his parents—as in sometimes, I'd catch him talking to his mother in another room, as if he was talking to her behind my back. I know Primo didn't want me to think that he was a momma's boy. Who grown man does? There was something incredibly emasculating about a man in his late thirties who still clung to his mother. He talked to both his parents everyday—he'd even give them hour-by-hour details about his day. I knew about this even when I wasn't around because I'd go through his recent calls in his phone. For crying out loud, he was a manboy who still watched cartoons—I've always wanted to use that expression in a sentence. However, that was what I loved about him, his youthfulness. After all, he was the only thirty-eight-year-old I knew who still got excited about video games. He'd play them for hours, especially whenever I had one of my monthly girl nights out. I leave with him playing a first person shooter or RPG—he was into shooter games especially—and when I returned home, loose off booze and wet as a clamshell from the idea of sitting on his face, I find him in the same exact position as before, with him kicked back on the couch, an empty beer bottle on the coaster and screaming at the TV while he murdered monsters. I didn't particularly mind that video games were an outlet for him. He was a real estate agent who spent his days sprucing up houses and blowing smoke up buyer's asses. He was entitled to a little man-time, I guess. His mother was the one who actually got him in the business. She knew a friend who knew a friend. Sometimes, that's how it works. You just have to know somebody. I was still teaching at Wendover, same assistant coach position on the varsity basketball team, same teaching position: ninth grade health. Back then I followed the curriculum to a T. I taught the same class at Central Agatha, however, with a slight sarcasm. A lot of things had gone on in my life between the time I started out teaching to the time my life turned into a murder mystery waiting to happen, but let me not get ahead of myself. As I tell my students—in a more polite manner—everything they learn in my class is based on eighty percent bull and twenty percent facts. My grandmother, Eureka Van Buren, a feisty thing spawned from a family of firefighters and police officers whose daily diet was a combination of meat and potatoes, smoked her whole life and drank cheap beer and ate red meat, and she lived to be eighty-three years old. Say what we will about cigarettes, all the harmful effects and whatnot—Grandma Van Buren smoked two packs of Virgin Slims in a day—but that wasn't even what killed her. One day, she fell while getting out of the bathtub. She slipped like they do in the cartoons on banana peels and broke her hip. They say you only live for about a year after you've broken your hip—that is, when you live to be as old and angry as my grandmother. She never got cancer, never developed emphysema. You can call it luck. Call it whatever you like. Grandma Van Buren was one tough cookie, a woman of true grit, and years from now, when the lights finally go out, the wanderers of the lost world will look back at women like my grandmother and say, "They don't make 'em like that, anymore." It's fair to say that I was close to my grandmother; however, I was nothing like her. I was never close to my parents like Primo was to his—after all, he was born with a silver spoon in his mouth—so, for me, of course it was new. Antonio was one of those "TV" defendants—yeah, one of those schmucks—mostly handled controversial cases, which attracted much public interest, including the famous Roger Palmer trial, the baseball player who allegedly murdered his wife. Jeanette is retired. Happily retired—was. She passed away from a major heart attack last year. I attended her funeral even though Primo didn't want me anywhere near there. She was an author of romance novels, the fabulous Juliet Sinclair—a pseudonym inspired by her grandmother, Juliet Fourier—who, after fifteen years in the industry, ended up hitting the mother lode when she decided to dirty up her beloved romance novels. Nobody likes a smut writer. It's lowbrow. Jeanette ended up patronizing her impressively large fan base—mostly retirees who talked about her books in staid book clubs—but on the other side where the grass is much greener, she gained worldwide fame. A lot of her fans called her a "sellout," but she was laughing all the way to the bank. Jeanette once said that she wanted to try something new. So, she took a stab at writing a smut novel. I'm not talking about your average lonely boy meets girl next-door type of romance. Boy wants to experiment with different sexual fetishes. Boy wants to borderline torture naughty girl. Let's just say there were a lot of whips, chains, and strap-ons involved. I never knew Jeanette was capable of writing such violence. The woman was so sweet, petite, and soft-spoken. The book became a major Hollywood movie—it was like *Basic Instinct*, *Fatal Attraction*, and *The Crying Game* with a strap on. Number one at the box office. She was sitting pretty for the remainder of her life. So, of course, they agreed to pay the tab for our wedding. Not like it didn't put any pressure on the wedding. I drank a lot over those several months of planning. I was a hot mess. The wedding turned out being great, despite the pre-hysteria. It's what happened after the wedding that sent me down the rabbit hole, so dark and ugly, one that could've finished me if I didn't make a drastic change in my life. I started to change. Primo changed. He used to be so handsome. I didn't even think he was that attractive when I first met him. We met the same way he ended up in the real estate business. I had this teacher friend who bought a house from one of Primo's real estate friends. She told me about this cute Jewish guy who was on the market. We had sex on our first date—I'm aware it's sort of a no-no because most of the guys, as in smart guys will either pigeonhole a girl as a slut or think of her as extremely desperate for getting in the sack on the first date, but Primo was the first guy I dated since my last boyfriend who turned out being a controlling psychopath. The sex wasn't all cream and strawberries, but it definitely could've been much better. Sex between strangers is never that great anyway. It takes time to find one another's rhythm. It's all a race. Usually, one of the other is trying to get off before they get on. Primo was a quick learner, though. I'd say he caught on by the second date.

Over a year together as a couple, Primo became "Simply Irresistible," like the song. That song used to be one of our many songs, most of them being songs from the 1980's—Phil Collins, Hall and Oates, Foreigner. Love has a magical way of turning an average man into a king. It's amazing what we did to each other. I turned him into the man he always wanted to be. And he turned me into the woman I always wanted to be: a wife, a lover.

But *not* the other.

The sounds of gunshots bring me back. I close my eyes and calm my breathing as I take myself back to a time where things made sense.

I fall deeper into another flashback and find myself going through a series of flashbacks. I think it's my way of trying to piece together where everything went wrong—our downward spiral.

As we're on the way home from the doctor's office, we're discussing the news from the doctor that there's a problem with the growth of our baby, but we're optimistic. We haven't named the baby yet. We know that it's going to be a boy. Just the other day, I bought a textbook-sized book of baby names—mostly for reference—and Primo and I literally spent our entire Sunday night lounging on the couch, cradled in each other's arms while we shoveled gooey gobs of Ben and Jerry's ice cream into our mouths and sorted through a list of names, Primo making sure to write down his favorite ones on a piece of paper, I, on the other hand, stepping outside the box by mixing and combing names—normally, our Sunday nights were filled with us going through a bottle of Cabernet Sauvignon and having lazy sex that lasted for hours, usually in my favorite and most preferred position while laying on the couch and watching Netflix, Primo laying directly behind me while giving it to me from behind. I'm not so keen on all of the names from *Kama Sutra*—after all, it's someone's opinion and opinions are entirely irrelevant. I call the position Sunday Sex, but I welcome others to use their own imaginations: Banana Sunday, Sunday Funday, Bloody Sunday—if it's that time of the month. With all of the drinking, the sex, and all that great nastiness aside, it was one of the best nights that we ever spent together.

As of now, Primo and I have narrowed down the names to Jacob and Izzy—the differences in the names clearly exploits our opposite personalities—but the doctor has planted a grim notion in our heads that it might be neither. Doctors always have a villainous way of looking at things.

Later that night, Primo and I get into a fight. It's one of our first heated fights as a married couple. Every fight from here on out is like a Pay-Per View event.

Is this where it all started?

The news.

The pieces are getting more rigged, crooked.

I slip farther and farther down the hole.

A month later I'm having my very first stiff drink in six months—bourbon on the rocks. I've come to realize that I'm a bourbon girl. I get hammered that night and have another fight with my asshole of a husband, Primo the Screamo. He goes out with some old pals and comes back the next morning reeking of pussy and regret.

By the following day, I'm incorporating three drinks into my excruciating long days. Then four the next. It becomes a routine for me, drinking everyday, earlier in the day. I know that if I don't control the drinking, I may never recover.

The following night, I pull my car into the driveway after having a night out without Primo. I wait for hours in my car, afraid to see his face. I don't want to see his face anymore. I just want him to finally turn off the lights.

Our fights have gotten to the point where I actually enjoy them. I enjoy watching Primo get mad. He finally has some color in his face. I wish Primo showed that much emotion months ago.

I know that any minute now, he's going to storm out of the house and fade into the night. Where does he go? I've often been wondering that while I sit alone in my wet misery. Even now, I'm wondering if Primo will ever come back home to me. Why would he? I wonder if these fights give him an excuse to see another woman.

Lately, our sex life has taken a turn for the worse. Sex is no longer healthy for me. It's been overrun by one red flag after another. I'm starting to turn into my own victim.

While I was pregnant, Primo didn't have much time with his video games. Taking care of me was like a job in itself.

Then, after everything happened, he no longer resorted to taking out all of his frustration on a joystick. I think the job was making matters worse. A week after our world started to fall apart, Primo made his A+ attempt to act as if things were back to normal when they weren't. I continued to be the stay-at-home wench while he became the breadwinner. I took yet another extended leave to refresh my page but mostly because I was afraid to show my face at school. I didn't want to deal with all the sympathy talk—gooey teachers hovering over me, watching me, waiting, all of the attention, every teacher waiting for me to do something out of line.

While I was at home finding a way to fix my failing marriage, Primo went back to selling homes to couples starting new chapters in their lives or families starting over. A new home can be the best remedy for saving a relationship that's gone stagnant. I think everybody's entitled to a fresh start; however, once a family is broken, there's no repairing the damage. Seeing that kind of pageantry day in and day out got to Primo when it should've been inspiring him to fix his own problems. I think that's when he started to use me for sex. It was no longer about making love. There comes a time when you just stop receiving any pleasure and you just lie there on your back and take it, like all the boys say, "like a man." Even the way he screws me has changed. He's turned into something primitive. I think it's his way of punishing me for what I did to the life growing inside when, in fact, I had *no* control over what happened. I've become the punching bag of the marriage. Something to toss around. An outlet. An object. Whenever he wants to release all of that manly shame, he takes it out on me. Sometimes, I'll even have to stop what I'm doing just to satisfy him. Besides sex or whatever you wanted to call it, we couldn't even be in the same room with one another. We became the couple that we said we'd never be. He'd never land a finger on me in that way—I wouldn't allow it after Glenn—but I know he wants to. Boy! He so desperately wants to slap me across the face like he really means it, slam my head against the wall, crush my skull, pick through each painful thought as if he's sifting for gold, or carry out whatever sickness that goes on in his mind. I can see it inside him, that red rage buried deep beyond those once beautiful brown eyes. Once, we were the 'it' couple. A hot item. The "look how cute they are" couple.

Once, I used to love pleasing him. Even when I was on my period. I was a team player when it came to getting my hands dirty. At one point, I was a man's woman. Then, weeks after when I was feeling piping hot and ready to jump his bones, he'd return the favor but go the extra mile. Primo would build a tent between my legs and bury his head inside me until every fiber in my body was greased and just right. The release was always, *always* worth the wait. Now, we're *that* couple you whisper to your spouse or significant other never to be like. If I had a chance to go back in time and confront the old me, Ms. Happy Idiot, I'd grab that bitch by the shoulders and shake the stupid out of her. I would scream at her to 'wake up.' To 'quit living in a fantasy world.'"

Another bullet skips off the concrete and brings me back to the beginning. Primo's pissed. He's shouting at me. He's making a list, checking it twice. His defense is making a good case. I've been avoiding him for quite some time. He's starting to question why I married him in the first place. It's true—in some way or another. Primo won't win the fight, but he makes a very good point: I'm starting to become one of those women. Always hated the type. The ones who don't work, who piddle around the house all day and spend all of their husband's hard-earned money on fruitless things that she doesn't need. Things that try to fill the void in her life. I do have a void, a massive one, and it feels like an obese monkey on my back.

I keep slipping. Into a stinging darkness. I'm older now, not the spring chicken I used to be. The memory is much more fresh and vivid.

I find myself waking up on a warm Sunday morning, naked, sore, and sprawled out over a cold bed, thinking about Primo and those glorious Sunday mornings we used to share together, making plans with what we wanted to do for the rest of our lives. I'm sure me waking up alone was not what I imagined. Funny how life does that, how it takes what you fear the most and it makes it a part of your reality.

My hangover is mild enough to get rid of the headache without any drugs. I turn to my left. The sight of the wrinkled sheets of an empty space covered in damp stains causes my gut to twist in knots. I don't remember the guy's name nor do I even feel like wasting any energy trying to rehash his name among the haze. He was in his early twenties, that I know, old enough to legally have a drink. He left somewhere between coming and zipping up. Some of them stay the night while others dip out before sunrise. When I wake up, I prefer not seeing their face to remind me of how pathetic I am as a woman who sleeps around with strangers who I meet at bars. It's become a whole new level of guilt. I'm starting to think that it's a disease or something worse, something mental, but knowing me, I'll go through an entire week cleaning up my act and by next Saturday night, I'll tell myself just one drink. I've been working all week. I could use the fresh air, an hour spent around new faces, new places. It's a vicious cycle, living in complete and utter denial. It's like your body has turned on itself. Then, you look in the mirror and start asking yourself: *Do I want to live like this? Is this my sick way of punishing myself?* I'm scared that one day I'll wake up and I'll be alone forever, forgotten. I know there will come a day when nobody will want my body or my company. I'm starting to age more noticeably. Only the decent ones stay for a while, I think out of guilt—some grab a cup of coffee with me, then they scrape me off the heel of their loafers. Sex never used to be a bargaining chip.

What happened?

I remember the first time I gave head. I was only seventeen years old, shy and insecure. I didn't have many friends who I could call my best. Only one or two girlfriends whom I hadn't talked to since my first year at Carolina—and a guy friend, Hunter, a geeky kid who lived down the street from me, a couple of years younger than me but he tagged along with us everywhere we went. These friends didn't associate with any of the other group of kids, like the jocks, cheerleaders, or stoners.

Regardless of these temporary friends, I felt like the everyday Teenage Ghost. Mainly my pizza faced acne. I had it bad for about two years. I had pimples that would have their own pimples, as if a new colony of pimples migrated onto my face. They'd pop up at the worst times: yearbook pictures; several days before prom; Friday nights at The Paramount. Garry Porter didn't mind my acne, though. I remember the kids used to call him Porta Potti, which is a terrible nickname to have in high school. I don't really know why they called him that. I can only imagine he was involved in a porta-potti accident. Kids can be so mean. Acne face and all, I followed Garry into the woods. I always fantasized about my first time, whom it would be with or where it would happen. The woods were the last place I expected to do it, but I had to take wherever I could get. Before he finished, Garry never gave me a heads up like he said he would—I remember his feet curling into the moist earth below me as he grew three inches in height—all of his warm vigor caught me directly in my right eye, temporarily blinding me, while the rest of it went down my throat. It didn't exactly turn out the way I imagined it in my mind.

At the time, I didn't feel the *least* guilty about hooking up with Garry mainly because I was completely obsessed with Garry. I would let him do anything to my body. We hooked up a couple of times after that—last time we were together-together was at a end-of-the-year party at Michael Puckett's house, both of us tipsy as car signs; Gary rounded third base and I waved him home. It was Garry's first time, my second, and he was surprisingly bigger than I expected, despite what his ex-girlfriend, Eliza "Bitch" Simpson, told me when she saw us holding hands at the party. One of the worst attributes about Garry was that he didn't make a sound during sex, not even a peep or a grunt or a moan. His body was trembling, I remember; think Garry was about as terrified as I was. After Garry, I moved on much bigger and better things. The college skank. I was never good at giving head. Late-bloomer. Wasn't until I was sophomore in college when I mastered the so-called art. Even with Primo, especially during the beginning stages of our relationship, I'd never felt the least amount of guilt about my promiscuous days.

Why should I?

He was my husband.

Then after Primo, everything I did either casually or physically was accompanied by some twisted form of guilt that either bludgeons one from behind or creeps into one's day.

At times, I couldn't even bring myself to look at myself in the mirror the morning after.

At times, though, I miss waking up next to his face, even his distinct smell, but I know it's a face that was doing more harm than good.

Should a woman really get used to sleeping alone?

I haven't.

On nights like last night, I usually overdo it whenever I get a cold shoulder at the bar, like I'm not even worth somebody's time, like time is too short to be spent on a person like me. It makes me feel worthless, as if I don't deserve to be alive, as if I'm something to be brushed aside.

Whenever I experience nights like these, I usually pick out the most wretched jerk at the bar and feed the hungry monkey. I once spent the night at some kid's dorm room—that's all he was, really, a barely legal kid who was studying criminal justice. I think he wanted to become a police officer or a lawyer. Not sure. He was that type who watched *way* too many cop movies to actually believe that a cop's reality is as glamorous as the movies. As soon as he was finished, I got the hell out of there. I can imagine what he was thinking when he woke up. I'm sure he felt like the luckiest guy on campus. Me, on the other hand, as empty and crushed as a soda can on the side of a road.

I'm replaying the same flashback over and over.

I don't know why my mind keeps accessing this one memory.

For some reason, it's one of the most important ones ever since the loss. . .

Primo grabs a chair from the dining room table. I bought the new set from the spring catalogue of *Collective Bargain.* He flings the chair across the kitchen; the chair grazes my shin, causing me to take cover. I know it's not his intention to hit me. He'd never do that to me, but I don't know what he's capable of anymore. This time, Primo comes really close to hurting me. Way too close.

The chair skips along the hardwood floor and strikes the island, forcing me to bolt upright from the darkness.

Rays of sunlight warm the sides of my numb face and cause me to squint. I think I try to shield the sun with my hands, but my hands feel as if they don't belong to me. I take a deep breath and try to make sense of what's happening to me. I do a lot of trying and it seems as if it's all I can do right now. Just try, Pam, I tell myself as I gather all of the commotion around me. It becomes too much to handle, overwhelming.

I suddenly get that tingly sensation throughout my body like I'm about to pass out. I ignore the streaks of light pulling along the sides of my vision and focus on two military boots next to a tire underneath the car.

I hear the girls screaming over my shoulder.

I turn toward the bus. The girls look okay. Stew doesn't look too well. His body's slumped over the steering wheel. Half of his face is covered in blood. At first, I think he's dead.

I notice a massive hole in the front windshield, then the broken glass scattered everywhere on the street.

The world around me gets shaky, but I focus on the military boots and take in another deep breath.

I try to move, but pieces of glass dig into my palms and send a fresh wave of pain through my wrists.

Most of the pain is coming from the top of my head.

All I can remember was Stew swerving the bus around a car that had crossed over the line, then the bus plowing into a barricade. I was telling the girls to get down and hold onto something. I didn't have any time to react and take cover.

Next thing I know, my body was thrown like a rag doll from the bus. Blood charged through my veins, once when I was shot through the window, then another time when I bounced onto a soft grassy hill along the embankment, then blackness, then my vision began to drift in and out of blackness as I crawled my way back onto the street, then I'm having an argument with Primo.

As more gunfire *pops* all around, I stay as low as possible by crawling on the sharp concrete.

I ignore the pain, ignore the screams, ignore every thought that enters my mind.

I make my way to the rear tire closest to the bus. Stew's starting to come to, I see, and then he starts yelling my name, I think. It's hard to make out what he's yelling even thought the bus is only five car-lengths away.

Strings of blood start to run down my eyes once I find the strength to find my feet, and I'm having trouble seeing. I pinpoint the source of the bleeding on the top of my forehead.

I run my hand across my forehead and wipe away a palm-full of blood. I rip off the bottom of my shirt and wrap it around my head as tight as I can.

Whatever that creature was, it came out of nowhere like a boulder of flesh falling from the cliff of a mountain.

My vision starts to come back a little.

I can only see through my left eye. The other one is not so good.

I desperately try to find whatever the soldiers are shooting at throughout the chaos.

I take a peek around the bumper of the car and witness an army—perhaps National Guard—firing at something to the left of me.

I duck behind the car before a stray bullet can strike me. I check underneath cars, only to find the bare feet of a woman casually walking around parked cars, as if the gunfire is nothing to her. Maybe she's in shock.

Gray and brass droplets splash before her feet and soon I realize the droplets are bullets melting before they hit her.

I try to get a closer look.

Lots of trying but not much accomplishing.

Finally, I find a moment of pause and sit upright in a kneel position.

Then, I witness the very same woman emerge from a wall of fire, all of the black smoke before me makes her look wavy.

I ignore the gunfire and peer closer. She becomes clearer. She's naked, early thirties—give or take—and she's walking directly toward another group of heavily armed soldiers. She has short hair, nearly scalped.

All of a sudden, she robotically turns toward me and we share a glance but only a glance for she directs her attention back toward all of the action in front of her. In that moment, as brief as it is, her face becomes a still image in my mind. I can't rid the thought of her and it feels as if she's still looking at me even when she's not. Her eyes are demonic-like. She doesn't appear human.

I don't who she is.

Whoever or *whatever* she is, she is everything.

I snap from my daze and turn to my head toward the black female FBI agent.

"What was the question again?" I ask her.

"I asked you if you got a good look at the suspect's face."

"No," I tell her. "I did not."

Before the FBI agent can ask me another question, my eyelids suddenly get heavy and I find myself drifting asleep. The slam of a door causes my eyes to snap open. I'm no longer lying in a hospital bed; instead, I'm on the floor of a room the size of a prison cell. I sit upright and check out my attire. I'm wearing a hospital gown, which is odd because the last thing I remember wearing was a raggedy dress shirt and blue jeans. I'm slow to stand to my feet. I'm a little unbalanced, but I go straight to the door. It's locked. I bang on the door, but nobody answers.

## 24. AFTER / PAMELA

I was leaving Lowe's when they grabbed me.

For the past two days, I had been laying around the house and doing some reflection, which is probably the worst thing to do. I didn't want to be around anyone nor did I have any ambition to leave the house. The nausea would come in small waves each time I tried to wrap my head around the attack—an attack on what? I have no idea. The media is calling it a terrorist attack. They said the terrorist might have links to the terrorist organization, Crisis, but it doesn't make any sense whatsoever. I needed to put my mind to good use. Not only that, I was starting to get cabin fever. I cleaned the house and then, after the house was spotless, I decided to redecorate and shift around furniture to keep my mind busy. First, I went to a local nursery and bought two indoor plants to help spruce up the house, as well as a couple of hydrangeas to plant in the backyard. I've needed new mirror frames, as well. The ones I owned looked too new looking and I felt as if it was time for a change. Plus, I was getting sick of looking at all of the new and polished things around the house. Everything I owned, from the new sleek-looking multilayer coffee table in the den to the new futuristic-looking toothbrush holder in my bathroom, was bought to match my new modern home. I was sick of the new look. Every since the divorce, I've wanted to make something look old and rustic.

While browsing through eBay, I came across gold frames, which would fit nicely with the chandelier in the dining room.

I watched a couple of DIY videos on The Tube, instructing me how to make new frames look old. Turns out, it was much more simpler than I thought. All you needed was a can of spray paint, a sheet of sandpaper, and just a little bit of what us women call elbow grease. I also needed to buy a new hand trowel since the one I had was all bent and crusty and destined to be food for trashcans.

So, I gave myself an excuse to splurge.

A woman has her needs.

* * *

This Roger guy asks me the same question again, but I chose to ignore him. I can't stop thinking about the moments leading up to the abduction. My mind is completely overwhelmed with a bunch of *what ifs. What if* I paid more attention to my surroundings instead of wondering if the cashier gave me the correct change? I hardly use cash. I try to stay up with the times, especially in this digital age. I know credit cards leave paper trails. But who would even think like that? It's not like I'm not running from the law. *What if* I did use a credit card to pay for all of my supplies? If so, then I would've been more aware of what was going on around me, the unmarked van that sneaked in behind me like a cold breeze. I could've used my new hand trowel on him. A good whack across the head would've sent him away.

*Ms. Van Buren?*

Ronnie's calling my name again—or, is it Roger?

Whatever his name is, he wants me to answer the question. He's starting to get anxious, I see. It's not like I get any pleasure out of watching the frustration slide over him like a winter's cold. I'm still a little pissed from the way they chose to bring me in. Only two types of people resort to such actions: first, murders or serial rapists, which, to me, fall under the same category, however, I seriously doubt these men intend to do me harm but I've been wrong about men before; second, the kind of people who have way more power than we think. I'm talking the government, CIA, Feds—scratch them off—Secret Service, black market assassins, hitmen—anybody who's in the disposal business. Nobody snatches people from behind and tosses them in the back of a vehicle without a reason.

Once more, the question is thrown at me: "Did the strange woman say anything when she confronted you?"

"No," I say, finally. "She just stared at me."

"Stared at you?"

"Yes," I say. "She stared at me."

I don't remember much at all after I was thrown through the window, except for her face, those two dark eyes peering through me.

The Roger guy leans back in his chair while the other one starts to grill me.

"Anything else, Ms. Van Buren?"

"I made an attempt to get back on the bus—"

"—Why didn't you?"

"She closed the door right as I was about to enter."

"Did you see anything inside?"

"No," I tell them. "I did not. In fact, I couldn't see anything."

"Can you give us a further explanation?"

"I thought maybe blood had gotten into my eyes, at first," I say, trying to think back to the moment where I was standing outside the bus, trying to get a better look at what they're calling the 'strange' woman.

How does one even define strange?

"And what else?"

"I looked again," I say abruptly, "but I couldn't see anything. The windows appeared tinted."

"Tinted?"

"You know, *tinted*," I say. "Like the kids do to their car windows."

"Could you hear anything?"

"Hear anything? No," I answer. "It was quiet inside the bus."

"Quiet?"

"Yes. Quiet."

"What happened next?"

"I pressed my face against the glass. It was dark inside," I say, thinking.

I remember seeing these tiny lights glowing inside like stars.

"Ms. Van Buren?"

"I don't know," I say. "Just darkness. The door opened a few minutes later, the girls exited, unharmed, and then—"

"—Then what?"

"Then she drove away."

"She was inside the bus for approximately eleven minutes, according to the report."

"That sounds about right," I say. "I really don't know. I wasn't keeping track of the time."

"How did the girls appear to you? Did they look any different?"

"They were in shock," I say. "How'd you want them to look? Excited?"

"What do you think this 'strange woman' was doing inside the bus for eleven minutes?"

"How should I know?" I return the question back to him. "She could've been seeking cover from the people who were shooting at her. She looked *scared.*"

"Scared?" the other guy, Roger, finally opens his mouth.

He leans up in his chair and acts as if, all of a sudden, he's interested in what I have to say.

"Yes," I tell him.

"Describe what she looked like?"

"I thought I told you—"

"—Her expressions before she entered the bus," he says. "How did they seem?"

"I told you," I say. "Scared."

"Scared how? Scared like 'I'm scared of riding roller-coasters,' or scared like 'I'm scared of spiders.'"

"I didn't know there were different kinds of being scared. I thought it was all the same." Another detail comes to mind. "Panicked," I say. "She looked extremely exhausted too, like she was about to pass out."

"When she walked past you, did you feel anything?"

"Really? Did I feel anything?"

"Just answer the question," he says over me.

It's complicated to capture how I feel in the current moment, let alone a moment that happened several days ago. The big ones are the most obvious: sadness, anger, grief, annoyance, disgust, fear, joy, serenity, love. It's fair to say that right now I'm feeling a combination of emotions, and I can't just pinpoint one. Literally, I could spin a wheel of emotions and wherever the needle landed, that was probably how I felt for a moment. I take myself back to that one moment in time when my eyes meet *her* eyes. Her face went blank as if somehow her mind had left her body, and I found myself drifting away from her, yet colliding with her in some other realm. It felt as if she was trapped inside my head, digging through each thought like a nose-hungry cadaver dog digging through dirt, accessing all of my memories, each one like a tiny knot of life. She reminded me of a curious child going through a spool of tangled wires. A feeling came over me, swiftly like a doubt. Even now, I can still feel the very remnants. I believe certain feelings have certain tags attached to them, like smell or touch. When I looked back into her eyes I saw myself sitting in the hospital. Doctor Park stepped inside the room with his head held downward and I knew the next words that were about to come out of his mouth. He informed me that I lost my baby. Everything beyond that point went past me. I canceled him out, not because I was scared of the future, but because I was scared of the truth. Someone had thrown a bomb into the room and everything around me was one massive hum. I've heard of women having abortions. I had this friend who had one—different story, long story, really, had two children of her own, couldn't afford a third one, desperate times called for desperate measures—but I've never heard of a woman losing one of her own. I'm talking about life that she so eagerly wanted to bring into the world. I felt polluted. I felt as if somewhere beneath the shadows of my thoughts, my own flesh didn't want a child. So, in return, my body turned on me and rejected the life I had inside me. The following days, I felt infected by what was lost inside me. I brought death into the world, not life, not hope. I think a piece of me died on that day. A piece that was fertile and full of life. It wasn't until just days ago that the feeling came back to me, that feeling of carrying death.

Earlier that Tuesday—in fact, before we went to Middleton—I pulled Emily aside. She didn't seem like herself. She was talking weird, saying things that raised concern. I know how some girls can be melodramatic and say things that they don't mean. But when Emily looked me in the eyes, I saw myself. I saw the same exact look I had on my face the day I lost my baby.

Even now, as I sit in this claustrophobic room, I can feel her, Emily. She's trapped. She feels as if she's cornered into a wall. I don't know how I can feel her, but I can.

I snap from my trance.

"—I don't know," I tell him, trying to make sense of the strange woman's face, the expression, the fear.

I answer with more clarity and confidence. "No," I say. "I didn't feel anything."

"How about this strange woman?" he says. "Can you explain more about her?"

"Like I said, she was scared," I say. "She seemed scared like any other person who was faced with death. I think she was aware that she was about to die but she wasn't ready. Not yet. She was scared and yet, if it came down to fighting to the bitter end, she was ready to put it all on the line." I turn away from the lie detector and face the one doctor. "I want you to answer *my* question. Who is this woman or 'strange' woman, as you call her—"

"—Wait a second," he says. "I was just repeating what you said to me."

"The strange woman," I say after gathering my thoughts, "those were *your* words."

"No," he says. "They weren't." He holds up the notepad. "I have the words written down, Ms. Van Buren. Would you like for me to repeat what you said—"

"—Why does it matter who said what first?"

"It doesn't—"

"—Who is she?"

Roger nods at the guard behind me.

He doesn't answer my question.

I don't expect him to.

* * *

Fahim says, "Her name is Frankie."

The other doctor looks at Fahim as if he's lost his mind. His cheeks get all red. He turns away from Fahim and looks at me, like Abe would sometimes look at my dad whenever he got caught hitting me.

Fahim opens a folder and pulls out papers containing the statements I gave to the Feds.

"Before we talk about Frankie," he says slowly, almost cautiously, to me, "let's talk more about what happened prior to the event on Tuesday, November Eighth."

"I'd love to," I say before he can finish his train of thought.

"Right," he says, looking down at the piece of paper in his hand. "The morning before school started, you were spotted walking a mile outside the blast site. Care to explain what you were doing there?"

"I wasn't there."

The needle's skipping around all over the place like some methhead.

"We know you were, Judith. We've talked to many witnesses saying that they saw you in Benjamin Creek."

"You think I had something to do with the gas leak?"

"That's not what we're implying, Judith," Sy says, but he's implying something all right. "We want to know what you were doing in Benjamin Creek an hour before school started."

Is there a connection? Must've been a coincidence.

"I don't know."

"You don't know?"

"Yes."

Fahim takes in a deep breath.

He's obviously frustrated with me now. Good.

Sy says, "You are aware the terrorist, Frankie, she released a chemical weapon leaving you and your entire team exposed to a highly contagious virus. Don't you?"

"Yeah," I say. "You keep telling me these things, but why didn't the two FBI agents mention anything about a virus?"

"Let's just say the FBI were kept in the dark."

"In the dark? I thought they knew everything—"

"—*Not* everything," Fahim says. "And that's why it's vital that you remain here for observation."

"And where is here?"

"I'm afraid we're not at liberty to say, Ms. Ilderton."

"Okay, so if I was exposed, then why aren't you infected?"

"We've concluded that the virus is *not* airborne—"

"—Boy! That's a relief!"

Sarcasm was never really my strongest suit.

"The only way to contract it is through. . . " he pauses and looks at the other doctor as if they know something that I don't, ". . . sexual intercourse."

I can tell he's lying, but I decide to play along.

"So, you're saying I have like HIV?"

"Not HIV," Fahim says. "Worse."

"What do I have?"

The doctors look at one another. Confused.

"We honestly don't have a name for it yet."

"Well," I say, "you shouldn't have to worry."

"I know, Judith, all of this may come as a shock to you, but let's take a step back." Sy runs his hand across the bottom of his chin. I don't know whether or not to believe them. They keep telling me I have this virus, but I don't feel sick enough to be in bed. "First, please explain to the best of your recollection, what were you doing in Benjamin Creek on the morning of Tuesday, November Eighth?"

The door cuts through the silence.

Behind me a guard is standing at the doorway, motioning to the doctors.

As one of the doctors stands up, three gunshots suddenly *ring* out!

Another guard enters the room, heavily armed. He takes out another guard.

His face looks very familiar. I've seen him before.

Whoever he is, he doesn't belong here.

Then, he turns toward me and aims the gun at me.

He approaches me. He stops a few feet away from me and holds out his hand. He tells me his name is Kris Solles, and he's here to set me free.

# PART TWO
## MURMUR

# 1. THE HIRED GUN / KRIS

I'VE lived long enough to understand that humans can be way more complicated than they need to be. It's easy to say we've mastered the art of survival. It's easier to say we've created loops for ourselves, certain routines to keep us in check, comforts and necessities remaining viciously constant in our daily lives, the binds keeping us entangled in the ghostly remnants of those who came before us. The human race, as we know it, has reached its pinnacle when Man set sail across great oceans in search of new worlds, only to discover Men less advanced than His own and far more adapted to lands in which He or She occupied; the loop was introduced, and now, Man is free-falling through a relatively new yet volatile world in which its singular purpose is to collect, control, devour, a world manifested from an idea inside the mind of a wannabe god.

In spite of our many faults, we shall not tread too far from our creator, for every person—whether it be man, woman, or child—has a story he or she can call his or her own, a story in which the individual telling it has the most supreme power. It's a story not taken from the pages of history, instead created from the constant choices the individual makes along the unwavering timeline of Man. I often wonder what the timeline would look like if I was to turn it on its side: stories glowing like ornaments in glimmering light, each one fingering outward as if they were roots in the earth—different routes leading toward different ends, as well as beginnings.

Is it fate or free will?

I believe we are all given directions, different routes, stories. One may feel good or promising; one may end in certain doom, only to plant a seed farther along the timeline, whereas one may flourish into something poisonous by means of persuasion. The other may be left unknown, one that questions everything we were taught.

As for me, my story landed me in the middle of an intersection, between not right and wrong but fact and fiction. I've taken many routes in my life, some that have brought me back to the same route I started, while others steered me down dark and sketchy roads, which have forced me to seek a clearer path.

My niece, Lanett, three months shy of twelve years old, used to be a heavy reader, a full time bookworm before technology withdrew her from the world. One day, I was picking her up from school: a typical niece-uncle afternoon consisting of a trip to the ice cream parlor followed by a pit stop at the used bookstore. I'd buy her one book of her liking—two, if I didn't have to kill anyone that day. We decided to skip the bookstore. Lanett said she was already nose-deep into a book that one of her friends had loaned her and she didn't want me to waste money on another book—Can you believe that? Only twelve years old and giving me pointers on unnecessary expenses—otherwise, Lanett said, it'd just go in a book pile and be pushed aside until Jackie (Lanett called her mother by her first name because apparently she had picked it up from being around her mother's friends all of the time) threw it in a box with the other books and hauled them to the nearest Goodwill. I didn't know at the time, but by the time Lanett got around to the book, her interests would already change to vampires—last year, it was fairies. The year before that, it was dwarfs, then elves, then wizards. Point being: I would come to know all about this loaner book when I dropped off Lanett at her house. The strap of her bookbag got caught on the handle of the passenger car seat, causing all the contents inside to spill out over the floor, as well as the street.

Later, when I got back home, I found the book underneath the passenger seat. Old, crinkled, and tagged with dog-ears. I must've missed the book while I was helping Lanett gather her notebooks and textbooks. Out of curiosity, I decided to keep the book for the time being—at least until she phoned me once she found out the book was missing. The book was called *The Girl Who Converged.* Halfway through reading the story, I realized Jackie would definitely not approve of it—the themes were rather adult for a twelve year old. The story was about a dare gone wrong. The daree was a girl named Noelle, didn't have many friends—only one or two, one of them being a neighbor—so, she did about anything to try to fit in with the other girls: pranks, vandalism, and all sorts of mischief. The dare came about during lunch. A girl sitting at the same table as Noelle handed Noelle a caterpillar and dared her to eat it. Pressured to fit in, Noelle was left with no other option. So she did. Days later, Noelle became violently ill. Her parents thought it might have been a cold. Days passed. She couldn't shake the sickness. Her parents thought it was the flu. Then, weeks passed and Noelle was still sick. Both her parents were baffled, unsure about their daughter's health. They tried everything in their power, every over-the-counter drug and holistic remedies. With no other choice, Noelle's parents took her to the hospital. Doctors ordered an X-ray of her chest. During examination, something extraordinary happened to Noelle. A pair of wings suddenly sprung up from her back. Noelle was mortified. She didn't know what was going on. Doctors were baffled. They had no other option than to clip Noelle's wings. Then, she died two days later. I ended up returning the book to Lanett; however, the story stayed with me. I couldn't help but think if a story, as fictional as it may be, could become reality. When did an idea take shape in the mind before it turned into reality? Was there a line between fact and fiction? Or, was it one giant blur?

When I was first given intel on Frankie, everything I knew about the world, about humanity, had turned out to be one hundred percent bullshit.

Understanding Frankie was like taking a giant leap backward and relearning everything that I learned as a child.

💣 💣 💣

My ears are ringing something fierce when I come to. I'm not sure how long it's been since I lost consciousness. Flashes of horror flickering in blackness come at me in steady jabs when I finally put my eyes on the bleak surroundings. In my mind's eye, I'm standing among the dead in a blood-drenched hallway as a massive fleshy *creature* charges at me. Couldn't have been her. I don't know what it is, but it isn't human.

Plymouth was right all along.

But did I listen?

Treetops rise into grayness as if the trees themselves are hanging from the sky.

I blink the crud from my eyes, but it only makes it worse.

I pull my hand to my face.

As I desperately clear away the crud with the backside of my hands, a bolt of pain shoots up my side, causing me to cry out.

The sting in my eyes gradually subsides, but another pain sits on my shoulders.

I am alive.

So says the pain.

I lift up the upper part of body and locate the pain by feeling around my body. I come across an object digging into my ribcage like a tick on steroids taking a chomp out of my flesh, and each time I move or rotate even the slightest fraction, an electric bolt of pain surges through my body.

I love the pain, yet I hate it. Right now, it's all I have. The pain. Always there. Reminding me that I'm still alive.

Pull yourself together, Brixx.

Concentrate.

I focus on my pain and how to reduce it. My other senses come back to me. First, the smells. Smoke in the air. Gassy smells. Fumes. Dead bodies. Hair and flesh burning in flames. The mixture of smells brings forth haunting memories, which I packed up and locked away so many years ago: *a destroyed house full of women and children, blackened and contorted. Drone strike gone wrong. Their black faces etched with suffering. Their mouths gaping like a yawn. The meat on the bones still red and raw underneath all the char. Soon, they'll be coming for me. A death squad ready to pick me apart on national television for the entire world to see. They're going to make an example out of me. I count my ammunition before the enemy reaches me. I'm low. Outgunned. I'm dead.*

I cancel out each memory as it fires at me and concentrate on the moments leading up to her escape. I can make out the fragments, however hazy they may be—it was her, that creature. It had to be! Orwell had been keeping us in the dark. Why did he not tell us about her *other* features? She was changing form as she pounded through each corridor, ripping through each one of my men. We were unprepared.

More sounds come at me.

A couple of thuds volley back and forth, the sounds muffled out and hard to distinguish.

I press my hand against the soggy earth and manage to push myself upright.

Chatter building all around me!

The place is swarming with law enforcement and fire fighters trying to contain the fire, now inching its way closer to me. Whatever remains of Mt. Olympus Research Institute is all but smoke and ruins.

I check for injuries next.

My left ankle is sprained—possibly even broken—but the origin of the pain is coming from my lower abdomen where a piece of wood about the size of a candy bar is protruding from my side.

More flashes of horror: *I'm chasing her down through a maze of corridors; the chase went outside of the facility; then, I unload on her in the compound; she turns around, then hell hath no fury like a woman scorned.*

I don't remember much, but I remember her eyes, the rage and then the air being knocked out of me. Must've caught a branch during the fall.

The injury doesn't appear life threatening and hasn't punctured any main organs; however, if it goes untreated, there's a chance it could worsen.

I attempt to pull out the wood, but the pain is too great.

I check my radio, hoping to make contact with my team. The radio is dead. Must've been from her. She still must be jamming the signals.

I check the time, my watch. I can't find my watch. I check my phone next. The screen is completely shattered and unusable. I manage to gather enough strength to stand. My side hurts like holy hell but I remind myself that I've been through much worse. This is nothing.

Commotion suddenly breaks out behind me!

A group of local police officers have come across a body—or what looks like a body. Another officer finds the remaining half of the body nearby.

I grab a long tree branch from the ground and use it as a cane and create much needed distance from the officers.

I only have three rounds left in my Berretta and a knife. And I'm definitely in no shape for combat. All I need is one bullet, but that's my last resort.

I make my way through the mountains and head toward Iredell.

I must make contact with the others—that is, if they're still alive.

Luckily, I break free from the party without getting spotted by any of Orwell's highly, yet sufficiently trained guards. For all I know, he's got the police department under his finger.

I follow a running creek for about two miles until I reach Antioch River.

Another helicopter skims the sky above me. They're closing in on me. It feels as if I've walked a 10K from the injuries tugging at me with every move I make. My gut tells me to quit being overly dramatic.

You've been through worse, Brixx.

Keep moving, wimp.

I rally myself more strength, stay extra close to the river, and make my way downstream until I reach a bridge with several cars passing by. The cars don't appear military. They appear like any other cars civilians would drive, which gives me a timely sense of hope.

Police helicopters have been buzzing overhead for the past two hours.

They're searching for me. I just know Orwell has gotten to them. His way of cleaning up his own mess.

Who knows what he's telling the authorities right now?

Call me a terrorist.

Call me whatever.

I was just doing a job.

Since my heart's working overtime, I decide to rest underneath the bridge for a few minutes and catch my breath.

Two large trucks—something between a dump truck and a Ram—pass overhead. Tires squeak over asphalt. The trucks come to a stop at the other end of the bridge. I don't think anything of it until I hear a door slam shut and a man with a resonant voice telling a person—a pedestrian—the street has been closed. I get a closer look at the people above and find three men who work for a power company, two are blocking off the street with barricades while another one—the deep-voiced man—is carrying on a conversation with a pedestrian. Everything about the servicemen reeks of Orwell, the words he uses, scripted, the way they carry themselves. They don't come across as an average Joe who works for a cable company. Nothing slang or casual in their dialogue. All business. The name of the company also appears bogus—Tower Cable?

Never even heard of the company.

I sneak back into the woods.

At least I have a clearer direction where I'm headed.

I don't know how much longer I can go on. My legs are getting heavier, my injuries heavier as well. Soreness sets in over my left shoulder. My body's screaming at me to rest or else it's going to completely shut down. So, I find a tight crag and try to rest.

When I close my eyes, all I can see is the horror flashing throughout the blackness: *I'm firing a couple of rounds at her while she storms away. The sprinkler system hisses above and then water starts to rain down on us. I keep firing and she keeps walking. She appears unfazed by the gunfire, like it's nothing to her. When she reaches outside, she finally stops and then turns and we share eye contact for a moment—* yes, I remember—*then she keeps walking. I keep pushing forward, then out of frustration, she lands a blow to my shoulder, which sends me in the air. I am nothing to her. A bug. Nothing more than a gnat.*

How am I still alive?

Is there a reason why I'm *still* alive?

What the hell is going on?

* * *

I make sure to stay close but not too close to a two-lane highway as I make my way through the woods.

Occasionally, one of those Tower trucks will pass by, forcing me to seek cover. The road is pretty desolate; nonetheless, each vehicle could pass as a front. What looks like a family of four in a minivan could be actors working for Orwell. I can't take any chances.

Five excruciating miles down, and I'm stuck with two options: rest or hitch a ride. I pass a gas station not too far away from the woods. I trudge through dense shrubbery along the highway and keep as low as possible. I notice a restroom behind the convenient store. I should be able to reevaluate my injuries inside the restroom. Plus, only two cars remain at the pump. I study each individual: one, a middle-aged man; another, a woman with two children in the backseat of her station wagon. Locals maybe, but again nothing's what it seems anymore. I no longer have the luxury of assuming. If my instincts are right, more than likely the locals don't know what's happening or what's about to happen. So, out of desperation, I make a go at the restroom. The gas station is backwoods-old and I don't see any surveillance cameras around the convenient store. I keep my head down anyway and sneak into the restroom where I wash the woods from my body. I search the restroom for a first-aid kit, but I come up short. Just a toilet covered with piss stains, a faucet that spits out water as murky as brine, and a rusty trashcan overflowing with wadded up paper towels.

* * *

The clerk's eyeballing from the moment I enter the store. I limp my way through the tight aisles until I can come up with a reasonable story to tell the curious clerk. Some kind of accident should do. Don't have to explain much about the accident, but if the old man's wanting a story to keep his mind occupied, then I can tell him that it involved fishing. Hence the wet clothes. Fishing strikes me as a popular activity to do here. I run with the story: "Tripped and fell while I was fishing. I was wondering if you had a first-aid kit."

I make sure to conceal the wound the best I can; otherwise, he'll insist on me going to a hospital.

"Think I sprained my ankle."

"You don't look too well, mister."

He reaches for the phone.

"No," I tell him. "Just need a first-aid kit. That's all."

Suddenly, I hear tires rolling over gravel outside the convenient store.

The car is black with tinted windows, doesn't scream local. Two men step out of the car. Suits. They got Orwell written all over their faces. The clean-up crew.

As the two men enter the store, I duck behind a shelf of cleaning supplies and chemicals inside a recess in the back of the store. They approach the checkout counter and ask the clerk if he's seen "this" man before.

I peek around the corner and see one of the men holding up a photo in front of the clerk's face.

I check my Berretta. Three rounds. Two for the two looking for me. Each one has to be a kill shot. Then, if I make it that far, the last one for me.

The clerk shakes his head over a second's thought.

"Ain't seen him."

"Can you take another look?"

"I told you 'I ain't see him before.' You deaf?"

The other man taps his partner with his elbow and whispers something in his ear.

"Thanks for your cooperation," the man says to the clerk.

They leave.

I breathe a sigh of relief and make my way to the front of the store where the clerk slides an ancient-looking first-aid kit across the counter.

"Old friends?"

"Something like that."

The clerk nods.

"Here ya go."

I watch the car drive away, kicking up clouds of gray dust.

"Why are helping me?"

"You look like a decent man who just going through a little blip."

"Blip, right? It's more complicated than that."

"Who were those two gentlemen? Cops?"

"No," I tell the clerk. "Worse."

💣 💣 💣

As I'm examining my wound in the restroom, the door suddenly opens behind me!

"Room's occupied," I say and turn toward the door.

The door's closed.

I turn around toward the mirror and find the same door open. I do a double-take. The door is closed behind me, yet it's open in the mirror. I have trouble focusing.

In the reflection of the mirror, I witness a woman stepping into the restroom. Tall and thin. Her face like a vague blur.

I concentrate on her face, but the more I attempt to adjust my eyes the dizzier I become.

I splash my face with cold water. She's gone. The restroom door remains closed. I check the outside just to be safe and she's not there. She never was.

Or was she?

I check my bloodless face in the mirror and I can't even recognize the person looking back at me.

Suddenly, I feel something pressed against my chest and I have trouble catching my breath. Everything in the restroom starts to spin and I have trouble keeping my eyes on one certain thing. This isn't a panic attack or me freaking out. This is something else. I can't control myself. My vision starts to wash over with gray.

I clutch the sink before my feet give out below me, and I drop to one knee. I brace for impact. I'm going down.

* * *

Two people are murmuring over a distant ambulance siren. I open my eyes, only to find two paramedics looming over my body on the floor, working on me, checking my vitals, keeping me alive.

Behind the two paramedics stands three other people, one is the clerk from before and the others are a man and a kid.

Adrenaline kicks. The pain lessens. I feel like punching a hole in a wall.

In one lurch, I roll onto my feet and push aside the paramedic's arm, causing his shoulder to snap out of place. The other one tries to keep me grounded.

"Sir, please, for your own safety, take it easy. Sir, I need for you to try to relax. You've lost a lot of blood."

I push aside the paramedic, who feels as light as paper, and scramble from the restroom. I spot a strung out young woman pumping gas into an emerald green Mazda. I hurry toward the Mazda as the other paramedic grabs at me.

In one swift motion, I push the paramedic in the shoulder. The push sends him flying in the air, causing him to fall into the other man.

While gripping his shoulder, the other injured paramedic tends to his partner.

I get inside the Mazda, close the door behind me.

The young woman's shouting out at me from outside the car. She's banging her palms against the roof.

The keys still remain in the ignition. Lucky me. I turn on the ignition, switch the gear into drive, floor it, and get the hell out of there. The hose detaches from the rear of the car as gasoline sprays all over the woman. She tosses the nozzle on the ground and chases after me, but I'm already gone.

* * *

I pass another one of those Tower trucks, as well as a couple of sketchy-looking unmarked cars, but no cops. They don't bother turning around. I probably have a good five minutes before police get word about the stolen car. I end up reaching an intersection. I have three ways to choose from. The town of Iredell two miles to the left. Straight takes me down a stretch of a road, mostly countryside. Right takes me into another small town—Dustin, I think.

I decide to take a right toward Dustin. More than likely, the Iredell Police Department will respond to the dispatch. I step on the gas. Punch it. No cops in sight. The adrenaline's still racing through my veins; however, the pain's starting to set in. I check my injuries. The wood has started to split in half and three-inch long splinters rub against the flesh. I tell myself I need to ditch the car and do it fast. I pass ranch-style homes along the highway, several vehicles in the front lawns overgrown with dead weeds, some of the vehicles are rusted from the inside-out or gutted or appear as if they hadn't been run since the end of the Cold War.

I decide to keep driving and the first building I pass is a brick structure.

The sign in the front reads, "Town Animal Hospital."

Next to that is a tire store. The parking lot is full; however, several vehicles are parked along the side of the building. It's not ideal, but I'm out of options.

I pull into the parking lot and get out of the car. I find a Nissan Frontier—a much older model, which works out in my favor. Around here, keyless ignitions are something that only exist in science fiction movies.

I take my chances and break the driver's side window.

A lady carrying a cat carrier turns to me as she's walking from the hospital.

"Locked my keys inside," I tell her.

Strangely, she smiles.

"I hate when that happens," she says and continues to her car.

I get inside the truck, rip off the panel from underneath the steering wheel, and hotwire the engine.

I drive away, driving past the lady as she places the carrier inside the back of her car.

"Have a nice day," she says as I drive away.

As I'm pulling out of the parking lot, I pass a cruiser on the highway. Sirens blaring. Pushing at least twenty miles per hour over the speed limit.

I check the rear view mirror and it keeps driving.

Two hours have passed since I've been on the road and I start to get nauseous. Helicopters are constantly passing overhead. Police helicopters, several military, one a medical helicopter.

I pass a road sign that reads ASHEBORO, 12 MILES.

I need to stop. Something else has happened and I get the feeling that whatever happened, it's much bigger than what occurred in Iredell.

I take an off ramp and stop at a payphone outside a two-story motel called The Inn. I gather loose change from inside the truck and give Felicia a call. It's not the best choice—it's pretty much the only choice I have right now. She doesn't live far from here. She'll hate me for seeing my face again—especially after what happened between us—but I need somewhere to hang my head until everything quiets down.

A raspy-voiced man answers the phone.

Surprisingly, she's moved on with her life.

"Can I speak to Felicia?"

"You got the wrong number."

"Is this 704-846-5—"

The man hangs up the phone.

Must be the last three digits, two-three-two, not three-two-three.

I try once more.

A woman answers the phone with a drawn out *hello.* I detect a tremble under her voice.

I listen closely to her breathing.

She speaks again.

Felicia.

I listen closer and hear a few people talking in the background. Three of the voices are clear. Two men, one woman. At first, I think she has company. Maybe she's having some friends over. Drinks and appetizers at her house. Last time I checked, she owned a tile and countertop company, worked like a dog during the week, drank like a fish during weekends. Business usually slowed down around this time of the year; however, Felicia never had a lot of friends, especially guy friends. She had maybe one or two girlfriends but even they teetered between overly sympathetic and fair-weather. She doesn't have much of a family either. She lost her father when she was a girl. Raised by her mom who is no longer living. She has a cousin—or at least, *had* a cousin—but she hadn't talked to her in many years. Felicia mentioned that her cousin had a lot of money. Lived in New York City, the nice part, Greenwich Village. She worked in the publishing business. A part of the whole in-crowd. Rubbed shoulders with rubbery-faced people represented by agents. Not once did she ever reach out to Felicia even though Felicia was so proud of her and her accomplishments. Her cousin wasn't the woman whom she once knew, who'd play with her over the holidays. She came across as another person. No different than a stranger. The type who wouldn't even show up to her funeral.

Just before Felicia hangs up, I hear laughing and I realize it's not the people who are laughing. It's an audience.

* * *

I finally arrive at Felicia's house.

She's still driving that same off-blue Accord that used to break down on her all the time. Nothing has changed.

As I'm backing into her driveway, my fingers become cold and tingly. The sensation stretches up both of my arms. The pain doubles me over.

I can't concentrate. Can't do anything.

I feel myself going down again.

* * *

I jolt upright from to the sound of a blaring car horn. Felicia pulls me from the car seat and lays me down on the driveway. She pops the hood of the truck and shuts off the engine by disconnecting the battery.

"Kris. . . " she says as she kneels down to me. Both of her eyes trail down my abdomen. "Oh God! You're bleeding—"

"—Felicia, I'm fine. . . "

I don't remember anything after that.

Just murmurings.

* * *

I wake up on a familiar bed with familiar smells in the air, the smell of strawberries and watermelons, and familiar sounds, the hum of an air purifier running like white noise. I remember waking up in this environment many times. I remember secretly rolling out of this bed. I remember each dent, each spring of this bed, each squeak.

I turn to my right where Felicia's approaching me with a white hand towel in her hand. She's wearing a hot pink tank top and black yoga pants. She looks good—great, actually—she's much thinner, healthier. She places the cool and damp towel over my forehead. The coolness feels good on my skin. Behind her, a TV is playing in the living room. A snappy anchor is talking about an explosion.

"Where am I?"

"You're at my house. You came here, remember?"

I look around and realize that I'm, in fact, in Felicia's bedroom. A wave of comfort comes over me and I almost miss being here in this room, with this smell, on this bed. Just the thought alone of how Felicia acted toward the end of our relationship squashes the nostalgia, the longing of being deep in the flesh.

I make an attempt to sit up, but the streak of pain shoots through the left side of my body.

"Relax," she says and props another pillow underneath my head.

I have a better view of my body, the wound. I lift up the cream-colored sheet and notice the branch has been removed from my side. Felicia has placed a dressing over the wound. The dressing is soaked with dark smelly blood and looks as if it needs to be changed.

My left ankle, swollen blue and purple, has been carefully propped up by a pillow.

I'm stark naked, too—that's what sends a shiver down my spine. She must've stripped me down after she managed to lug my body into the bed. I'm sure she didn't mind the free peek. We're all grown-ups here.

But what else did she do while I was unconscious?

"Your face is all over the TV."

I don't understand what she's saying.

She clarifies for me, "They're saying you shot an unarmed man—"

"—What? What are you talking about?"

She turns her shoulder toward the living room.

On the television, the same surveillance footage's playing in a loop. A man who looks like me is walking into the convenient store. The same clerk raises both of his hands in the air and then he's shot twice in the chest. The mysterious man exits the store and as he's exiting, he shoots a glance up at the camera. The freeze frame on the television is a spitting image of my face, but it's clearly *not* me. I know for a fact. I passed out in the restroom. The clerk was there when I woke up. I remember seeing his face over the paramedic's shoulder. He was alive when I drove away. Orwell must've gotten to him.

"They framed me," I tell Felicia.

"Framed you? You're on TV, Kris—"

"It's not me, Felicia. You have to trust me."

"*Trust* you? How can I trust you after what—"

Her cheeks start to flush. She's doing all she can to not lash out at me.

I make another attempt to sit upright. I try to block out the pain, but it cuts at me like a knife.

"Kris, you have to lay down and rest—"

"Just look at the footage, Felicia. Take a closer look at the man. Look at how he's walking. Please, Felicia, I'm telling the truth. . . " Another streak of pain knocks the wind out of me. I grab Felicia's hand, hold it tight. "I did *not* shoot that man! I swear!"

Felicia slips her hand from my grip and walks over to the television. She watches the footage again. Studies the man in the footage. She walks back over to me.

"How do I know you didn't have this," Felicia nods at the wound, "accident after you shot him?"

"You don't know, but you know *me*, Felicia. I know I have a lot to explain. I know you're wondering why I came here—"

"And why did you come here, Kris?"

"I had nowhere else to go."

"What if the cops find out you're here? I can't be aiding and embedding a criminal. I will lose my job, Kris—"

"—I'm aware of the repercussions, but you have to believe me." She doesn't say anything. She wants more out of me. "I know this is a lot to take in," I say, "but you have to understand, these people, they don't care about people. They don't care about you and me. They can make it look like I shot that man. They're *that* good."

"Who did this, Kris? I deserve the truth."

"Why are you helping me?"

"Why wouldn't I help you? You were hurt."

"You could've taken me to the hospital."

"You don't remember anything. Do you?"

I don't remember anything after I passed out.

She says, "You specifically told me not to take you to the hospital. You said your life was in danger."

"I don't remember saying that."

"Well, you did. You were in bad shape." She takes a seat next to me. She places her hand on my forearm. "What happened to you, Kris? Who is after you? Tell me everything."

## 2. THE AGENT / RASHIDA

It's only eight o'clock and so far it's been one of those days that I wish would end before it even begins. Lord, help me!

Before I even have a chance to start my morning routine, Bo's sleaze bag of a lawyer, Moody Broderick, who's disturbingly persistent in spite of his reputation throughout the Triangle, phones me yet again—by the way, who names their son Moody?

Twice now Moody's done this to my ass and each time he's left a rather abrasive message on my voicemail: same message as the one before, only spoken after a shot of hot sauce. Bo's already signed the papers. Good for Bo. I got a star sticker waiting for him. I'm just another thing he can stick under his belt or check off his bucket list. Not like Bo can't easily find another woman—when I mean easily, I mean like picking up a number from the twenty-something barista before heading into work. Most single men like Bo now, or soon-to-be single, looked at marriage as if it was an accomplishment, something they just had to do in their lifetime because either a) they had friends or siblings who were already married—particularly the older sibling who smeared his or her kids in their faces—or b) they had a nosy parent who was pressuring them for grandkids—and, of course, we all know it takes a woman to make a child, so sorry, boys, you can't just spit one out into a cup and wash your hands clean—or c) for some ridiculous reason, they thought marriage was going to be a piece of cake, a Brothers Grimm fairy tale where the prince always steals that poor ole white girl's heart, then both sides of the aisle get along and live happily ever after or, my favorite one, d) they thought marriage was going to be Nookie On-Demand and every time they got horny, they knew it was *always* there, 24-7, 'round the clock, whenever they got home from work, whenever they were feeling the urge, whenever they got bored to death, frustrated, whenever we had a fight—make up sex was about the only joy we had going for us—so pretty much whenever the thought popped in their head. Divorce isn't the least pleasant and it's the one option both sides should try to avoid, if they don't wind up killing each other first. Divorce is no different than a new mole that has surfaced on a noticeable part of your body, like on your cheek or neck or a place where people can see it without a trained eye—that ex, or soon-to-be, if I can finally get my shit together, being the mole. You don't know how long it has been there; nevertheless, it's there now and you have to do something about it; if you ignore, then there's a possibility it might grow into cancer; each day, you look at the mole, wondering if it's gotten any bigger or darker. So, you finally decide to get it looked at by a professional. You want to get it removed from your body, but you're having second thoughts because you kind of like the mole. It kind of makes you stand out. Makes you unique. In a way, you love it. Yet, you hate it. It's a part of you now, your life.

I so desperately wanted to cut it out and move on with my life but right now, I don't have the strength to do so.

I grab a bite to eat before hoping in the shower. Most of the shower is spent mentally traveling to a far-off island in the middle of the Atlantic where materials are things only spoken by futurists. Native men would have to chip away at my heart the old fashion way, like impressing me with their strength or humor, not bling. Back to reality, and I'm wondering how my face got so old—would the mirror count as part of the whole material world? If not, it damn well should be. I can already see the disappointment starting to sag in different parts of my face, underneath my eyes especially. I'm not even a settled woman with a settled man, yet I carry all the right features of a woman seven years past settled.

☼ ☼ ☼

Since it's been one of those slow days at the office—mostly wasting time by flipping through the hot files from one of our resident agencies in Raleigh—I take a late lunch with Benny. I meet Benny at Carlz, this hole in the wall diner not too far away from my work. My brother works as an audio engineer at a boutique post-production studio next to the Channel 8 TV station seven miles from downtown Raleigh, about a fifteen-minute drive depending on construction. I swear Benny's so lucky, probably one of the luckiest men alive. He never has to answer to anybody, except for every now and then an uptight producer telling him that this package needs to sound louder and that sound, like a splash effect, needs to be cleaned up or raised in volume, nothing that he can't fix in literally a matter of seconds with a couple of clicks or tweaks. He's one of those "quick key" guys. He's got a short command for everything, and the keyboard is like his magical wand. He does a lot of voice-overs too—V.O.'s, Benny calls them. He's met a lot of local celebrities, former actors or athletes, while on the job, some come into the studio and lay down a couple of lines for a car commercial or whatever. Last week, he recorded a V.O. for an eye lens commercial with that once famous soap opera actor, Stanley Stevens. Turns out he's not the masochistic asshole who every housewife in the country wanted to scratch his eyes out like the one he played on TV. Benny also said he was a lot shorter than he appeared on the TV. Once, Benny tried to explain what he did on a daily basis, but it was like he was speaking another language. I guess Benny takes up more after my mother, the left-brain, the more analytical part, whereas I take up after my father, the lonely and miserable part. Benny has the rest of the day off; he's worked his little faders for a couple of hours, then it's pre-happy hour for him. Sometimes I wish I had a job like Benny's. You do your job and then you're done.

As an agent for the Federal Bureau of Investigation, the job is *never* done.

Only twenty-six, Benny's been through his share of problems, some that most everyday folks don't experience in a lifetime. If there was one thing Benny took away from it all—the hustling, the time he spent in jail—it made him one heck of a listener. In the past, Benny wouldn't give me the time of day. Now, he doesn't mind listening to all of my problems. Even gives me advice when I ask for it. He thinks I should move on with my life while I'm still young—he doesn't exactly refer to me as *young*, which isn't much of a surprise considering most of the twenty-something population thinks people older than thirty are priming themselves up for retirement. I'm thirty-five years old and soon-to-be a single woman with one failed marriage under her belt. I don't have any kids—technically, I'm on what us women call the clock. I have at least another year or two before I can forget about spitting out a kid. And, I know I'm at that age where good men are few and far between. I'm not into online dating. I'm old fashioned when it comes to finding Mr. Right. It's strange how women nowadays will go out of their way just to let another person find a match for them; then they use the excuse that they don't have time to find a man. If you don't have time to find a man, then you don't have time to be with a man. Bo wasn't Mr. Right nor was he a prince by any means, but he did show me the woman who I could've been—if only for a minute. If I could have that minute back, I could've stretched it to a lifetime. I met Bo while I was grocery shopping. It was a rainy Saturday. Isn't that how all the romance movies start? Lonely woman bumps into Man on a rainy day. The perfect day for new beginnings. It's cold, too. A soup and sandwich kind of day, which normally keeps most people at home. I didn't want to leave the house, but I was out of bread. I didn't bother to put on any makeup. I threw on some clothes. I did look as if I rolled out of bed, but apparently, I made quite an impression on Bo. I was sorting through a bin of fresh butternut squash when this handsome man wearing a Mr. Roger's beige cardigan came up behind me and said that he knew a great recipe. My eyes met with his sparkling blue eyes. Black men with blue eyes are hard to find. Not only that, he had money. He came from money—not like it mattered, but his father owned a home improvement business called The Pot; had a chain of stores all across the East Coast. Bo was well-off as a bigwig for an insurance company. He could've been rich or poor. I still would've been very interested in him. But he found me; right then and there, I knew it was the beginning of something special. A romance? A fling? Something. This handsomely attractive man with Caribbean blue eyes called himself Bo, but it was short for Robert. A name with only two letters had given me so much than I deserved, yet he ended up being one of the worse things that ever happened to me.

❂ ❂ ❂

The discussion of who's paying for the meal comes up while Benny and I are eating peach cobbler. Benny insists on paying for lunch—he doesn't give me any reason but I know it's his subtle way of trying to cheer me up—but I'm the big sister and big sister always has the last word.

As I'm paying for lunch, Benny taps me on the shoulder and tells me to take a look at the TV.

I turn to Benny, unaware of the TV. His jaw is set in a position that would only suggest awe or disgust. His wide eyes are staring at the TV above the cashier.

My phone suddenly rings, then his phone rings right after.

Then, a quarter of the people in the diner's phones suddenly ring!

I pull out my phone from my pocket and I see that it's a 704 number.

I answer the call. It's Pelham, the Special Agent in Charge from Charlotte. The next few words that come from Pelham's mouth sound like murmurs. The only thing that I make out is when he tells me that he needs me in Burbane ASAP. He's got a chopper waiting on me close by. Says traffic is blocked up. Chopper will be quicker.

I toss more than enough money on the counter, turn to Benny, and tell him thanks for lunch.

"Gotta go, little brother."

"Rashida," he says, "what's going on?"

I tell him, "I don't know. I'll keep in touch."

On the way out, I give Bry a call. He's out of breath. I can hear other men yelling in the background. I already know what he's up to. Of all days he calls out: his yearly "Bro" Fest. All of his macho guy friends use their sick days for Bro-Fest. The rules are simple: no women allowed. Everything else is fair game. Why in the world would a grown man call off work to spend his day filled with testosterone-fueled activities such as golf cart bumper cars, paintball, zip-lining, extreme fishing, all accompanied with coolers of beer? Bry is the answer why. The epitome of a man's man. Bry has what I like to call anger issues. I figure Bry needs days off like today to take out all of that manly anger he's got buried deep inside him. Said he keeps it in there so that he can access it whenever he needs to—the anger helps "keeps him on edge." So, I know he's not going to be too pleased.

He's already voicing his complaint through the side of his mouth.

Apparently, I've called him during a game of Capture the Flag.

Someone is screaming out in the background to grab the flag.

"Calling at a bad time, Rashida—"

"—I'm not interrupting, am I?"

"No," he says. "Not at all."

Bry suddenly lets out a grunt. Someone is yelling in the background that he shot him. Visualizing Bry as we speak is amusing to say the least: a bright-colored ball of paint, probably lime green or pee-yellow, splattering all over Bry.

"Didn't I not tell you those things were distractions, Bee?" another person says in the background. "Don't you Feds ever listen?"

Frustration creeps in. Playtime is up.

"Bry?" I say, more demandingly. "You there?"

"Yeah," he says, catching his breath. "Here."

"Drop whatever it is you're doing," I say. "There's been an attack."

"Attack? What kind of attack?"

"No time to explain," I say.

Bry drops whatever he's doing, tells the fellows he's sorry.

"I'm on my way," he says.

I get in my car and head toward the closest helipad.

☼ ☼ ☼

Agent Ryette is looking as if he's anticipating the worse, as he should. I don't blame Ryette for showing concern about my current state.

You stick me on a train, and I'll be just fine. Stick me in a racecar going over hundred miles per an hour on a racetrack. I'd probably manage. Sailing or riding a boat. Depends on the circumstances. Never been a fan of cruises. Nevertheless, I'd find a way to make it work. As far as flying, planes I can do but only under the right conditions. Give me two gin and tonics—I'm talking liberal with the gin—and I can make due until the alcohol wears off.

But helicopters. Different story. I hate them. Just something about flying in a giant peanut M&M attached to two rotary blades that just gets me thinking about what life could've been like if I didn't join the FBI. A desk job during the day. I'd probably get a dog to keep me company at night. Weekends consumed by binge watching TV shows that I miss during the long week. A vicious cycle of unadventurous minutia. More than likely, I'd be safer in a helicopter than any of the other vehicles I mentioned but still—how safe can a racecar actually be? Besides tailgating and getting shitfaced off cheap beer, aren't car crashes one of the reasons why a person pays good money to watch a bunch of cars drive around in a circle? As for trains, I've heard about more train derailments in the past year than any other year. Engineers dozing off or texting while operating passenger trains. Mass causalities on separate instances. It'd make me feel a whole lot better about trains if most accidents weren't caused due to human error.

I make sure to keep a close eye on the pilot. Theoretically, helicopters may be safe considering the probability of getting involved in an automobile accident is far greater than a one-way flight from New York to LA; however, the one issue that would beef up the statistic would be a rapidly growing number of commercial drones shaving the sky.

Ideally, helicopters aren't really for me. I swear, Orville and Wilbur must've been completely out of their minds when they decided to build an airplane!

Let's face it: humans weren't meant to fly.

I focus on the other things inside the helicopter, hoping to settle the nerves, and all I get in return are feverish flashes of randomness brought on by a soon-to-be full on panic attack: a fingerless gloved hand tightening over a stress-relieving plush toy; a pink scar in the shape of a crescent moon on the side of a neck; a smirk rising over the side of Ryette's face. At least he's not laughing. Bry always gets a kick out of watching me fly.

I already know the words that are about to come out of his mouth.

Ryette finally voices his concern: "You okay over there, Jones?"

He's talking to me in one ear and my stomach's talking to me in the other.

I feel a cat-like poke on my arm, which causes the nerves to race throughout my body.

"Just think of something peaceful, like fishing."

"Humans weren't meant to fly, Cassius—"

"—Come on, Jones. How bad can it be?"

No, Ryette. It's *that* bad.

I glance at Agent Ryette and his once tolerable smirk has now turned into one hideous-looking grin.

"You're not helping," I tell Ryette.

Below me, treetops pass at a dizzying rate. We start to descend, and that's when my stomach feels as if it's grazing my throat.

I make myself think of peaceful things, as Ryette suggested, but I can't rid the thought of what's going to happen next. I'd say it's easy to leave the job at the door, but I'd be lying.

My eyes catch the billow of black smoke not too far away, and I realize that such a yearning notion of peace doesn't exist anymore.

"There," Ryette says, pointing out the obvious.

I turn toward the so-called specialist from Langley, better known as Rambo, sitting across from me. He releases the toy in his hand and readjusts the assault rifle.

"Just hitching a ride?" I say.

"This isn't Hogan's Alley, Agent Jones."

"Sure," I say, doing the best I can to maintain my big girl face.

The helicopter approaches a massive wreckage right where Church Street turns into Highway 70. From where we're flying, the wreck looks as if a section of the highway has been stuck inside a giant garbage disposal, and then someone made a poor attempt to put the chewed up remains back together.

Finally, we touch ground outside what they're calling the "Containment Area."

The nausea fades. Agent Denmark, who's from the resident agency in Greensboro, is already waiting for us.

"Looks like you made good timing, Denmark," I say over the helicopter.

"Any word on Agent Corbin?"

"He's going to meet me at the blast site."

Two men approach us from the rear. Denmark introduces us to three guys who say they're from the NSA and then two others from Homeland Security. He tells me their names but they go in one ear and out the other. I'm too concerned about what happens next. One of them has two prints of satellite images, an unidentified heat signature, or heat bloom, taken over our precise location, then another one taken over Benjamin Creek.

With our heads down, we make our way to the tents. More agents inform me about the causalities, all of the players involved. So far, a containment team has rounded up fifteen eyewitnesses; however, six of them badly injured during the shootout—the total number of eyewitnesses is still pending, but for now, they're going with twenty-one. For now.

Those are the two things that stick out the most: the number, first. Approximately twenty-one eyewitnesses. I tell myself that it's going to be a long day, but I remind myself over and over that there's no time to sleep. Then, secondly, the eyewitnesses were transported to Arthur Barrow Hospital.

Next, Agent Whatever informs me about the blast site, precisely seven miles away.

The blast, the agent says, nearly destroyed half of a town.

Causalities unknown at this time.

The thought alone causes my stomach to lurch.

After we're suited up, we're escorted to the crime scene. Nothing getting in or out. The entire highway has been shut down for miles, and police have already created a detour for the afternoon rush. Coroners have already covered up all of the victims with white sheets. Most of the victims, as seen, are fellow FBI agents as well as the soldiers from the National Guard who were activated by the resident agency in Greensboro. I liked to say that they died bravely, but it's hard to attach words to people who are no longer recognizable. Limbs and other appendages scattered along the blood-splattered highway have been covered up as well.

Several technicians are making quick sweeps with particle detectors—one would expect it be like Chernobyl times ten or even far worse especially after being informed on the heat signature taken by the satellite, but there is absolutely no indication of radiation.

I nod at Agent Whatever.

"Take me to the blast site," I tell him.

☼ ☼ ☼

I make it to the blast site in good timing. Bry's already waiting on me. The man changes fast. I give him that. As far as the hygienic department, he could use a shower.

We scope out the site, me keeping my distance from Bry's natural funk. A few pieces of the bus have been tracked down and marked. No bodies so far. A report came in that a piece of bus was discovered in a lady's backyard nearly two miles from the site. No injuries so far.

A couple of news helicopters are scraping the sky, trying to get a money shot of the aftermath.

Where to begin? How do you even explain such an event?

I'm certain all sorts of rumors are buzzing the airwaves or flooding the Internet. I reckon the most logical one is a gas line broke and something ignited the gas, causing a massive explosion. Point the finger at fracking. Yeah, Internet. Sure. Slap a hashtag on that, if that makes you sleep better at night. Another technician is already at the scene, checking for radiation. Again, you'd think particle detectors would be off the charts, picking up dangerous levels of radiation. The particle detectors are indicating levels of radiation but nothing more than what a person would get from flying in an airplane.

"What's your theory, Bry?"

Bry looks as dumbfounded as I am. I tell him that the only thing that I can think about: This terrorist *obviously* felt as if she was cornered.

According to witnesses, she didn't have any explosives on the scene.

"Could've been planted on the bus without anyone knowing?"

Why would she lead police out here?

That's the seventy-five thousand dollar question.

Bry's still waiting for further explanation.

She wanted to minimize the casualty rate, I put it as simply as I can. That could be why.

"Why would a terrorist want to kill less people?" he asks. "Doesn't make any sense. These extremists tend to take out as many innocent people as they can drag to hell with them."

"Not sure about the 'innocent' part, Bry."

I find what appears to be a license plate to the bus underneath the rubble. The plate is dented and blackened, barely recognizable.

"Why you mean, Jones? You think a group of high school kids had something to do with this?"

"Not what I'm saying."

"Then what are you saying, Rashida?"

"I'm saying that I don't know what to think about all of this," I say. "Right now, we need to keep an open mind."

"Open mind, huh? You're not gonna start getting weird on me, are you?"

I ignore Bry and make my way to the massive crater in the earth.

"What used to be here?"

"A rundown industrial park," Bry says. "Place shut down eight years ago. According to several sources, the only things living here were the weeds—"

"—Sources, huh?" I interrupt. "That's unlike you, Bry. Now, wouldn't that require a little bit of work? I'm thinking you should have these Bro-Fest events more often."

"A man's gotta get his dopamine some way or another."

"You know some guys spend a night out in town and find themselves a cute lady or have a stiff drink." I correct myself, "I forgot you don't drink."

"Maybe you can help me out, you know, since you're about to be on the market and all," he says, trying to get a rise out of me.

"Please," I say. "You're not my type."

"And what type is that?"

"The FBI type."

"You like those sensitive guys, don't you? Tormented artists who think their shit smells sweeter than everybody else. Am I right?"

"Wrong," I say, trying to change the subject.

"So, what type you into? I'm a curious guy."

"I'm not going to have sex with you, Bry."

Bry acts as if he's surprised by the comment when I know he's not.

"Whoa, Rashida. Let's pump the brakes. Where do you think this relationship is going? As your partner, I advise that sleeping with a colleague could create a very uncomfortable workspace filled with endless regret and humiliation—"

"Are you through?"

"Sorry," he says as if he just lost his puppy. "So, partner, give me your best shot. What's your theory on all of this?"

"Honest?"

"Honest."

"I don't think she wasn't trying to kill the witnesses," I tell Bry. "She was protecting them."

"Protecting them? And how did you come up with that conclusion?" Bry points to his temple. "Let me guess. Open mind, right?"

"I don't know, *partner*," I tell Bry, "but let's find out. Shall we?"

## 3. THE CURATOR / ROGER

WE follow the breadcrumbs to the fallout of a deadly shootout in Burbane where a team of scientists is wasting their time by combing the crime scene with particle detectors. We've seen enough.

After Fahim and I leave undetected, Fahim tails FBI agent, Agent Rashida Jones, while I check on the six witnesses at the Arthur Barrow Hospital—not sure if that's the correct number but that's what one of the news reporters had told Fahim, so I'm expecting the number to change drastically.

By the time I make it to the hospital, the emergency room is flooded with cops and civilians from across the entire Triad area. The ones sustaining the most significant injuries were medevacked to the hospital; however, each patient ranges in illness from severe to overactive imaginations brought on by a mass hysteria spread through major media outlets. My face hasn't reached the cops just yet; but soon, after the Feds start digging deeper, my face will be plastered all over TV. I fully take advantage of the situation while I still have my freedom. One of the nurses informs me that one of the doctors called several other doctors from neighboring towns to pitch in since they're well understaffed. A small window of opportunity opens when I least expect it.

As I make my rounds through the clutter and blend in as best I can, I search for Frankie's whereabouts, hoping to find her hiding somewhere in plain sight for me to find like someone who would stick out like a sore thumb, like a clown who broke his big toe while entertaining a crowd. She's made it incredibly hard. I can't sense her presence anywhere. She's known to give off certain energy whenever she's frightened—similar to that fuzzy sensation you get whenever you run your hand over a plasma globe. She's also been known to stop pacemakers from time to time. It's hard to explain, but it just happens. Each one of the six witnesses were injured during what they're calling an attack—at least, that's what the media is calling it, yet it appears nothing like an attack. One cop is missing an arm. He doesn't look good. Doctors are having trouble stopping the bleeding. He doesn't have long before he succumbs to his injuries.

I check for the most obvious signs that Frankie has laced herself inside witnesses' bodies: some suffer from tremors—mostly hands and feet—similar to the effect of experiencing a trauma or severe alcohol withdrawal, others suffer from heat flashes to muscle spasms ranging from mild to incredibly violent. Some spasms can be strong enough to break bones.

My window is closing; and as each minute passes, more and more cops make their way into the hospital, most of them checking on their blue brothers.

I check on each witness: the first one is Florence Brown, prefers to go by the name "Flo," a thirty-one year old black female who works as a hair stylist, shot in the arm, lost a great deal of blood but she'll live to fight another day; the second, Sandy Whitmaker, a former teacher at Riverbank Elementary, now retired, gunshot wound to right femur; third one, Cassidy Becknell, a college student studying journalism, severe lacerations to her neck and face; fourth, Julio Perez, painter, doesn't appear to have any legal status, shot in the shoulder—an "in and out" wound, as they call it—and the fifth witness, Lenny Mayor, a professor at the Greensboro Day Academy; he teaches film history, lost three toes after being shot in the foot. The sixth and final witness, who wasn't injured during the shootout: David Whitmaker, former businessman, retired like his wife, Sandy Whitmaker.

From all that I've gathered, each one of the witnesses doesn't appear to have any life-threatening injuries.

After I'm finished asking preliminary questions, I go into further detail about what they witnessed. The questions turn off several witnesses; nonetheless, each one of them describes June spending about ten minutes inside a school bus.

Even though I can't trust a single one of the witnesses, I believe them. They don't show any signs of being in contact with Frankie. Their injuries aren't out of the ordinary. Soon, Feds will be paying the witnesses a visit. Right now, I have to trust my gut and my gut is telling me that all fingers are pointing at these high school kids on the bus.

✲ ✲ ✲

I make contact with Fahim from a safe line. He informs me the Feds are holding all of the remaining witnesses at Naples Center. Two of the witnesses are missing. Both of them are coaches on the JV lacrosse team. I track down the two witnesses inside the emergency room before leaving the hospital. The hospital is now swarming with cops and FBI agents from all across the state. The only information I manage to gather is their names.

The seventh witness is Stewart Tabby. The other witness is Pamela Van Buren.

They know something, but they're not telling me.

✲ ✲ ✲

Fahim and I meet in a safe location a few miles from Naples Center and go through all of the names on the list. The ninth witness is Malick Bowie, a swimmer for Chelby Swim Club. The tenth witness is Anne Polinski, a stay at home wife, former clothing designer from New York, now owns her own business, a clothing line for babies called Skye Clothing. The eleventh witness: Daniel Ratliff, unemployed, music buff, says he wants to be a music producer. The twelfth witness: Arjun Joshi, born in Mumbai, then moved to America at the age of six, a family practitioner, trusted. The thirteenth witness is Manuel "Mase" Turner, stepson of Anne Polinski, no relation, father's name is Reece Turner; he is homeschooled. So far, eleven out of the thirteen witnesses show no signs of Frankie. The other twelve witnesses, including the two coaches, who happened to be on the bus while June entered, are questionable.

"This is all the information we have on them?"

"So far," says Fahim. "Yes."

"It's not enough."

"I'm aware, Roger—"

"—I need you to get a closer look."

"Closer? How close?"

"Close-*close.* Full concealment. I'm talking about a badge, background. The whole works. I want you to become one of them."

"Can't we obtain these statements another way?"

"I hate to break it to you, Fahim. There is no other way."

"I can't—"

"—You will."

"Isn't this more up Bloch's alley?"

"I need Sy to help me conduct the assessments."

"Are you forgetting what happened to Freeman?" asks Fahim. "What she did to him?"

Nobody has the ability to unsee such violence. I can imagine the war going on inside Louie's mind before she tore him to shreds. All of that *don't think* mumbo-jumbo that Fahim spoon-fed him. I can see Louie repeating those lines over in his mind as everybody was dying around him. Louie won't even be given an open casket, not unless the mortician pieced him back together like a jigsaw puzzle. Poor bastard.

"She did what she had to in order to survive."

"And if she is hiding inside one of these witnesses, then she'll sniff me out."

"She won't. She trusts you."

Fahim starts pacing around. I want to do the same, but I need to exude confidence in front of him.

"I don't feel comfortable with any of this—"

"—And you think I do?"

"It's *too* risky, Roger. You think I look like FBI material."

"I didn't know the one of the most revered agencies in the United States federal government hired people based off their looks."

"Well, they do," says Fahim. "And my presence will raise red flags and not to mention, create more attention than—"

"—We have no other option, Fahim. She saw something in that bus that changed her mind. I know it!"

"We can't make decisions based off your instincts, Roger!"

"Right now, my instincts are all we have."

"Then, what do you think she saw?"

"You really want to know what I think?"

"Yes. Of course."

"I think she saw a way-out."

"Okay. So what now?"

"We keep eyes on the twelve until we know what in the hell's going on."

✪ ✪ ✪

Fahim thinks I'm insane. Don't break out the ice pick just yet. I don't blame him for his concern in my well-being. Besides, he wouldn't be the first. We do, however, agree on one thing: Frankie is possibly hiding in one of twelve witnesses on the bus, ten of them being female players—athletes, fitting—and the other two, coaches, one male and the other a female. On the other side of the argument, there is the possibility that Frankie is gone. Self-sacrifice. Destroyed in the explosion at Benjamin Creek, which, by the way, is considered to be rather small in scale for a character like her. The odds of her survival are clearly not in her favor. She has always been a dark horse, the one who always finds a way to prove us wrong even when the odds are against her. My gut is telling me that she's still out there. Alone. Confused. Somehow, I can still feel her energy whenever I think of her and it's beating like a faint pulse. She's telling me that I'm close.

Keep going.

Don't give up.
Never ever give up.

☼ ☼ ☼

Apparently, one of the girls on the bus—Judith Ilderton—had a seizure a day after she had spoken with the FBI. I pay Judith a visit at the hospital and tell the doctors that I'm a friend of the family. According to Judith's chart, this wasn't uncommon for her. She has suffered from amnesia in the past. Troubled sleeper. Two years ago, Judith was treated for sleep deprivation. Usually, a large amount of stress or even experiencing a stressful event, like the one in Burbane, can trigger all sorts of issues in the human body. It can even bring out illnesses that remain dormant in the body—strange but not uncommon for a teenager to have trouble sleeping. I find that teenagers have a strange way of putting themselves under unnecessary stress. This kind of stuff is more in Bloch's department. The doctor ended up ordering a CAT scan. I can't do anything until I see the results.

☼ ☼ ☼

The CAT scans show several abnormalities. The neurologist can't explain what's going on inside Judith's head. They release Judith from the hospital anyway, but strongly advise her to do a follow-up next week. They want her to see a specialist. Funny because I know just the right person.

☼ ☼ ☼

Sy has brought to my attention that one of the girls has been acting strange. He suggests that we go ahead and start with the process, which, depending on the witnesses' cooperation, could last from days to weeks. Sy did a little more research on the other girls on the junior varsity lacrosse team. There are twelve players altogether, one of them ended up calling out sick. Her name is Donna Lambert. The other one, Elle Isley, didn't show up at school.

That makes ten players and two coaches.

Twelve people.

"She's hiding in one of them (the twelve). It's our job to find out which one she's hiding in."

"Where do we even start?"

I look over the backgrounds of the two adults, Pamela Van Buren grabbing most of my attention.

"Which one was driving the bus?"

"The head coach," says Sy. "Stewart Tabby."

"We'll start with him and then work our way down until we find her."

"Roger, we are not prepared for this," says Sy with unease in his voice. "If she is hiding in one of them, she will do everything in her power to escape."

"That's why we lie. Lying is the only thing we have left to our survival."

"And if she finds out?"

"She'll revert back to her most basis instinct, which is survival. We'll have to make due until we can transfer them to a more secured facility."

"Secured facility?" says Sy. "We're on our own, Roger."

"Fahim may know of a good location but I'm all ears if you have any other ideas."

"How about the West Division?" asks Sy.

"Too obvious. Orwell probably has men there right now as we speak. For now, I want you to team up with Fahim and find out everything you can about the twelve. I mean 'everything.' Their favorite color. TV show. I want to know what they do for fun. Hobbies. I want to know their habits, their patterns, routine, friends, family. Everything. We need to roll up our sleeves and get down to the root. Understood?"

"Roger, that could take months—"

"—Well, you're wasting time."

Sy turns away in frustration.

I catch Sy before he walks away. He's scared, like the rest of us.

"Remember, Sy, there are eyes everywhere," I say. "Keep your head down and stay focused."

He attempts to walk away. I call out to him again.

"And don't trust anyone," I tell Sy, "including yourself."

## 4. THE HIRED GUN / KRIS

I'M the best money can buy: that's the line I use on this young sad-faced Peruvian with a tight body that ranks an eleven. She buys the line. Then, she's all mine.

Fast-forward two months later after our first salut, Felicia and I are strolling through the raggedy entrails of Peril's Palace at Fantasy World, tracking each one of the scribbly lasers randomly moving along the hallways. I've never seen her so happy in the brief amount of time that we've spent together. I place my palm over the ground as each string of light slithers across the backside of my hand. Felicia kneels down beside me and places her hand over mine; both of our hands glowing like embers. I slowly pull my eyes upward into hers. Everything feels so surreal, as if I'm sitting on a small pile of stones with a sketchpad in hand outside Church of Paraportiani on the island of Mykonos within the Aegean Sea, sketching each detail of white houses climbing along steep hillsides, being submersed in the moment, as if in that moment I witnessed a soul. My observation level is out the roof. Even the slightest movement she makes is everything, down to the crease in her lip, the flicker of her eyelid, and then the melody of her every breath. Every detail is fleshed out, more vivid than any other memory. My eyes get lost in Felicia's eyes. Her pupils suddenly swell, her eyes now big and black. Each memory I have of Felicia presses against eyes like a jagged timeline. We used to come here—to this very place—in the summer before it got unbearably hot. We also came in the fall when the park was decorated in Halloween drag. She loved riding rollercoasters in pitch-black, loved messing with all of the undead meandering toward the living; loved luring me into the haunted mazes, those flashes of horror was like sex to her. Her nostrils flare as she inhales through her nose. I can feel her energy pulling me closer—magnetic in its bite. The hormones. I lean in for a kiss. Her tongue is wetter than water, and every inch of her starts to consume my body. I'm no longer basking in my most basic urges or admiring the colorful lights at the Laser Show. I'm drowning in black sludge.

Rewind two months earlier, Felicia and I are nothing more than strangers having drinks at a swanky restaurant on the top floor of the prestigious Belmont Hotel owned by the billionaire, Baron Orwell. I'm sipping on a margarita while listening to Felicia talk about tile. I've never known a lady who knew so much about tile. She lives just south of Asheboro, but her business brought her here. She's good at what she does. We share similar qualities in that we're both highly recommended in what we do. Not once does she ask me what I do for a living. Once, it crosses my mind that she may think I'm in the flesh trade but I keep her guessing. Normally, it's one of the first questions asked. She's different. She doesn't care about money or materials. And that's what I like about her. She's a worker. I can't shake her from my reach. It may be the alcohol. At this point, I've lost all judgment or rationality. I can't stop staring at her, the way Charlotte's uptown lights reflect off the glare in her eyes, as well as the diamonds of her black dress. I can't help but think about Felicia without a dress on, lying next to me as naked as the day as she was born, what it would feel like to be inside her. I gently place my hand over her's. The blood rushes through my veins like an indomitable current. I can feel parts of my body growing taller, stronger. Every inch of her makes me feel deadly.

Later that night, I wake up to the sirens of an ambulance outside the hotel. I roll to my right where Felicia's sleeping—*what the hell is a paramedic doing in my room?*

He's not real.

I tell myself he's not real and he vanishes in the shadows of the room.

I'm brought back by the city lights reflecting off the sweat of her back and with my finger, I trace each and every contour of her skeletal structure, as if I'm discovering the female anatomy for the very first time.

The next morning, I can't shed Felicia from my body quick enough. She wants to spend more time with me, but I tell her that I must get back to work. I know it's a mistake as soon as the words reach my lips. Me leaving her alone like this is only going to make her want me even more, especially after a night filled with one orgasm after another. Felicia wanted me to do things to her that no man has ever done to her. I took her to paradise.

Felicia and I spend most of the evening sharing past stories and laughing at observations at a cocktail bar, getting lost in the sound of her laughter, unbridled and carefree. I can't describe how it makes me feel. The pain vanishes now, like it was never even there to begin with—if only for a moment.

Another long night of sweating out each drop of alcohol from our bodies.

The next day, I find myself thinking about Felicia, as I'm about to pull the trigger.

His screams sound like the cries of a baby as he drops to his knees and begs for the life I'm about to take away.

What has she done to me?

Felicia wants to take things up a notch—dinner first, then possibly a movie or another activity besides sex. One side of me is ready to take the next step. Another side of me wants to cut loose from her and destroy every trace of her. We have an early dinner at one of her favorite spots—a small dive called Rooster's Chicken. Greasy fried chicken and waffles washed down by artificial-flavored lemonade. A thought pops in my head while we're eating, leaving me nauseous. I'm starting to become close to her. I haven't had a drink. Yet, I feel so intoxicated when I'm around her.

Is this the start of something?

A life full of getting old and fat together?

We go back to her place and spend the entire night burning off calories. I'm more aggressive than usual. She doesn't mind the roughness one bit. She acts as if she enjoys it. I'm mad at myself for getting this close, and I take it out on her.

Weeks pass.

Months.

Felicia and I are still seeing one another. Days are filled with activities, like grocery shopping or going to the movies on a regular basis. We are like-minded in regard to having a wild side. She always picks out a movie that doesn't draw a crowd, something lame or cliché, like a poorly acted, overly sentimental melodrama that's been in theatres for a couple of weeks or a movie that hasn't grossed much money at the box-office and is destined to spend an eternity of being shuffled and tossed around in the five-dollar bin at Wal-Mart. Most of the time Felicia and I have the entire theatre to ourselves. It's starting to become a thing for us: finding new places to have sex in public. She's cooking me meals, buying me things to wear or throw away. She says that she wants to start going on vacations together. I mention a cabin near the mountains. I have a job close by. Three marks. Shouldn't take that long. I hold off being intimate with Felicia for the entire day. I need my physical stamina as well as mental sharpness to complete the job. The thought of coming back to Felicia, being nine inches inside her, being close to her, just being with her, is what keeps me going. The job doesn't go as planned; nonetheless, the job is carried out according to my client's wishes. Normally, I'd find a place to stay on my own for the night. I want to get back to Felicia, though. I make sure to stay quiet. Not even a cat could detect me. As I'm washing up, the light switches on. Felicia is standing with her arms crossed at the doorway. She's asking me questions about my whereabouts, as well as the blood all over my hands. That's when I realize the fairy tale has come to an end.

My mind fills in the gaps. Felicia runs away. I chase after her. She knows too much now. But I catch up with her. She tries to fight me off, but my hands make their way across her jugular. I tell myself that she was just getting off on this kind of stuff the other day. She likes when I'm rough with her.

That night, I have a dream that I'm back in a shoddy black site somewhere in Afghanistan. Just when things couldn't get anymore extreme. The underlings of Crisis have stripped the clothes from my body, and I'm hanging upright with a noose tightly wrapped around my neck, the tips of my feet slipping and sliding over a block of ice like a puppet being controlled by a puppeteer with multiple sclerosis. They're asking me all sorts of questions about the American's next planned strike. As the ice painfully starts to melt before my feet, I think about the people who once loved me—*Will they miss me? What will my legacy be? Will I just be another white cross?* The thought alone of going back home in a casket wrapped in red, white, and blue causes the blood in my veins to boil. I will *not* die here by a bunch of intolerant religious savages! I can feel the block of ice getting wetter and wetter; the figures below me getting more blurry. I don't have to see them to know what they're doing. It's like one big-ass circle jerk. They get off on watching infidels suffer. The pressure builds around my jaw. The roots of my teeth dig into my gums like thorns. I'm having trouble breathing. As my feet start to dangle, I hear the muffled *pa, pa, pow* of gunfire dancing through the dark and dusty hallways. Screams sound like the cries of animals. A language that I've grown to love and hate. More gunfire. They've found me. The rage builds! Can't die here. I won't die here. As my executioner pulls out the AK-47, I suddenly swing my legs behind me, whip them above my head, and desperately climb up the noose as chaos unfolds below me. More gunfire rings out, much louder, closer. A firefight below me! More blood and gore. More everything. I watch one of the Navy SEALs slit the throat of my executioner. Once and for all, I want the violence to stop. Is this what we've become? The SEAL looks up at me, his face painted in a smear of black. He says something but his voice sounds like an alarm blaring out.

I suddenly bolt upright from sleep. The sound of a smoke alarm is still blaring out. Footsteps pitter-patter through the house. Felicia switches on a light. The kitchen's smoking. She grabs a towel from the dish rack and tosses a flaming object in the sink and dowses it with water.

"Felicia," I say, "what's happening?"

She comes back to the room.

"My phone charger caught on fire," she says.

"Phone charger? How'd that happen?"

"Don't know."

I force myself back to sleep.

✪ ✪ ✪

The bedroom door swings open! Felicia's shaking me by the shoulders, telling me that I'm dreaming. I'm cold and sweaty, more terrified when my eyes connect with Felicia's.

"What happened?" she asks, as she switches on the bathroom light.

I don't answer the question. I'm trying to wrap my mind around the dream and the time Felicia and I were together as a couple and the moment when things went terribly wrong for us. Felicia finding out what I did for a living had only made her want me more; whereas any normal woman would've run far away. Felicia wasn't like any other woman I've been with. She embraced that side of me, my violent past, the killing and why I chose to take away life rather than preserve it. In a way, she thought it was all a game. With Felicia, I can only see the bad parts, which stick out the most: the controlling, all of the calls—her checking up on me all the time, wondering if I was alive—the spying, the manipulation. I can't be here. She will put me in harm's way.

"Kris," Felicia dampens a hand towel with cool water and places it over my head, "how do you feel?"

"It was just a bad dream," I tell her. "That's all."

I hear a noise outside the window. For a second, it sounds like children playing.

"What's that noise?"

"Coyotes," she says. "They keep the cats away."

"Great."

"Let me check your dressing."

Felicia heads back to the bathroom, grabs a pair of gloves from underneath the sink, and checks the dressing on my abdomen. Her facial expression is one of surprise.

"What is it?"

"Your wound," she says, "it's nearly healed."

"That's a good thing, right?"

"It's. . . "

"It's what, Felicia?"

"It's. . . I don't know. . . " she carefully removes the dressing, ". . . looks like you're recovering faster than I thought."

She changes my dressing.

"I'll be right back."

She leaves the room and comes back with two pills in one hand and a glass of water in the other. Her face has dramatically changed. Her eyes appear somewhat vacant, but I don't put much stock into the thought that she's displeased about my speedy recovery.

I don't take the pills, at first. She says they're for my pain and she waits and watches me swallow them before leaving the room.

"Any news on the television?" I ask her as she's about to close the door.

"Last time I checked, you were still a wanted man."

"Felicia," I say as she attempts to close the door yet again.

"Yes, Kris," she says, her voice sounding bitter.

"Thank you for taking care of me."

"No problem."

She leaves the bedroom.

I decide to sleep with one eye open.

Old habit.

☼ ☼ ☼

The following day, I'm able to walk on my own. Felicia helps me at the beginning and then, after I get going, I'm like a baby taking his first steps. She talks to me about her business and how she's doing. She tells me about how she ended up expanding her business. Not only does she handle tile work, but she also does stone fabrication, including granite—says she met a man who works at a stone yard and he got her a great deal on stone. Even as she's telling me about this so-called "hookup," I'm thinking about whether or not he's a trustworthy man, if he's happy and married and has mouths to feed, or if he made Felicia spread her legs. She has to step out for a minute, which, to Felicia, can be hours, maybe all morning. Felicia's only doing a consultation, so she says that she won't be long. She's lying, though. I can sense the lie in her voice. What is she hiding from me? She hasn't been the same since last night. I'm starting to wonder if my presence is starting to change her. What did she see on the television?

☼ ☼ ☼

I spend all day watching the speculations develop on national television. The TV people even go so far as to report the latest chirps by celebrities who share their personal opinions on what they're calling the "Massacre on Highway 70," then, just minutes later, a mysterious explosion. If the TV people only knew how *wrong* they were about what happened, about everything. Yet, they continue to shove lies down their viewer's throats. They have a couple of things right, the death count, but that's about it. Everything else is mere speculation, truth in distortion, lies in embryo. No mention on what happened at Mt. Olympus. I swear, it's like these TV people live in their own little TV bubble, and that is exactly how Orwell wants it to be. To keep people less informed and misinformed.

Keep them guessing.

⚙ ⚙ ⚙

The headaches kick in after I waste about an hour resting on Felicia's new couch. I've never had headaches like these, like I have the end of baseball bat pressing against the inside of my skull. My pulse speaks to me, a murmur stirring in flesh. I pop a couple of Tylenols and splash my face with cold water, which helps ease the pain; however, it's still there, the pain, *always* there, lingering like a rude guest. I stretch out the skin on my face, pull down the papery bags underneath my bloodshot eyes. What the hell is happening to me?

⚙ ⚙ ⚙

Felicia startles me in the middle of the night by slipping into the bed.

"Felicia, what are you doing?"

"I couldn't sleep," she says.

Heard the line before.

Know the tone in her voice. The heat she's giving off.

As a couple, we spent our Friday nights listening to vinyl records from her mother's collection and going through a six pack of craft beer until our bodies were humming like amps.

After the music and Indian pale ales, the night usually carried into the bedroom where we engaged in more nocturnal activities.

My throat suddenly tightens because I know what Felicia wants and it's something I can't give her. Not now. The warmth of her body presses against mine. I can feel the heat between her legs underneath the covers. It's her body's way of pulling me closer, tempting me, begging me. I know all too well about the feeling, that urge. She even gives off a different smell when she's turned on. The little things Felicia does with her face gives it away: the gnawing on her bottom lip; the inflamed nostrils; that tiny devil trapped like a prisoner in her eyes. I can read her like Hemingway. I don't exactly know if it's the drama unfolding all over television or handling all of those bloody gauzes, or if it's from nurturing my flesh. She once said to me that she was terrified of blood. She loved to look at it in all those horror movies that she ritually watched. When it came down to getting something as small as cutting her finger on a rose bush or getting a paper cut while opening the mail, she couldn't stand the sight of a drop of blood coming from her own body.

I lie back down, ignore her, and shut my eyes. I feel her hand sliding underneath my shorts. She starts juggling my balls as if they're dice.

I grab her wrist.

"What are you doing, Felicia?"

"What do you mean?"

Her voice is sharper than last night.

I move her hand away from me.

"Felicia, I can't. . . "

"You can't? Really? You're serious?"

She throws the covers off her body and rolls out of bed.

"It has nothing to do with you," I say.

But it has everything to do with her.

She storms out of the bedroom and shuts the door behind her.

☼ ☼ ☼

Napalm with a side of regret. Felicia acts as if her breakfast is the worst thing she's ever stuck in her mouth. She asks me twice when all of this is going to end. She's carrying that look in her eye again, the one I'm so used rying that look in her eye again, the one I'm so used to, the one she held onto right before I left her. I tell Felicia one more day and I'll be good to go. I can't thank her enough for taking care of me. I get the feeling that I'm turning into the unwanted houseguest; and now, the shoe is on the other foot.

☼ ☼ ☼

It's started. Every single news channel, including both major and local, has officially released a photo of Dr. June Lugosi. She's considered armed and extremely dangerous. It's obvious that the media was pressured to release an image on the suspect after intense scrutiny once clips of the Burbane massacre had made their way onto the web. It's not uncommon for certain organizations to be persuaded by the public. It's human nature. People want the hundred percent truth, unfiltered, unbiased. People want answers. People want to hold other people accountable when things go terribly wrong. It's not the new normal. People have always been this way. People crave violence. The release of the photo takes more pressure off my situation. Either way, it doesn't change the fact that I'm a wanted man. Dead or alive, they won't stop looking for me.

Felicia's going to step out for a minute.

At this point, I don't know how long that will be—a minute, an hour, all morning, all day? We've been eating carryout for the past two days and she says she's in the mood to cook me a descent meal. I think it's her way of telling me that she still cares about me and that she's not giving up on me. Or, it could be her way of plumping me up before she shoos me off to the vultures.

After she leaves, I flip on the news, as I've been doing periodically throughout the day.

Three of the ten girls who were on the bus during the terrorist attack have been reported missing.

The local authorities have also had trouble locating the remaining seven girls, as well as the coaches of the

Central Agatha lacrosse team. I wonder if it has something to do with what happened at Mt. Olympus. Is there a connection?

☼ ☼ ☼

For the remainder of the afternoon, I piddle around Felicia's house. I go through her personal things, including her laptop, which is still warm. She hasn't closed any windows. I go through her emails. She wasn't born yesterday. She knows how to clear her history and whatnot, now that she has an indefinite guest living with her. What if she wants me to see these things? I make sure to put everything back in its proper place. I don't find any pictures of me. I expect to find some kind of trace of me left behind, like inside a jewelry box or underneath a panty drawer or a picture of us tucked away in a photo album. I do, however, find several sex toys inside the bottom drawer of her dresser: butt plugs, rubber dildos, and a vibrator about the size of a mixer. I can picture Felicia spending her Friday nights in bed with all sorts of sex toys and lubrication laid out next to her like instruments for a surgeon, fast-forwarding through an endless collection of porn on her laptop, pleasuring herself. Nobody deserves to be alone.

I keep searching but find nothing of mine. She's erased every trace of me.

As I head back into the living room, I come across a book on the bookshelf. *Moby Dick*. I don't know why I'm so drawn to the book, but I can't keep my eyes from it. I take the book to the couch and start reading through it.

Once I read the first page, I read the next and next thing I know, I'm already halfway through the book.

I'm starting to feel like Ishmael right now.

The only difference: I'm not hunting my white whale.

It's hunting me.

✿ ✿ ✿

Felicia and I eat dinner in a mouthy silence. Steak and russet potatoes. My kind of meal. The potatoes have been roasted with olive oil, sea salt, and rosemary. Soft and seasoned. A baby couldn't mess up a potato. The steak, however, is overcooked.

During the entire meal, our jaws do most of the talking. I have to stop halfway through the meal to rest my jaw. Felicia knows that I like my steak medium rare. I think she knows that she deliberately overcooked the steak, but she knows that I won't say anything because I'm not her boyfriend. I'm only a guest here.

Every Saturday night—if it wasn't Mexican or Italian—it was steaks with red wine. Red meat and red wine go together like peanut butter and grape jelly. It became a tradition for us: Steak Saturday. If we decided to stay in, she'd stop by the meat market early that day—that is, if Felicia wasn't hungover from the night before—and she'd pick up freshly cut T-Bones or Filet Mignons, meat so tender that you could cut it with a fork. I didn't even have to tell Felicia how I wanted it. She knew that I liked it with a little red in the middle. Pink all the way through. One time I showed her a neat trick on how to cook a steak by touching the backside of her hand as a guide. That meaty place between the thumb and index finger, a good indicator whether a steak is rare or well done based off feel and tenderness. Since any cook—good or bad—doesn't know what's going on inside a steak while it's being cook, it's easy to say cooking a steak is based on touch. The softer it is in the middle, the rarer it'll be. The harder, the more cooked it is. It's Cooking 101.

So, of course, it's deliberate.

Not only that, Felicia hasn't said a word, which is unusual. She always has something to say, a story about her day. I find it comforting to listen to her keep my mind at ease while I'm eating. Something is seriously bothering Felicia and I know that it's not just me being here. Something else is going on with Felicia. Something below the surface.

Overcooking the steak is a prelude as to how the night is going to be.

☼ ☼ ☼

All of the tension between Felicia and me is fleshed out after I power through the meal. I can feel the tension, as if it has its own entity.

As Felicia grabs the plate from the table, I grab her by the wrist and tell her that I'm sorry.

She acts surprised by the comment.

"Sorry? Sorry for what?"

She already knows the answer.

"I'm sorry for how things ended up between the two of us. I'm sorry for not being more forthright with you in the beginning. I'm sorry for not treated you the way you deserve to be treated. I'm sorry for not *being* there when you needed me the most. I am sorry, Felicia—"

She pulls her hand away from me.

"—You can't just show up in my life after I spent a whole year trying to forget about you, Kris!"

She has every right to be angry. She storms out of the kitchen. I chase after her. I know it's a mistake. I know I'm opening a door that was closed a long time ago. I follow her into the guest room where she's crying on the bed. I sit next to her on the edge of the bed; wipe the tears from her eyes. I lean in closer for a kiss. She resists by pushing me away. I ease away and give her the space. Her eyes glaze over. She can't hold herself back any longer. Felicia suddenly comes at me in a fierce move. She's on top of me, kissing me, straddling me, grinding on me. I kiss her back. She can't remove her clothes quick enough. I don't realize that it's happening until our clothes have been stripped away from our bodies. I'm sore, but it doesn't take me too long to find her rhythm. I know Felicia's been waiting for this moment. I make sure not to disappoint her.

✿ ✿ ✿

Felicia and I lie in bed. She reaches in the top drawer of the nightstand and pulls out a pack of old Marlboros and offers me one.

"You've been saving these for a special occasion?"

"No," she shrugs, "I forgot I had them. Here. One won't kill you."

I grab the cigarette from her hand.

"I started smoking after we—you know—then I gave them up. I recently got into yoga. Cut out red meat from my diet." She lights up the cigarette, then hands me the lighter. I light up mine. She says from the corner of her mouth, "Except for tonight, I think the last time I had a steak was with you."

"That must've been hard for you then."

She shrugs again.

"Not really."

Silence swells over the pillow talk.

"It takes a while to get back into the swing of things."

"And is this what this is, a thing?"

"It could be," I say.

I don't know if it's the truth or if it's just what she wants to hear but it certainly comes out of my mouth without any hesitation whatsoever.

"Felicia, I don't want to be a bad influence on you."

She turns serious and says, "You were always a bad influence on me, but that never stopped me. . . "

Her words start to rattle down the base of her throat.

"Stopped you from what?"

Tears form in her eyes. Her lips are shaking.

She looks me in the eyes.

"You know. . . "

I pull Felicia close to my chest and hold her in my arms.

"I wish things could go back to the way they were between us," she says quietly, her face pressed against my chest. "Like the time we first met, you know, when things weren't so complicated."

"Me too," I say as I run my hands through her hair. "Me too."

We lay in a more comfortable silence.

I don't feel the need to start up a conversation or put an end to the silence.

"Kris?"

Felicia finally breaks through the silence. Her voice suggests that she has a lot on her mind.

"Yeah, babe."

"The man who hired you to kill this doctor character," she says as she plays with the hair on my chest, "Orwell—"

"—What about him?"

"Does he have anything to do with those girls who went missing?"

"I don't know."

"What if—"

I sit upright, causing Felicia to sit up as well. I grab her by the shoulders and reassure her that nothing is going to happen to me.

"We can leave," she says. "We can head south, drive until we *hit* water."

"I can—I can't put you in harm's way."

"Besides work, I have no ties here. I don't have any family here. I don't have many friends here. I can come with you."

She's already started to create fantasies in her head. Once she starts, I know she won't stop. She's already setting herself up for disappointment.

"Out of the question," I tell her. "It's too dangerous."

"You can't just hide here for the rest of your life."

"So, you're saying that you would come with me?" I gently place my hand against the side of her face. "If it came down to surviving—out there, just the two of us, no walls to protect us—you, Felicia Rosado, you would fight off each and every one, killers whose sole purpose is to make a person disappear without leaving a single trace?"

"Hey," Felicia says, a ghost of smile growing underneath her face, "I know how to use a gun. I would take on every last one of them if I had to."

Laughing, she lunges forward and smothers me with her breasts.

I hold her tightly, kissing every inch of her face. I roll over on top of her, pull my lips from hers.

"This isn't a game, Felicia," I say closely.

A short and quick burst of a smirk flashes across one side of her face. She shrugs one of her shoulders, tears forming in her eyes.

"So what?" she says playfully.

She has that same look in her eyes, the look she had when we first met.

✩ ✩ ✩

Felicia and I are wandering through the Asheboro Zoo, making our way through one exhibit after another: a polar bear swimming through crystal blue water; gorillas standing next to the pane of glass, one gorilla is messing with us by picking its nose, flicking buggers at us; lions lounging on rocks; endangered red wolves; monkeys hanging out. We come across a black panther, and I'm completely left in awe from the sight of the leopard as it approaches us. Felicia is left speechless. I remove my hand from Felicia's hand, step closer to the barricade, and stare into its piercing eyes. Everything around me stops. For a moment, I stop breathing.

✩ ✩ ✩

I wake up gasping for air. I'm choking on my own saliva. I'm having trouble swallowing. I bolt upright and roll out of bed. I hurry to the bathroom, trying not to wake Felicia. I don't bother turning on the bathroom light either. Something feels off about my breathing. My body's wrapped in a cold sweat. I splash my face with water. The feel of the water against my skin is numbing. I take a few sips of water straight from the spicket. The water tastes strange—metallic. I cough and spit out the water. The sounds would definitely wake Felicia, but surprisingly she doesn't stir one bit. She's sound asleep, not snoring, not even moving from all of the racket I'm making. She's a kicker, too. I used to wake up with bruises on the side of my calves or tiny lacerations on my ankles from where her toenails cut me while I was sleeping. The room has a gassy smell to it, as well.

I switch on the bathroom light for a better look. I notice a smear of blood along the light switch, as well as the doorway.

I follow the stains to my forearms, then my hands, both of them covered with dark blood. I direct my attention toward the mirror and realize the left side of my body is bloody! The lower part of my face, mainly my chin, is covered in blood. . .

I frantically scan my body for injuries, looking to see if I've been cut—maybe my wound had opened while I was sleeping.

The blood isn't coming from my wound. The blood isn't mine. . .

I rush back into the bedroom, flip on the lamp, and find an unrecognizable Felicia spread out on the bed. She appears to have been mauled by an animal. Most of the bite marks are concentrated around her neck. She has several long gashes around her chest and arms from where it looks like she tried to fight off the creature while it was gnawing at her neck.

I check Felicia's pulse, but I already know that she's dead. The smell of excrement is potent in the air. Blood has pooled underneath her body, especially the upper part of her torso. She hasn't completely bled out. Whatever blood she still has in her body bubbles over the corners of her mouth, popping in tiny splashes along her cheeks.

I step closer, accessing the situation. She just died. Minutes ago. Ten minutes maybe. Fifteen?

I hear the sound of glass shattering in the kitchen. I grab my Berretta from my belongings and check out the noise.

I make it to the kitchen where I see a black beast sitting on top of the countertop, licking its paws. It's too burly to be a coyote. The echoes of the dream call at me and for a moment, I think I'm stuck in a dream. In my mind, I see the image of a black panther entering Felicia's house through the back door, which, for some reason, I had left open earlier that night. It makes its way toward Felicia's bed, climbs onto the bed, and stands over Felicia while she sleeps.

With the knife in my hand, I flip on the light switch!

The same black panther from my dream appears just feet before me!

It stops what it's doing. Its yellow eyes snap toward me. My heart feels as if it's about to punch through my chest.

"Take it easy," I say, adjusting the Berretta in my hand.

Even the words I speak have their own pulse. They echo like the beats of a drum.

I try to keep the fear at bay.

If I show it that I'm scared, it will sniff it out. I stay calm and resolute.

I display submission by standing still with my hands held outward, showing it that I'm merely a fearless observer.

Its ears curl back behind its head. It growls at me. Then leaps down from the countertop.

"Go on now," I say, keeping my voice as soft as possible.

If I show the least amount of aggression, it will sniff it out.

It prowls along the tile floor of the kitchen, leaving behind bloody footprints.

I mentally keep reminding myself—that if this really is a dream—then wake the hell up, Brixx!

It's *not* a dream.

This is real.

The black panther stops at the edge of the kitchen.

I backpedal—again, a clear indication that it's the one in charge of the show.

I'm an observer who means no harm.

We share the longest stare. Its ears release from the back of its head and point upright.

With its long tongue, it licks the blood from the side of its mouth.

Then, finally, it turns around and walks out of the cracked door. I follow the black panther, making sure to keep my distance. It walks from the porch, down the driveway. It stops once to look back at me and then it walks into the woods and fades into the night.

I don't realize that I stopped breathing until I find myself taking in a deep breath of air.

✿ ✿ ✿

I examine the entire house for clues as to how an animal entered the house.

Black panthers in North Carolina?

It had to escape from the zoo: that's my only answer as to what happened. Why do I feel that I was responsible for her death?

I can't think straight.

The back door is unlocked. No damage to the door or the doorway. No sign of break-in.

The footprints next to the black panther's paw prints are muddy. The prints lead into Felicia's bedroom. I follow the prints, both of them.

Next to the dresser are my boots lying on the carpet. The boots are muddy. Next to the boots are my clothes, including my pants and underwear, laying in a messy pile.

I find traces of mud on the bottom of my pants.

I turn to Felicia, lying there, dead, murdered.

All of it comes out, the emotion, the tears, the guilt. Everything hits me all at once and I realize that I can't even trust myself anymore.

☼ ☼ ☼

After I compose myself, the old me comes back and I treat the bedroom as a crime scene and put myself in the shoes of a detective. I need to destroy every trace of me indicating that I was here. I need to make myself disappear.

First, I grab the car keys from the drawer, grab the thickest comforter from the hallway closet, and cover the inside of the Accord's trunk, every inch from top to bottom.

The hard part: I find a pair of jogging clothes for Felicia.

I go to her bedroom and search through her closet. She owns a lot of dry fit shirts and power bras. It'll be harder to make the cuts look consistent with a dry fit shirt or the skintight stuff. So, I go with something that would tear easily, like cotton.

Shirt aside, I find a pair of leggings—she doesn't have any marks on her legs, so I won't have to make any cuts.

The story goes: Felicia was jogging the trails in the woods when all of a sudden she was attacked by some wild animal—in this case, possibly a leopard or what investigators will determine was a black panther. She put up a fight, dropped her car keys near the river. The investigators will determine from all the evidence they find scattered throughout the woods that Felicia was fleeing toward water. Felicia was overcome by her injuries while she was crossing the river. Her body was carried downstream until it finally came to rest on the shore. It's the only reasonable solution I can think of.

Who knows how exactly long it will take until her body is found. A fisherman a week later? A jogger, like Felicia? It could take weeks, maybe even months.

I can't leave her the way she is right now. It must look like a random attack. I leave the wounds untouched on her body and with the sharp end of one of the scissor blades, I cut the clothes according to each and every gash on her arms as well as her chest and make them look like claw marks.

Before I make my way to the lower part of Felicia's body, images flash through my mind: Felicia and I are making passionate love. I finish inside her. The thought alone of cleaning away the evidence inside her makes me nauseous.

I rush to the bathroom before I can contaminate the scene with my vomit.

Just hours ago, we were talking about a life after the media storm. Life together. Just the two of us.

Now, I'm trying to wipe every inch of me from her.

I pull myself together, clean her up, dress her, carry her to the car, and place her inside the trunk.

As far as the paw prints around the house, the only ones that I find are the ones on the driveway.

I grab a hose and wash off the mud, as well as the blood into a sewage drain.

Once I get back inside, the real work begins.

I start by grabbing a box of plastic gloves, as well as a box of garbage bags from the laundry room. I strip the bed sheets from bed and place them in a garbage bag. A couple of drops of blood somehow make their way onto the mattress. I clean the mattress the best I can with Clorox. The stains aren't significant enough to draw much attention. The stains could've come from menstruation. I don't stress too much over it. I place new bed sheets over the bed, as well as blankets. Once the bed is all taken care of, I start with the stains on the carpet. I cover the carpet with a heavy-duty carpet cleaner and let it sit until it's ready to be scrubbed. All of the bloody water I dump into the toilet. My bloody bandages in the trash are flushed down the toilet as well. I clean the entire bathroom with disinfectant. I clean every inch of the furniture. I leave no fingerprint left behind.

After the bedroom is all done, I make my way into the kitchen. I mop the floors. I clean the dishes. The countertops. The table. I scrub every inch that I have touched. Not only do I make it look as if I wasn't here, but I also make it look as if the black panther wasn't here either.

We are ghosts.

Right now, the black panther and I have the most in common.

I move into the living room, wipe down the television remote. The couch.

Once every square inch of the house is cleaned and then staged to appear as if Felicia brewed a pot of coffee, then set a coffee cup with an impression of her lips in the sink, then stripped the peel from a banana, placed it inside the trashcan, then spread an outfit along the already made bed—once everything is settled in its proper place—I take a steaming hot shower. I wash the dried blood from my arms and remove every trace of Felicia from my body until all I have left of her are the memories of the time we spent together.

After I shower, I grab Felicia's purse from the living room and empty out all of the contents over the kitchen table. I search for anything that might contradict her story, starting with her mp3 player. The mp3 player will be one of the many clues that I'll place around the vicinity of this so-called attack.

I reach for her phone on the new charger that she bought earlier in the day.

My hand grazes the charger and sends a tiny surge of electricity through my body. I pull the charger closer. It smells different, sweeter like butterscotch. A streak of pain suddenly shoots through my body as soon as I unplug the phone from the charger. A flash of an image comes to me: *Dr. Lugosi stepping through a pocket of fire, stalking toward me. The water from the sprinklers rains down on the both of us. Water drips into my eyes, causing me to clear my eyes.*

She's whispering words to me. The words are scrambled together and sound like a million wasps buzzing inside a hornet's nest. I snap from the trance and place the charger aside. Felicia's phone doesn't require a password, only a swipe of my gloved finger across the touch screen, then I'm in. Felicia was never the tech-type. I remember she created a MyCircle page for her business, as well as a Linkedin page, but that's about it. She didn't spend a lot of time on the web—at least, not that I remember. Whenever we were together, we were together. We weren't playing with our toys. She didn't care about trying to impress anyone by taking any photos of us and posting them on the web for strangers to us, which was another trait I liked about her.

I search through her social media pages. I don't find anything on them that will work against me. She didn't have any plans for the coming days. She had a consultation with a client next week, but I'm not too worried about that.

I tweak her schedule and add in a morning jog to her calendar.

Lastly, I scroll through her photos until I come across several photos of us together. I can't believe that she saved these photos. One of them was taken at Fantasy World. A selfie of the two of us standing outside Peril Palace, smiling ear to ear. We look so content with our lives, even though I know during that time whenever I wasn't spending time with Felicia I was anything but content.

I trash the photo. I go ahead and trash every photo of me in her phone.

As I'm about to delete the entire trash bin, I find a recent snapshot of an ad for a ghostwriter. The ad says, "Looking to write the next great American novel? Hire a Ghostwriter."

The photo was taken the other day, when she went in early for work.

Did Felicia really want to write a book?

If so, who or *what* was it going to be about?

⚙ ⚙ ⚙

I make sure I don't leave anything behind as I do one final sweep of the house.

I check on Felicia.

When I open the trunk, I notice that her body is missing!

Behind me, the sound of a bone cracking!

My body goes cold like ice. I slowly rotate around, only to find Felicia standing inches away from me. Her face is pale and covered with strings of blood.

"Don't answer the door," she says.

I suddenly wake up with a string of drool hanging from the side of my mouth.

The sun is out.

How long have I been asleep?

I sit upright and look around the kitchen. I must've dozed off while I was going through her purse.

I hear the *ring* of the doorbell!

I check the window.

A police officer's standing on the front porch!

The officer rings the doorbell once more, waits a second, then walks back to his cruiser.

Did I close the garage?

As he walks along the driveway, he scans the front lawn. Most of the officer's attention is focused on the ground where I washed away all of the blood and mud from the driveway. He gets back in his cruiser and drives to the next house down the street. I breathe a sigh of relief. Too close.

⚙ ⚙ ⚙

I save the truck for last and strip it clean. The license plate. VIN number. All of the owner's manuals and papers and receipts. I remove every single thing from the truck that would lead the detectives to me and stuff it all in a garbage bag, then wipe the inside down with Clorox wipes for safe measure—for all they know, Felicia was working on a special project on her off-time. After all, I wouldn't necessarily call her a pretty in pink-kind of gal. Every now and again, she liked to get her hands dirty. And that's what I loved about her.

As I'm about to make one last walkthrough, I spot the box of a GPS device on the shelf. The box appears untouched. I open it up and pull out a GPS. It still has the packaging and everything. I get the strangest feeling that I might need the GPS. So, I take it with me.

✪ ✪ ✪

It starts to downpour by the time I dump the garbage bags in a dumpster next to an apartment complex several miles from Felicia's house. I find a black Pathfinder with North Carolina license plates parked in a secluded area where there are no cameras or wandering eyes and with a screwdriver, I remove the license plate and then replace it with Felicia's license plate—it will take months for the driver to figure out he or she is driving with the wrong license plate. After all, who looks at a license plate before getting inside a car?

I remember passing a river before entering Asheboro. I drive to the same river not too far away from Felicia's house. I arrive at my destination just as the sun is about to set. I find a dirt road not too far away from the river and park the car away from the highway.

I put on a pair of gloves and carry Felicia's body through the woods, stopping several times to rest.

Once I reach the river, I place Felicia on the ground and start to scatter the evidence all over the ground. Mp3 player. I turn on the player and set the volume to a listenable level. I remove the running shoe from her right foot and wedge it underneath a rock. Finally, I carry Felicia into the river until I'm about knee-deep in water and then I set her body, clothed and all, into the river and ease her downstream.

The rest is out of my hands.

☼ ☼ ☼

The GPS makes a beeping noise as I cross the South Carolina border. I pull over on the side of the road, pull out the GPS box. Open it. The GPS has turned on all on its own. I don't think too much about it—at least not until I turn to my left and see the cell phone tower across the street. I feel enticed by its energy, incredibly drawn to it. I mindlessly step out of the car while the rain continues to come down harder.

I wait until the street is clear before crossing. I make my way toward the tower.

I touch the base of the tower with the palm of my hand.

Images flash through my mind: *I'm back inside Mt. Olympus, moving through one of the many corridors as the sprinklers kick on above me. I check my ammunition, then find one of my men missing his arms—it's Theo—but he doesn't have that long before he succumbs to his injuries. He's taking his final breaths. I grab him by the face and he musters out a couple of words.*

I don't remember at the time what he said, but his words are as clear to me as never before.

*Game over,* he says, grinning an awful bloody smile.

*I turn my shoulder and she's approaching me.*

Another flash of memory: *I'm lying on Felicia's couch, skimming through the book* Moby Dick.

*My eyes move up from the book and I'm no longer lying on the couch. I'm standing in a much older room with wooden bookshelves lining the walls. A study of some kind. A bibliophile's wet dream? Old hardbacks everywhere, each one covered in a thin layer of dust. Each window has been boarded up with large plywood and sheets of heavy steel.*

I reach to grab a book from the bookshelf.

As soon as I make contact with the spine of the hardback, it's night and I'm standing in the rain.

Out of desperation, I attempt to remove my hand from the cell phone tower but it appears stuck like a magnet.

I slide my hand downward along the metal and then give it one last tug!

Flashes of lightning streak across the black sky.

The rain comes down harder.

Rumbles of thunder choke the night air.

I finally release my hand from the tower and stare at my hand, now both of them shaking before me.

I know my purpose, where I need to be, and most importantly, what I must do when I get there.

## 5. THE AGENT / RASHIDA

BRY has the lights on throughout the entire apartment and the first thought that immediately comes to mind is this *better* be good.

When I make it to Bry's floor from the elevator, an unsettling vibe starts to sink in and my only reaction is to unbutton the strap from my holster. Something's going down—or went down. I inch my way toward Bry's apartment. The door is cracked open, very suspicious, however, no signs of breaking and entering. All of the training that I learned at the Academy kicks in and I find myself back in Quantico, waiting for cardboard targets of criminals to pop up or spring up out of a corner. That unexplainable sensation gnawing in my gut, one that I get whenever I sense the presence of a threat.

I place the cup holder filled with two cups of coffee and blueberry scones on the floor, remove my gun from the holster, and creep into the apartment where I find an overturned lamp without a shade on the floor. Other things are scattered throughout the apartment, papers, folders, little knickknacks. The place looks as if it's been raided by a pack of wolves.

"Bry?" I say, listening closely for a response.

All I receive is the rumbling of my stomach.

Pull yourself together, Rashida.

"Joke's over, Bry," I say, thinking of ways to lure a threat out of the shadows. "I'm putting my gun back in my holster." Too obvious. "Okay now, Bry," I call out once more. "Gun is going back. That way I don't shoot your funky ass."

Again, the sounds of indigestion.

I make my way into the living room where I find a body on the floor. I can't tell if it's Bry or not. A plastic bag has been pulled over its head.

Next to the body: two shattered mugs, as well as a bloody trophy.

I kneel down and remove the bag.

I rope of blood pours from the bag, revealing Bry's face.

"Bryan. . . "

I frantically check his pulse. I can't find one on his neck. He has several deep puncture marks on the backside of his head. I check his pulse once more. He's dead.

I inspect the rest of the apartment before calling it in. I check each room, bathroom, closet. The apartment is clear.

I rush back to Bry and check the trophy. I remember Bry talking about the trophy a couple of days ago when we hit a dead end in the case. His team won first place in a paintball tournament—*not* Bro-fest where he played solely for the bragging rights and a cheap fix, but from a league consisting of middle-aged masculinists who wanted to get away from the misses on the weekends. Bryan was a widower, lost his wife to the big C three years ago; once said he was going to dedicate his life to catching bad guys. The trophy was one of his many trophies that he had won. Basketball. Baseball. Football. Hockey. I check the trophy case in his office. Most of the trophies are from his childhood. I don't know why I don't feel anything from the sight of his body. I want to feel something for Bryan. I should feel something for the loss. Bry had only been my partner for three months. Once—I believe this was around the time I was first partnered up with him—I believe the thought crossed my mind that this could be a lasting partnership. We definitely had a Yin and Yang-type relationship going on. I'd like to think that in spite of our differences we had respect for each other. Maybe it's part of the training. Don't get mushy. Most importantly, if you do show any kind of emotion, bury it as soon as you feel it coming on.

I stay strong and retrace my steps. I don't find any clues of forcible entry on the doorway. Whoever did this to Bry *knew* Bry. This wasn't a random act of violence.

I make my way back to Bry's body and try to find anything that will lead me to his murderer. I take note of the shattered mugs on the floor. He appears to have been holding mugs in his hands the moment he was attacked. The splatter of blood on the walls suggests that he was directly struck from behind. He could've guessed that I was coming over. He knew I was sort of a pop-in partner who never called or gave him a heads-up before coming over—once I caught him jerking off in the bathroom and acted as if he spilled mustard on his pants and he was trying to rub out a stain. From that point on, Bry assumed everything. The other mug could've possibly been for me. Maybe Bry had an intuition I was coming over to discuss the details of the case. We had so much to go over, especially the laundry list of contradictories from each one of the witnesses' statements. I wish it were true, about Bry being overly courteous enough to make me a cup of coffee ahead of time. But Bry is fully aware that I'm a BYOC-kind of lady.

This was personal.

I check a lengthy wall of evidence in his office. He pinned a map of the East Coast to the wall. He's been tracking June Lugosi's every move with red thumbtacks, starting from the time she started working as an epidemiologist at the Center for Disease Control and Prevention in Atlanta, Georgia, thirteen years ago, to the time she fell off the radar nine years ago—basically, went off the grid—to the moment she popped up all over surveillance cameras in the Blowing Rock area to her ultimate demise in Benjamin Creek.

I pull out my personal phone and start taking photos of the map, each thumbtack over each location.

I take photos of one of the main suspects, Kris Solles, from the still of a surveillance video inside a convenient store between the towns of Iredell and Duggins. Kris Solles, the ex-marine who vanished like a cheap trick after being honorably discharged from the United States armed services, was caught on video gunning down a clerk, shot him twice in the chest, then a final shot in the head. Triple tap. Very professional.

I take a photo of the morgue shots of Ramon López, the young man who was found in his 1999 gold Nissan Maxima in a ditch in Tartersville.

I take as many photos as I can before I make the call.

Lastly, I check the papers on the floor, the empty folders. The folders are what really grab my eye. I know these folders because days ago Bry and I were going through each one of them. The statements of each witness were once inside these folders. Now, they're gone. Every one of them.

Whoever was responsible for killing my partner got exactly what they wanted.

☼ ☼ ☼

The clean up crew shows up at Bry's apartment after I inform Pelham about Bry's death. Pelham wants to know what happened. It's rare for an Assistant Director, let alone the Special Agent in charge, to show up unannounced; but when one of our own has fallen victim, anything can happen.

I follow him to the map on the wall—most of his interest is centered on a disturbing photo of Ramon López taken at the morgue.

"Who's the stiff?" he asks, pointing at the photo.

"That's Ramon López."

"How come he wasn't mentioned in the report?"

"We don't know exactly what happened to him?"

"Well, tell me what you know."

"What we know?"

"For starters, who is he and why the hell does he look like that?"

"Ramón Lopez was from Tartersville," I say. "The son of Mr. Pooper Scooper—"

"Is that right?" Pelham flashes a smile on his face. It's the first time I've ever seen the man smile. "You mean the one from the commercials? Scooping up dog shit?"

"That's right," I say. "The guy who thinks he's funny but he's not funny at all, you know, people are actually laughing at him, not with him: that Jorge Lopez. His son, Ramon, was carjacked outside Blowing Rock. He was forced off the road not too far from Burbane, crashed his car in a ditch. López was discovered looking just like that." I point at the photo. "It's like everything inside him was overcooked. Look at the burn marks. Look at the rest of his body. Untouched."

"How the hell does someone burn from the inside out?"

"It's freakish."

"I'd say." Pelham starts examining the rest of the crime scene. "So, the last time we spoke Corbin was talking about finding discrepancies in one of the witness's statements—"

"—I remember there was one girl in particular."

I frantically search through the papers on Bry's desk and find the list of witnesses.

"Rashida," Pelham says as he holds out his hands, "some other time. You've been through a lot—"

"—Bryan was onto something—"

"—Go home, Rashida," he says. I sense his patience starting to wear thin. "Get some sleep. You're way too close to this investigation."

I find the list.

"This girl here. Judith Ilderton. Bry mentioned that she was spotted less than a mile outside the blast site on Tuesday morning. He said he received a call from a witness—man who owns a local bakery in Agatha—claimed he saw Ms. Ilderton walking on the side of the road. He said she looked 'scared.'"

"Doesn't mean anything, Rashida. Kids wander. That's what they do."

"At six o'clock in the morning?"

"Yeah." He stuffs his hands in his pockets. "Why not?"

"What would she be doing all the way out there at that time of the day?"

"Who knows, Rashida? Where are you going with this?"

"What if June Lugosi was working with her?"

"Working with her? And why in the world would a former employee of the CDC be working with your everyday high school student?"

"I don't know. Maybe they knew each other."

Pelham gives me that look like I'm out of my mind.

"Go home, Rashida. Try to get some sleep. I'll call you if we find anything."

"But Pelham—"

"—I'm not asking you, Rashida."

Pelham gives me a cold shoulder and joins the other investigators.

That's my cue to leave.

☼ ☼ ☼

I leave Bry's with only the photos that I took on my phone. More than likely, Pelham's going to put someone else on the case. Why wouldn't he? I'm too close, even though I don't feel close at all. According to Pelham, my judgment is cloudy. The training has taught me that, when an agent has blood on his or her mind, then he or she cannot properly perform the task. The job wants me to be unbiased. How can I be unbiased? My partner is dead.

☼ ☼ ☼

On the way home, I stop at the ABC store and pick up a flask of vodka to help me sleep. I realize such an attempt as sleeping will be a fruitless endeavor—somehow, images *never* go away. How can I erase the violence that has taken place? It'll always be there, reminding me of why I decided to work for the FBI. The ghosts. It's relatively easy to erase the images of the dead. Most—if not, all—of them look the same. Bodies that have succumbed to stabbings, shootings, or any other bodily injuries which lead to their demise have a way of masking what was alive. It's much harder to erase—let alone hold onto—an image of someone who once laughed or cried or shared something deep and personal with you. Is this how Bry felt after he lost his wife? Only a man with so much drive as Bry must've held onto some sort of violence inside him, as he said, to keep him sharp. On the other hand, why the hell does the dead care about us when all they care about is consuming the living?

I must follow Pelham's order and at least try to get some sleep.

When I make it back home, the training kicks back in. I spot the same headlights outside the ABC in my rear view mirror. I keep my holster unbuttoned as I pull into the driveway. I keep a close eye on the suspicious vehicle. I can't make out the make or model. It slows down in front of my house, then keeps moving.

My plans are completely foiled by the time I get settled inside my house. I place the vodka in the freezer and turn off every light in the house. I set booby traps around the doors, as well as windows. If someone enters, then I'll be the first to know. I make sure the safety is off and rest on the couch with my gun in hand. A part of me wants someone to try something while I'm sleeping just so I can release all of the built up anger I have growing inside me.

Try something.

I double-dog dare you.

☼☼☼

I have a dream that me and Bry are going over the case when all of a sudden something comes over me, and the next thing I know, I'm on top of Bry, strangling him with my hands. I can feel the air in his lungs bottling up in the base of his throat right below my clenched fists. His bloodshot eyes glaze over and he stops breathing, then I wake up on the couch, gasping. I look around in confusion. I find my gun lying on the floor. I must've dozed off sometime during the night. I check the time on the cable box. I've only gotten four hours of sleep—not even that long—which is more than I thought I got.

While coffee is brewing, I check the booby traps and they appear unaltered.

☼☼☼

Another one of those days that I wish would end before it began. The only thing keeping me going is the thought of Bry, so I start off my morning by paying a visit to Judith Ilderton's parents in Agatha.

Mrs. Ilderton finally answers the door, as I'm about to ring the doorbell for a third time. She looks at me strangely, as if she's turned off by my presence. We spoke briefly, but she remembers my face from our first introduction.

"Hello," she says shortly. "Can I help you?"

"Yes, Mrs. Ilderton, I just wanted to ask you some questions about your daughter, Judith."

"Have you found her?"

"No, ma'am."

Before I can squeeze out another word, she says that she has already talked to the police. The first "off" thing I notice about her are the dark bags underneath her eyes. She looks as if she could use some sleep.

Who can blame her?

I ask her, "May I come inside?"

She lets me inside without any complaint and asks me if I want a cup of coffee. I've already had two cups at my house and I could use another one—a really stiff one—to muscle my way through the soon-to-be awkward conversation. Three is my limit. After three, my whole body acts as if it's about to go on freak-out mode, especially if I haven't eaten that much for breakfast. I ate an apple strudel before I came.

"You take it with cream or sugar?" she asks as she shows me into the living room.

"Just cream will be fine. Thank you very much."

I mosey around the living room, looking over photos of the Ilderton family. Cute family. Very white. Very Republican. Judith, however, strikes me as the outsider of the family. The black sheep. I know a thing or two about being a black sheep. Ask my mother.

"Is this Judith's brother?" I ask.

Mrs. Ilderton leans away from the sink and pokes her head from the kitchen.

"Yes," she says. "That's my son, Abraham. He's two years older than Judith."

"Where is he right now?"

"He stayed the night with a friend. You know how kids his age are. Do you have any children?"

"No," I say. "I don't."

Mrs. Ilderton doesn't seem too concerned about her own child—both of them. Seems odd. She acts as if her daughter is spending the night with a friend and soon, she'll show up. Like all kids who go missing do that kind of stuff all the time without telling their parents. Sneaking out when parents are sleeping. Go to friend's house.

She returns to the living room with coffee.

"So, how are you holding up?" I ask her.

"I'm managing," she says, letting out a sigh—which I can't tell is from me bringing up the subject or if she really is tired and stressed-out. "You know this isn't the first time Judith's done this to us?" Anger climbs in her face, around both of her cheeks. "She pulled this little stunt last year. She went missing for two days."

"I take it she's going through that stage."

"What stage is that?"

She hands me the cup of tepid coffee.

"The rebellious stage," I say.

"She's not the type. She's ah. . . she's. . . " she hesitates again, as if she can't find the right word to explain her own daughter, ". . . she's different than most girls her age."

"How so?"

"Well, she doesn't have many friends for one. She's very reserved. Like her father. Doesn't do drugs. Doesn't drink. I take that back. She takes up more after her grandfather on my husband's side. He had the personality of a fish."

"What does Judith's father do for a living?"

"He's a Surveyor."

"Surveyor?" I say, sipping from the burnt coffee that tastes like diesel fuel. I clear my throat and try not to make much of a scene. "What's that? Like someone who examines land."

"That's correct," she says. "He just finished surveying that spot near Jacob's Crossing. Some big wig from 'up North' bought out the land," she says 'up North' as if she describing a cesspool. "The rumor has it that they're going to put a new shopping mall in there. Just what we need, am I right? More shopping malls. One of the reasons why Eddie and I moved to Agatha was to get away from that big city lifestyle. Here. It's simple. It's not complicated. People mind each other's business."

"Where are you originally from?"

"I was born and raised in a small town outside Dayton, Ohio. My family moved to North Carolina when I was around seven years old. I immediately fell in love with the Carolinas. I met Eddie while I was at a fraternity party in Cullowhee. "

"Cullowhee? Where's that?"

"It's small town outside Sylva. It's home of Western Carolina University."

"I see. So, how's the relationship between you and Judith?"

"Listen, Agent—"

"—Jones."

"Agent Jones," she says, "you appear to be a nice person. I went through all of this with the two police officers who came by the house yesterday. So, if you don't mind me asking, why are you really here?"

"Your daughter was rushed to the hospital on Wednesday. Is that correct?"

"Yes," she says. "That's correct. We think she had a seizure."

"Is she prone to seizures?"

"No. Never. Honestly, we don't know what it was. The doctors ran tests. They kept her overnight for observation. Tests came back fine. They sent her home the next day with a clean bill of health. They said they want to do a checkup later in the week or so."

"That's good news."

She says out of the corner of her mouth, "I hate to see the hospital bill. . . "

Her daughter was not only hospitalized, but has also been missing for forty-eight hours and she's complaining about the bill. Something else is on her mind. Her eyes don't lie.

I ask her, "Is something else going on that I should know about?"

"You want my honest opinion, Agent Jones?"

"Absolutely."

"I think she's doing it all for attention," she says with a sudden pause, as if she misspoke. "I mean, when things don't go Judith's way, she's been known to get back at Eddie and I. Last year, she wanted a new phone. I told her no. Next day, she didn't come home from school. Hours passed. She never came home for supper. All night I was worried sick, wondering if something had happened to her. I called police, even filed a missing persons report. Then, the next day she shows up like nothing ever happened. In my opinion, it was her way of giving us the middle finger."

"Well, kids that age are filled with a lot of emotion."

She says again from the corner of her mouth, "Sometimes I wonder if she feels anything at all."

"Where was Judith?"

"Where was she?"

"Where did she run off to before you filed the missing report?"

"She said she was staying at a friend's house, but I didn't believe her."

"Well, you must realize, Mrs. Ilderton, this isn't her getting back at you for whatever it is you did or didn't do to her. She witnessed a traumatic event, and I'm sure all of this is taking an extreme toll on her, as well as the other girls." I pause and think carefully about my next words. "Tell me. How was she acting before she went missing?"

"Agent Jones, have you found anything that would help me find my daughter?" she asks. "Any evidence suggesting that she might've been abducted?"

"None so far," I answer.

"Then, answer my question: 'Why would all of those girls on the bus go missing after all of this mess?'"

"The two coaches have also been uncounted for."

"It just seems fishy to me."

Something's fishy all right.

"You don't think it's strange, Agent Jones?"

I try to think of something diplomatic to say.

"I wouldn't call it 'strange,' but it's not uncommon. People do uncharacteristic things after experiencing trauma."

"Running away is *not* uncharacteristic of Judith."

"Say Judith did run away. Same with the rest of her team. Where do you think Judith would go?"

"I tell you the same thing I told the police. I have absolutely no clue."

✡ ✡ ✡

The old way of investigating is going nowhere. I need hard evidence that will stick to the wall.

So after the splendid conversation with the more than unhelpful Mrs. Ilderton, I decide to follow up on Bry's work and make a road trip. I drive west toward the Appalachian Mountains. Once I reach the town of Iredell, I stop at the local police station and talk to one of the detectives who was working the Kris Solles case and follow up on one of Bry's leads. The detective, a laidback man who acts as if he doesn't want to be there, tells me one of us—as in, another FBI agent—had already come by asking questions. I ask the detective if it was Bryan Corbin. He shakes his head no and tells me that it was some other guy.

"Dark skinned," he says, as he flips the black cocktail straw in his mouth and the other chewed side looks like the end of a tiny broomstick. "You know, like Middle Eastern."

I ask him if he got the agent's name but he doesn't recall.

"Do you remember what exactly this agent wanted?"

"He wanted everything I had on Mr. Solles."

"Everything?"

"Wasn't that much," he says and pulls up the file on Kris Solles on his computer.

"I don't know if this will help, but a 2004 Nissan Frontier was reported stolen not too far away from the scene of the crime. I have one witness identifying Mr. Solles from a photo I.D."

"What color was the truck?"

He looks at the computer screen.

"Silver," he says.

✡ ✡ ✡

I leave the station and stop by the convenient store where the clerk, Melvin Gaffney, was allegedly gunned down by

Solles. I investigate the area, ask the locals if they knew Mr. Gaffney. Most of the people who knew him said he was a simple man with a simple life. A man in the wrong place at the wrong time. I continue to ask around—mostly keeping a low profile and asking passing civilians and motorists if they've been noticing anything out of the ordinary. Anything out of ordinary in a town like this would be headline news. One civilian tells me about some construction that's been going on these past couple of days and it has all the right qualities of "out of the ordinary." The civilian says, "Big ole trucks been zoomin' on by." With a swollen, arthritic finger, he motions at the road in front of the convenient store. "One of 'em damn near ran me over da otha day."

"Is that so?"

"Yes, ma'am," he says.

I take a mental note of the civilian's observations and head west until I reach a sketchy road with a heavily guarded fence. Two armed men are standing post outside the gate. They're wearing shades and camo jackets, as if they're hunting deer; however, they don't look at all like hunters. I know the type. At the Academy, I started a close relationship with a woman who went by the name of Sara Bradford. Last time we talked, she was working a nice, cozy analyst job in Baltimore. When we were doing the daily grind in Quantico, Sara used to talk a lot about her family back home, as in Clemson, South Carolina. Her father was a hunter and his father before him was a hunter and so on. Me, being a city girl, never liked the type—actually, I despised any individual who killed animals for fun, even if he or she was trying to control the animal population or kill coyotes just because. Sara had frequently talked about a certain type of hunter, trophy hunter, which her father was not. He was the other type, the meat hunter. Whatever her father shot, he ate. Grilled it. Stewed it. Sautéed it. I guess I could respect that about her father, me not being much of a meat eater, but still, I'll eat chicken from time to time. So, I mean, someone had to kill it before it wound up on my plate.

Someone had to do all the dirty work that goes into preparing a meal. She'd go on for hours talking about hunting, what her father caught that weekend, and she'd go into freakishly extensive detail and paint a vivid image of her father and men like her father. So, based on what Sara had told me about the hunter, I had a solid grasp on why exactly they did what they did or how they acted, what they looked like, straight down to their posture.

Even though these men may dress like a typical hunter—either trophy or meat hunter—they look like neither.

Both men leave their post. They could be military in the way they carry themselves in a stern business-like vibe, but I don't know. One of them walks to one side of my car and the other approaches the driver side in a flanking position.

"This is a restricted area, ma'am."

"I'm sorry," I say. "I'm looking for Webster Hill."

"Sorry," he says. "Can't help you."

"Thanks anyway."

Not too long ago—actually, the same day Mr. Gaffney was killed—there was a wild fire not too far from here. The fire was contained within two days.

Again, the training kicks in. Something's not right about this place. I do a U-turn and keep driving until I reach a side road.

I park the car on the side of the road and check the map. A large question mark is written exactly in the spot where the two men were guarding the fence. Why would Bry circle that one place on the map? What did he know? What did he uncover? Solles was spotted in the vicinity. I need to find out what's going on behind that fence.

✪ ✪ ✪

For the rest of the trip, I decide its best to go on foot. I grab my bookbag with snacks and water and start to hike through the woods. I don't have much cover since most of the trees have been stripped thin. I spot the same two armed men at a distance and make sure to stay out of sight as I proceed from this point forward.

I pass a yellow sign posted on a tree: PRIVATE PROPERTY. NO TRESPASSING.

After about a half of a mile in, I reach a mangled barb-wire fence.

I squeeze my body through the fence and remove my gun from my holster. Some of the trees are black with soot.

The farther I walk, the blacker the trees get.

I'm getting close.

✪ ✪ ✪

The sunlight momentarily breaks through all of the gray above; and in that moment right before the sun hides behind the thick clouds, I catch a glimmer of light in the corner of my eye. I follow the glimmer to a wristwatch underneath the charred wood and broken tree branches. The watch is similar to the one those two wannabe hunters guarding the gate were wearing. Droplets of dried blood are caked over the screen. I pocket the wristwatch.

I keep moving forward until the woods finally open up and reveal a spread of land roughly cut out in a circle. A building used to reside here. All that's left is mostly rubble, bricks and mortar, steel beams warped and bent like clothes hangers.

Whatever was here has been demolished.

*Big ole trucks*, I remember the civilian's words. All of that construction and noise. All that "out of the ordinary" stuff.

I locate the tracks of what looks like a bulldozer, as well as two sets of tire tracks of what looks like the tires of a dump truck. The tracks are concentrated mostly around the empty space in the middle of the land. All of the tracks lead to a dirt road, possibly the same road leading toward that gate.

I pull out my phone and start taking photos of the site.

As I'm taking photos with my phone, I hear the *snap* of a tree branch!

Following the noise are the sounds of crisp leaves rustling around in the woods.

I track down the sounds and notice a deer standing statue-like not too far away. It's looking directly at me.

As I'm inching my way closer to the deer, I notice a dark indention on its side. A wound perhaps?

I stop and take a couple of photos of the deer with my phone. I switch my phone to video and record the deer as I cautiously approach it. I get a much closer look at the side of its body. I realize—after a thorough study—that the deer has no side. The entire right side of its body is completely missing. Part of its ribcage is exposed. It appears as it had a sore and that sore is starting to eat away at its body like a resilient infection. I immediately think of radiation exposure and then those guys in the hazmat suits at the blast site—who were they really working for?

Can what happened here be related to what happened in Burbane? What's the correlation?

The deer's ears suddenly twitch. It starts breathing faster and faster. Before I can take another step, it's gone. It's just a black woman. Why you so scared, deer?

The first thing that immediately comes to mind is Chernobyl. All of the radiation and the effects it had on its wildlife. I watched a documentary on *Nature* Channel about the mutations brought on by high levels of radiation.

If that's true, then why hasn't it had any effect on me?

I don't realize what the deer is running away from until I glance over my shoulder and witness the same man from before aiming an assault rifle directly at me.

I raise one of my arms in the air. I keep the other hand holding the gun down by my side.

I hear similar sounds from before, leaves rustling.

Footsteps!

As I'm about to turn my shoulder, I hear the voice of a man behind me: "Drop the weapon."

I drop my gun to the ground as the two men approach me from my front and my rear. Both of them have guns on me. I have nowhere to run.

"What'd you say? Another journalist, huh?"

"Nah," one of the men says as he's checking out my backside. "She's way too spunky. She might be one of those environmentalist, you know?"

I keep my hand in the air as the other man, the one with the scraggly beard, checks my pockets.

He finds my wallet. Opens it. He laughs while the other one looks me over with utter amused expression on his face.

"What do you know? She's with the F-B-I. You're a long way from Raleigh, Agent Jones?"

He doesn't check the rest of my body. Soon, he will pay dearly. But I make sure to keep them in suspense.

"I like that name, Agent Jones. It has a certain roll to it, don't it? Like a song." The man starts singing: "Agent Jones! Agent Jones! She put quite a shiver in my bones! Ms. Agent Jones!"

I turn my shoulder and find the other one staring at my ass as if it's a succulent prime rib. I'll remember that for later.

"Let's just call this a misunderstanding," I say, keeping my calm. "Let me go, and I won't tell a soul about this place."

"And what do you think *this place* is, Agent Jones?"

"You tell me."

"If I told you, then I'd have to kill you."

The other sketchy man standing behind me giggles.

"Isn't that right, Matty?"

I turn to the man behind me and he's bobbing his head.

"Oh yeah," he says and he starts licking his crapped lips. "We'd have to kill you, but with you," he looks me over again, "we can make exceptions."

The other man brushes the hair from my eyes, then takes a smell of my neck.

"I can smell you from a mile away," he says as he takes the barrel of the rifle and runs it up my abdomen, then my chest, then my throat until the barrel comes to rest underneath my chin.

"Poor Agent Jones," he whispers. "I admire your tenacity. But I'm afraid we have our orders; however, my friend here, Matty, has this thing. It's like ah, you know, a sickness."

I wait for my opportunity.

The other man, Matty, grabs me from behind and throws me to the ground.

"Do your thing, Matty Boy, then I get sloppy seconds."

My window of opportunity starts to open.

Poor Matty Boy makes the mistake of tossing his gun aside and starts to unbuckle his pants.

I backpedal and play the role of the helpless woman with a hole between her legs.

"Please. Don't hurt me."

"I'm not going to hurt you, Agent Jones." He gets on top of me and starts kissing me. I turn my head away in disgust, but he still kisses the side of my face. He grabs a handful of my hair and seethes in my ear, "You hush now, my black angel. . . "

As he starts to take off my pants, I find my opportunity.

"Let me do it for you. . . "

I unbuckle the belt, then unbutton my pants.

As I bend my knees upward and start to remove my pants from my body, I reach for the gun strapped to my ankle and roll over on my back. I withdraw the gun. I shoot the man in the chest! The other one opens fire on me, but I use Matty as a human body shield as he lunges forward and aim over his shoulder. I prop my shooting arm on his shoulder and shoot the other man dead!

It all happens so quickly.

Three seconds—max!

Once they're both alive and ready to bust a nut and then they're taking their final breaths. No time to think, only react. I'm alive. All thanks to my training.

☼ ☼ ☼

I make it back to my car all in one piece. I can't even think straight. I don't even know what happened. My hands can't stop shaking. I'm tempted to go to Pelham and tell him about everything that happened. A part of me thinks—I take that back—a part of me *knows* Pelham won't believe me. He's going to start asking questions about why I was out there to begin with. He'll ask for my two most precious things, both my badge and my gun.

I have no other choice than to keep my mouth shut.

Right now, I'm on my own.

☼ ☼ ☼

I need to find out more about Solles and what he was doing all the way out here. Since both of his parents died after he came back home from doing a tour in Afghanistan and he has no siblings, I drive to his hometown in Mercy, Texas. I pay a visit to his high school, Red Springs. I inform the principal about Solles and tell him that I'm trying to track down some of his old high school friends or people who knew him. The principal has only been at the school for two years and I don't expect him to be any help. I pull up as many records as I can from the four years Solles went to school here, starting with the yearbooks. I come across a photo of Solles and another young man named Beaumont Lafel. His nickname is Bo—what are the odds? The bottom of the photo reads: "Kris and Bo experimenting with Bunsen burners." I look up Bo's name in the index and find two other photos with Bo and his friend, Solles, standing in the background. They both played on the football team. Solles played quarterback and Bo was a wide receiver. They clearly hung out in class and played together outside of class. To me, the two appear as if they were close friends. It's not a break in the case, but it's a good place to start.

✲ ✲ ✲

I look up Bo in the yellow pages and find just three Beaumont Lafels living in the Mercy area. I call each one of them. The first Beaumont had "passed away in a car accident," according to his mother. The second one is in jail. The third one: jackpot. I ask Bo if we can get together and talk about Kris. He tells me to stop by his work.

✲ ✲ ✲

Bo works at a family owned business called Bo's Auto-Repair. His father, Bo Senior, handed down the family business to his son, Bo Junior. Business isn't exactly booming, but it sure is running like a fine-tuned instrument. From what I've gathered so far, it seems like a tight knit community. Each employee couldn't be any nicer toward me and even though the Southern charm can only go so far I don't mind the attention.

When I finally meet Bo, he's doing paperwork in his office in the back of the shop. I do the formal introduction and display the badge. Surprisingly, he doesn't act displeased by my company, rather quite the opposite. I start to wonder several things: first, I wonder if he doesn't see too many women my age nowadays, especially women with badges—after all it's fair to say that he is a handsome man in a ruggedly cowboy sort of way—and second, I wonder if I'm not the only face from the Triangle that has paid him a visit. I ask Bo about Kris, but he refers to Kris as Brixx, as in Brixx with double x's. I ask about the nickname, how he got a name like Brixx.

"He was a bricklayer back in the day." Makes sense. "He'd throw up them houses like it was nuttin'. Somehow the name just got branded on him. Everybody 'round town know him as Brixx."

"Fitting."

"So, how can I help you, ma'am?"

Lately, I've been called ma'am.

Am I that old, really?

Or, is it just Southern hospitality coming out in full force?

I tell him that I'm looking for Brixx. He knows about what happened. He tells me that Brixx is an innocent man. He's a hundred and ten percent certain that Brixx isn't the man who shot Melvin Gaffney. We talk a little about Brixx, his family, when he left Mercy, if he ever came back. Last time Bo saw Brixx was two years ago when he came back home to bury his father.

"The other day," he says, "two men came by here, asking about Brixx."

"They weren't FBI by any chance. Were they?"

"No. Honestly, I don't know exactly who they was but they sure as hell ain't FBI."

"Can you remember what they looked like?"

"Two men," he says simply. "White folks. One had a scar on his face, looked like he meant business. I told him I didn't want any troubles. So, I gone ahead and told the two exactly what I be telling you. Then, they went on their way."

"That's it? They didn't leave behind a card or number?"

"No, ma'am."

He's a gentleman. I give him that.

"Agent Jones. Please."

"Sorry. Didn't mean to offend."

An awkward silence comes between us.

I immediately break it with a question: "Was Brixx seeing anyone in Mercy?"

"You mean like a lady friend?"

"Yes. You can say that."

"Brixx saw 'lots' of ladies. Last time I saw him, he mentioned this one in particular. Felicia was her name. She was from North Carolina."

"Did this Felicia have a last name?"

"Well, I don't remember exactly. But I know she was definitely from North Carolina because he mentioned something about the two of them getting back from Grandfather Mountain a couple of weeks ago."

"We've been a great help Mr. Lafel—"

"—Bo," he says and reaches out his leathery hand. I shake it. "You can call me just Bo."

I leave my card with Bo.

"Just in case you remember anything else."

He grabs the card.

"Sure thing."

I say so long to Bo.

Hopefully, it's not a final goodbye.

✪ ✪ ✪

After a much-needed deliberation, I decide to stay the night in Mercy and let everything that I absorbed today fester over until I can come up with a more sensible plan of action. I buy a room with two beds at a cheap motel right off the highway and make sure to keep an extremely low profile. I still have to answer for two murders that were carried out in self-defense. I still have to find Solles. I believe Solles is the key to unlocking the mystery surrounding what was going on in the mountains.

✪ ✪ ✪

I grab a hat and step out for a minute to grab a drink. I pass a couple of dive-like bars within walking distance from my motel—they got "lots" here in Mercy. I've been asking around all day about Solles and I don't want to draw any more attention than I already have. Plus, I'm not in the mood to be talking to drunks. Being around people in general right now would not be good for anybody. So, I stop at the nearest liquor store and grab a much-needed drink and take it back with me to my room. I don't even realize how angry I am until after my second pour. Alcohol has a keen way of bringing out the worst in me, especially whenever I'm feeling a little on edge before I have a drink. Alcohol highlights emotions—actually, it spotlights them in the most hideous light. It's like standing underneath a fluorescent light and that light exposes all of the blemishes on your face, every scar or wrinkle, every unwanted mole. Alcohol is the fluorescent light of my existence. I say three is enough. Three pours turns into four. Four turns into five. By the sixth pour, I'm stumbling all over the room like an idiot.

I spend about an hour talking smack to the TV. I should turn off the TV and call it a night; go straight to bed, get some much-needed sleep.

Instead, the fluorescent light shines down on my sorry ass and exposes every shade and shadow of the human disease: the annoyance, the anger, the rage. I have so much rage clawing around inside me, so much that it feels as if it's a mini-me kicking around in there, trying to break free. Another pour. I'm loose. My nerves are tight. I want to fight, but the only person I can fight is myself. Boredom sets in as I flip through the media circus shows, then the disgust sets in and partners with the anger, then the loathing.

I keep flipping through each channel, attempting to rid the thought of what happened in the mountains. I had no other choice. They were going to rape me. Who knows what they would've done after that? Kill me? The thought of that disgusting man—Matty—and his little redneck pecker being inside me forces yet another pour. Then another. I can't stop thinking of Matty, his body on top of mine. I want to block him out but I can't. The more I think of Matty I think of Bo—my Bo. The thought alone of Bo on top of me causes my skin to heat. I'm back in the woods, about to be raped but not by Matty or that other strange man. Bo's raping me. I tell him to stop but he does the opposite. Emotion floods over me, the anger squashed by every shade of sadness. I curl myself up into a ball on the bed, wrap covers around my body, and I try so hard to cry myself to sleep but for some reason my tears have all but dried out.

☼ ☼ ☼

My phone is first to wake me up. Next is a streak of sunlight lazily pouring in though the crack in the curtain.

Hungover, I sit up and look around the room, wondering how I got here, wondering how I got so messed up last night.

I check the phone. I don't know the number. It's a local number, though.

"Hello," I say, the dull ache in my head starting to weigh down my eyes.

"Agent Jones?"

"Speaking."

"This is Bo."

"Who?"

"Beaumont. We talked yesterday."

"Yes. How can I help you, Beaumont?"

"Am I calling at a bad time?"

I check the time. It's a little after eight-thirty.

"No," I say.

"Rosado. Felicia Rosado was her name."

"Who?"

"Brixx's girlfriend. Her name came to me last night, but I didn't want to disturb you."

"No. It's fine."

"Anyway, I believe she was from Asheville."

"Asheville, North Carolina?"

"I believe so."

"That's all?"

"That's all."

"Thank you very much, Beaumont. Really, it means a lot."

I write down the name, Felicia Rosado, on a piece of paper with a motel pen and hang up before Bo can say goodbye.

I shut my eyes for about an hour or so, most of the time spent thinking about Bo. I don't even realize I had a conversation with him until I finally gather enough energy to roll out of bed. I come across a piece of paper with Felicia's full name and then the empty flask on the floor.

How much did I drink last night?

☼ ☼ ☼

I can't hold much food inside my stomach. Even a sip of water is a challenge. I leave the motel and bum Aspirin from the motel clerk. He feels my pain.

Once I'm on the road, I give Agent Faraday a call. A couple of months ago I gave him two free tickets to a Warhawks game. At the time, I was going through this phase where I wanted to at least make an effort to heal the wounds I had created in my relationship with Bo. In the brutal end, doubts won. I lost my spine and got cold feet. I knew Faraday was a fan. The man would never shut the hell up about his favorite player, Sebastian "The Fist" Ames. So, I gave him the tickets. He said that he'd owe me a favor. His words. When someone owes me a favor, I always hold onto it like a rain check.

☼ ☼ ☼

Agent Faraday calls me back as I'm about to cross the Mississippi border.

"I narrowed down the search and found a one Felicia Rosado who lives in Asheboro, North Carolina. Could be her?"

Asheville and Asheboro.

The two are easy to get mixed up.

Even Steven gives me the address.

Now, we're both even.

☼ ☼ ☼

I drive through the night and make it to Asheboro in good timing. I locate Ms. Rosado's address. I check my gun before exiting the car and make sure the safety is off. I ring twice, but I receive no answer each time. So, I resort to knocking. I make my presence known by informing whoever may be inside that I'm with the Federal Bureau of Investigation. Again, no answer. Faraday mentioned to me that Ms. Rosado owned her own business. Stone fabrication. She could be at work, but I decide to check out the place anyway. Might as well. Since I'm here. I first start with the garage and peek through the dusty windows. I notice the same silver Nissan truck that was reported missing in Iredell. I take out my gun. I don't bother calling for backup. I remind myself I'm on my own. I take out a pick from my back pocket and pick the lock to the backdoor.

When I'm inside the house, I make sure to let my presence known once more.

"Ms. Rosado," I say, "this is Agent Jones of the FBI."

I check the entire house. I check every room, but I don't find any sign of Felicia or Kris. I check the name on the mail and make sure I'm in the right house.

As I'm searching the house, including the garage where the Nissan truck has been completely stripped of all identification, I can't help but notice all the cleanliness of the house. The house appears way too clean. It even smells too clean. I check the sink and find a coffee mug with the smudge of pink lipstick on the brim. The mug is partially filled with cold coffee.

Once I finish my search, I grab a photo of Felicia in a picture frame and take it with me.

✿ ✿ ✿

On the way to Bry's apartment, I get a call from Faraday. He tells me that a body was found not too far away from Ms. Rosado's house. One of the local police officers believes that it's Felicia. He claims he knew her; however, they're still waiting on her next of kin to identify the body. The local authorities are certain that it's her."

"Where is she?" I ask Faraday.

"She's currently at a morgue not too far from Asheboro."

✪ ✪ ✪

I stop by the morgue and check on the body. When the pathologist reveals the body, my stomach churns from the sight of the wounds. I swear, as long as I've been working with the FBI, I've never seen a body as mutilated as this one. I use the photo of Felicia to compare the body. Yeah. It's her all right.

"Who the hell did this to her?" I ask the pathologist.

"It's not a question of who, Agent Jones, but what."

"You think a wild animal did this to her?"

He points at the lacerations around her arms.

"These right here, they're defensive wounds. She was trying to shield her face—"

"—From what?"

"It's hard to say right now—"

"—If you had to guess. . . "

"Mountain lion perhaps," he says, throwing the name out there. "The claw marks are much too narrow for a black bear. Whatever killed her wasn't—how should I put this—hungry. See." He points to bite marks around her jugular. "Whatever the creature was, it wasn't messing around. It saw this young woman as a threat. It went straight for the kill. It's as simple as that."

He covers the body back up.

"It doesn't make any sense, though."

"Sure it does. Young woman jogging in the middle of the woods, had ear buds stuck in her ears. She was completely defenseless. She was completely oblivious to her surroundings. You know, some of the boys down at the station think it's the leopard that escaped from the zoo."

"Leopard?"

"Black panther, actually."

"Are they known to attack people?"

"No. Not really. They're extremely elusive creatures from what I've read; but, nevertheless, I believe if any animal feels threatened, it has every right to defend itself."

"She doesn't seem like much of a threat."

"Maybe not to you, but to it, that's another story."

☼ ☼ ☼

Felicia Rosado is dead. Her many wounds suggest that she was mauled by a wild animal—possibly the black panther that escaped from the Asheboro Zoo. The evidence suggests that she was attacked while she was jogging through the trails. As far as the Nissan Frontier, I'm still not certain that the truck is stolen based off the lack of evidence.

Unless I can pull a fingerprint off the truck, then all I'm doing right now is trying to find a conclusion based off pure speculation.

I don't have enough hard evidence to bring to Pelham.

Not just yet.

Right now, the search to find Kris Solles has gone cold.

☼ ☼ ☼

Before heading back home, I grab a bite to eat. Fast food. Cheap. In the drive-thru lane, I order a number one combo with a large lemonade. You can never go wrong with a number one—that's why they call it a number one. After I pay for my food, I pull into a desolate parking lot where I park the car and begin to mix the rest of the vodka from the other day into my drink. As I'm about to dig into to my cheeseburger, some jerk pulls up behind me with halogen headlights. I put the burger aside and shield my eyes from the bright light beaming through the rear view mirror. A dark figure suddenly appears in my blind spot. I remove the gun from my holster and conceal the gun in my lap while a man stands outside the passenger side of my car. He's not making any sudden movements. I can't get a good look at his face—at least not until he leans down into my range of vision and reveals a scar in the shape of a lightning bolt running down the side of his face. I immediately think of Bo, the other one, what he said back in Mercy. The stranger politely knocks on my window. I roll down the window, still ready to plug him if he tries anything. I ask him if he needs any help.

"Out of the car," he demands.

"Excuse me," I say, as my finger touches the trigger.

"I'm not going to say it again."

I open the car door; and as I'm about to turn, another man steps in front of me.

"The gun please," he asks, as he holds out his hand.

I pause.

"Now," he says.

I turn to the other man, the one with the scar. He unpeels part of his coat and exposes the gun that he's carrying.

"Don't make this any harder than it has to be," he says and points to the SUV. "He just wants to have a word."

"Who?" I ask.

The man doesn't respond. He's still holding out his hand, waiting for me to hand over my gun.

I hand it over.

"Thank you," he says.

The scar-faced man pats me down for other weapons. He finds the sassy one on my ankle, the one who doesn't take shit from anybody, then hands it to the other man. The sight of another man touching my weapons only feeds the rage.

Once I'm free of my weapons, he escorts me to the SUV.

I notice two other cars—black, tinted windows—parked not too far away.

Both cars have their engines running and they're both facing the SUV at an angle. He opens the backseat door for me. I get inside. He closes the door behind me. Seated inside is a man pushing sixty or seventy—I can't quite put a number on his age for his quite dapper and well-groomed.

"Looks like we're both having trouble tracking down the same man."

Before I can find the words to speak, he turns to me and smiles.

"I must apologize for the disturbance, Agent Jones. Gerald isn't much of what I like to call a 'people's person.' Regardless of Gerald's lack of personality, he gets the job done and that's all that matters. Right—"

"—Who are you?"

"I'm the man who knows how to get things done and I'm here to make you a proposition, Agent Jones, one that will very well change the course of mankind as we know it."

What the hell is this guy smoking?

He looks me straight in the eyes and it feels as if he's looking right through me.

"After all," he says arrogantly, his forehead slanted downward, his eyes sharp like a snake, "what other choice do you have? You killed two of my men. They were loyal; and now, they're dead. With that said, your compliance is the least you can do—"

"—I was defending myself."

"You were trespassing on private property."

"What property? What used to be there before it was torn down—"

"—Not torn down," he says. "Burned down. Before it was destroyed, it used to be a research facility called Mount Olympus."

"Mount Olympus?"

He lets out a heavy sigh.

"You see, Agent Jones, I believe you and I have a lot in common—"

"—You don't know me."

"I know enough. Daughter of a full-time drug addict and a hospital clerk. Your younger brother, Jonah, was shot by a stray bullet when he was only an infant which resulted in your family being split apart."

The sound of his name lands an uppercut to my stomach. I'm doing all I can to myself from lashing out at this arrogant son of a bitch.

"Then," he says, reeling me back into the conversation, "at the age of ten, a man gunned down your father in the street, left him to die. Till this day, his murder has gone unsolved. You decided to dedicate your life to the law. You were Valedictorian at Lethem High. You did so well in your class that you were given an academic scholarship to the University of Virginia where you majored in criminal justice—"

"—Anybody can find a person's background on the Internet."

"Really? What was the name your father used to call you whenever you would frequently visit him while he was in jail? Was it 'Little Bear'?"

Nobody knows that name besides me and my father.

"What do you want from me?"

"Agent Jones, I admire your passion to find the truth and I believe that passion can be useful not only to me, but also the FBI. Just think of it like this: You'll be doing the entire world a—how do I say—quite a favor. You'll practically be in their debt as long as this rock keeps spinning. There is a man who you've been trying to track down—"

"—Kris Solles."

"That's correct. It is important that this man be found."

"Why? So, you can kill him?"

"My interests in finding Mr. Solles are of no concern to you, Agent Jones. However, I reassure you that you will be greatly rewarded for your services. So, what will it be? How would feel about creating an alliance?"

"Alliance?" I say. "What is this? A joke? *Who the hell are you?*"

"My name is Baron Orwell," he says, reaching out his hand to shake mine, "but you can call me Barry."

I don't shake his hand. I don't plan on it either.

I throw a pop question at him, hoping for him to take the bite.

"*Who* took the girls? *Where* are they?"

"I don't know where they are, Agent Jones," he says, "but I might know someone who does. If you and I can work together as a team, we can find the people responsible for their disappearance."

"And who are they? These people?"

"These *people*? I'm afraid that they don't qualify as people, Agent Jones. They would have to be human first of all." He extends his hand once more, his eyes flick downward at his hand. "But we'll get into all of that some other time," he says as he holds out his hand. "So, what do you say, Rashida? Are you in or are you out?"

## 6. THE CURATOR / ROGER

ONCE the first assessment has concluded, Sy pays me a visit to my office as I'm going through the footage on the recent assessment.

He has a look on his face.

"Infected by an unknown virus that—if not contained— would create a massive ripple effect throughout the country, then the world?" says Sy, grinning like that Cheshire cat from *Alice in Wonderland.* "Nice touch."

"A little too much?"

"It's perfect," says Sy. "You think he bought it, though?"

I stop the video and turn to Sy.

"For now," I say, "I don't know. Maybe. If we keep telling them that they're sick, then sooner or later they'll start believing it. I read an article on a controversial scientist who went by the name Floyd Haggard—"

"—I've heard about Haggard. He was the definition of a mad scientist. Went to jail for life."

"Have you heard about the Monkey Trials?"

"Briefly."

"Well, it was pretty simple. He would place two objects in front of the monkey, a banana and a knife. Naturally, monkey grabs banana. Eats banana. However, every time the monkey grabbed the banana, it would be shocked by an electrical current. The voltage would be no greater than, say, two to five thousand volts—almost similar to what any dog would receive through an electrical fence—not enough to kill the monkey but just enough to scare the living shit out of it."

"Sounds barbaric."

"To us, yes, but I guess when you're trying to rewrite the brain for the sake of science, then sacrifices have to be made."

"Every time the monkey reached for the banana, it would receive an electrical shock. Days later, the monkey eventually caught on. It finally grabbed the knife from the table and you know what happened?"

"What?"

"Nothing. Nothing happened."

"So, then it starved to death. Without food, it wouldn't be able to survive—"

"—No," I say. "Later that day, another monkey was found in its cage. Dead. The other monkey had eaten it."

"That's a dark story."

"Tell me about it."

"What are we going to do with this one?" asks Sy, pointing at one of the monitors. The surveillance camera shows Haley pounding at the door and screaming to the top of her lungs.

"Give her time. She'll settle down."

"And if she doesn't."

"She will."

"Shouldn't we give her something to calm her down?"

"If Frankie is hiding inside her, Sy, then she will be harder to detect. We can't mask her. We need her to surface. Naturally—"

"—She's scared."

"Of course she is, Sy."

"Well, I think we need to reassure her that everything is going to okay."

"We will. All we can do now is wait."

"We don't exactly have the luxury of time, Roger."

"We can buy time. We still have enough money leftover from Baron's wonderful contribution."

"And what exactly happens when all the money runs out? What's the end game, Roger?"

"We'll find another pretentious power hungry philanthropist who wants to change the world. It's not like the world is running out of a short supply of assholes." Sy's growing impatient with me. It's understandable. I pat Sy on the shoulder and reassure him. "Have patience, Sy. We're exactly where we need to be." I step out into the hallway and motion to Sy.

"More coffee."

"Yeah," says Sy, looking down at his empty cup. "Sure."

Sy and I grab a cup of coffee in the break room.

✪ ✪ ✪

Log Entry #27: *It's been three days since the assessments have begun and I haven't found any significant evidence indicating Frankie has laced herself into any of the twelve key witnesses who were on the school bus during June's meltdown. So far from what I've gathered through around-the-clock observation, each one of the candidates' behaviors have remained relatively stable—except for the occasion outburst. It's also come to my attention that Frankie had previously tried to walk inside the body of a man before the showdown in Burbane. His name was Ramon López, according to Fahim. His body was discovered in his car on the side of the road. Every single orifice of his body, including his face, had been completely fried like an electrical socket. Coroners said his eyeballs had completely melted inside the sockets of his skull. I recall several test subjects a couple of years ago experiencing similar symptoms; however, they were—more or less—accidents that could've been avoided. In other words, it was Frankie's way a giving Orwell the big bird. I've also learned that Candidate #2, Rhea Johnson, has developed an unusual stutter, which may be due to her confused state; nonetheless, it definitely warrants further evaluation. Candidate #11, Stewart Tabby, appears to be showing signs of anxiety in his cell, but it's nothing out of the ordinary. There is still a chance that Frankie will rebel if she takes over their bodies. Right now, it's fair to say that the candidates don't know what's going on, but soon they will and it's my job to make sure nothing tragic happens to them. After all, Frankie is my sole responsibility.*

✡ ✡ ✡

Sy catches me watching him as he carefully watches the monitor of Judith's cell.

"What is it, Sy?"

"She reminds me a lot of Carolyn," says Sy.

"She's probably around her age. Am I right?"

"About."

"Sy?"

"Yes, Roger," says Sy, as he pulls his eyes from Judith.

"Don't make this any harder than it should be."

Sy remains quiet. I nod at Judith sitting in a fetal position in the cell. She's staring at the floor. Not moving.

"Based off your assessment with her, where does she stand among the others?"

"She's a lot more mature than the other girls, that I know."

"Besides that, anything else that would suggest she's been compromised?"

"I think she's telling the truth."

"You think? You're not in the business of guessing."

"I know you don't have any kids. I admire your devotion to her. I really do. But do you ever regret it, not having any children?"

"Not a day goes by that I regret not having kids."

"Well," says Sy, as he tries to add some comical relief to an otherwise tense situation, "I hope you brought plenty of Aspirin with you."

Sy attempts to exit but I pull him back into the office with a question that's been heavy on my mind for the past twenty-four hours.

"She seemed anxious," says Sy.

"Anxious about what?"

"It was one of those gut instinct-things that she has from time to time. A foresight. I don't know. You know how she gets?"

"What did you two talk about?"

"Talk about?"

"Did you not talk to her before she escaped?"

"Yes."

"Well, the monitor was turned off."

He takes a step closer to me, his dull eyes narrowing in concentration.

"Where are going with this, Roger?"

"I don't know," I tell him.

I don't know where I'm going with the subject. What I do know is that Sy's hiding something from me.

☼ ☼ ☼

"Why books, Roger?" asks Fahim.

"Distraction," I say, as the both of us carefully watch Candidate #5 checking out the library in the first main room. She appears interested in the books, however, unsure whether or not to read them. "Sometimes, distraction fills in the gaps of people's lives or even blocks the things that they chose to forget. When you look at each cell, what do you see?"

"It's just a cell," says Fahim.

"Exactly. Like a prison cell, it's empty. The walls are pale. They're as blank as an artist's canvas. Nothing to do put think and stare at the reflections of your own skull. The very foundation of what makes us 'us' is molded around the decisions we've made throughout our existence, and these decisions—whether right or wrong—have either stirred us in a direction of self-growth or a direction of self-destruction. What if we lost the ability to control our own decisions, to shape our future? What if someone else was pulling our strings? What if we—like these people—were trapped in a confined space with only ourselves? Would we learn to love ourselves? Or, would we hate ourselves? Would we turn into nothing more than a stranger? Would we go mad? *Now,* if Frankie is hiding inside one of these bodies, then the cells will help bring out shades of Frankie." I show Fahim the monitors of the other candidates' cells. Lastly, I point at the two main rooms. "Then we put them in here, a room filled with one distraction after another. If Frankie decides to use one of these stories as her own, then we'll know by the candidate's answers to each one of our questions. We'll know who's lying based on, not only his or her previous statements to the FBI, but also from the personal articles that we've collected."

"Their statements could change based on further memories or even if it's as banal as the change in environment."

"If these candidates lied in their original statements, more than likely they'll stick to their story. The books, however, are there to guide Frankie, to inspire her, to help Frankie manipulate the thoughts of the host, to confuse her from fiction to reality. After a while, she'll learn how to fill in the gaps on her own."

"Then, what about the polygraphs?" asks Fahim. "If she can manipulate all the data, then wouldn't she just change the results according to the candidates' answers?"

"Distraction, Fahim," I say, pointing to my temple. "Remember?"

☼ ☼ ☼

Rhea's assessment is, by far, the toughest one so far. The barrette brought a flood of memories.

The first time I met Frankie she was wearing a red barrette in her hair. Her hair was jet black and shined like diamonds whenever the sun hit it. She had a bob cut, which made her appear much younger than her age suggested. She was thirty-seven years old at the time—I just turned twenty-five—but with the hairdo aside, she appeared at least ten years younger. I didn't know it at the time—and even if I did, I still would've stayed with her—but soon I'd come to learn that age would no longer play a factor in the love I had for Frankie. Hard to love someone who didn't carry any emotion, pain, or sorrow, none of the emotions that humans constantly experience everyday; somehow, I knew deep within her, she had the capacity to love. I showed her a way. I showed her what could be gained from love; and each and every day, I watched that red barrette slowly slip away from her hair.

After I wrap up the assessment, I decide to pay a visit to the blast site in Benjamin Creek. The place is still roped off from the public. The FBI, as well as Alamount County Sheriff's Department and the Burbane police, have dirtied up the entire scene with footprints. I search the scene for anything that can lead me closer to Frankie but end up coming short.

✪ ✪ ✪

When I get back to Four Lakes, I come across Sy in the media room. He's sitting in the chair, refreshing his mind with disease and violence. He says he only needs five more minutes, then he's good to go. I tell him to take all the time he needs. It's better safe than sorry.

✪ ✪ ✪

Log Entry #42: *Candidate #7, Haley Shapiro, tried to escape right before her assessment today. I put on the song "(Don't Fear) The Reaper" by Blue Oyster Cult through the loudspeaker. I thought it was not only a catchy song but also quite fitting, considering my history. Sy said that she saw the Chair. Just in case, we're going to keep her in the cell and skip evaluating her. If Frankie is, in fact, hiding inside Candidate #7, there is a possibility that she may come in contact with one of us. If that's the case, everything that we're doing will be for nothing. She will find out that everything that we're telling her is a lie. The virus. Everything. I must use extreme caution while dealing with Candidate #7.*

✡✡✡

I spend the rest of night going through old videos of June days after her transformation, mostly searching for any signs of disturbance—something I missed. I focus my attention on the last video, Test 8b, of THE AMPHIBIAN TESTS. First, I start with TEST SUBJECT FROG. In the video, two frogs sit in front of June, who makes contact by touching the back of the frog with her finger. All of a sudden, Frankie momentarily leaves June's body and laces herself into the other frog, Frog A, which, in return, begins to slowly consume Frog B, stretching and popping its jaw out of place similarly to the anaconda eating the deer in the other video.

Sy suddenly interrupts from behind, as I'm about to reach the gooey part.

"Jesus!"

"Sorry. I didn't know you were in here," says Sy, standing at the doorway.

He enters my office. Shuts the door behind him.

"Anything I can help you with, Sy?"

"I just wanted to let you know that Ms. Shapiro has been restrained."

I stop the video, but Sy doesn't follow up with any other comments. He sees that I'm busy; then he walks away. I suddenly stop Sy before he exits.

"Sy!"

"Yes, Roger."

"Do you remember anything else the day Frankie escaped? Anything unusual?"

"Why do you ask?"

"Just curious."

"No," says Sy, thinking. "Not that I remember. It felt like any other day." He takes a step back into my office. Leaves the door open. "What's on your mind, Roger?"

"You were the last person to see Doctor Lugosi before she escaped. Did she seem, I don't know, different?"

"She seemed fine to me."

"You sure?"

"Twice you've been on my back, Roger. What are you implying?"

"I'm just trying to put all the pieces together. It's just—what I don't understand is that if Baron wanted to stop funding us, if he thought it was necessary to cut us loose after all the research we gathered, why would he hire a team to try to take out his greatest investment? For example: If you invest all of your money into a product and over time that product doesn't live up to its fullest potential, why not just leave it alone? Why destroy it after all of the time and effort put into it?"

"Maybe he wasn't trying to destroy her," says Sy. "Maybe he was trying to set her free."

"I don't think so."

"Men like Baron Orwell don't care about people. Men like that would rather stand on top of a mountain while watching the valley burn below. Why? Superiority. *Control.* When a man doesn't have control, then everything can feel like chaos to him. Bottom line, Roger: we'll never have complete control over Frankie. We may think we do, but we were wrong about her. I mean, did you ever stop and question whether or not we were supposed to use Frankie for the greater good? What if her purpose has nothing to do with us? What if there is something else going on?"

"How can you say that after everything you've seen?"

"I'm just saying, Roger—"

"—What are you saying, Sy?"

"I'm saying she doesn't have the answers to life's greatest questions. She doesn't hold the key to our future. She's a freak of nature, Roger. Plain and simple—"

"—Watch it."

"Did you ever stop to think: *What if* there are no answers? What if we've spent all this time trying to seek an answer that doesn't exist? We had our chance, Roger."

The thought alone of what Sy is saying leaves me with no words.

"Did I ever tell you about the first time I met your father?"

Still, no words.

"Roger?"

"Yeah," I say, trying to hold myself together in front of Sy. "Africa, right?"

"That's right."

"*Briefly.*"

"In 1984," says Sy, as he leans up against the doorway, "the Americans dropped a bomb deep within the Congolese Rainforest in order to prevent a deadly outbreak from spreading throughout Central Africa. Never have I seen anything like it. The inhumanity. We ended up tracing the host to a ruthless regime called Kenwanawha. They were killing off their own people, 'depopulating,' through Entomological warfare, a type of biological warfare used to defeat enemies with insects used as vectors to infect enemies with deadly diseases. I was one of the lucky ones to evacuate before the bomb was dropped. I went back after everything was destroyed."

"Why'd you go back?" I ask.

"I don't know why I did," says Sy deep in thought. "I just had to. You spend months surrounded by these people. In a way, you grow to love them like family. So, I went back after nearly half of Zaire—which you may now know as the Democratic Republic of the Congo—was wiped out. That's when I saw them, the Reapers. They were burning the bodies of the ones who managed to survive. Women. Children. It didn't matter. Your father almost killed me, you know? He was a much older man at the time. Worn down by life. I saw pictures of him from when he was much younger. But the man I saw looked like a stranger—"

"—What's the point of the story, Sy?"

"My point: nature has this unique way of correcting itself. And those who get in the way of nature will feel its wrath."

"What's that supposed to mean?" I ask. "You think nature chose my father? Is that it? You think it was nature getting back at him?"

"Your father was a complicated man."

"Don't talk about him like you know him—"

"—And you did?"

I can feel my cheeks turning red with anger. I try to hold myself back from lashing out at Sy.

"If Frankie is supposed to live—if nature really wants her to live in order to sustain the human race—she will. And she will survive by *any* means necessary. But come on. Seriously, Roger," says Sy, taking another step closer. "Haven't we done enough to her? What if she isn't supposed to be here?"

"She's *not* a freak, Sy."

"But what if she is, Roger? Shouldn't you allow nature to runs its course?"

"Nature doesn't care if you're different."

"No," says Sy, his eyes widening with madness. "Nature is nature. Her nature is death and destruction. And when it comes down to it and our nature waits in the balance, who do you want on your side?"

I don't respond to Sy's comment.

He says quietly, "I think maybe it's time for someone else to take over. Roger, what would your father think of you if he found out what you were doing to her?"

"You think you know my father. You don't know shit?"

"I think it's time we call a meeting and reassess the situation. We might as well be blindfolded in there, Roger—"

"—Get some shuteye, Sy. I'll pretend we didn't have this conversation."

I turn away. Sy attempts to leave. He turns back around.

"Just curious, Roger. Of all the years you've been by her side, did it ever cross your mind to ask her what she wants?"

I ignore Sy until he finally leaves the office.

I play the video.

Suddenly, Frog A explodes!

Frog blood and guts splatters all over June's face.

Then, Frankie laces herself back into June, who, in return, turns to the camera and smirks.

☼ ☼ ☼

I turn the burner back on as soon as I clear the power lines surrounding Four Lakes and give Fahim a call when I reach a safe and secure distance.

We meet up at Silver Pines, a once heavily occupied, now abandoned, train station not too far away from the refuge.

Fahim informs me about Agent Corbin's former partner, Rashida Jones, and how she may be a threat. Baron has possibly gotten to Agent Jones.

☼ ☼ ☼

"She's been cooped up in there all day," says Fahim. "What do you think she's doing in there?"

"Digging up our deepest and darkest secrets." I admit my sense of humor is like how I like my scotch. "Who knows?" I say to Fahim. "Sooner or later, she'll call it a night. She can't stay in there forever."

I can see the agent's shadow pacing back and forth around the living room.

"Any progress with the twelve candidates?"

"One of them tried to escape again—"

"—Get out of here. Let me guess. Shapiro?"

"No," says Fahim. "Smart. Brittany Smart. I think she and a couple of others are trying to hatch up a ruse."

"How'd you know?"

"Their behavior's more suspicious. Some girls aren't eating. McDonald's been stashing her food inside her mattress. I think we need to be up front with them—"

"—Not yet," I say. "It's too soon."

"Yesterday, I was skimming over Shapiro's profile. She comes across as the rebellious type. Don't you think?"

"It's that age, I guess."

"Whenever she sees an opportunity, she's going to take it."

"No," I say. "She won't."

"She's scared, Roger. They're *all* scared. Think about it: they've been taken away from their homes, family and friends, social lives, their little gadgets and their toys that consume their daily lives. If I was taken away from all of that, I guess I'd be pretty scared myself. I'm worried about one of them. Akea. She's showing classic symptoms of contact. She kept looking down at her hand."

"Her hand, huh? Makes sense."

"You think it's Frankie?"

"No," I say. "Did you see her social media pages?"

"I don't see what that has to do with anything."

"It has everything to do with it," I say. "She has over fifty thousand chirps on her Chatterz page. According to records, she purchased her phone two years ago. Tally up the chirps in one day. That's over sixty-eight chirps in a single day. So, sixty-eight times in a day she was looking down at her phone."

"What about her computer?" asks Fahim. "Anybody with a computer can have one of these ah Chatterz account. The computer was purchased back in 2007."

"Akea created her Chatterz account in September, 2014. Seven years after the computer purchase. Two years before she purchased the phone. So do the math, Fahim. It doesn't take a genius to figure out what's going on. I mean, you saw her."

"So, you think she's experiencing withdrawal symptoms?"

"Yes," I answer. "I do. Not Frankie. Could be? I don't know."

"Okay," says Fahim, "if that's the case, then think about your everyday drug addict going through withdrawal. Take a heroine addict. Take away the drug from him or her; then, after a couple of days, the body starts to shutdown. First, it's the shaking, the fever, the restlessness. The body has become so dependent on the drug that it can't survive without it. The chemistry inside the brain has changed and the drug that was once helping him or her normally function has either become the greatest enticement or the fiercest repellent. In their suffering, they have a choice whether to live or die. Essentially, they have an option. If they choose the drug, they ultimately die. And if they don't, then there still might be a chance for them on the other side—depending on whether or not they have willpower to survive without any of these enticements. *You*, Roger, you've given them no choice whatsoever. No option to improve or better themselves."

"I've given them a chance to be true to themselves."

"And there lies the one thing you and I will *never* see eye to eye on. People like having options. It makes them feel included. For some, it makes them feel special."

"So, are you blaming society?"

"I'm not blaming anybody, but it's the world we live in today."

"Society has taught people to pick and chose what's acceptable and what's not. It's been going on for years, centuries. Now, we're starting to grow accustomed to putting labels on everything, whether it be the people who we associated with or the things we consume. If you do this, you're labeled *this.* If you don't do that, you're labeled *that.* But when you take away everything from them—the labels, the insecurities—it is at that moment you start to understand who they truly are."

"Did you ever think: What if you're wrong about them, the twelve?"

"When have I ever been wrong, Fahim?"

"I'm sure you've been wrong some time in your life," says Fahim. "If you haven't, then that doesn't make you human."

"If I am wrong, then everything that you and I take for granted will be no more. The entire world that you seem to know so well will be nothing more than a gray rock floating out in space. So, what good would it be to just hit the reset button? In the end, we wind up back in the same place. I'd be lying if I said that it would be a tragedy to see that next comet to come our way, shake things up a bit, like it did with the dinosaurs. Make us realize who's boss. I believe Frankie can be that comet, that reset, if she's provoked, if she suspects that there isn't a single shred of hope left for humanity yet an ongoing cycle of history repeating itself. When she finally reaches that point of execution, she'll do *all* of us a favor and kill every last one of us, including me."

"If that's the case, Roger, and everything you're saying is a hundred percent accurate, do you think it's wise to keep them locked up down there?" asks Fahim.

I know Fahim's right. I would never admit it, but he's as right as any.

Fahim continues: "After years of research—knowing what she's capable of doing—we still don't know *who* or *what* she is or *where* she came from. Even though your father found her after the bomb was dropped on Nagasaki, how certain are you that she didn't come from another world? Another time—"

"—You and I, Fahim, have seen firsthand what she can do. There's no denying that." I think about when I first laid eyes on Frankie, how I couldn't look away, the instant connection, that innocence. It was like a magic trick. "When I found out my father was lying about what he did for a living, I remember I was angry at first. I was mostly angry that he lied to me. Then, once all of the anger wore off and I started to imagine him out there, killing, I realized that my father was doing these people a favor. Then, I started to wonder what kind of individual would want to do that for a living. It only made me more interested in wanting to know what drove a man to do such things. What's the reason behind it all?"

"Maybe he felt as if he was protecting others," says Fahim.

"I'd like to think that were true, Fahim." I think back to when I was younger and much dumber. "As hard as I tried to find the answers as to why my father did what he did, I realized I could *never* understand why he chose to be a Reaper. I wasted years of my childhood wondering if it was brought on at an early age. Just imagine that, Fahim: A young boy stressing over his father whenever he wasn't around to guide him, to play with him, instead of playing outside with other kids. It was pointless trying to make sense of him and the choices he made. A man can spend a lifetime trying to find that moment in time where everything started to change. I can only assume that when my father laid eyes on Frankie underneath all of that rubble, he had a change of thought. He saw change. He saw life, *not* death. He saw God."

✿ ✿ ✿

After hours of waiting in the car, Agent Jones finally steps out of her house at exactly eleven-fifteen. I give Fahim a tap on the shoulder. "Fahim," I say, "wake your ass up!"

He bolts upright, eyes billowed open as if he's been electrocuted.

"Wha—what happened?"

"It's time."

Fahim grabs the tranquilizer bracelet from the glove compartment.

"No," I say. "We won't need it."

Agent Jones gets in her car. She doesn't even wait for the engine to warm up. She drives away in a hurry.

✿ ✿ ✿

Since Fahim is more skilled when it comes to picking a lock, I step aside and let him do his handiwork.

After we sneak inside, we check each room, searching for any intel Agent Jones might have on us. We check the living room last. The room appears as if a bomb has gone off. Papers scattered everywhere. It's a complete mess! She has an entire section of the wall devoted to a man named Kris Solles, starting with a map specifically tracking his progress. She has one file after another on this one man, tours in Afghanistan, background checks; looks like he served in the United States Marine Corp, then suffered from PTSD when he returned to America. Why would she be so much interested in this man? Ex-marine gone rogue? Perhaps Baron is using Agent Jones and her FBI resources to bring in Kris Solles. Even worse, hand-deliver him to Baron on a silver platter. What does he know? If this Solles guy was at Mount Olympus the day it was attacked—sent by Baron to wipe us out—then he must know everything about Frankie. He must know everything about Baron, too, and all of his investments around the world, both at home and abroad. I'm sure he knows about his ties with the Saudis. Rumor has it Baron was funding several terrorist organizations, like Crisis. I'm not in the business of speculation. What I do know is the guy's an energy buff. He knows energy is what powers the world and without energy, there is no power and without power, there is no world. Only darkness and despair. A world so bleak. Terrorized by nocturnal animals—

—Fahim startles me by calling out my name.

"Who's the kid?" asks Fahim, as he shows me a photo of a young child lying in a hospital bed. Several aides are standing next to his bed. Fahim comes across another photo of the same child in a wheelchair. I see a younger version of Baron standing beside the child.

I take a closer look.

"That's Orwell's son," I say.

"He's a paraplegic?"

"Yeah."

"How?"

"He was horseback riding. Fell off. Broke his back."

"Orwell looks much younger in the photograph," says Fahim. "How long ago was this?"

I continue to search through the living room while trying to ignore Fahim and a soon-to-be barrage of questions about the kid. Fahim's completely aware that me not answering is my way of telling him that the conversation is over.

"Roger, come take a look at this," says Fahim with more urgency, as he makes his way to the coffee table.

Scattered on the table are aged photos of my father—ones that have obviously been *given* to Agent Jones. Amazing what power can do. Sometimes power comes in the form of a custom tailored suit. Next thing you know you're nothing more than a handkerchief in a pocket. Some of the photos I haven't seen before. One photo of my father standing among his other fellow Reapers in black hazmat suits, holding assault rifles against their shoulders, agents of death.

Fahim grabs one particular photo from the pile, hands it to me. It's a much older photo, crinkled and brown with age. In the photo, my father is standing with Sister Diane in front of the convent, Order of Our Lady, with Frankie, who's around four years old.

"Is that your—"

"—Yes," I say. "That's him."

"And the girl?"

"That's her," I say. "That's Frankie."

I come across a more recent photo of myself taken from a distance. Baron's evil minions must've taken it after I came to him for money. It was Baron who first came to me, trying to strike a deal with me after he heard about Sam Lieber. I sat on it overnight. I remember I had the most vivid dream later that night about changing the world and becoming a worldwide celebrity. Not like I didn't bring all of this upon myself. Not like Baron held a gun to my face.

I pick up the photo and hold it close to my face.

In the photo is a much younger version of me exiting a cafe. A cup of coffee in each hand. One for me. The other for Frankie.

"What do we do?" asks Fahim.

I place the photo back in its proper place while Fahim's frantically skimming through more photos, tossing them aside and making a mess over an already mess. She has photos of Baron and me striking deals, money exchanges, hauling prisoners in the back of armored trucks, photos of a younger Fahim from his early, more radical days at Four Lakes when it was operational, even photos of Sy as well, one file after another. She's basically got all of the dirt on us—most of it, at least.

"If this woman has information on me, Roger, it's only a matter of time before she finds us!"

"Leave it," I say.

"Roger, we have to destroy all of this."

"We leave it and act like we were never here."

"If she knows about me, she knows about Four Lakes—"

"—We need to get back."

"How long do you think we have?"

"Two days tops. Regardless, they'll be coming for us and when they do, we'll be ready."

"What about the twelve?"

"We begin Phase Two of the assessment."

"Phase Two? I thought you said—"

"—I know what I said, but we don't have a choice."

Fahim points at the map on the wall—a red Sharpie circling the town of Gibson.

"Least we know where she's headed next," says Fahim.

## 7. THE HIRED GUN / KRIS

I'M getting closer.

I can feel it in my mind.

In my body, my bones, my heart.

I don't know what's going on with me. Whatever this force is, I can feel its grip taking hold on me, tightening like a knot. Even when I make any reasonable attempt to put my mind on something else—like Felicia, my beautiful Felicia, all those memories we shared together—I wind up in the same place with the same thoughts, images, same feelings. . .

I find myself trapped in a cold, dark prison and I'm shaking and I'm scared. Flashes of panic creep into my bones and I find my vision spiraling out of control. The only thing that keeps me going is the life around me. I have to constantly remind myself that it's not me. I'm not someone else.

I am Kris Solles.

But why does it feel as if these thoughts and feelings are as much a part of me as I am a part of them. I don't see any clear indication of them letting go. The signs are everywhere, showing me, guiding me the way: 12 miles to New Cherry.

Why the number 12? Why does the number seem so appealing? Why not 11 or 13? Why 12?

I pass another sign, a billboard with a cartoon drawing of a smiley yuppie riding on skis as he's being dragged through a lake by a jet ski. The yuppie's waving and smiling this hammy fake smile at drivers below, this goofy cartoon bubble over his square-shaped head reading, "*Come on and take a dip! The water is always pristine at Lake Augustine.*"

A song plays on the radio. The lyrics intrigue me. I turn up the volume, gradually. A whiny man's droning about finding "my road" and "calling it my own."

I don't know what the singer means by that, but he sounds as if he's singing directly to me. He sings about waking up in bed next to a beautiful, long haired brunette named Felicia with a pair of legs that stretch on for miles and a smile like the rising sun and lips that taste sugary-sweet and go down like mimosa. Only horror remains. No sunshine. No sipping mimosas on a sugary white beach. No romance. Only a haunted love.

I block out images of Felicia being torn apart by a black panther and turn off the radio and focus on the road ahead.

It's all I can do from losing it.

✡ ✡ ✡

I pass New Cherry and drive through the small downtown of Gibson. I roll down the window and get a smell of the town. The town reeks of cigarettes, fumes, and pork. I pass a Fifties era diner, which appears as if it's been frozen in time. I pinpoint the source of the savory smell to the diner. I tell myself I need my strength. Pork isn't really the ideal food to give me that boost I need—a belly full of pork would more than likely send me straight to bed for a nap—however, I need to at least eat something that had parents.

I park away from the other cars, keep my head down, and walk to the diner.

Along the way, I pass an electronic store. Rows and rows of televisions are playing a BREAKING NEWS report. The police have found Felicia's body. A camera crew is hanging around a familiar dirt road next to the woods. Yellow police tape is pinned from one tree to the next. Investigators aren't letting anybody near the scene. A glum-faced news reporter's talking about a young woman named Felicia Rosado, how Ms. Rosado was running through the trails while she was viciously attacked by a wild animal—which a team of zookeepers at the North Carolina Zoo believe to be a black panther that recently escaped. They're calling the black panther, Oscar. This animal—Oscar—still has not been found or spotted and specialists are warning civilians *not* to approach the animal. There's also a camera crew at Felicia's house. Cut to other feed. FBI agents are scattered all over the scene, but I don't think it had anything to do with the black panther. The reporter's saying Ms. Rosado might've been "aiding and embedding the wanted man, Kris Solles."

Shit.

All of that work, for nothing. The cover-up. They have no proof that I was there with Felicia. It's not like Felicia and I never broadcasted our relationship. Not once did I ever hang out with her friends. She never hung out with mine. So, I know they didn't get the information from any of her friends. And forget her cousin. She acted like the Ghost of Felicia's Past. I stripped the entire truck clean and removed anything that would lead back to the same truck that was stolen. I made sure to cover up every single piece of evidence leading back to me, every single fingerprint, every fiber, every hair. It doesn't make any sense—unless Orwell has already gotten to the FBI. For all I know, he has the FBI in his pocket.

As I turn around, I'm startled by two shadowy figures!

Before I take a step back and access the situation, this girl wearing a pink jacket and a black Mona's Arch tee shirt suddenly bumps into me! The collision sends a surge of electricity through my body!

The girl—who can't be much older than twelve years of age—drops a glittery-covered mp3 player, causing the ear buds to rip from her ears. I kneel down to pick up the player off the ground as her father brings her in close to him, repeatedly apologizing as if by him not acknowledging how sorry he was about the accident was only going to provoke a confrontation.

I excuse myself. Hand the girl back her player. Then tell the guy not to sweat it.

During the exchange, the girl overreaches and part of her hand grazes mine.

Another surge of electricity shoots through my body!

A flash of an image comes to me: I'm staring up at a *scary man dressed in black. His face looks similar to mine but it's somewhat blurry.*

I snap from the trance as my knees are about to buckle and I'm looking back down at the mp3 player gripped in the girl's hand, the title of the song on the player's screen: "An Everyday World." I recognize the artist, *Rembrandt,* even though I have never heard of him before. I can't stop thinking about this artist, Rembrandt. He's a genderless man who considers himself to be part of the "they" group; forget pronouns, they don't belong to a he or she, instead someone who can change their appearance or sex based off whatever mood he or she's feeling at the moment. When he first started playing music, he was a kid with a keyboard, playing old renditions of jams from the 80's. How I know these things is beyond me. Why I'm even interested in this individual is even more troubling, especially when a guy like me wouldn't even pay much attention to someone like Rembrandt who was simply trying to get attention. Not too long ago, he, Jeremy Brinker, changed his name to Rembrandt and followed the current trends of society and dressed himself up into a pretty little girl. His identity somewhat evolved over the past few months, first a he, then a she, then somewhere in between—*they.* I recognize the satellite channel as well, *Pop Delights.* I know everything about the artist—I don't how and why I know these things but I do. Somehow, I know more about Rembrandt than I do about my own self. It's all because of this girl here, Angela, who likes to go by Angie. She's his number one fan. She follows him in whatever he does. He's what most call a social media whore. He's considered popular on the Internet. He spends a lot of his time on PhotoBag. On his page, Rembrandt posts photos of his daily activities, including ones of him hanging out in the studio, which he calls the Laboratory, hanging around all of his high-end equipment. It's his way of seeking approval. He wants people to think he's a well-off musician even though he's barely getting by. When he was thirteen, he wanted to be a rock star. The glamour. The girls. The money. The lifestyle. He realized it wasn't what he thought, like on the television. He's known to post many photos of his two children, going to the park, going to a restaurant, going to coffee shops. His first child is a three-year-old girl. The other is a two-year-old boy who takes after his mother more than Rembrandt. She's the breadwinner of the household. Works as a website developer for start-up businesses. Rembrandt never posts any photos of his wife on the Internet. He has lost the desire to pleasure her. According to the recent text message on Coralline's phone, she's having an affair on Rembrandt with one of her colleagues. Rembrandt even wrote a song about his wife's suspicious behavior and called it "Faithless." The story behind why Rembrandt posts so many photos of his children is that he wants his fan base to think that he's a normal yet cool father. Whenever Rembrandt's children are at day care, he logs onto his son's computer at exactly ten-thirty and he trolls the Internet, picking fights with other kids by using his name, Vain_84. He gets off on making fun of others. It's developed into a routine for Rembrandt, a sickness.

Rembrandt has become a perfect escape for kids like Angie, who are completely unaware of his double-life as Vain. She, like Rembrandt, discovered music during a dark time in her life. Her mother had a problem with booze, so bad that it had rendered her utterly useless. She got the right treatment that she needed but whatever demons she had still lingered in the relationship with Angie's father—the manipulative behavior, the constant looking for arguments, and even worse, the lack of competency. She ended up getting good at sneaking around, finding ways to sneak in a sip whenever nobody was around. Angie's father had enough. His wife was still living in college and he was trying to raise a child on his own. So, he filed for a divorce. It was better that way.

Angie's currently angry with her father for not letting her go to Rembrandt's concert next week. Angie's never been to one before and from what she's heard from her friends, Rembrandt was known to put on quite a show. Her good friend, Paula, bought two tickets. Paula's looking for someone else to go to the concert with her.

I suddenly pull my hand away and take a couple of steps back.

Angie makes eye contact with me.

What the hell was that about?

"Is everything okay?"

"Yeah," I say, still hanging onto the strange effects of the trance. "Sure."

Both the father and daughter move along.

I can't remember what I'm doing, where I am.

I walk back to the car.

I peek over my shoulder along the way and notice the girl putting the ear buds back into her ears.

✲ ✲ ✲

My body's telling me that I need to eat when I make it back to the car. I sit back in the seat and close my eyes for a minute. I listen to several cars pass by with the radio blaring. That's when the idea comes to me. I think I know what's going on with me.

I pull out Felicia's phone. I'm sure the FBI agents may think it's suspicious that they didn't find her phone either at her house or at the crime scene, but I couldn't go through with planting it at the scene of the crime. I don't know why, but I know why I need it. I know that when I turn the phone on, I will risk putting myself in harm's way. Surely by now the FBI is trying to track down Felicia's phone. I have to find out if it's true. If something did happen to me when I made contact with her at Mt. Olympus, then whatever entity wormed its way into my body is starting to show its ugly head.

I hold my breath as I turn on the phone. I pull up the music app on the phone. I scroll to the one station, *Pop Delights,* turn up the volume.

One of Rembrandt's songs is playing.

I close my eyes again and focus on the song, the lyrics, and each instrument, guitar, synthesizer, and sampler effect.

Suddenly, I find myself being yanked out of the car, as if my body is attached to a pull cord!

I'm being shot at a lightning fast speed through the street, dodging one car after another. Then, I zoom down the sidewalk, passing pedestrians, weaving in and out of traffic until I find myself speeding directly toward the diner.

I brace for impact as I charge at the door. . .

Nothing happens?

I slide right through the door like a phantom. I keep moving until I find the source of the music.

The girl—Angie!

She's sitting across from her father in a booth.

Before I can make any sense of what's going on, I'm sitting in the booth across from the girl's father.

He's telling *me*—not her, Angie—to take off my ear buds.

I look down at my hands and they are not my hands but the hands of a girl.

Is this really happening to me?

My father keeps talking to me, but I ignore him. I want him to go away, far away, to leave me alone, to just let me be. He doesn't understand me anymore. I'm getting older now—I mean, soon I'll be thirteen years old!—he's afraid one day I'll be gone from his life forever. I have a life. I don't understand why he continues to control me like this. I cannot be controlled. I won't be! He points at my buds and does that annoying thing where he tilts his head to the left and keeps it there. I stand up from the seat and walk to the bar and order two roast beef sandwiches. I tell the waitress that I want one order to go. The waitress asks if it's for the gentlemen sitting with me in the booth. I shake my head and tell her that it's not for my father. It's for a friend.

☼ ☼ ☼

I wake up with a girl tapping me on the shoulder.

I realize it's the same girl from the diner—Angie!

I wipe a string of drool from the side of my chin and grab the bag of food from the girl's hand.

"Thanks," I say.

"You're welcome," she says flatly.

"How did—"

"—Don't worry," she says. "Your secret is safe with me."

Like that, she walks away.

I look down at my hand—my actual hand.

You got to be kidding me!

As I'm about to open the bag of food, I hear a couple of men laughing in an alleyway.

A local gang is terrorizing some poor kid. One of them has a knife to the kid's throat.

I look down at the phone in my lap, then look back to the gang. I have another idea.

Might as well.

While my hands are clean.

## 8. THE AGENT / RASHIDA

WHAT have I seriously gotten myself into?

Turns out a missing case intertwined with the most peculiar murder case has become much more complicated than I would've expected. I can't help but ask myself: Who is this man, Baron Orwell? For starters, you can call him a power-junkie—I've seen his type many times before at the Academy, the more control, the more power, a power-junkie—and like every power-junkie, they thrive on the thrill of success.

Every man—and woman—has a drive, a fire inside him or her; it's the *y* in why they do what they do.

For some of us, I guess that drive will take us as far to the edge as possible and it will push us to go just a little further and defy limits. I don't know why Orwell is so obsessed with finding Kris Solles—did Solles, a trained killer, somehow get his hands on whatever June Lugosi was working on or what? The next cure for cancer? Did it have anything to do with this orphan from Nagasaki? Or, do Orwell and Solles have a bromance they're trying to keep secret? I seriously doubt it. Or, is it something as pedestrian as getting back at Solles for not doing his job—revenge for not taking out the rogue doctor in the first place? If that's the case, whatever happened to the saying *you're fired*? Just two words, then it's over. Move on, kid. It's not that simple. There's something else that Orwell is not telling me.

So many questions with very little answers.

Frustration aside, Orwell turns out being a lot more helpful than I had originally thought he'd be. So far, I have just enough information on each one of the key players involved in the disappearance of the lacrosse team to take to Pelham, including quite a page-turner of a résumé on Seymour Bloch, former virologist of the United States Army Medical Research Institute of Infectious Diseases—I mean we're talking about a man who handled not only the deadliest diseases on the planet but also super bugs that could literally wipe out mankind—as well as the shrink who was responsible for murdering my partner. I have more important matters to handle, but soon, his time will come.

I go to Pelham with a timeline of events.

Does he take me seriously?

What do you think?

Orwell's right.

I'm on my own.

And maybe it's better that way.

☼ ☼ ☼

Kudos for Agent Faraday for coming through once again. He managed to track down the signal to Felicia Rosado's phone inside an abandoned hotel in the town of Gibson. He sends me the coordinates and gives me a "thirty-minute head start" before he notifies Pelham and the rest of his cronies. The catch: I end up agreeing to going on a date with Agent Faraday. Word has traveled fast around the office about Bo and I and I'm sure people are starting to suspect whether or not I'm going to be on the market. I know Agent Faraday will probably want to hook up with me—I know Faraday, young and full of come—but if it results in me finding Solles by the end of the day, I guess when it comes down to it, then a lady's got to do what a lady's got to do—even if it means spreading her legs for a hot minute.

As soon as I arrive at what was formerly known as The Golden Cache at the outskirts of Gibson, training kicks in and I get the feeling I shouldn't be here.

I grab the shotgun from the trunk—my only backup—then empty the box of shells into my palms and stuff a handful into my pocket.

The front door of the hotel has been boarded up so I try to find another way in. I make my way through out a three-story parking garage next to the hotel. I can't find a single car inside the garage. The vast emptiness causes the hairs on the backside of my neck to stick up like quills. I'm not alone.

Something sure is creeping on me and I can't shake it.

I suddenly hear the sound of footsteps doubling over my own and whenever I stop, the footsteps stop as well.

"Hello," I say, my voice being squashed by concrete beams around me. I try once more, this time louder. My voice manages to travel through dark passageways. "Anybody there?"

Any ghosts there? The Boogeyman?

No luck.

Where are you, Solles?

Of course, if there was anybody stalking me, he or she certainly wouldn't come out and say it.

I move forward, making sure to keep my footsteps to myself. Heel rolling into ball. Not a complete step. More like a slow waltz. My backup in hand. My handgun within reach.

I locate a way in into the hotel via a side door, which has been locked with chains so rusty that even the rust has started to eat through the metal, causing several links to break like aged bones. I give the door a nice giggle; although I can tell the door has been put to good use for the chains are as loose as an amateur knot. If I didn't skip dinner, then more than likely I probably wouldn't be able to slip my body through the crack. I manage. I make my way down a stretch of dark hallway that has a gassy stench of farts and body odor hidden underneath a heavy waft of urine and something synthetic and chemical. I can't exactly pinpoint what the smell is, but it sure does burn my eyes. I peel the scarf from my jacket and wrap part of it around my nose and mouth.

I get about halfway down the hallway until I see a shadowy figure moving throughout the darkness.

Following the soft stirring is the bloodcurdling sound of the growl of what sounds like a dog—a really big one, too!

Four beady glowing eyes emerge from that hellish darkness. I aim my shotgun at the dog.

Suddenly, the dog sprints from the darkness!

I can't tell what it is, really. It's a dog—a rottweiler, from what I can tell—however, two dogs in one?

"Heel!" I yell out.

The rottweiler keeps charging at me.

I fire a warning shot toward the ceiling, but it doesn't stop the wild mutt.

As the rottweiler gets ready to pounce, I realize it's not two dogs. It's one dog with two heads!

The creature leaps at me. I have no other option. I shoot it in the chest before it can take a bite of my throat. The creature falls to the floor in a loud and dusty thud. I check on the creature, the two heads. I check to see if it's still breathing by placing my free hand on its chest, the shotgun barrel tucked underneath its throat. If the creature does make any sudden moves, then I'll blow it straight back to whatever hell it came from. I can't feel any air in its lungs. It died a quick death. The texture of its skin, I notice, is slimy to the touch. Dark secretions heavily concentrated around its jaw and underbelly. I pull my hand away and carefully place it underneath my nose. My hand smells like oil.

We're definitely not in Kansas anymore.

☼ ☼ ☼

I head toward the light until I reach a main lobby where several oil drums burn tame fires. I come across raggedy sleeping bags and various piles of trash scattered along the lobby, as if each pile of trash belongs to a certain homeless settlement. Occasionally, I'll step on the glass of a syringe or crack pipe or other paraphernalia underneath the sole of my boot. I check all corners of my vision, the playful shadows dancing in and out of the firelight.

I suddenly hear the sound of man imitating a monkey behind me!

Followed by the animalistic noises is the sound of what sounds like a metal pipe or a crowbar rhythmically tapping along a row of steel bars.

Different sounds start to manifest all around, to my side, to my front and my back: a man whistling throughout the archaic darkness; another man letting out short bursts of bottled-up giggles, which sound like smothered coughs; another one tapping the head of an aluminum bat against the palm of his hand. Then, finally, in front of me, I witness a man dragging from a cigarette in the darkness. He's staring at me, as if he's been there from the very start. He comes forth from the darkness and arrogantly flicks the butt of cigarette toward my direction. The light from the fires brings his face in and out of the darkness. The other men come forth and reveal themselves. They're wearing holey trench coats with red bandanas wrapped around their right biceps. One man has a purplish sheet wrapped around his waist. Two of the men have tattoos on the side of their faces. One of them, I notice, has a tattoo of a pyramid in the center of his head—a tattoo that I've seen in several inmates before I joined the FBI. A prison gang called the Prophets, a crew of doomsayers who believed in all of that end of the world nonsense back in 2012, according to the Mayan calendar. The firelight hits a curved blade in one of the man's hands and causes the metal to glitter.

The smoker, which I reckon is the leader, steps forward in the light. He raises his chin to display male dominance and then he peels back the bottom flap of his coat, revealing a handgun tucked underneath his waistband.

"You lost, sweetheart?" he says in a surprisingly charming voice.

"I'm looking for somebody."

"You came to wrong place," he says. "Nobody here worth looking for."

The man, now standing directly behind me, stops tapping the bat against his palm. I peek over my shoulder and notice that he's got both hands wrapped around the grip.

I listen closely to the mouthbreather in one ear. I listen to the grit skidding along the sole of his boot, the baseball bat in his hand. I keep all these sounds close to me and know that whenever the sounds stop, it's showtime.

While the man stalks behind me, I keep my other ear on the leader.

"Four against one," I say, sizing up each junkie. "Not exactly a fair fight."

The giggly man lets out another high-pitch laugh, causing the others to laugh, masking the stalker behind me.

I check on the stalker once more, making sure he's being a good boy.

"Fair?" the leader says. "You killed my dog. I liked that dog, too."

"Well, maybe you should've taught it some manners. It was going to attack me."

"Attack you? That dog doesn't have a mean bone in its body. Now, it's dead."

"I'm sorry," I tell him. "Let's just call it a misunderstanding. I'll be on my way. Deal?"

He says, "Does it look like we the type of folks who make deals, sweetheart? Down here," he looks around the place in awe, "we make the rules. Down here, we're gods."

I'm not sure what he means by "down here." I keep reminding myself that these guys aren't playing with a full deck.

"I'm just looking for Kris Solles," I say. "You seen him?"

The leader pauses. His eyes drift in thought for a moment, which strikes me as odd because he doesn't look like the type who puts thought into anything. Then, he acts as if he just caught himself thinking.

"Nah," he says over a long pause. "Never heard of him."

One of them says to my side, "You a cop or something—"

"—You sure don't look like a cop—"

"—Yeah. Where's your badge, Ms. Piggy?"

I find the one who called me Ms. Piggy, eye him down, and say to him, "Why don't you put down that knife and I'll show you where my badge is?"

More laughs.

I'm losing patience.

The one with the blade flinches at me as if he's about to do something. I don't take him too seriously. If he was going to try something, he would've done it already.

"I don't have time for games. Kris Solles. Have you seen him? Yes or no?"

The leader nods to the man behind me.

I feel the silence pressed against me.

Showtime.

I drop my shoulder to the right, only to find a man swinging a bat at me. I dodge the bat and kick him in the back of the knee, causing him to fall in a matter of milliseconds. I take the butt of my shotgun and throw a hammering blow directly to his throat, crushing the rings of cartilage of his trachea. That delicate and ever so precious passageway from his throat to his lungs now shrunken to the size of a snare-drum tight sphincter.

Another man makes an attempt to charge at me while the other incapacitated one reaches for deeper and more crucial breaths.

I aim my shotgun at him.

"Don't even try it." I tighten my grip. "I will blow your fucking head off. . . "

I notice the man on the ground still choking. His eyes are glowing; however, he's trying to shield them from me.

The inside of the hotel starts to rumble!

A deep groan erupts from the insides of the man. I'm not sure if it's that crap in the air that's turning my mind against me or if it's some unknown drug I've ingested—maybe something new on the streets—but I start to see things that don't appear exactly normal.

As I check on the man, his arm suddenly shoots out and hits me between my upper abdomen and chest, sending me, as well as the shotgun, in the air.

While I'm soaring in the air, his arm, which is still extending, rushes past me and all of the veins and ligaments of the arms are blown up out of proportion; and by the time his arm is fully extended, it has to be at least twenty feet long!

I catch my breath and shake off the blow while the man's arm slowly retracts into his body. He rears back again. Gets ready to throw another punch.

I search for my shotgun but can't find it anywhere in sight. I check my holster for my handgun but it must've fallen out during the blow. I find it resting against an oil drum. I dodge another attack, roll toward my handgun while the aged hardwood below me cracks in half from the thunderous blow.

I grab my gun. Aim. Pull the trigger.

I shoot the man directly between the eyes!

He falls down, this time for good.

I turn to the other three and they're slowly fading into the darkness. Their eyes are lit as well, like the other man.

"Who the hell are you people?" I ask the leader.

The leader only responds with a boyish smirk as his body falls into darkness.

I can sense all three of them circling me as if I'm tonight's main course.

I move closer to the oil drum of fire and constantly check my surroundings.

The moonlight cuts through a large pane of glass along the lobby and shines on one of the men.

From all that I can make out, he's no longer a man or not even the shape of one. Both his arms and legs are long and stretched and contorted, like the other man, the dead one.

I listen carefully to the footsteps all around me and they're much wider and heavier in stride.

Before I can turn around, I'm tackled from behind. One of the scumbags is now on top of me, his arm is as thick as a tree trunk. He rears back and slams his hard fist down in a deathblow. I manage to roll out of the way at the very last second. Pieces of floor shoot up beside me! No man has the strength to do these things!

His arm gets stuck in the floor, which gives me an opportunity to counter by kicking the oil drum of fire onto the man. He burst into flames and rolls over the floor, trying to put out the flames but they end up overtaking him!

Two left, I tell myself as I stand over this man-thing and watch him burn to a crisp.

I hear yet another one—not sure which one—doing laps around me but, like before, I can't quite tell where he is.

I stay on the move, my finger never leaving the trigger.

As I pull out my phone, I hear what sounds like an ill man screaming in agony!

The scream only lasts for a couple of seconds and then it fades into the darkness.

I stay alert—still mindful of the other two whom I presume are dead, but I'm still not a hundred percent positive—and I dial Felicia's number.

The phone starts to ring.

I pull away the phone from my ear and listen closely.

I hear a ring tone!

I track down the source of the ringing coming behind two doors. The ringing stops. So, I redial the number, place the phone in my pocket, and adjust the grip on my gun.

I make my way into a dingy ballroom with old cables and wires hanging from the ceiling. Hundred of tables fill the entire room, most of them untouched despite all of the vandalism and waste and ruins caused by an underbelly of criminals who have turned to the hotel as their own private sanctuary. The tables are covered in lavender-colored tablecloths, I notice as I run my hand over the dusty tablecloth. One of the men was wearing it more as a fashion statement than trying to stay warm. More junk scattered everywhere, however, not as bad as the lobby.

I inch closer and closer to the ringing until I finally locate the source.

Of all the tables inside the ballroom, one of the tables is pulsating ever so faintly with a pale blue light. Either I was right about Solles about leading me into a trap or the other.

I keep my gun close to me as I approach the glowing table.

"Solles," I whisper, hoping to find a reaction from underneath the table—a stir, a twitch, a murmur, anything!

The only response that I receive is a light pulsating with the ring of a phone.

I place my finger on the trigger and take in a deep breath.

On the count of three, I kick over the table. . .

No Solles.

No nothing.

Only a cell phone ringing on the floor.

My number is visible on the screen of the phone.

I pull out the phone from my pocket and end the call.

As I reach down to pick up Felicia's phone off the floor, I hear *squeak* behind me. . .

I turn my shoulder and rise to my feet.

In the distance, a lanky dark figure is standing in front of the doorway, staring at me with menacing eyes.

"Solles?"

The figure takes a step forward.

Not Kris Solles. Not human for that matter.

I lift my gun and tell the creature to freeze.

"I'm warning you!"

I give my final command.

Suddenly, the creature charges at me!

I can't make out what it is, for it keeps low as it runs, sharing similar characteristics of a gorilla running on all fours. It plows through one table after another like a fullback. One by one, each table is flung into the air in domino-like fashion.

As the creature nears, I take aim. I let out a warning shot, but the creature is not stopping, nor is it slowing down!

I shoot the creature in the shoulder, but the gunshot has no effect on it. I aim for the head and chest area. I pop off seven rounds to areas of the body that would easily put down any average man, but the shots have absolutely no effect on it!

Before it makes impact, I curl my arms close to my body, dig both of my heels into the floor, and brace myself.

Before I can get a closer look at what's about to hit me, the blood charges through my veins!

Once more, I'm flying through the air!

I land on a table about five tables away. The table helps cushion my fall. The relentless creature comes at me again. I realize it's not a creature at all but the same man from before, the one with the knife. Like the man before, his limbs are much longer; parts of his body are severely blown out of proportion. He looks modified—mutated almost. I don't know if they've taken a radical drug to enhance their bodies. Maybe he's jacked on PCP.

I realize that I don't have time to figure out what or who they are. First, I have to survive.

This man-thing comes at me yet again and throws a jab at me from at least ten feet away. At the last second, I notice the glittery object in his hand—the knife!

I quickly move to my right. The knife stabs the broken table behind me, the edge of the blade nearly grazing me!

I return fire on its stringy forearm while the knife remains stuck in the table. He lets out a deep, staticky screech. He releases his hand from the knife. His arm stretches back into his body. He charges at me once more. He leaps in the air, both hands intertwined in the shape of a mallet. He goes in for a deathblow. . .

As he soars closer to me, I search around me. I finger a piece of wood broken off from one of the table legs. I grab the wood, and just as he's about to strike down on me, I hold the sharp piece of wood in front of my body. Brace myself.

The piece of wood penetrates the center of his chest. He gasps for a moment, struggling to catch his breath. Then, his eyes roll over white. I slide from underneath the dead body and catch my breath.

As I'm gathering myself, a gunshot *rings* out!

The bullet whizzes by my head, causing me to duck.

I take cover behind one of the tables and take a peek at the shooter.

I hear a voice coming from the doorway.

"You have nowhere to run, *Agent Jones.*"

How does he know my name?

"What do you people want?"

I sneak behind another table and try to keep out of sight.

Three more gunshots go off!

Bullets skip around!

"Who are you people?"

I check my magazine and find only two bullets left.

"We are free men, Agent Jones, free men who have been given an opportunity to turn a wrong into a right," the leader says, his voice sounds much closer. "Without wrong, there would be no right. And we are the right, Agent Jones. God has spoken to us. You wanna know what He said?"

I crawl toward another table.

More gunshots ring out!

One nearly hits me.

"He said, 'Join Me and I will give you powers to destroy the evils of the world.'"

I look around, trying to find a way out. I spot an exit door on the other side of the room. I won't make it. I sneak a peek at the leader, who's stalking closer with a gun in its hand. It stops underneath a cobweb-infested chandelier.

I find my opportunity and count to three.

I aim at the chain holding the chandelier.

I pull the trigger. . .

I hit the chain with one shot, causing the chain to break in half!

The chandelier comes crashing down on the leader. It's not moving. I check on the leader. The needle of the chandelier has pierced his throat, instantly killing it. I take its gun away and make my way back to my car, trying to make sense of what in the hell just happened.

✡ ✡ ✡

As I'm passing through the lobby area, I can't help but notice one of the dead men on the floor. His body appears as if it's changed back to normal. His limbs are normal and not freakishly blown out of proportion.

Something's approaching me!

My skin starts to crawl from the sound of a pitter-patter of footsteps. I turn in all directions, trying to find the noise.

Everything stops.

Silence.

I turn toward the window and see another dark figure staring at me. The figure is much smaller. The first thing I notice is its chest puffing in and out, as if it's trying to catch its breath; then, secondly, the horns on its head.

My eyes adjust to the darkness.

A beam of moonlight basks over the figure.

Not horns, I realize.

Pigtails. . .

A little girl charges at me!

"Stop!" I shout out. "Stop right there!"

I can end her life with one shot to the head, but I decide not to waste my last bullet on her. Instead, I rip off a plank of hardwood from the chewed-up floor and stick the end of the wood inside the oil drum until it catches on fire.

The girl suddenly leaps at me. . .

I rear back and smack her upside the head with the flaming piece of wood. She crashes to floor. She lays motionless. Then, suddenly, she starts violently convulsing and screaming. She screams so loud that I have to cover my ears. The scream intensifies, like a ground loop blaring out of control.

Suddenly, the windows shatter all around me!

Tiny shards of glass rain down, forcing me to take cover.

While I cover my head with my jacket, I witness something leaving the girl, moving like smoke in the way it slithers into the air. Yet, when it leaves the girl, it does so in a matter of seconds before it fades into the night sky. She stops screaming, stops moving—from what I can tell, she stops breathing.

Another stark silence fills the lobby, which forces me back into defense-mode.

Another *squeak* behind me!

I turn, only to find two of Orwell's goons standing in the foyer, aiming guns at me. How long have these two assholes been standing there? Surely, long enough to witness firsthand the freak show that just happened. One of them whispers something into the other's ear. I can't entirely make out what he's whispering—something about a girl—but whatever it is, it's important enough for one of them to get on his phone and make a phone call. The other nods his head at me and tells me Orwell needs to have a chat. Not like I have any say-so in the matter.

☼ ☼ ☼

By the time I decompress, the two bodyguards escort me to a SUV where Orwell is cozily waiting inside. They take away all of my weapons—both my guns, as well as the other one that I collected from the freak, one of them even found my shotgun. Two men seated in the front, one in the driver's seat, another waiting in the passenger seat, while Orwell remains seated in the back. I enter the vehicle. The door closes behind me.

"No luck in finding Mr. Solles?" Orwell says to me.

The comment gets me riled up.

"I was attacked back there!" He doesn't seem surprised by my response. "I want answers right now! What the hell am I up against?"

"I apologize, Agent Jones. I needed to know whether or not Mr. Solles was who he said he was."

"What do you mean? Who is Kris Solles?"

"He's not the Mr. Solles you've been hunting. He's only a puppet now, being controlled by a force beyond science."

"So you knew what was going to happen back there? You used me as bait?"

"It was the only way to find out the truth about Mr. Solles, Agent Jones. You're alive, right? That's all that matters." He pauses for a moment and acknowledges my current state. "I apologize. I should've told you more about her and her—how do I put it—her uncanny abilities. You must agree. She's quite the individual—"

"Her abilities? So, are you telling me that was June Lugosi back there—"

"—Not Lugosi," Orwell says. "Those men back there—and girl—were being controlled by Mr. Solles.

I'm afraid he has been compromised. He is *not* who he says he is—"

"—Then who is he?"

"He's *her*, Agent Jones. He is Frankie—"

"—The girl?"

"Yes."

"I don't believe you. That's impossible."

"You should know, Agent Jones, that a word like *impossible* doesn't exist in this world anymore."

"So, did this girl's power have anything to do with what happened back in Benjamin Creek?"

Orwell doesn't answer.

I tell him again.

"Answer me!"

"Frankie had everything to do with what happened in Benjamin Creek."

"If she detonated this bomb as some sort of distraction or decoy, then how is she still alive—"

He holds back his laughter with a smile on his face.

"—Am I missing the joke? What's so funny?"

"She didn't detonate a bomb, Agent Jones."

"If not a bomb, then what?"

"It was Frankie—a momentary hiccup, if you will. If only a fraction of her set off that explosion in Benjamin Creek imagine what the rest of her can do?"

"She's a weapon?"

"That's one way of putting it." He pours himself a scotch. Offers me one but I'm close to telling him that he can shove that glass of scotch where the sun doesn't shine. "My team hasn't quite figured out where she comes from but what we do know is that on August 9, 1945, three days after the bombing of Hiroshima, we dropped another bomb on Nagasaki, which led to the end of World War II. Death and despair wasn't the only thing that rose from the ashes, Agent Jones. Among the rubble rose a girl who was given the extraordinary ability to harness one of the greatest properties that mankind has taken for granted: energy."

I grab the door handle and make an attempt to escape.

"Relax, Agent Jones," he says. "You wouldn't want to do anything that you might later regret."

I think of ways to escape, how to protect myself. The glass in his hand would be a good place. Shatter it and use it as a weapon.

"I've done what you asked," I say. "I can't find him. He's a ghost."

"Not a ghost, Agent Jones. Mr. Solles is just like any ordinary man. Only difference is that he's under the influence of a power so great that he can—and trust me, he will, if necessary—destroy an entire world without batting an eyelash —"

"—What do you want from me?"

"Tomorrow, I want you to meet me in Haden. There's a commercial development off Graham Street. You won't miss it. I have a special project for you, Agent Jones. One that will be less strenuous."

"The hell with you. I'm *done* here."

"Very well," he says coldly.

Orwell rolls down the window and holds his gloved hand outside.

One of the guards hands him my gun. He rolls up the window. He checks the chamber. He lets out what I believe is a laugh but I can't tell if he has any sense of humor.

"I'm sorry, Fernando," he says to the passenger.

The passenger grins and replies, "Sorry for what—"

Orwell aims my gun at the back of the passenger's head and pulls the trigger.

He shoots the passenger in the back of the head!

Blood and brains splatter over the windshield.

The passenger's body flops against the driver's shoulder. I can't tell if the driver is in shock or if he's flat-out disgusted by the man in the passenger seat.

The driver pushes the dead body away from him, causing the body to flop against the other door. Then Orwell expressionlessly turns to me and hands me my gun, the barrel facing the other way.

"I'm afraid, Agent Jones," Orwell says, "you don't have a choice."

☼ ☼ ☼

I manage to get home in one piece after such an insane night. I go straight to the fridge and pour myself a glass of vodka. I could use about ten drinks right now, but I drink just enough to keep me right.

Once my nerves have calmed down, I jump in the shower. Everything comes at me all at once. I've never been an emotional person—even Bo used to tell me all of the time that I should smile more, that it looks better on me, he'd tell me to laugh more also. Everything that took place tonight has gotten to me. I can't even remember the last time I've cried, like really cried, like bawling. My eyes start to burn and the pain grips hold of me. I start thinking about the things that have happened throughout these last few months of my life, with Bo, losing my partner, Bry. I haven't had time to have a single moment with myself, to absorb everything that has happened. I heard that work sometimes covers up the grief. Eventually, it'll be as if it never existed. I wish that were true. I really do. I just want to see his face one more time. Just once.

☼ ☼ ☼

After I step out of the shower, I put on a bathrobe and start to lather myself with lotion.

Halfway through, my hands start to shake yet again. I stop everything that I'm doing, remain frozen. There it is again! A *tapping* noise coming from the backdoor!

I rush out of the bathroom and grab a gun from the nightstand. I make sure it's loaded. Then, I turn off the safety and check on the noise.

More tapping!

I realize someone's gently knocking on the door.

I peek through the curtain and see a dark figure standing outside. My heart starts to beat a little faster. I remind myself to remember the training.

*Keep calm*, I tell myself again as I approach the backdoor. I switch on the light and unlock the door.

With my finger close to the trigger, I open the door. . .

A man dressed in a black hoody is standing on the porch.

“Show me your hands, motherfucker,” I say and take aim.

He removes the hoody from his head and reveals himself.

Roger Sonnenberg?

“Why are at my house?” I ask.

“We need to talk,” he says.

I keep the gun on him.

“Whatever Baron Orwell’s said about me, it’s not true.” He points inside. “Please, Rashida. We need to talk. It’s important.”

I lower my gun and let him inside.

✡ ✡ ✡

As soon as I realize that he’s not going to be a threat, I put on a pot of coffee. I do my best to keep him from the living room where I have information on him, including photos, records, and background profiles on each one of his associates neatly tucked away inside folders—all of it meant to be handed over to Pelham, that is before he rejected my idea that a bunch of mad scientists were behind the abductions, as well as Bry’s murder—but my workspace is the first thing that he notices. He skims through a folder on the coffee table and acts as if it doesn’t bother him that I’ve been sticking my nose into his life. I ask him, “So, are you gonna tell me why you’re really here—”

“—I know you’re working with Orwell,” he says, examining the table full of his personal information.

"Clearly," he says and removes a photo of himself from the folder.

"If you're just here to tell me that Orwell can't be trusted, you're wasting your time," I tell him. "I know now what he's capable of doing."

"Did he blackmail you? Threaten you? What was it?"

Does using my own gun to kill a man count as blackmail?

I don't answer Roger's question. I think he already knows my answer. He walks over to the map on the wall. Remains rather quiet.

"Why are you really here?" I ask.

"Let me ask you something, Rashida," he says, ignoring my question. "Did Orwell tell you about how I met Frankie?"

"He said you met her through your father," I say.

"Yes," he replies. "That's right. As you may already know, my father worked for an elite unit of professional assassins called Reaper Squads."

"I heard. The world's last line of defense. Some people called them *Black Suits. Angels of Death.* They have no country affiliation. They are, essentially, men without country."

"Not bad."

When I imagine Roger's father as a Reaper, only one image comes to mind: a man dressed in a black hazmat suit with a oxygen mask and assault rifle gripped in hand. Surrounded by other Reapers, like himself, marching through the smoky gray lands of a nuclear winter, moving their way from ruined village to another, killing off the sick or dying.

"My father," he says, shaking his head. "Mr. All-American. It was all a lie, a front. Did you know Reaper Squads were disbanded after one of the members attacked the United Nations?"

"I did not."

"Two hundred and thirty-one people slaughtered," Roger says.

"Why?"

"Who knows," he says. "A sleeper agent? Or just a soldier with his brain wired all wrong? PTSD? It could've been anything. Anyway, Reapers lost all credibility. Undermined the very thing they fought against. My father was out of a job. I'll tell you one thing about my father: he was good at hiding, like Frankie. The best."

"If he was so good, then how'd you find out?"

"Never underestimate a child's intuition."

"I'd say some of those characteristics rubbed off on you?"

"You can say that," he says, pacing around the coffee table. "When I was a kid, I had an idea that something wasn't quite right with him. All of the sneaking around. He was good at what he did, though."

"Your father sounds like a real humanitarian."

He picks up the sarcasm in my voice.

"Frankie did that to people, made them stronger, better at what he or she did." He finally takes a seat on the couch and makes himself comfortable, which makes me a little less nervous. "You know, after the Americans dropped the bomb on Hiroshima, the Reapers were called in to contain the fallout. Eradicate every man, woman, and *child* on sight. They were exactly what their name said they were: Reapers, the very personification of death." He takes a moment to himself, picks up one of the photos of his father. Looks it over, not with reflection but more or less repulsion. "When my father and his team were deployed to Nagasaki, he came across a girl underneath the rubble. He couldn't bring himself to kill her."

"Why?" I ask. "Why not kill her? That was his job, right?"

"I don't know the reason why, but I think that, if he did kill her, he would be killing one of God's greatest creations."

"That's what you think she is, a creation? Seems more like a mutation."

Roger narrows his eyes. I've clearly hit a sore spot.

"So, like I was saying, he rescued Frankie, smuggled her home with him."

"Okay." I ask, "So, I'm curious. Why the name Frankie?"

"She liked franks and beans."

"Franks and beans?"

"Yeah," he says, a smile trying to break through all of that sternness. "Used to eat them when we were younger. I hated them. This lady who took care of me at daycare forced me to eat them; but apparently, Frankie, she loved them. She only ate the franks. So I've heard." He catches himself laughing, but he gets serious again. "She was like the daughter my father never had," he says. "To protect her, he placed her in a convent where she was raised by nuns."

"Why didn't your father bring her to his house with him? Why the convent?"

"I thought maybe he was embarrassed of me," Roger says, carrying a heavy sadness in his eyes. "He hid her from me for so many years. I don't know." He shrugs, hangs his head. "I think he did it because he didn't want to expose Frankie to the real world. After my father died, he sent me a letter with pictures of Frankie; he told me to watch after her. We hadn't spoken in years. The last time we did, I dropped out of medical school to pursue a career as an artist."

"Artist, huh?"

"I was young and confused," he says. "I mostly dabbled in painting and sculpting. My father was right—and wrong. My heart was pulling me in one direction, my brain the other. Being a doctor was the most logical choice. Anyway, I got into a fight with my father. Hit him. It was bad." His eyes drift off, as if the thought alone of what happened to him years ago still weighs heavily on him. "Can you imagine that? A son striking his own father, hurting him?"

"Why'd you do it?" I ask Roger.

"He was upset about me dropping out of school. He said that 'no man can have a career in art, only a life full of pain and suffering.' Like he should know anything about pain and suffering. I think he hated me because he saw too much of himself in me. After I found out what had happened to him—the cancer he was hiding from me—I felt as if I needed to give him a chance. I never gave the man a chance in life. So, I felt obligated to give him a chance in death." He reaches for another photo. Holds it close. "When I first met Frankie, I understood why he did it, why he wanted to keep her from me, from the world. She had this way about her, like a pull, to draw people closer to her, as she did with me. The second I laid eyes on her, I knew she was special. She *is* special."

"I'm sure she is," I tell Roger as he starts to tear up. He wears his broken heart on his sleeve. He wipes the tears away as soon as they reach his face.

"Once," he says, "I realized what she could do, I decided to dedicate the rest of my life trying to understand Frankie—"

"—Then why'd you kill her?"

He turns to me, baffled.

"I know all about it," I say. "Orwell told me. I tried to run a background check on you and you know what came up?" I answer for him, "Nothing. You don't even exist, Roger."

"If I could take back that night, I would," Roger says, as he hangs his head. "*But*, if I never got into that car on that rainy night, I would've never found out what she was capable of."

"So, what was so important that you needed to drive under the influence of alcohol?"

"We were celebrating, Frankie and I," he says. "Imagine, Rashida: a single drop of her blood curing cancer. Just imagine the power she held, then being able to harness that power for the greater good."

"You sound like all of those other whackos out there trying to save the world," I say. "Let me skip to the ending, Roger. It doesn't end well."

"You should know, Rashida," his eyes sharpen over mine, "nothing ever ends."

A tense pause in the conversation.

"So, why'd you run?" I ask.

"We just left the bar a couple of minutes after midnight," he says. "We were literally two miles away from home. I took my eyes off the road for a second, that's when I crossed the yellow line. When I realized that she was dead, I freaked out. I checked on the passengers in the other car. The husband was out of it; the wife didn't look good. So, I ran. I ran because I had to."

I say, "You ran because you couldn't own up to what you did. You were a coward who was afraid to face punishment."

"No," he says. "Not a coward. A survivor."

I bite my tongue on this one.

"Three days later," he says, "the husband wakes up from a coma. Has absolutely no idea about the death of his wife. He doesn't even know he has a wife. Somehow, after the wreck, Frankie metaphysically transferred herself into Sam Lieber's body."

"What? You mean, like bodyswapping?"

He shakes his head—not sure if he's shaking his head no or shaking his head from the tone of my voice. I think he's more or less embarrassed by the term.

"I call it 'lacing.'"

"Lacing?"

"To us, it happens so quickly it may look like a floater in the corner of our eye," he describes. "To her, it's like lacing up tennis shoes."

"How does she do it? This lacing?"

"There's an indigenous tribe that resides just off the Yellow River. They practice the art of self, cancel out thought, letting the mind go blank, body loose, just being, not being 'distracted' by any outside forces, to let go of one's self. Fahim believed that was the only way to prevent her from taking over; otherwise, she'd just pass over the body. Like wind. In theory, she transfers herself by touch. She can even transfer herself by simply looking you directly in the eyes."

Roger moves his eyes toward mine and holds them there. I find myself looking away.

"If that's the case," I say, not looking in his eye but more or less just looking in his vicinity, "then she could be inside you and you not even know about it?"

"In theory, yes."

I look into his eyes once more. Hold them there. He tilts his head to the side and smirks at me.

"How do I know that I'm talking to you and not her?"

"She's not flesh and blood like you and I—"

"—Who is she?"

Roger—or whoever the hell he may be right now—doesn't answer my question. For some reason, I don't expect an answer from him because I've asked the wrong question. Not a who but a what. What is she? I decide to leave the question hanging in the air for him to answer whenever he feels as if he can trust me.

"Two days later after the accident," he says, "Sam Lieber is discharged from the hospital with a clean bill of health. I pay Lieber a visit at his house. I asked him certain questions. He knew things only Frankie knew. Things that Frankie and I shared together. Personal things. That's when I knew *who* he was. He was her. Sam Lieber was Frankie—"

"—Sounds like what happened to Sam Lieber was more along the lines of religion. More of a spiritual experience, if you know what I mean."

"For years, I questioned my faith," he says, more passionately. "I didn't know what to believe anymore. I believe in Frankie. I believe she has a purpose. I don't know what it is yet. Maybe it's better that way, me not knowing what happens next—"

"—If you are right, Roger, about everything you've just told me, and this Frankie girl is truly one of a kind—I mean truly a gift from God—then why in the hell does Orwell want to destroy her so badly?"

"He never wanted to destroy her," he says. "He wanted to save her."

"Save her from what?"

He pauses—not sure if it's hesitation or him simply thinking of the right words to use—then he answers: "From me."

"She's inside a man named Kris Solles, ex-marine turned assassin. The same man who Orwell sent to Mount Olympus to—how do I say—exercise his power."

"Orwell doesn't give a shit about him or what he can do now," he says. "He wants her. He wants to trap lightning in a bottle. That's all. Like all businessmen, all he cares about is results. She's an investment to him. He promised to expunge my record, in exchange I'd give him all the cures to every disease known to man, years of research toward finding answers to life's questions: Where we came from? Who we are and what's our place? When we weren't giving Orwell the results he wanted, that's when things got out of hand. He started cutting deals with prisons, inmates carrying out life sentences to volunteer as guinea pigs. I guess when you're locked in a cage you'd probably do anything to have a taste of freedom. It was an utter disaster—a circus show. They signed their life away to science. That's exactly what happened to them, they were signing their own death sentence. It had gotten to the point where she was doing more harm than good. We were nothing more to Orwell than a bad investment that needed to be liquidated. Instead of cash, he wanted blood. My blood. My entire team's blood. No witnesses. No survivors. Luckily, some of us managed to escape before the bloodshed. Others weren't so lucky. He wanted to take Frankie away from me and hold me, as well as everyone I was associated with, responsible for Frankie's lack of progress."

"Then, why not just give him what he wanted? Why not give Frankie to him?"

"After a while, Frankie knew what she was turning into?"

"And what was that?"

"A monster." He turns away, trying to keep his shit altogether. "She didn't want to be an experiment anymore. Who would?" he says. "I guess you can call it Frankie's way of getting back at Orwell. I mean, after all, the best way to get back at a man is through his pockets. Am I right?"

He moves his now sharpened eyes toward mine and holds them there again, as if he's trying to pull something from me, a reaction or maybe it's him just studying me—not sure what he's doing or why he's really here besides informing me about stuff that I mostly already know.

At that moment in time, when I locked my eyes onto his, that's when I realize he may think he knows more about me than I do about him, but the truth of the matter is he doesn't know a damn thing about me.

## 9. THE CURATOR / ROGER

IT'S happening.

Soon, the entire world will know about us, about Four Lakes, what went on here; they'll know about what we've been up to. I'll admit that Fahim's right to a certain degree. This time when they do find us, they might succeed. We will be completely outnumbered, but I'm still holding onto what very little faith I have left. As soon as I get back from Raleigh, Sy and Fahim agree to commence the beginning stages of Phase Two while I search through each video for any possible clues that might suspect that Frankie is hiding inside one of the members of the lacrosse team.

While Sy and Fahim wait for orders, I point at the monitor. There.

"Start with her," I say. "Judith Ilderton."

"Why her?" asks Sy. "If you don't mind me asking."

"Of all the girls, she's the strongest. Survival of the fittest, remember? The strongest always finds a way to survive."

"What are you going to do, Roger?" asks Fahim.

"Like I've mentioned, I'm going to go back over the videos and try to see if I missed anything."

"That's hours of footage—"

"—I didn't say it was going to be easy, Sy."

Sy's hands are shaking.

"Is everything all right?"

"Yes," he hesitates. "I'm just a little nervous."

"No reason to be nervous." I try to reassure Sy. "Just look at this way: Death will come to us swiftly, no matter the outcome. If Orwell and his men find us, then we're dead. If the FBI finds out, we're dead; however, if we find Frankie, then—well—maybe we can reason with her; and if she doesn't comply, then there will be absolutely nothing left of us. As for the fate of the world, I'm hoping that maybe—just maybe—Frankie sees something in these twelve candidates that will make her change her mind about us, about mankind."

"What's the point in all of this, Roger?" says Sy, growing more upset. "Seriously? If we find her, how are we going to sit her down and explain to her that we're not 'bad' people, especially after everything we've done to her?"

"I'm not going to have this conversation with you, Sy—"

"—She deserves the truth, Roger!"

"Yes," I say, remaining calm. "She does. She deserves the world. Sooner or later, someone else will come along. Someone with more power. Someone far worse than Baron Orwell. And when that day comes, they *will* find Frankie. They'll lock her up. They'll exploit her, her gifts. Do you understand, Sy? They'll bleed her dry. Is that what you want?"

"If it's meant to happen, it's meant to happen," says Sy. "You can't protect her forever. The truth is you're going to die, Roger. Not now, but eventually. And when you do, she'll be out there on her own."

The thought of Frankie trying to make it all on her own doesn't scare me. A part of me yearns for Frankie to lace herself into the body of another person, restart a brand new life, healthy and carefree, live a full life without fear or regret.

What scares me the most: Frankie meeting a man like me.

## 10. THE AGENT / RASHIDA

TWO miles outside the quaint town of Haden rests a massive stretch of land that once used to be a rundown golf course but now soon to be home of a new shopping center with affordable townhouses, two grocery stores, a game store, beauty salon, new Thai restaurant, coffee shop. The townhouses have started development. The land has been cleared, pipes and whatnot already buried, the foundation has already been laid down. I meet up with Orwell and his goons in a cul-de-sac. I don't exactly know why a man of Orwell's stature would put his money into this commercial development in the middle of nowhere. To me, it seems a little beneath him. I can't help but wonder if it's all a front for something far sinister. I notice the cement mixer truck when I first pull up. The truck is parked in an empty lot and it appears as if it has no earthly business being there. The mixer, I notice, has already started to rotate. A group of Orwell's men are gathered around the mixer. One of Orwell's guards—Gerald—greets me as I get out and escorts me to Orwell, who's standing outside the SUV and watching the mixer from a distance.

"I'm glad you made it, Agent Jones," Orwell says, not even acknowledging my presence.

"What's so important that you had me drive all the way out here in the sticks?"

A couple of manila folders are resting on the hood of the SUV.

Orwell picks up one of the folders. I can't keep my eyes off the mixer pouring cement into what looks like a rectangular box with a wooden coffin inside.

I turn to Orwell and he's staring at me.

"Don't worry, Agent Jones," he says, surprisingly wearing a grin on his face. "It's not for you."

He opens the folder. Inside are papers and photographs.

"I have a new job for you, Agent Jones."

Orwell pulls out a black and white photograph of a petite Japanese woman—possibly closer to the younger side of seventy. He hands me the photo.

"It's simple. I want you to track down this woman in the photograph. She was last spotted in Tokyo."

"What if I say no?"

"It would be in your best interest that you don't. Besides, I'm starting to really like you, Agent Jones. If you decide not to help me, then you will no longer be working for the FBI."

That's the least of my worries.

Orwell deliberately shot the man in the back of the head to make his death look like an execution. Clearly, he wasn't shot out of self-defense—doesn't take a genius to figure out that he was murdered in cold blood. They'll trace the bullet back to my gun. I can't sneak my way out of this one, at least not anytime soon. Hate to say it but Orwell's right. I have no choice other than to help him.

"So, who is she, the woman?" I ask, nodding at the woman in the photo.

"She's Frankie's sister—twin, actually." He hands me another photo of the same older Japanese woman walking along a crowded market street. "These photos were taken last year by one of my men. They were the last photos given to me before he went MIA."

"Where the hell did he go?"

"I lost contact with him," he says. "More than likely, he's probably dead."

"Does Sonnenberg or the others know about her?"

"Only you, Agent Jones." He speaks directly to me: "And I plan on you keeping it that way—"

"—What do you want me to do?"

"I want you to go to Japan, find Frankie's twin, bring her to me. Can you do that for me, Agent Jones? Can you bring her to me?"

"Bring her to you?" I say. "So, what? So you can perform your experiments on her?"

"No," he says. "I have other plans for her, ones that will benefit the both of us."

"Care to tell me what these plans are?"

"Let's just say, she'll be in much better hands."

Vague much. The guy is straight out of a movie.

"And if I do, what's in it for me?"

"Your life," Orwell says to me. "So, what's it going to be, Agent Jones?"

The weight of cement suddenly caves in the coffin!

✪ ✪ ✪

Once I make it back home, I grab a bag of frozen peas from the freezer and place the bag over my head. I still can't wrap my head around today—let alone last night. The strange men and the things they did with their bodies. I'm still left wondering what Orwell meant after he told me when I left Haden, that he'll take it from here. He wants me to track down some woman who's possibly Frankie's twin. Maybe he's doing it so he can just get rid of me. I get the feeling that something has happened. There's been a break in the case; a change in Orwell's original plans. They know something I don't know. It doesn't occur to me what exactly has transpired until I find myself standing in front of a map of North Carolina. I recognize the town of Burch Valley, which isn't too far away from Gibson; in fact, it's only a few miles away. I fish through my notes until I come across the devil himself, Bry's murderer. I dig out an old newspaper article about all of the controversy surrounding Four Lakes. The mental institution was forced to shut down by public outrage in October of 1997 after it had come to light that several of its patients died during lobotomies. They were also known to perform other barbaric operations, but there wasn't enough evidence to prove such claims. He was one of the doctors who had lost his license due to malpractice. Now, apparently, the mental institution has been boarded up. The legend goes that Four Lakes is haunted, and thrill seekers have been known to sneak into the now decrypted institution and film horror movies or whatever kids do nowadays. It can't be a coincidence that Solles was in the area.

Four Lakes happens to be located a couple of miles from Burch Valley.

## 11. THE CURATOR / ROGER

THE clock is ticking.

So far, I've been through every single assessment of each candidate and still, I haven't found anything significant.

In the monitor, I see the first candidate, Judith, starting to succumb to the gas. She lies down on the couch and finally, she goes to sleep.

As soon as she's out like a light bulb, the three guardsmen enter the main room and drag Judith into the hallway.

While on this is going on, Sy enters the surveillance room.

"Roger," says Sy, "it's time."

The guardsmen set Judith in the wheelchair and escort her toward West Wing.

"Remember, Sy," I say, "she's going to be confused when she wakes up. So, you're going to have to ease into the question."

"You sure you don't want to join me? I'd feel more comfortable with you being there."

"I'll be right here, watching you—"

—There's a chance Fahim might say something—"

"—Just let him follow your cues," I say. "I'll be watching her every move through the monitors. If I suspect anything—I mean anything—I'll notify one of the guards." I can't stress enough. "It's going to work."

Sy doesn't have much to say. He nods his head.

As he's about to exit, I tell him, "Good luck."

"Thanks," says Sy as he walks away. "I'm going to need all the luck I can get right now."

I get back to work.

✡ ✡ ✡

At ten minutes and thirty-two seconds into the assessment, Judith smiles at a question she is asked. I can't explain why, but for some reason, I take a mental snapshot of the smile. I know that smile. I've seen it before. Then she smiles again at exactly eleven minutes and seventeen seconds. It's—more or less—a smirk than a smile. That's the clue. . .

The smirk.

June.

I rewind the video and watch the clip again and again until I see June in Judith's smile—hiding.

I grab the polygraph results from each one of the candidates' answers and conclude that around the eleven-minute mark of the assessment the results look similar, if not, the exact same. She's talking to us. . .

I go back and watch other videos of past subjects.

The frog.

Before that, the salamander; then each reptile, the snake, the alligator.

The guard before the alligator.

I watch the video of the old man whom Frankie laced herself into when we were taking a walk in the park.

The autistic boy.

Then, the mouse.

The monkey.

Each person or even animal that Frankie took over had left a trace or characteristic of the prior host. Certain attitudes or cues. Behavior patterns. Signature gestures. Or even nervous ticks such as the guard cracking his jaw whenever he felt uncomfortable.

When the Frankie entered the guard after having just been inside an alligator, the guard displayed unusual immobility. I thought maybe it was just another side effect of an individual being in contact with Frankie. I was wrong! Frankie isn't just using her ability to play just another game of soul tag, tagging her way from one host to another—You're it! She carries a piece of the host with her wherever she goes. . .

Once I figure out the clue, I pull up every assessment from Phase One, starting with the assistant coach, Pamela Van Buren, and then work my way back.

I watch each video until I find the one characteristic—the smirk.

While Sy works his way up to informing Judith Ilderton of Frankie's presence, I reach the eleven-minute mark.

Then, I see it!

I pause the video.

The freeze frame shows Pamela bending one side of her mouth in a smirk. I rewind the live assessment with Judith and pause the tape at eleven minutes.

I watch the assessment until she smirks at eleven minutes and seventeen seconds.

I compare the smirk with the freeze frame of Pamela.

They match!

I do the same with each assessment and look for the smirk in each one of the candidates' faces.

The second candidate, Rhea Johnson, displays the same smirk when she's talking about her auntie. I match the facial expression with the same one on Judith and Pamela's face.

I pull up the next assessment and find the same smirk on the third candidate's face—Yadira Santiago.

The smirk on the fourth is easy to spot.

The fifth candidate is much harder. I have to zoom in for a closer look. The smirk is faint, but it's there.

The sixth candidate.

The seventh.

I fast-forward through the assessment of the tenth candidate, Ebony Acres; discover the smirk; then go back and forth from one screen to another, comparing each freeze frame.

"She's in all of them. . . "

I end with the last candidate, the eleventh, Stewart Tabby, and search for June's smirk. Strangely, I'm unable to find the smirk throughout the entire eleventh minute. I go back and watch one more time. I can't find anything. I watch yet again but still can't find any indication that Frankie has taken over his body.

Suddenly, the lights flicker above while I'm going through Stewart's assessment!

I check the live feed on the monitors. A couple of screens start to act up. The video goes fuzzy and scrambly and several surveillance cameras flicker. One of the monitors grabs my attention: Pamela stands up from the bed and strolls toward the door. She places her hand over the door. She robotically turns her head toward the surveillance camera.

The camera suddenly fills with static!

Each and every monitor of the cell fills with static. . .

I check the camera above the staircase leading toward the basement of West Wing. A strange man is walking down the stairs. He enters a long stretch of hallway leading toward the interrogation room. I notice the man's carrying something in his hand. I get a side view of his face.

Kris Solles?

An alarm suddenly goes off!

One of the candidates has escaped. . .

I search the other monitors, checking the hallway cameras. The door to Haley's cell is open. I frantically check the other monitors but I can't find her anywhere. I finally locate Haley heading toward West Wing. Two guards are approaching her from the north. If they run into her, who knows what Frankie will do to them.

I quickly grab the tranq gun.

As I'm about to leave the surveillance room, I spot movement coming from one of the outdoor surveillance cameras. I check the monitor. A black SUV parks in front of the gates. A team of heavily armed mercenaries dressed in black rushes toward the gates while three suited men pour from the SUV.

The last man to exit is none other than Baron Orwell himself.

☼ ☼ ☼

Before I reach West Wing, I hear the sound of a man screaming bloody horror. I arrive at an intersection of hallways, the lights still flickering with a pulse of dim light; however, I can only make out two silhouettes at the end of the hallway.

One of the guards—I can't tell which one—is pointing a gun at Haley. He's yelling at her to put up her hands. Haley's not cooperating.

Suddenly, two gunshots flash through the darkness, each flash bringing Haley in and out of a soft light; in those two briefs moments, I witness Haley widening her stance, her left leg sliding forward while her right leg slides backward as if she's bracing herself for the incredible energy that's about to be released from her body; and then, the second flash, Haley lowering her head and opening her mouth in a gaping yawn.

A high-pitch scream suffocates a dampened explosion, creating the sound of a numbing quake that cuts throughout the facility. A tremor races through my entire body, causing each and every nerve to fire up like a million fire ants biting at me all at once!

The wake from the surge of energy forces me a couple of steps back in my already supported stance and the notion of what's about to happen next turns my blood cold as ice.

I get a closer look, flickers of the shoddy fluorescent light highlighting scenes of gore. Whatever remains of the guard is nothing but pieces of flesh, crushed bones, and blood splattered over both the walls and ceilings.

She literally turned his body inside out!

"Frankie!" I suddenly call out, hoping to draw a rise from her.

Haley turns to me. She stands still and acknowledges me with a pensive gaze before she takes off and runs the other direction. I don't know if it's her way of telling me to chase after her or if it's just her wanting me to play a game with her. Right now, I don't think she knows the difference.

## 12. THE HIRED GUN / KRIS

AS soon as I arrive at the basement floor of Four Lakes, two gunshots ring out!

Following the gunshots are the familiar screams of a man. Soon, the screams taper off; and before I can track down the source of the commotion, I come across what I think is a man. The only thing I can make out is a hand with a silver watch on a wrist. The rest of the arm has been torn to shreds and appears as if it has been ripped off a body, which remains completely unrecognizable. The thought of Theo comes to me in the image of him flashing through my mind; me watching him die in my arms, taking his final gasps as he bleeds out.

Blood is everywhere: oozing down the walls, dripping from the ceiling, covering the floors. I think about Oscar, the black panther, wondering if the wild animal is responsible.

After examining the scene, I realize no animal is capable of such horror. Whatever it is, it's more powerful than the creature at Mt. Olympus. I concentrate on the magnetic pull—the same one that's been tugging at me ever since I arrived in the town of Gibson—and it's telling me that I'm getting close. *Keep moving.* I keep moving.

I get about halfway down yet another hallway and hear the sound of footsteps coming my way—fast!

I dart to the end of the hallway—away from the noise—and peek around the corner only to find a guard approaching me.

With the butt of my gun, I knock him out cold, drag him into a janitor's closet, and strip the uniform from his body.

Once I'm dressed, I keep moving. Two other guards rush past me. They don't pay any attention to me. I round a corner and find even more guards perched outside a door. Two of them, both appear on high alert. Their guns are drawn too, as if they're waiting on me.

That tug feels the strongest it has ever been.

I don't waste anytime. I make my move.

Once I'm spotted, one guard hurries into the room behind him, closes the door, while the other one calls out, "Stop right there!"

I ignore the guard's demands and take him out with a single gunshot to the head before he can return fire. I shoot out the lock to the door and bust it open.

The guard's gun is drawn on me. He squeezes the trigger, but nothing comes out of his gun.

As with the other guard, I shoot him directly between the eyes.

I step farther into the room. I see the same two men from my original hit list, Doctor Bloch and Doctor Ahmad, standing next to a desk with cameras pointed at a sickly girl hooked up to a polygraph machine.

They don't appear as if they're going to be threat. So, I rip the wires from the girl's body and reach out my hand.

"Name's Kris Solles," I tell her. "I'm here to set you free."

She grabs my hand.

We exit the room.

"This way," I tell her, motioning toward the hallway where the other captives are being held.

"Your name is Kris?" she asks.

"That's right, but you can call me Brixx. And you?"

"Judith," she says. "Judith Ilderton."

"Pleasure to meet you."

Another voice yelling out from behind: "Freeze!"

I stop in my tracks and turn around. The same two guards I passed earlier have guns on us.

"Let her go," the guard says.

I let go of Judith's hand and hold my hands up.

"Now, drop the gun! Do it or I'll shoot!"

I kneel down and drop the gun onto the floor.

In the corner of my eye, I witness another girl around the same age as the other one inching into the hallway. The girl creeps behind the guards with both of her hands curled into fists. Her body is trembling. Her forehead leans forward. Mind heavy. Jaw clenched tight. Both of her eyes sharp and filled with rage.

One of the guns starts to melt in the guard's hand!

Before the other guard can turn his aim, his head violently snaps to the right—*ka-ka-runch*—causing his neck to snap like a twig; part of his spinal cord now sticking out of his skin; the other one is twisted and contorted in the air and flung against the wall, hitting the wall so hard that he shatters every bone in his body. Not only that, the girl doesn't even lay a finger on them! She doesn't even land a single blow!

We share a moment. She stares at me, yet I don't seem the least frightened by her presence. I seem the opposite. I'm comforted by the sight of her.

I think of the only word that comes to mind.

"Thanks," I tell her.

The other one, Judith, calls out the girl's name, "Haley."

While the two embrace one another, I grab the pair of keys from the guard's belt.

This girl, Haley, pulls herself from Judith and walks up to me.

"We have to free the others," she says, brimming with confidence. "Can you help?"

"—Yes," Judith says before I can utter a word. "He's here to help."

"Here," I say and toss her the keys.

The two doctors cautiously step into the hallway. The girls turn their attention toward the men.

Haley hands the keys to Judith and does that thing again with her eyes. She holds out her hand in a halting position, tosses the two doctors in the air as if they weighed no lighter than action figures. One of them slams against the wall. The other one gets the wind knocked out of him.

I don't know where to begin to even try to fathom how a teenage girl—who's probably pushing around a buck-thirty—is able to release enough energy to send a grown man in the air like that. Maybe it's just one of those things that I'm not supposed to understand.

Maybe I'm just too old to understand.

Maybe there's something else going on behind the scenes.

Something that will soon come to light.

Whatever it is, I feel as if I'm going to find out pretty soon.

## 13. THE CURATOR / ROGER

WHEN I make it to the interrogation room, I find both Sy and Fahim lying on the floor.

Sy is holding the side of his head and trying to sit upright. He's bleeding badly from his head, but from what I can tell, the wound doesn't appear life threatening.

Fahim, however, remains unconscious.

I rush over to Sy and ask if he's good.

"Yeah," says Sy, out of breath. "Good. Check on Fahim."

I check on Fahim.

I pat him a couple of times in the face until he comes to.

He looks around, confused.

"What happened?"

"What happened is Frankie," I say. "That's what happened."

I help him sit up, slowly.

"It's Kris Solles—"

"—I don't think he's with Orwell."

"He seemed like he was helping them escape," says Sy.

"I think you may be right."

"What?" says Fahim, still confused. "Why?"

"I don't know."

"What now?"

"We have much bigger problems now. We have to get out of here. It's Orwell," I tell them, "he found us."

"Just wonderful," says Sy.

"How about the girls?"

"Frankie," I tell them, "she's in *all* of them. I'm not sure about the coach, though."

"How is that possible?" says Sy, who's stricken with disbelief.

"I don't know how, Sy," I say. "Let's find out."

## 14. THE HIRED GUN / KRIS

"WAIT!" a voice calls out from the end of the hallway.

The doctors manage to catch up with us. There's another man with them, not a doctor, but more important than a doctor. They catch up to us while the other girls seek cover behind me. Like the other two doctors, he doesn't strike me as a man who wants to do any harm.

Once I get a better look at his face, I realized it's the other man from my list: the one and only, Roger Sonnenberg.

"Stay away from them," I say.

"Frankie," he says as he approaches both Judith and Haley, "it's me, Roger."

"I said, 'Stay away!'"

"She's in you, too, isn't she?" Roger says, pointing at me.

I don't know what he means by that.

"It's okay," he says. "You can feel her, can't you?"

I turn to the doctors.

"What's he talking about?"

I keep my finger on the trigger and wait for him to make a move.

I know he won't, though. It's not his style.

"Something happened at the research institute. Didn't it?"

Another image flashes through my mind and suddenly, *I'm face to face with the doctor.* A grainy still of Frankie trapped inside the body of June Lugosi. More images pour in, following the one before in a turbulent sequence, moving like a video being fast-forwarded, a circle jerk of violence, unrecognizable at first, then I slow down my thoughts and I take myself back to the first corridor, that same still of Frankie, then start from there. The video slows just enough and I see myself chasing after June Lugosi. The chase moves outside the research facility. Then, *she suddenly strikes me in the chest with a club of a fist, causing me to soar through the air, my back catching jagged branches.* The thought alone causes me to flinch from a momentarily flare of pain in my side. I put my mind on something else besides the pain, which, in return, causes the pain to lessen to the point of nonexistent. Mostly, I start thinking about the time I first found myself in June Lugosi's presence. I'm not sure if it was the blood rushing through my veins at that initial *impact* or Frankie making a lasting impression. A staticky sensation coursed throughout my entire body, I recall. Ever since I left Mt. Olympus, I haven't felt the same. If whatever Roger's telling me is, indeed, true, then something happened when June Lugosi made contact with me.

Something unexplainable. Something beyond science or faith.

"We need to free the others," I clarify.

"Right this way," Roger says, "but there's one thing—"

"—He's here. Orwell."

"Yes. You can feel him. Can't you?"

"I can," I say. "I don't know how, but I can."

"What do we do?"

"What we do," Haley cuts in, "is we kill these three for lying to us." She turns to me. "Do you know what they did to us? We can't trust them?"

"Please," Roger says, "I kept you here for your own good. I know it may be easy to point the finger at us. I realize what we did was wrong, but you must understand that we're *not* the bad guys here. The people waiting outside, if they find you, they will kill you. That's a fact."

"Why do these 'people' want us dead? What did we do to them?"

"You didn't do anything wrong, Haley," I say before Roger can answer. "As much as you may disagree with this man, he is right. Orwell's crew will kill each and every one of us."

Haley starts crying.

Really?

"Why?"

"To them, you're an investment—"

"—You are all an investment," Roger interrupts.

"We didn't give Orwell the results that he wanted, so he decided to cut all ties between himself and Roger and Roger's crew. It has absolutely nothing to do with you, Haley. It's what's inside you what they really want. What's inside us—"

"—Then we give it to them," Judith says calmly.

"I'm afraid it's not easy," Roger says. "Frankie is now as much a part of you as you are to her. She is a guest. And you are merely just a host."

"Then, how do I get rid of her?"

Roger says, "You have to die."

"Okay," I tell Roger. "Clearly, that's not on the table."

Haley asks, "What other options do we have?"

The entire building suddenly shakes!

I grab Judith by the hand.

"We get the hell out of here," I say.

✡ ✡ ✡

We manage to free six of the ten captives, one of them being Pam. One of the girls, Akea, looks as if she's at death's door. Another one, Rhea, is completely bald. Haley asks Rhea what happened to her hair. Roger cuts in before Rhea can answer and tells her that it's one of the many side effects of Frankie.

"I thought my auntie put a curse on me," Rhea says.

We keep moving forward.

By the time we reach the remaining four, Orwell's motley crew has already breached Four Lakes. We take cover behind a corner of the wall, watching carefully.

"So, who's left?" I whisper to Roger.

"The coach, Monica, Brittany. . . "

"Emily Nyquist is the last one."

Orwell's hired guns, who are armed to the teeth, shoot out each lock to the cell. They open each door and line up in firing formation.

"We can't just sit here and do nothing!" Haley cries out.

One of the girls, Yolanda, makes an attempt to rescue the captives, but I grab her before she can be spotted.

"Lemme go," she says.

Suddenly, I hear a commotion coming from the end of the hallway.

More gunshots ring out!

The four guns who had lined up in front of the remaining cells are lying on the ground. They're not moving.

"Agent Jones," Roger says from behind.

"FBI?"

"Looks like she had a change of heart."

I witness a black woman—this Agent Jones—coming forward, gun drawn.

"How do you know her?" I ask Roger.

"Agent Jones and I share a common interest," Roger says and breaks free from the group.

"Which is?"

"We're both outsiders."

Roger rushes toward Agent Jones.

I follow.

## 15. THE AGENT / RASHIDA

MY knuckles are throbbing—*What have you done, Rashida?*

I turn my attention away from the dead bodies, only to witness a familiar face coming closer. Solles has found the girls on the lacrosse team, and he doesn't appear as if he's taking them against their will. They all sprint toward me—the other girls clinging to Solles, along with Roger and his partners in crime, Bloch and that murdering son of a bitch. My attention is drawn away from Ahmad by the gasps of a girl in one of the cells. I ignore Ahmad, try my hardest to think of something other than avenging my partner, and hurry to the sound. One of the girls is holding her chest. Strings of blood are pouring through the cracks of her fingers. Blood is coming from her mouth as well. The blood is really thick, too, almost frothy in the way it bubbles and moves like lava from the corners of her mouth. The sight of her dying rips right through me, and an image of Jonah, so stark and so real, comes to me. I block out the images as soon as they manifest and I realize the poor girl doesn't have long. She only has a minute or two before she bleeds out.

"One of them has been shot," I tell Roger, trying to ignore Ahmad.

Roger hurries to the second cell where the girl Monica has been shot. He removes his sweater and presses hard against her chest.

"Can you save her?" one of the girls asks with desperation.

"I don't know," Roger says, pulling the sweater away for a brief moment. He examines the gunshot to her chest before he reapplies the pressure. He looks at me with an expression of dread on his face. I know the look. I know he wants to tell me the grim news, but I know he doesn't want Monica to hear his words. He grabs a hold of Monica's hand and tells her to hang in there. I know he's not speaking to Monica. I don't know how I know this, but I know that he's speaking to her, to Frankie.

"Please," the poor girl says, "I don't wanna die. . . "

The blood keeps coming, strangling her every word.

"You're *not* going to die," he reassures Monica, but I know from taking another glance at the wound that she has about a minute to live before her heart stops beating.

Roger has Bloch switch hands with his hand. While Bloch is applying pressure to the gunshot wound, Roger calls in the other members of the team to help comfort Monica while he runs to the Med-Lab to grab medical tools.

As he steps out of the cell, another group of Orwell's men approaches the cells. Solles picks up the assault rifles from one of the dead mercenaries and lays down an impressive cover fire, while Roger makes a run toward the laboratory. The resilient mercenaries push even closer, bullets ricocheting off the metal doors. One of the mercenaries manages to catch Solles with what looks like a lasso of some sorts around his neck. The metallic rope tightens around Solles's throat, causing him to drop his weapon; and then, in the blink of an eye, Solles is hoisted from his feet and pulled through the hallway.

"Brixx!" one girl—Judith, I believe—calls out to him.

Solles holds out his hand as he's pulled farther and father away. Finally, he disappears in the shadows of the hallway.

I grab a grenade from a dead body and toss it in the other mercenaries' vicinity.

That stops them, for a while.

I'm tempted to chase after Solles but Ahmad yells out to Roger before he can reach the laboratory.

"Come quick," he says.

Roger hurries back to the cell where something strange is happening to Monica. He shoulders his way into the cell as Monica starts to convulse—which reminds me of the girl back at The Golden Cache before she screamed blood Mary. Her body stiffens; her hands and feet curl inward, as if she's having a seizure or even a posturing attack one would experience after a brain injury. Her jaw clamps down so tightly that I can hear the teeth grating against one another.

In the flip of a switch, she stops moving. Her entire body appears as if it deflates.

Roger grabs Monica by the cheeks, holds his fingers underneath her nose, then presses his ear to her chest.

Roger's eyes billow open as Monica's chest pushes out in one giant inhale. I can see her dying. With Jonah, my parents were hovered over his body. I think he was already dead by the time we reached him because he wasn't breathing and his limbs were loose and lifelessly dangling when my father held his tiny body in his arms. With Monica, I *see* her die.

Whatever this thing is inside her body—this Frankie girl—tugs like an invisible string from her body. The air is incredibly warm around her, warmer than any other space, and I can feel that staticky feeling against my skin, like when I was a girl touching the screen of an analog TV, the static tickling the palm of my hand, then my frizzy hair sticking up in the air like that one woman in all of those Frankenstein movies. Her body starts to levitate in the air!

However, she doesn't quite reach the point of floating, but she nearly does. The backside of her wrist and ankles remain pinned to the floor while this warm force pulls itself from her body—that's all I can think of it, a force, a pull, like Roger described, because I can feel it slowly moving through the air as if it's tangible. Her body falls back to the floor and she lets out her last rattling breath. Her head flops to the right. Her glazed eyes pinned open. The other girls, as well as the two coaches, are crying behind me.

Roger checks Monica's pulse, but he doesn't bother administering CPR.

"Did she just die?" one of the girls asks.

The assistant coach, Pamela, consoles her.

"I'm sorry, Brittany," she says to her.

Another girl is trying to make sense of Monica's death.

She asks, "Would someone please explain to me what just happened?"

"She's dead, Akea."

"People don't do that when they die."

"Oh yeah! Like you would know!"

"Give it a rest, Akea," the coach says.

Behind us, Bloch is struggling to catch his breath. I realize he's choking. His face turns pale and sweaty. He backpedals and reaches out his hands, as if he's about to brace for a fall.

Ahmad grabs Bloch before he collapses. He helps lay him against the floor.

"Fahim," he says, "what's happening to me?"

If Bloch was choking, he wouldn't be able to speak.

Something else is going on with him.

He looks down at his hands in shock.

Ahmad turns to Roger.

"Roger?"

"My skin in burning up," he says. "My heart," he grabs his chest, suggesting that something may be going on inside his chest. A hear attack perhaps?

"What's wrong, Sy?"

"It can't be. . . " he murmurs as he continues to stare at his hands. He turns to Roger with a look of betrayal on his face. "Why me?"

Bloch directs his attention to the other nine girls who are looming above him and they're staring down at him with vacant expressions.

The top of his forehead cringes, an expression that appears uncharacteristic, especially coming from a grown man.

"Frankie," Roger says to Bloch, "are you in there?"

Bloch faces Roger.

His eyes big and glossy like the eyes of a stray dog.

"Luke. . . "

"No, Sy," Roger says. "It's me, Roger."

"Roger?"

"Yes."

"Where am I? What happened?"

"She chose you, Sy," he says as he tends to him.

"Me? Why me—"

"—Chose you?" Catherine blurts out. "What are you talking about? Who chose him?"

Roger turns to the rest of the girls.

"Frankie," he says to them. "She chose *all* of you."

The other girls look around at one another, half-amazed, half-confused.

"Why us?" Judith says. "Why are we so special?"

"I don't know, Judith," Roger says, "but she chose you all for a reason. One day, you may know what that reason is. I guess it's up to you to find out."

All of a sudden, Bloch starts crying, looking around, both paranoid and confused. Then, he frantically scratches the top of his scalp, pulls wads of hair from his head. Holds the hair in his palms in awe.

"It's normal, Sy."

He pulls more handfuls of hair from his head. He looks down at his palms. He ignores the stringy hair. Looks at the backside of his hand.

"Holy shit, Roger," he says. "You have no idea what you're missing."

"Can you stand?"

Bloch nods.

"Yeah," he says. "I think so."

"What about Solles?" I ask.

"Whatever Orwell plans on doing with him, it's out of our hands—"

"—But Frankie," I tell him, "she's inside him, remember?"

He doesn't respond. He acts as if he doesn't want to hear the truth right now.

As Roger helps Sy stand, the entire place starts to shake.

I hear helicopters swarming above!

"We have a bigger problem on our hands."

"What the hell is that?"

"Roger," I say, "there's something I need to tell you. It's important."

"Does it have to do with whatever that is outside?"

I don't answer at first. Roger demands an answer.

"I tried to warn them—"

"—Warn them? Warn who?"

I pause and try to be as diplomatic as possible.

"*Everyone*," I tell Roger.

As Roger attempts to speak, his mouth opens and remains open in a yawning gap. His eyes widen. I follow his eyes to Bloch, who's violently shaking on the floor.

"What's wrong with him?" one of the girls asks.

"I think he's having a bad reaction to Frankie."

A rope of foam is dribbling from his mouth. His joints are popping out of place. His muscles stretch and tear like elastic bands. His eyes roll over white. That's when everybody starts to freak, when his body starts doing things that no man can do. The temperature in the air suddenly gets warm, even hot to point of unbearable.

I turn to the other girls.

First, it starts with Pamela, then it slowly spreads to Akea, then another girl and then another. Lastly, it sucks Judith into the mass.

Whatever is trying to break free from their bodies, I don't want to be anywhere near when it finally surfaces.

## 16. THE HIRED GUN / KRIS

ONE second I'm picking off each one of Orwell's guns—and doing a pretty good job at keeping them away from the others. The next I'm being strangled by a wire and dragged away as if I'm a calf being strung up by a rancher. I manage to get one hand underneath the wire before I choke to death. I'm unable to cut through the wire with my blade. Even when I dig my blade into the wire, it sends an electrical shock through my body, forcing me to drop the blade. Eventually, I come to rest outside Four Lakes. I follow the end of the wire to the back of a tow truck. Next to the tow truck is a concrete mixer.

Before I can pounce to my feet, three other scumbags are bearing down on me. One of them pokes me in the neck with a needle and then applies these metal cuffs to both my wrists and ankles. Whatever drug is racing through my veins, it hits me in a matter of seconds.

Another gun puts an oxygen mask over my face.

I can hear Orwell somewhere in the middle of the haze.

His voice is cloudy but I can still make out what he's saying to his crew: "Give me a gun!"

I track down the voice and watch one of the guns handing a furious Orwell a pistol.

"If I'm not back in five minutes, take off."

The gun: "Sir, what about the agreement?"

Orwell's voice gets much cloudier: "Talk to Maron. He will be the one to continue my legacy. . . "

Maron?

He must've meant Baron.

I'm not sure what he means.

Orwell rushes inside Four Lakes.

The other two hoist me inside a cold metal box.

My eyelids get heavier and heavier.

Everything around gets cloudier and cloudier.

They close the lid.

The sounds start to slowly fade.
Then, I'm out.

## 17. THE CURATOR / ROGER

TWO of Orwell's heavily armed mercenaries sneak up behind Stewart and unload on him as he throws his body in front of Frankie. Stewart goes out in a glorious blaze of glory. His body stretches out in a Jesus Christ pose, his arms flapping around. The bullets cut right through him. The bullets that zip overhead catch Frankie, but they act like mosquito bites to her.

Agent Jones grabs me by the arm and advises me to come with her.

I take her advice; however, I can't help but watch the horror unfold before my eyes, the madness, each one of the girls, including Pamela, reacting differently to one another, some of them fleeing while others embracing each other; then Sy, making his best effort to break free from the crowd of bodies, but he's immediately sucked into an enormous network of flesh.

Emily makes a run for it, but Frankie uproars within and takes control over her body.

The force of Frankie causes Emily to *slam* against the wall!

Emily's head smacks the wall, causing her to fall into an unconscious state.

Frankie pulls Emily's lifeless body closer to the dog pile, one of her feet lifted in the air, as if it's the sole force driving Emily.

The remaining two girls, Yolanda and Judith, are the last ones to be driven into the flesh. Screams, moans, and groans of agony, a combination of noise, emit from Frankie. Arms and legs stick out from the mass like tree branches. Several hands reaching out to me, the desperate cries of a girl—Rhea or Haley, I can't tell which one—shouting for help. Eyes and other facial features scattered everywhere, disjointed, pulling a part like putty, an eye next to an ear, an ear next to a nose, everything being shuffled and stirred within the mass of flesh.

The sight of her gross transformation causes both extreme fascination and nausea.

After a while, it gets to a point where I can't make out any of the girls anymore.

They've all become one!

A giant ball of chaos!

"I don't understand what's happening—"

Another force is tugging at my arm.

"Come on, Roger!" yells Agent Jones.

"Something's not right," I tell Agent Jones over all of the tumult. "I've never seen this before—"

"—Let's go, Roger! We have to leave right now!"

I resist Agent Jones and stand and watch Frankie turn into a monster.

"I'm sorry, Frankie. . . "

Agent Jones pulls me in the opposite direction.

I go with her.

Directly above us, the helicopters start their descent over Four Lakes.

A medley of foot stomps storm closer. We head away from the chaos.

"Did you call the goddamn army?" I say, trying to keep up with Agent Jones.

"It's Pelham, my boss," says Agent Jones says. "The satellites must've picked up on Frankie's heat signature, the same one that goes off whenever there's a nuclear explosion. . . "

"That can't be," I say. "She wouldn't—"

"—Oh yeah!" shouts Agent Jones. "Well, we can't stay here to find out! Any moment, this entire place is going to be swarming with soldiers!"

As we make it to the surveillance room, Orwell's standing directly in our path. He's pointing a gun at us.

"I'm surprised to see you here, Agent Jones," says Orwell. "Guess that's what happens when you put your trust in people."

"It's too late, Baron," says Agent Jones. "Looks like you won't have your vengeance."

"Funny you bring that up when you're standing next to the man who murdered your former partner. Do yourself a favor and shoot that man," says Orwell, as he turns the gun toward me. "While you're at it, you can also shoot that son of a bitch for committing treason."

Agent Jones doesn't look at all surprised about the claims that Orwell is making.

"Fahim didn't kill your partner," I say. "I did—"

"—Roger," says Fahim, as he steps in front of me with his hands raised in the air. "Don't!" Fahim says to Agent Jones, "I was the one who shot your partner, not Roger. That's the truth. If you want your revenge, Agent Jones," he lowers his arms and motions to Agent Jones to shoot, "you can have it."

"Before you die, Roger, why don't you tell me where she is?"

Agent Jones turns her gun to Fahim.

"I *know* it was you who killed Agent Corbin."

Fahim entices Agent Jones by waving at her, as if he wants her to shoot him.

"Rashida," I pull Agent Jones' attention back toward me, "he was just doing what he was told. Please. Don't do this, Rashida. This is what Orwell wants—"

"—I'm not going to kill him."

"Where is she?" Orwell yells out as Agent Jones turns her aim toward Orwell.

A *thud* against the wall!

The floor shakes!

Suddenly, Frankie appears behind Orwell.

As Orwell's about to rotate around, Frankie has him by the throat. He manages to fire off three rounds before his body is completely ripped in half!

Frankie tosses both pieces of his body aside, his torso one way and his lower half the other.

As Frankie stomps closer, I turn to Fahim and tell him to get Agent Jones out of here.

"I'm staying," I say, as Frankie approaches.

"I'm not leaving you here to die," says Agent Jones.

"Fahim, get her out of here!"

Fahim grabs Agent Jones by the arm.

"Come on," says Fahim.

Agent Jones and Fahim make a run for it as Frankie slowly waddles closer to me.

I witness a familiar face within the ball of flesh—Sy's face!

She moves even closer to me, timid at first, like a shy creature.

More faces within the ball of stirring flesh, past faces, faces of great anguish and suffering, hundreds of faces.

Among all of the warped faces, one of them comes forth throughout all of the chaos and confusion and it's as clear to me as never before, the one face that I fell in love with when I was just another ungrateful kid cast from an era of rebellion, a kid who never displayed an ounce of respect for his own father even though I had an entire world of respect for him, a kid, nonetheless, even though I was old enough to be a man.

Before I can map out every detail of Frankie's original face, it falls back into a swirl of flesh.

Behind Frankie, a platoon of soldiers line up like a firing squad, take aim, and fire at Frankie; however, bullets bounce off her thick hide. If they knew that each shot is making her that much stronger and larger. Portions of flesh start to darken and harden around random areas of the body. Portions of flesh turn to scales. Yellow dots randomly pop up on parts of the body, similar to dots on a salamander.

I yell at Frankie, tempting her closer, to take me.

To my left, I see light flickering from one of the monitors inside the surveillance room. I look closer while soldiers continue to fire at Frankie.

In the monitor, Agent Jones and Fahim are racing through Four Lakes trying to find a way out. What they don't realize is an entire army is waiting for them outside. More soldiers. Hummers and tanks and helicopters. I doubt their orders are to take prisoners alive. They run into another platoon in the lobby.

I dart into the surveillance room for a much better look at the monitors. I watch another platoon open fire on both Fahim and Agent Jones.

Fahim steps in front of Agent Jones and acts as a human shield.

## 18. THE AGENT / RASHIDA

AHMAD takes a bullet for me.

In his dying breaths, he apologizes for murdering Bry. He tells me that it was the only way to save Frankie from the world.

His last words before he dies: *Whatever Orwell has told me to do, do not do it.*

I try to get more out of Ahmad, but he falls to his knees, bleeding profusely from his chest.

I carefully ease his body onto the floor and watch his final breath leave him.

His eyes glaze over and fixate on mine.

I call out my name to the soldiers and tell them that I'm a FBI agent.

Like they care.

They keep firing at me.

That's when I realize that they have been ordered to kill every last person on site.

This isn't a rescue crew.

It's a cleanup crew.

## 19. THE CURATOR / ROGER

As bullets fly all around me, I watch Agent Jones step away from Fahim and take cover behind a wall.

The soldiers continue to fire at her, despite her being on their side. She manages to squeeze through a basement window without being shot by the soldiers.

I track her down on the next monitor.

She runs to her car.

Then the next monitor: Agent Jones gets inside her car.

As she's driving away, a sudden *blast* of what sounds like a grenade launcher causes the entire facility to tremble!

Pieces of foundation start to break apart and spit dust and handfuls of debris from the ceilings.

The entire facility is falling apart.

It's only a matter of time before it collapses.

## 20. THE AGENT / RASHIDA

I floor it through the barricades in the middle of the road.

The impact flattens my front right tire, but the car is still drivable.

I check the rear view mirror.

The soldiers aren't following me.

Strange.

They get on their radios and turn to Four Lakes.

They grab their rifles and rush the opposite direction.

I figure I'm in the clear for now.

I keep driving.

☼ ☼ ☼

I barely make it to the next town.

An alarm is blaring throughout Main Street. Civilians are frantically running around, dropping whatever they're carrying to scramble to their cars. They've been ordered to evacuate.

It's a zoo.

## 21. THE CURATOR / ROGER

THE war continues to rage. I peek my head from the surveillance room and notice Frankie, who has now grown twice the size she was before. Even though the gunshots are only making her stronger, the soldiers keep firing away. She eats each bullet as if it's candy. At this rate, she's going to be the size of Four Lakes by the time the army breaches West Wing.

Suddenly, another rocket is launched at Frankie!

The rocket misses her by inches and heads directly toward me. . .

Frankie suddenly grabs the rocket in mid-air and rams the nose of the rocket against her body.

Billows of flames come charging at me!

The explosion lifts me off my feet; and I find myself trying to grab hold of something, but all I grab is air.

Blood rushes through my veins.

The ringing intensifies in my ears.

The shock sets in.

Then, the blackness.

## 22. THE HIRED GUN / KRIS

ANOTHER *ka-runch*!

Another thunderous vibration forces me to wake, but all I can see is blackness all around me.

Gradually, a sunbeam pierces through the blackness.

Wet concrete slowly pours over my body.

It starts to fill the container; then, before I can make sense of what's going on, I'm drowning in a thick and heavy nastiness.

Before I'm completely smothered by concrete, I'm yanked from the box.

I feel my body being hoisted back in the air, but this time I keep soaring higher and higher.

At first, I think I'm dead.

Must've been buried by concrete.

And now, it's just my soul flying through the air.

Then, I look down and see that I'm lying on a giant palm of what is supposed to be a hand. Within the palm, there are other much tinier hands reaching at me, grabbing at my body, rubbing me, comforting me.

I follow the hand to a fleshy creature nearly half as tall as the Empire State Building. The creature pulls me closer to its massive swell of a body.

Another hand suddenly reaches out from its body, tempting me to grab it.

I reach out my hand and I grab the hand.

The hand pulls me into the flesh, which slowly consumes my entire body.

I'm sinking through a pink jelly-like substance. I can still breath, even though the flesh is covering my entire body.

A surge of energy flows through me.

Never have I been so alive!

## 23. THE CURATOR / ROGER

SLOWLY, I wake to the distant crackles of gunfire.

I can't move my legs.

I can't move anything.

The flickering light of a monitor highlights the clouds of dust being kicked up from each breath I take. I realize that an entire piece of ceiling is on top of my body.

I finally regain feeling in my legs. My ankle, I realize, is pinned underneath a piece of chewed up concrete.

Every single monitor has been ripped from the wall. I take a closer look and realize that there is no longer a wall, only chunks of debris.

I manage to pick up certain images on one of the monitors. The screen is cracked down the middle, but I can make out Frankie. She's more than three times the size of the Titanic, stomping on soldiers, tossing tanks in the air with the flick of a finger. She's hit hard twice with two large missiles!

The impact shakes whatever's left of Four Lakes, causing the piece of debris to loosen from my ankle.

"Frankie!" I yell out as I try to muster the strength to free myself from the rumble.

Somehow, I manage to slip free.

My ankle is broken as well as several ribs and each breath I take in stings.

I manage to crawl my way through the debris until I reach sunlight.

I make my way to the surface where I come across a graveyard. Bodies are torn apart and lay everywhere. Fires burning. The thick black smoke making it hard to see, the blood dripping into my eyes making it even harder to see.

Through the smoke, I witness Frankie stumbling through the woods.

She's heading toward the lake!

She's looking for water!

I chase after Frankie, but I can't keep up with her for the pain is too great.

So, I stop and take it all in. A huge cylinder-shaped object blots out the sun above me. . .

I follow the dark shadow moving its way closer toward the earth, toward Frankie. I shield my eyes and look up, only to find a bomb falling from the sky.

I watch the bomb make its way toward the earth.

I don't have any time to react. I don't have any time left to do anything but stand there and watch death approach.

White light flashes through my eyes!

And in that final moment of life, I think about Louie and how wrong he was about the water.

# PART THREE
## ONES AND ZEROES

## ? / 2 . 0 1 . 2 . 0 / ?

PUNCHING and kicking my way through cold darkness, I reach the warm surface. I push myself through a hard, slimy shell that appears to have been congealed over my skin. I embrace the hot air. Even the swell of gray looks bright and alluring compared to the cold dark earth. The lower half of my body remains attached to a scaly tomb. I grab handfuls of clumpy pieces of dead hide from my body and break through the rest of the hardened earth and remove both of my legs caked with dry mud.

Somewhere among the ashy gray all around me, the wood is *crackling* and *popping*. Beyond the sounds is a great silence. It's so quiet I can hear my body speak to me: blood moving through my veins, a tight lump of balled air rolling down the base of my throat, the pulse pecking away behind my ears. I can't hear any sounds of life, except the life thriving inside me, as well as the fire, as it chews through the ruins. I remember I used to go on these walks deep in the woods—so deep that even the foggy mornings after spring felt as cold as any winter's day. The trees holding in all of that cold from the night before, then, as the sun rose high in the sky, slowly releasing the coolness from underneath the coarse layer of bark. I used to listen to nature speak to me, the birds, the squirrels, and other tiny creatures, as well as the trees as they creaked or cracked. I tried to make sense of what these things might've been saying about whatever, about me, about life. All of these sounds used to sooth my ears, used to remind me of the life outside my room, always moving, always there, comforting in its presence, yet so violent in its progress.

Now, the lack of sounds haunts me.

Is this the sound of death?

I always wondered if death spoke or made a noise, a low snarl or a moan that carried you to the other side.

I clear away the dry mud from my eyes and peel the rest of my body from what used to be a shore. Now, all that's left of the lake is a contaminated pool of water with a city of shriveled roots and debris cast from the woods.

Around me, the woods have been mostly stripped of trees. Remaining are charred tree trunks like gnarled claws protruding from a black earth covered in a blanket of smoldering embers.

I stand to my feet, stagger at first, then regain my balance. I examine my body, only to find myself without any clothes. I try to find something to cover myself, but I can't find anything to wear or cover myself with.

I look down at my hand and study each groove and wrinkle of my hand with great fascination, as if this is something new to me. I peel yet another slimy layer of skin from my hand—gelatin in its texture yet thick and rubbery in its elasticity.

Once it's all peeled off, it hangs like a wet washcloth. I toss it to the ground and keep moving.

I work my way through a smoky landscape, trudging mile after mile through smoke and black char—occasionally stopping to catch my breath.

I keep moving until I come across a nearly dried-out river; then I decide it's best to turn around. Each step through the mud is strenuous and drains my strength, so I decide to follow the river.

I come across a more walkable piece of dry land and stay extra close to the murky stream of water until I reach a desolate highway.

From there, I take the road and follow it to a small town called Parish. The letter H looks like it's been etched away, making the word look like *Paris.*

I keep walking along the road, making sure to keep a quick getaway route in sight. A two-lane road widens to four lanes as I reach Main Street. Not a single car has passed me, which is the first indication something terrible has happened. The next indication: the litter, trash, people's belongings.

As I wander mindlessly through the deserted town, I come across various items on the street and sidewalks: a purse or a bookbag, newspapers—a dispenser has been knocked over—a hat, a scarf. I even come across a tennis shoe, only one out of two. The other is uncounted for.

Of all the items, though, one of them appears to be the most popular one of choice: Styrofoam cups with lids. Most of the cups half-full before they were dropped or even thrown to the ground.

I reach a couple of cars parked along a strip of local stores. One of the cars—a station wagon—appears abandoned. The driver's side door left wide opened. I check the inside. Most of the backseat is covered in breadcrumbs and children's toys. I step on something squishy. I pull my foot away and find a pacifier on the street.

Out of nowhere, a wave of panic moves through my body!

I get lightheaded from the thought alone of an entire town vanishing from the face of the earth. My breath shortens, and each breath I take in becomes more of a challenge.

The thought of death presses against my chest. I take in a deep breath through my nose, then blow out through my mouth. I do this three more times until the tension loosens.

The thought of being butt naked doesn't come to me until I find myself looking in the reflection of the car's window.

Somehow, everything else doesn't seem so bad anymore.

It's not the end of the world.
I'm still here.
Aren't I?

⬬ ⬬ ⬬

After I wash the soot and mud from my body with smelly water and runny liquid hand soap from a bathroom that looks as if it hadn't been cleaned in decades, I borrow a pair of clothes from an Army-Navy store at the edge of town.

As I'm leaving the store, my appetite comes to me with a furious growl of my stomach. I remember passing a sandwich shop a couple of stores down. I decide to give it a try.

⬬ ⬬ ⬬

With caution, I enter the store. Even though I can't hear any life, I'm still on guard, waiting for someone to pop out at any moment. The shop smells of something awful. I pass the deli meat, thinking the smell may be coming from old meat; however, it smells more like shit than something rotten. I'm not sure how fresh the meat is, so I take my chances with the refrigerator in the back of the store.

Inside are bottled waters and soft drinks, as well as cold cuts prepackaged with saran wrap. I grab a couple of waters and two sandwiches for the road.

As I'm about to leave, I notice a figure in the corner of my eye. Blood escapes my face. My heart starts to beat faster.

I turn toward the body behind the counter and he or she— can't quite make out which one—is not moving.

I place the food and drinks on the counter and inspect the body. An old man probably pushing eighty. He's lying facedown on the floor. The smell, I notice, is potent around him. Heart attack possibly—who knows? He has dark stains on the backside of his pants. I cover my nose from the awful stench as I check his pulse. I don't find one. He's been dead for a while and now, it looks as if everything inside him is trying to exit his body with one last retort. Even the blood has started to pool underneath his body, making his skin appear dark and purple and spongy. I grab a plastic glove from a box near the sandwich station and check his pockets. I find a leather wallet with the man's driver's license. His name is Sergio Palomar, a member of Sunny Lakes Golf League, and from what I can tell, an avid coupon collector.

I grab the thirty-seven dollars from his wallet, as well as the stuff from the counter, and I can't get out of there quick enough.

• • •

I constantly remind myself to "keep moving." One step at a time. My energy is low, even after I manage to hold down a few bites of food. I'm not much of a napper—if that's even a word and if it is, I'll add it to my notebook of new words—but I sure as hell could use a good nap right now.

• • •

I finally reach the next town, like the town before, completely abandoned. I move through the town and make my way back to an open stretch of road. About two miles down, I hear the low guttural rumble of an engine. A rust-colored truck suddenly pulls out of a dirt road and onto the street. The person driving slams on the brakes!

I try to keep my cool—probably just a local who decided to pull his or her head from the sand. The truck does a u- turn, and that's when I get a look at the driver. Two people inside the cab. Both wearing gasmasks.

The truck pulls up beside me.

I keep my head down and keep my cool.

A brown-toothed man dressed in camo lifts up the gasmask and ask me if I'm okay.

The passenger is a wide-eyed woman with shaggy brunette hair. She appears more dangerous than the man.

The driver asks me the same question again.

"Darling," he says, "you okay?"

"Yes," I tell him. "I'm fine."

I pull out the money in my pocket, the thirty-seven dollars and extend the money toward the driver.

"Can I hitch a ride?"

He turns to the passenger seated next to him. She's trying to shake her head no without me noticing, but she catches me staring at her.

"She's just a girl, Suz," the driver whispers to her through the corner of his mouth.

"Do we look like cab service?" she urgently whispers back. "We don't know what effect the radiation had on people. We could get, you know, sick—"

"—I'm *not* sick," I blurt out.

The driver looks at me, studies me.

"Please, Arnold," the Suz woman says, louder now.

"Hush," he says and throws up his hand as if he's about to smack her across the face. Then, he turns his beady eyes toward me. "Where you headed?"

"East," I say. "I'm headed east. Toward Agatha."

"That's at least two hours away—"

The driver holds up his hand again.

"I can take you to Raven Hills. That's as far as I can take you."

"Yes," I say. "Okay."

I wait for further instruction.

"Well, don't stand there," he says. "Hop in the back. And make sure to be careful with the gas cans."

I slide over one of the many red gas cans in the back of the truck and take a seat against a hump above the back left tire.

The truck drives off.

I listen to the gasoline sloshing around inside the cans.

I don't know why, but the sound is incredibly soothing to my ears.

⬬ ⬬ ⬬

We end up taking the back roads to Raven Hills, which puts us behind at least thirty minutes.

When I ask the driver, Arnold, about his erratic driving, he tells me that the military has these check points scattered all along the main highways. He's trying to get to his brother in Somerville, which is about forty miles off the North Carolina/Virginia border.

He reassures me by telling me that once we reach Raven Hills it should be much safer—whatever he means by that.

I just want to get back home.

⬬ ⬬ ⬬

Things seem close to normal the closer we get to Raven Hills. I see more cars on the road. Most—if not, all—of the traffic is headed away from the direction we just came from.

When we arrive in Raven Hills, an old textile town about forty-five minutes north of Agatha, the Arnold man drops me off. I wish him luck in finding his brother.

He hands me a pale blue pamphlet with the words *Trust the Lord.*

"God bless you," he says to me.

"Yeah," I say. "Thanks for the ride."

"Good luck," he says and drives away.

I crumble up the pamphlet in my hand and toss it on the ground.

After asking around for about an hour, I manage to find an old man who happens to be passing through Agatha. He tells me he can give me a lift.

During the entire ride, he doesn't say a word. He doesn't even tell me his name, nor does he once ask me for my name. It's, by far, the most interaction I've had with a human being.

Finally, after what feels like years of being away from home, I make it back to Agatha. Can't believe I almost miss the place. I expect the media to be camped outside my home, like soldiers standing a post and waiting for the action, but strangely I don't see any—at least no news vans parked in front of my house. I spot one camped outside our neighborhood, underneath an old oak tree, waiting. I keep my head down. There may be more lurking around like predators. I don't take any chances. So, I tell the old man to drop me off in front of the Peabody's house. The Peabodys are a typical grade-A American family who live directly behind us. Sometimes I wonder if my mother had an affair with Mr. Peabody before she had Abe. The Peabody's also have this dog that I've grown to despise. His name is Bruno, a horny terrier that treats my leg as if it's a lady terrier. I wish a car would hit that mutt. Often, I wish the mutt a terrible death, like getting stuck in a drainage pipe or whatever—as long as it died a most brutal death, then that was fine by me. It could even get caught in the chain link fence and starve to death. If having to partake in the ritual hump fest ever time it lays its devilish black eyes on me isn't enough to drive me crazy, then what it does at night usually does. Bruno will yap at the slightest disturbance. An owl. A car door. A mouse's fart. He's a night-stalker's worst nightmare.

Also, it's probably best if the old man doesn't know where I live anyway—just in case he turns out to be a creep.

He tells me to have a nice day. I can't remember the last time someone's told me to have a nice day. What does that even mean, really? Have a nice day? Why don't people start switching up the norm and tell other people to have a bad day?

Either way, I can't thank the old man enough. He reminds me a lot of the old folks from Agatha. So naive and generous. The type of people who'd go out in public to start conversations with complete strangers. They'd even pick up a hitchhiker and not think twice about whether or not he or she was a serial killer looking for the right moment to plunge a knife in their throats.

Now comes the hard part: trying to find the right words to say to my parents.

I noticed that both of their cars were parked outside right before we turned off our street. So, I know this is not going to be pleasant. If it was just my dad, I could probably get away with a half-ass story.

I walk past the Peabody's. Bruno's acting like Bruno. The little mutt appears almost happy by my presence. I stare into its eyes and all of a sudden, it lets out a whimper and runs back into the house.

That's a first.

I put aside Bruno's unusual behavior and keep moving forward. I make my way through our backyard. I get halfway toward the backdoor and still can't find the words. I honestly don't even know what happened. I remember being abducted in the middle of the night. I remember riding inside the trunk of a car. I remember regaining consciousness inside the trunk, having a severe panic attack. The only thing, I remember, that kept me alive was concentrating on the road, mentally mapping out each turn the car had made, remembering the feel of the road, each bump and turn, when the tread of tires rolled smoothly over asphalt or dug into gravel. My ears became my eyes. I don't remember anything after the car stopped. I *do* remember being held inside a cell without any windows. I *do* remember being asked questions by two men who claimed to be doctors. I *do* remember a handsome man coming to my rescue, but I don't know if that was a dream or not. So many things happened inside my dreams. There was this one time I had a dream of escaping from an abandoned mental hospital. After a while, though, the dreams started to blend into reality. And how I ended up on the shore naked and muddy is beyond rational thought.

So, what do I tell my parents?

*Where do I even begin?*

I have no idea.

Before I knock on the door, my dad slides open the patio door and calls out to my mother who's sitting on the couch with a glass of Chardonnay in her hand. She's usually drinking red wine. So, immediately, I start the process of wondering why she's switched over to white. I see Grandma Lynch has come out of hibernation to join the rest of the family in the living room. Surprisingly, she looks glad to see me. My dad looks glad as well, but seems to be in a state of shock, like those victims on TV after a tragic accident. He runs over to me and gives me a bear hug.

My mother breaks a rare moment between my dad and me by throwing a gazillion questions my way: "What happened? Where have you been? Why didn't you call us? Are you hurt?"

My dad calms down my mother and tells her to give me some space. My brother doesn't say a word to me. The furrow of his brows explains it all. I don't know if it's shock or if he's upset that I'm still alive or if it's a little bit of both. My first inclination is that he's upset that he won't get my room now. I make my way toward the house and notice the idiot box is on full blast in the living room. The news helicopters are flying over a massive crater in the earth. My brother's laptop is on the coffee table, receiving the most attention. There's a live video of a news report streaming on the Internet. So much has happened in the past twenty-four hours, and it all centers around me. I just wish I knew what the hell was going on.

Rumors are flooding the Internet: a military helicopter accidentally mishandled an atom bomb while transporting it to a military base located in Fayetteville. The blame: human error. The news on TV says another: the military was conducting a new drill—of all the places in America, they chose the rural North Carolina mountains—educating people of these chosen counties on the proper procedures to follow when being faced with a nuclear war. Nearby towns were evacuated in a timely fashion. Other rumors include that the government was testing a new hydrogen bomb, not atom bomb. Either way, there was an explosion that could be felt for miles. They're saying it was approximately *ten* times greater than the explosion in Benjamin Creek. Terrorist attacks came up in the conversation, but there wasn't any significant evidence pointing to a certain terror organization. Not only that, no terror organization had taken responsibility for the explosion, which is out of the ordinary since most of these backward assholes try to take responsibility for anything that involves mass causalities. The story nearly breaks the Internet. Several websites shut down due to heavy traffic. One conspiracy after another is swirling around Chatterzsphere. Hashtags like D-Day and WWIII are trending all over the Internet. People talking about the end of the world, pointing their fingers at who's to blame while, at the same time, demonizing certain groups with divisive rhetoric that paints these certain groups with a broad brush. It's as if people are acting the way they've always been; and yet, for so long, they had kept that side hidden from the public. The crazies have come out of the woodwork, while others have taken a sharper turn into the less practical by coming up with more amusing hashtags for their own comical relief. Hashtags like "3ThingsToDoBeforeIDie" and "BombASong" have gone viral. Another one that's getting a lot of attention is "Where's The Bread At." Grocery stores around the country have been gutted within two hours after the news broke. Crowd fights seem to be a popular trend; some videos have gone viral on the Internet. Even videos of the mushroom cloud have leaked onto the Internet, but nobody really knows if they're real or not. Even amateur videos of the initial blast many miles away, towns away before the blast knocked out power. Videos of people evacuating from nearby towns. More fights breaking out. Straight up chaos and pandemonium.

My story, on the other hand, is exactly what both my parents feared. I ran away. My parents want to know everything that happened, starting from the very moment I disappeared. They want the details, descriptions—an oral history of my "Final Days." I tell them as much as I can. I leave out the kidnapping part and the part where I woke up in the massive crater on TV.

The first emotion that came to mind was fear. And that's what I tell my parents. I tell them that I was scared and that I feared for my life. I tell them that I heard all about what happened to the others. The last person I talked to—Emily—told me that two men were stalking her. I told them that I thought people were stalking me even though that's one big-ass lie. I don't even have stalkers—not like I would want them, but I'm just saying. They want to know why I didn't contact authorities or, most importantly, tell my dad about it. Cue the tears. I tell them *all* about the way they've been treating me lately, how they don't listen to me, how they act as if I don't exist anymore, and how they constantly put Abe first instead of me; and the whole time I'm telling them these things, Grandma Lynch is in the background rolling her eyes. It's really a simple story. The first driver won't mention anything. He came across as the type who only trusted one person and that surely wasn't his own government. If the other driver, the old man I hitched a ride with, decides to come forward, he doesn't have one thing he could pin on me. Not even a name. As far as he knows, he was taking a lost runaway back home to her nest. So, with all that said, I *was* the lucky one. I can't say the same about the others. I know the story won't stick for long. Sooner than later, I'm going to have to explain myself to people far worse than my parents.

For now, though, I stick to my story.

I was lucky.

After all the explaining, I bathe in warm water until my skin prunes. During the whole bath time, I can see shadows under the doorway. Both my dad and my mother hovering over me like a rain cloud. They've been saying that I seem different behind my back; I'm carrying a certain "glow" that apparently I haven't carried before. I guess I am different. I feel much different. I don't blame them for being so curious. I guess if I were in their shoes I'd be pretty freaked out myself. My own flesh and blood running away, wanting absolutely nothing to do with me. I guess it would feel as if I had failed as a parent. I have to constantly remind myself that it was nothing they did.

I sense at least one of my parents looming behind my bedroom door as I step out of the bathtub. Listening. I wonder what's going through what I assume is my mother's mind. I wonder if she's caught me in a lie. She has been known to have a racing mind and jump to conclusions the first second something rubs her the wrong way. She's seen every movie out there, especially the mysteries and true crime TV shows. She's been known to go on Friday night binges. She'd drag my dad into watching one with her. At times, I've walked in on her watching the same crime show that she watched just a week before. So, I know she's thinking like one of those clichéd detectives on one of the TV shows: *If my daughter was kidnapped by the same people who kidnapped her teammates, then maybe she's created some kind of sympathy for her kidnapper and now, she's covering for him or her.* It makes total sense on TV, but nothing in the TV world makes any sense in reality.

Before I throw on a pair of pajamas, I stand in front of the mirror in my room and remove the damp towel from my body. I find myself staring at every little detail of my body, studying my body, like my hand before, like I've never seen it before. I grab the phone from the top of my dresser and take a selfie of myself.

As I'm about to post the photo, I hear a knock on the door. I turn off my phone and hide it inside my underwear drawer.

"Yes!"

My mother's waiting outside.

Go figure.

"Is everything okay?" she asks.

"I'm changing."

"Supper's about ready."

"Okay."

My mother has made supper? Can you believe that? Like she cares. More than likely, they've ordered out and like she always does whenever the whole family's together, she's taking full responsibility for the upcoming event—in this case, it's supper, because that's what it feels like sometimes, a rare event, and I know she's going to act as if she's the one who killed it, prepared it, cooked it, and served it. Did I say I miss this place?

⁂

The total idiot in the idiot box is acting up again when I join the rest of my awesome family downstairs. My dad's banging on the side of the flat screen as if it's an old analog TV. Natural habit, I guess, to give a nice smack to something whenever it's not working properly. I could use a nice smack upside the head myself. The TV starts to glitch. The images of screen scramble, shift, distort, and freeze. The volume is next to act up. Every other syllable coming from the sultry and sharp-tongued news anchor, Charlene Storm, of Channel Nine's news team cuts off as if it's being bludgeoned by the clearing of her throat. My dad has a serious crush on Charlene, but he'll never admit it. He'll stop everything he does to watch her at six o'clock. He'll practically ignore everybody in the room to catch a glimpse of the bimbo. He gives one last smack on the side of the TV before calling it quits.

"After all this time fixing the lousy thing, it starts to do this crap again," he says in disgust. "I swear, they don't make 'em like they used to."

"Yeah," Abe says, glaring at me, "it was working just fine before *Judge Judy* showed up."

"It's probably made in China," my mother contributes to the nightly bickering.

I can tell she's working her way through yet another bottle of wine. Usually, she polishes off about one a night. But this is a special occasion. This is my homecoming!

They've ordered my favorite: Indian food. Abe can't stand Indian food; in fact, he hates it with a rather innate passion. He has the diet of a third grader. Hamburgers, hot dogs, anything in tube-form—basically, anything that you can eat with your hands and has the word *dog* in it, basically, anything in the shape of a penis—and then, last but not least, pizza: Abe has three basic food groups. The most exotic food he'll ever eat is Mexican.

So, of course, Abe's pissed off.

As he's obnoxiously scooping rice on his plate, he says to me, "I coughed on your curry."

"Really?" I say.

"Yeah," he says. "Really."

"Fantastic."

I dish out the chicken curry on my plate and start eating in front of Abe.

"Yum," I say, holding the plate in front of his face. "Can you be a dear and cough on my curry again? It taste so good the first time around that I'd love some more. Please—"

"—Get a life," he says and walks to the table.

"*Judith*," my mother says sharply as if I'm Queen Instigator.

I've only been back three hours, and they've already had enough of me.

During supper, all of the anger starts to build up inside me and I can't stop thinking about how everything is back to the same crap. They've had their little moment of showing that they cared about me. They get their nod from the Academy; then, once the cameras are all gone, they remove their plastic masks and reveal to me who they truly are. I just want to run away. I mean, for really real this time. Run far away from this place and never look back.

I can't even look at them anymore. It's even a struggle to move my eyes from my food and make eye-to-eye contact with any of them.

I catch a sneak peek of Abe deliberately chewing his food with his mouth opened. My parents don't even say a word to him. He's such a spoiled brat who should be joining his other spoiled brats on the streets, protesting. He has no reason for the things he does. He does them because he's a sheep like everybody else.

My dad finally gives him a tap, not a bang or a smack or a whack, but an innocent tickle on the side, and says in his fake deep fatherly voice, "Abe, be nice to your sister. She's been through a lot."

Like he knows what I've been through. Like any of them have a clue what's going on!

I can't be here anymore!

I get up out of my seat before I lose it.

"I'm not feeling well," I tell them and hurry up to my room.

As I make my way upstairs, I hear my mother talking about me: "What's *wrong* with our daughter?"

Like she has any room to talk. Some mother. She spends her nights getting wasted to make it a little bit easier to deal with her children, like we've—meaning "I"—have become this Rubik's cube that is impossible to solve.

I go to my room and I put on Reelspace to help rid any thought of my family.

I flip through all of the suggestions until I reach the 1980's remake of *The Fly*.

I get through about two-thirds of the movie until I hear a car door slamming shut outside. I check the window and see a black car parked on the street. Other cars pull in front of our house. Men dressed in black suits getting out. They look like they work for the government.

The doorbell *rings*!

My dad answers the door.

Then, I hear footsteps outside my room.

My mother says that it's the FBI and they want to have a little conversation with me.

## 2. ? / RASHIDA

TWO weeks have passed since the fallout at Four Lakes Mental Institution, and even after Baron Orwell's death, his influence manages to extend beyond the grave.

After Four Lakes, it feels as if my own agency is out to get me.

Pelham has started his own witch-hunt against me, especially after disobeying direct orders. The FBI wants to make an example out of me, but I won't let him.

In my case, it'd seem appropriate to take a vacation, go to the beach, get some sun, clear my head, put all of this in my rear view; then, once everything is swept under the rug, come back where a job as a greeter at some big box retailer awaits me.

What better way to get away from the rat race and go on that much needed vacation.

My first stop: Tokyo, Japan.

When asked, I tell the official at customs that I'm here in Tokyo strictly for pleasure, not business.

They buy it, all thanks to Orwell's timely resources.

Not like I'm hooked up to a polygraph.

♟ ♟ ♟

I spend four days bouncing from one hotel to another along the Sumida and Arakawa River, as well as the many other rivers that snake their way into Tokyo Bay. I avoid the expensive hotels and stay away from travelers. The last thing I want is to stick out like a tourist. By the fifth day in Tokyo, I come to the bitter realization that I may never find Frankie's twin. From the beginning, I knew it wasn't going to be easy. The language barrier doesn't help at all either. My day starts early in the morning by asking locals about Frankie's twin, showing them pictures of her. I do this all day long, late into the night. I catch only three to four solid hours of sleep.

Then, I'm back at it again.

On that hustle.

Some locals send me on wild goose chases while other locals simply shake their heads and go about their lives. One man—an older gentlemen who had nothing else better to do—spent hours trying to help me track down Frankie's twin. Unfortunately, we had no luck.

On the eight day, I finally find a significant lead. A local who speaks a little bit of English directs me toward an elderly man named Gorou, an artist—or what he calls a "badass, like Japanese version of Jackson Pollock." Immediately, I'm intrigued—mostly by the fact that he knows Jackson Pollock. In college, I had a minor in art history (it didn't look too good on my résumé, you know, since my major was criminal justice—even at the Academy, fellows grilled me about it, thinking I was an uppity bitch who thought she was better than everyone else because I was this art buff—but, at the time, art was something that fascinated me and still does till this day).

The local takes me to Gorou's studio in a much sleazier, sketchier part of the city. The studio is like a hoarder's wet dream, cramped and cluttered with these pornographic paintings and disturbing sculptures.

As we trek our way farther into this dingy studio, we walk through a hallway with thousands of pieces of phallic-shaped origami with wings suspended from the ceilings. We make our way into a larger studio with high rafters. The local takes me to Gorou, who's working on a new piece that covers an entire wall. A collage of faces.

Gorou calls the piece, "*Konseki*," which in English means vestige or face.

The local introduces me to Gorou, an unpleasant man who carries the stench of a man who hasn't showered in months. He's missing a lot of teeth and the ones he's still clinging onto are brown and as crooked as old Western tombstones.

The two start speaking in Japanese; however, I can't keep up. I have a translator app on my phone, but it doesn't work half the time.

I hand the local a photograph of the twin, then he hands it to Gorou. His ink-stained hands ruin the photo, but as upset as it makes me, I don't get all over Gorou mainly because I'm hanging on the fringe of desperate.

Gorou takes one glance at the twin and immediately recognizes her by bobbing his head.

"Aimi Hayashi," he says, turns to the wall behind him, and points at the twin's face in the collage.

I match the face with the photograph.

What do you know? It's a match!

"Aimi Hayashi? That's her name?"

"*Hai*," he says.

"You know where I can find her?"

He doesn't understand me.

I ask the local.

"Can he tell me where she is? Where is Aimi?"

The local starts translating for me. He asks Gorou—or at least, I think that's what he's asking—where I can find Aimi Hayashi. I only speak a few words of Japanese, and it sounds like a kindergartner trying to push out words.

The local translates for Gorou: "He says Mrs. Hayashi died three weeks ago. Says doctors discovered an inoperable tumor on the base of her spine. In a matter of days, the cancer spread like a spider throughout her entire body. She was put in hospice to die peacefully. Every face you see on this mural," the local points behind Gorou, "is the face of the deceased."

"Aimi Hayashi is dead?"

"*Hai*," the local says, bowing. "Yes. Dead."

I ask him to ask Gorou, "Can you ask him if he knew Mrs. Hayashi? Anything?"

The local asks Gorou for me.

"'No,' he says," the local translates. "He says he spent a lot of his days hanging around the cemeteries."

Gorou bursts out laughing and says something to the local.

"—With the cats," the local translates as he joins in on the laughter.

▲ ▲ ▲

Now that the difficult part is over—finding out the twin's full name and the name of the cemetery where she was buried—finding where she lived is the easy part.

▲ ▲ ▲

A woman a few years older than me answers the door. First, I ask her if this was where Aimi Hayashi lived. She becomes somewhat hesitant and timid by my presence. She thinks I'm a journalist and she wants nothing to do with me, but I explain to her as simply as I can that I'm on her side. Her English is just okay. She's not totally fluent, but I manage to pick out certain words and I put them together myself.

"What is your business?" she asks me.

I pull out the photo of a younger Frankie. I tell her that I'm from America and that I knew Aimi's sister. She tells me that Aimi didn't have a sister. She refuses to let me inside the house—in fact, she tries to shoo me away as if I'm as worthless as the sensationalistic journalist whom I tried to describe, the desperate hack trying to get attention by stirring up controversy in order to promote divergence, even worse, create conflict between groups of people.

I persist, though, and remain curious—maybe even to the point of being nosy.

I even have the audacity to wedge my foot in the doorway as she attempts to shut the door. I tell her that Aimi's sister has died. Again, I have no luck.

As she's about to make an attempt at shutting the door, a fiery older man shouts at the woman. She turns to the man inside, submissively lowers her head, then struggles to make eye contact with me. She starts acting servant-like.

"My father-in-law would like to speak to you," she says, her head still lowered.

The woman steps aside and lets me inside.

♟ ♟ ♟

Aimi's daughter-in-law, Fumi, puts on a pot of tea while I sit with Aimi's husband, Ken Hayashi, who wants to know everything about Aimi's twin. So, I tell him as much as I know. Of course, I leave out the part where Frankie transformed into a ginormous monster that looked just like something you'd see straight out of a *Godzilla* or *King Kong* movie—not to mention, this thing nearly destroying an entire town in its rampage. I leave that part out. Trying to describe the events that transpired at Four Lakes is like trying to give a brief synopsis of the movie, *In the Heat of the Night*, without using a single noun or trying to replicate the painting of *Mona Lisa* with a broad paint brush and a holey canvas. I'm going to leave out all the fine details that make Frankie's story unique. If Aimi Hayashi were known to display any kind of special gifts or talents, like Frankie, then it'd be easily justifiable to bring up that part of her life as well as her demise. But, in the eyes of Aimi Hayashi's family, Aimi was an average person. Dare I say, normal. Not special or gifted or rare. Just *just*. A decent person who married a carpenter named Ken at the age of twenty-three, then, together, had a son named Ichiro.

Mr. Hayashi asks about the man, Roger, in the photograph. He has many questions about him and Fumi tries to keep up with the translation. I keep the details limited on Roger—the American—and how his father—a photographer who wanted to capture and chronicle images of war—found Aimi's sister amidst the fallout in Nagasaki and then brought Frankie back to the States with him. He gave her a place to live. He helped raise her along with the sisters from the Order of Our Lady. Then, Frankie met Roger many years later. They fell in love.

They didn't have any children. Nonetheless, I tell them, they lived a quiet life together. Frankie died of a stroke days after Roger passed from a heart attack. Doctors called it a stroke, but ones close to Frankie knew she died of a broken heart.

Now the question that's really on everybody's minds, including mine: Did Frankie's death have anything to do with what happened to Aimi? Perhaps it could've had something to do with being a twin? If one twin dies, then the other one dies too. But I think that's all urban legend—bullshit you tell other kids to get a rise out of them. Mr. Hayashi's daughter-in-law has been taking care of him ever since Aimi's death. He tells me that Aimi never talked about her family. He was fully aware that she once had family in Nagasaki, but he always assumed the worst and he never brought it up. He knew it was a wound that needed much time to heal and he didn't want to prevent that wound from healing because the memories were too painful. Fumi tells me that her husband Ichiro has taken the death very hard. As of lately, he spends most of his time at work. According to Fumi, he is a producer for a late night television show called *The Happy, Happy Hour.* Mr. Hayashi isn't fond of his son's work or accomplishments, which seems as if it has caused a rift between him and Fumi.

"He's very work-driven," Fumi says, referring to her husband. "What Americans call 'workaholic.'"

"Yes," I tell her, as I glance over the various picture frames on the table. "I know all about it."

I come across one photo in particular: a photo of a young girl holding hands with Ichiro.

I pick up the picture frame.

"Who's the child?" I ask.

Fumi gets quiet. Silence builds. I've clearly brought up a subject that nobody wants to talk about.

"She's my daughter," Fumi finally says.

"Is she currently at school?"

She doesn't answer right away.

Mr. Hayashi says something to Fumi but she doesn't translate it for me. They get into a minor argument in front of me. Mr. Hayashi insists that Fumi translate—*kanojo ni iu,* he keeps saying, *kanojo ni iu.*

Fumi turns to me, both of her cheeks blushing pink. "He thinks cellular phones did something to Mina." She points to her head. "Her brain."

"Is she okay?"

Fumi avoids the question and walks over to me. She holds out her hands. I hand Fumi the picture frame. She bows her head and looks over the photo almost in reflection.

"She was close to her grandmother. She loved her with all her heart. Right before she passed, an American came to visit Mina. He said he was a friend of Aimi's, but Aimi acted like she had never seen the man before."

"Did this American have a name?"

"Orwell," she says. "Maron Orwell."

"You mean, Baron Orwell?"

"No," she says. "I don't think so."

"By any chance was this man in a wheelchair?"

She thinks for a moment, then shakes her head.

"No. He was walking."

The handsome blonde-haired man in the shiny silver suit from the airport immediately comes to mind, sitting a couple of seats away from me as I was waiting to board my plane to Tokyo. I remember trying to make sense of the rectangular creases along his legs. He was wearing something underneath his pants, some kind of brace that covered both of his legs. He was a man brimming with charisma and joking about how much of a pain in the ass it was going through the metal detectors. I didn't know exactly what he meant by that. I never got his name. I was too smitten to ask for it. My zone was called. I got up. Walked away. I looked over my shoulder and he was gone.

"Did this man," I say, trying to paint his face in my mind, "did he mention anything about why he was here? What he wanted?"

"No," she says, shaking her head. "He wanted to see Mina. After Aimi passed, Mina started to—she started to act ah. . ."

"Strange?"

"Yes," she says. "Strange."

"How so?"

She doesn't respond.

I persist.

"How did Mina change?"

"All day she wouldn't leave her room," she says. "Her behavior became more erratic. She would start yelling at me for no reason. She have moments where she stare for hours at her phone. I try to pull it away from her," Fumi pulls up her sleeve, revealing a scar running across her forearm, "and she stab me with scissors."

My final question: "Where is Mina now?"

♟ ♟ ♟

Aimi's granddaughter, Mina Hayashi, is currently residing in a psychiatric hospital called Anzai Hospital.

I decide to pay a visit to Mina during visiting hours. Anzai Hospital is located west of the city, away from the grind. The place is like another town, I swear. There are more trees and vegetation, an entire community of both doctors and patients living together. They have a pond next to the hospital. In the backdrop is a skyline of Tokyo from a distance. It's nice.

♟ ♟ ♟

When the orderlies take me to Mina, she's standing in front of a window. Mina is only eight years old. You would never tell by the way she carries herself.

I pass a table of crayon drawings and doodles.

I look over one of the drawings: a reddish orange backdrop of what looks like flames with a demonic black figure emerging from the fire. Three other dark, lanky figures—more gray than black—are emerging behind the black figure, two on the left and one on the right.

I put the drawing aside and sort through other drawings, most of them similar—if not—identical to one another.

Filling the entire piece of paper are rows of ones and zeroes scribbled with a black crayon.

I take a closer look and realize it's binary code.

I place the drawings aside and walk over to Mina.

The tips of her fingers and the grooves around her nails are covered with black from the crayons. I ask Mina about the drawing, but she remains in a trance-like state. I tell her that I recently talked to her mother, Fumi. Again, I get no reaction from the girl. I assume it's the drugs—an antidepressant or antipsychotic. She's a zombie. I try again and ask Mina a couple of simple questions: How are you? Do you like it here? Are the people treating you well?

Again, I get no reaction. Not a blink or even a bat of her eyes. It's like everything that was once thriving inside her had been completely sucked out of her like a vacuum and now, all that remains is this shell of a person.

I show Mina a photograph of Frankie, hoping it may draw a reaction.

Again, I get nothing but this cold, empty stare from a girl who has lost more than her marbles.

Lastly, I show her the only photo I have of Maron Orwell when he was just a boy.

She doesn't even look at the photo.

I decide to give up. It's pointless. Her brain is like scrambled eggs.

As I leave the recreational room, a voice calls out to me in near perfect English: "How did she die?"

I turn back around and Mina's still staring outside the window.

At first, I think my mind is starting to play tricks on me.

Did she actually speak?

Was it someone else?

Another patient?

I walk back to Mina and ask her, "You say something?"

She robotically turns toward me.

"How did she die?" she asks.

"She died of a stroke," I lie.

Mina cracks not even a half of a smile but more like an attempt at a smile. Her face is still slack from the drugs.

"So, how did she *really* die?" she asks again.

I sharpen my gaze.

"Do you know something?"

"I know your life is in danger."

"What kind of danger?"

She turns to the window. Goes back to staring outside.

"Would you like to go for a walk?"

"We have to stay here."

"We don't have to. We can get some fresh air, if you want. I can ask the order—"

"No," she says sternly. "We *have* to stay here."

"Okay," I say, holding out my hands. "Whatever you say."

"Did my grandfather tell you the story about what happened to my grandmother last year?"

"No," I say. "He did not."

"My grandmother was abducted," she says. "Then, three days later, she returned. She had been tortured, starved. She was unrecognizable. The man who had abducted my grandmother was found dead in Tokyo Bay a week later. What the authorities didn't know was that the man was working for an American named Baron Orwell. My grandmother *never* went to the authorities. Instead, she told me to keep a secret. So, I did. I didn't tell a single person. She said that when she was being held captive that her captor said there would be others. He said they would keep coming for her and they wouldn't stop until they had what they wanted."

"Like Baron's son, Maron Orwell, the man who paid you a visit before her grandmother's passing?"

"Yes."

"What did Maron Orwell want from you?"

"He didn't say, but I could read his mind. He wants what was inside my grandmother, now inside me."

I clear my throat and ask carefully, "What's inside you—"

"—Let me ask you, Ms. Jones, are you here to take what's inside me?"

"No," I say, my heart beating faster. "I'm not. I'm here to help."

"If you want to help, then you can kill that man standing next to the poker table."

"What man?"

"The orderly. He's been watching you ever since you've been here."

I turn my shoulder and notice the orderly standing next to a poker table. Both his arms are crossed and his hands held in front of him.

"I'm sure he's just doing his job," I tell Mina.

"That would make sense, but he's *not* an orderly."

"If he's not an orderly, then who is he?"

"Who do you think he is, Ms. Jones?"

"I don't know. You tell me."

"The minute you leave, he is going to escort me back to my room, but he's not going to go back to my room."

"Where's he going to go?"

"There's a burgundy van parked near the loading dock."

I remember passing a van on the way in.

How could she know these things? Maybe she saw the van from the window?

"Inside are two men," she says. "One a driver. The other a man currently speaking to the orderly through an earpiece. He's reminding the orderly to make it look like an escape. He wants to trick the others—"

"—The others, as in people like Maron Orwell?"

"Yes."

"How do you know all of this?"

"I can hear him."

"Hear who? I don't hear anything."

"I can hear his thoughts." She looks at me as if I'm dumb, like I haven't been listening to a single word she's said. "He's anxious. He's mapping out the plan in his head. He's talking about you."

"He is?" I say. "And what is he saying?"

"He wants you to leave. At any moment, he's going to end the visitation."

I glance at the orderly and notice he's touching his ear.

I turn back around.

"Here he comes."

The orderly approaches us.

"Time's up," he says from behind.

As I make my way toward the exit, I bump into a table and knock over a couple of crayons.

The orderly kneels down and picks up the crayons. I look closer at his ear. I don't see any earpiece. He has nothing in his ear. Maybe he took it out. What am I even talking about? What is this girl even talking about? She's the one in a psychiatric hospital.

I say goodbye to Mina.

"Take care of yourself," I say.

I leave the recreational room.

As I open the door, I suddenly see a reflection in the window. The orderly is dragging Mina through the hallway!

Other orderlies and guards stand in my way. I remember what Mina told me, and now I surprisingly find myself believing every word that she said. I rush outside. I spot the van parked outside the loading dock. Burgundy, just as she said. I get in my car and drive toward the van. I floor the gas and brace for impact.

*Bam*!

I end up ramming the side of the van. The air bag goes off inside the car. I'm okay, more so startled. I get out of the car and check on the driver. He's more dazed than me but alive. There's a man in the back of the van. He's unconscious and bleeding from his head. I notice all of the equipment, radios, monitors. They've been watching me the entire time!

Mina was right all along!

The driver starts to come to.

I grab the gun from his holster and pistol-whip him in the side of the head.

Suddenly, I hear a door *squeaking* open!

The orderly!

I shoot him in the arm before he takes a blindfolded Mina to the van. I remove the blindfold from Mina's eyes and rush her back to my car. She resists getting inside, but I force her into the passenger seat. I'm surprised the car still runs after the collision. A strong odor is coming from the vents. Possibly something leaking from the engine. I don't have anytime to look at it. I need to get the hell out of here!

So, I floor it away from the hospital, occasionally checking on Mina's condition.

"You were right," I say. "How'd you—"

"—This is all wrong."

"What do you mean?"

"I don't know," she says. "It feels wrong."

"Wrong? Now's not the time to start questioning yourself. Focus, Mina. Where do we go?"

"We find Frankie, right?"

"She's dead," I say. "Frankie's dead."

"No," Mina says. "Not dead. Alive. *Very* alive."

"She can't be. I saw the explosion with my own eyes—"

"—Not an explosion. It was all a smokescreen."

Smokescreen? Who is this girl? Another lunatic obsessed with conspiracy theories?

I don't respond. I'm way too confused right now.

"How do you know all of this stuff?" I finally ask.

"I know it because I've seen it in my dreams."

"What else have you seen in your dreams?"

"I've seen *you* in my dreams."

"Me? Really?"

"I have dreamt of this day in my dreams."

"Is that so? Then what happens next?"

"Pull over."

"I can't."

"Pull the car over right now!"

"There could be more of them. . . "

She touches the interface of the touch screen.

The engine suddenly shuts off!

Then, the steering wheel locks up.

With all the strength in my body, I manage to gain control over the wheel.

I pull over on the side of the road.

"Whatever she's done to you, you have to fight her."

"It's too late," she says. "The future is already set. I have to make it look like one of them shot me while I was trying to escape."

"You don't *have* to do anything!"

She steps out of the car. I follow.

She stops and faces me. "Can you think about a person in your life who has betrayed you?" she asks. "Something that's made you the person who you are? It doesn't even have to be a person. It can be an idea or whatever. It's something that brings you great pain and anger and sadness."

"I don't understand—"

"—I need you to do this for me."

"Why?" I say, as cars zoom inches away from us.

"Just do it," she says. "For me. For Frankie."

I close my eyes and think about the person who has made me the person I am today. Not Bo. It'd be too easy to think about Bo and everything we've been through together. The fights. The manipulative behavior. Bo trying to control me. Bo wanting a baby from me and me not giving him one. He knew what he signed up for, yet he made me feel as if I was less than zero—even driving past the playground on the way to the office started to get to me all because of Bo's behavior. Normally, I'd ignore it and not even glance at the playground; then, after all of the pressure from Bo, I couldn't stop staring at them whenever I passed them on the way to work or wherever, fantasizing about sitting on a bench close by, watching my very own creation play before me, nursing him whenever my own fell down or scrapped a knee. It had gotten to a point where I even had to change routes to work. After a while, I couldn't stand the sight of playgrounds, the other moms with their tight leggings trying to smooth out their celluloid thighs and sipping on their afternoon lattes. If I stayed with Bo and turned into the woman whom he wanted me to be, I don't even know if I could've carried on living a decent life. It would be easy for me to point my finger at the man whom I once loved. The man whom I envisioned spending the rest of my life with. I travel deeper into myself. I rush past my college years, past the turmoil that was currently going on in the country. The police brutality. The unrest. The division. If it wasn't for Mr. Raspberry, my criminal justice teacher who encouraged me to pursue a career in law—guiding me through all the noise and following what I felt was right in my heart—I would've strayed onto a much different and dangerous path. I rush past high school. The fights. The many times where I disappointed my aunt. I wanted to do right, but I felt helpless. I travel deeper and locate my first pain: *I'm standing over my little brother, Jonah, as my father tries to administer CPR. My mother is hysterical. She's on the phone with the 911 operator, trying to explain what happened while her baby boy lies lifelessly before her eyes.* I reach deep and grab a hold of the pain, all accompanied by the anger that I shed many years ago and rediscover what it felt like to watch Jonah die. Minutes ago, we were playing Nintendo. Now, he's dead. I think about the days after, the cops arresting the man who was responsible. According to the report, he was targeting another man. The bullet grew wings. In my heart, I know he didn't mean to kill Jonah; but he showed no regret or remorse when the judge handed down his sentence. I travel deeper, trying to find the reason why a person would resort to killing another person. It all washes over me and the thoughts are so strong I have to turn my thoughts to something else before I pass out.

I catch my breath. The thoughts come back to me, pulling me in, reminding me: Jonah was *not* murdered by a black man but an individual who had absolutely nothing, an individual who felt as if the entire world had given up on him based on the color of his skin, an individual who was desperate for control in a cruel world that wanted to control him even though he was out of control. He had no one to guide him, like Mr. Raspberry did with me. All he wanted was an opportunity to play his part in society. It had gotten so bad that he stopped caring. Essentially, the animal took over the man. His actions don't feed my anger. I'm angry at society, how we got to be this way, how trivial issues have masked important ones. I'm angry at the injustice. I'm angry that one day when it gets so out of control the ones remaining will look back at these days and say to themselves: "This was the time we had a chance to resolve our issues but we sat back and watched a country tear itself to shreds."

"Okay," I say to Mina. "I got it. I'm ready."

"Now, hold onto it. Never let it go. It's a reminder. It's a tool. A weapon."

She turns to the traffic beside us.

"What are you doing?"

"It's the only way. I'm sorry."

"What are you doing. . . "

"I have to die."

"Please, Mina. Take a step away from the road. Let's get back in the car."

"Remember," she says to me.

"Mina, don't do this—"

"—Remember."

"Mina! Please—"

Mina takes a step back into traffic. . .

A truck suddenly rams into her!

The thunderous *thud* ripples throughout my bones. I can hear things cracking and crunching.

I turn away, trying to force away the thought of Mina splattering all over the road. The truck ends up dragging her body at least twenty feet—leaving a long streak of red blood along the road—before the truck spits her out from the rear tires.

As the driver stops and gets out of the truck, I race over to Mina's broken body. I can hardly recognize her. Everything is stretched and bones are shifted out of place and sticking out of her skin. I drop to my knees and try to stop the bleeding, but it's spewing from every orifice of her body. There's nothing I can do to help, except stay by her side in her final moments and comfort her as she dies.

Mina tries to speak but she ends up letting out a death gargle before she fades away.

I pull my hands away and look down at my chest.

Blood is covered over my shirt.

I touch my damp shirt and pull away my hand.

My palm is stained with not Mina's blood but mine.

I look down at her bloody hand, then mine.

I notice I'm holding a gun in my other hand.

I try to catch my breath but I come up empty.

I have trouble focusing on an object.

My fingers get all tingly.

My vision starts to double.

I get dizzy.

The world suddenly goes gray.

I close my eyes for a moment.

In darkness, I hear the word softly spoken to me, "*Breath.*"

I open my eyes, gasping for air.

I'm lying on the side of the road.

I look down at chest, my shirt, but I can't find any blood.

Two men are looming over my body.

One of them is the same truck driver as before. Another man is a pedestrian who has pulled his car over on the side of the road to check on my condition.

I turn toward Mina, who's lying next to me.

She's gone, but I'm not.

I'm here.

I'm alive.

The truck driver helps me to my feet.

I look around, disorientated at first.

I look down at my hand again.

This can't be happening!

The sound of police sirens gradually builds behind me. . .

I rush to the pedestrian's electric car.

The engine starts as soon as I enter the car.

Instead of turning around and driving away from the police sirens, I drive back to Tokyo.

Two cop cars are blocking the road.

Three officers are standing behind the cars, aiming guns at me.

I don't slow down.

I don't stop.

Can't stop.

Won't stop.

*Never* stop.

3 . 2 . 0 / ?

I so want the week to be over already, and yet the week hasn't even started. If I hear anyone ask me if I have the case of the Mondays or even bring up the day as a comparison to my behavior or demeanor, then I'm going to snap.

After spending days being grilled by FBI agents and going through extensive tests, including these psychological evaluations and scans of my head, I'm supposedly cleared to go back to my daily life. For all I know, I'm still on their watch list. I mean, I could be on their naughty list—honestly, I don't see why I wouldn't be on it, especially after everything that happened. So, I can go ahead and start planning my getaway to Canada in the near future. For now, though, I want to crawl in a dark hole and never see anybody else ever again. Just me going through all of my answers. I basically ran with the same exact story that I told my parents. The FBI agents bought it—I think. I don't have to worry about surveillance cameras putting me in the vicinity of a pretty sizeable explosion or what they're now calling "a mechanical malfunction." The public bought the story. Man, did they buy it? The one fallback was that it caused a majority of the public to distrust the government even more, which is baffling since they work for us, not the other way around. Fortunately, though, there weren't too many casualties—not enough to make headlines for an entire week. If it weren't for the mountains shielding the blast—the radius, according to the news reports, was about roughly five miles (if you do the math that's about nearly half the size of Burbane)—and if nearby towns didn't evacuated as quickly as they did, then there would've been a way higher death rate. No surprise that the Internet was having a field day with what happened at Four Lakes. People have tried to sneak into the restricted site. From what I've seen on the news, the military has set a perimeter of the radius of five miles around the blast site. Finger waggers—or whistleblowers or whatever you call them—and the wannabe journalists trolling the Internet have come out of their caves, trying to get a shot or a selfie or "hot" footage of the fallout. Each video that has been posted on the Internet has been immediately removed by watchdogs.

Who would've thought that I, a girl from the small town of Agatha, was in the middle of it all?

What can I say?

I've always been good at hiding in plain sight.

At nine o'clock tonight, Central Agatha is hosting a candlelight vigil for my missing teammates and coaches. Most people are aware of the statistic being thrown around the school, the ninety-nine percent chance that they're dead. Still, there are some who keep all of the cynics second-guessing if they're dead.

In other news, the hashtag, "Pray for Central Agatha," was started by none other than those two class clowns, Sebastian and Julia, to commemorate the members of the junior varsity lacrosse team—like those two imbeciles care about us? They haven't even spoken a word to me all year long; in fact, everyday I pass Sebastian on my way to Second Period class and he doesn't even acknowledge me. I don't want to attend the vigil tonight, but I don't want to draw any more unnecessary attention to myself. From what I heard, the varsity team is going to be there to show their support. I figure Elle and Donna will more than likely show up. They have absolutely no idea what we've all been through. A part of me is glad they were spared from the grief of the whole ordeal. So, I follow what my dad told me at breakfast, and just get it over with—like it's so easy, to just put all of this behind me. I guess the sooner I get back to my life the sooner I can forget about Four Lakes. That'd be easy, but the thing is, I can hardly remember what exactly happened.

Only fragments.

It reminds me of waking up after sleepwalking.

Acorn starts the morning announcements with a moment of silence for the JV lacrosse team.

One of the kids, Brandon, makes a sound of a baby crying in the back of the classroom, like a *bah* of a sheep, only with a w, not a b, and drawn out more for effect. The noise causes a couple of muffled laughs.

Red-faced, Mrs. Potts springs up from her chair and asks the classroom who made the noise, but nobody comes clean.

As Mrs. Potts sits back down, Brandon, who's seated behind Shauna, grabs her tit, causing her to laugh.

"Stop!" she whispers.

"Shauna," Mrs. Potts calls out.

"Sorry, Mrs. Potts."

"Show some respect please."

Shauna apologizes again.

Sorry? You? You're sorry? I don't think so, Shauna. Before class started, I overheard her telling Brandon about how "glad" she was after she heard about us.

"Good riddance" and "Do they have Stairmasters in hell?" were just some of the plethora of unkind comments Shauna used while talking about what happened at Four Lakes. She doesn't think anybody heard what she said—except for Brandon—but I heard every single word.

I get through the first part of the day without any problems. People have started to notice me more, which is unusual to say the least. Sebastian manages to throw a snooty horse nod and a long *ohhai* my way as I pass him. I know it's all for show, though. He thinks I don't remember what he did to me, but I do. I remember that one time I tripped and dropped all of my books on the floor and he kept on walking, he and all his pretentious theatre pals, who think their shit smells sweeter than everybody else's, frolicking right past me as if I was an obstacle. I know Sebastian's on the clock. To him, the red light of the camera is on, and he wants to make an impression. He makes sure other people see him when he makes his gesture toward me. He doesn't want to come off as an opportunist who takes advantage over other people's suffering.

Several students draw their eyes on Sebastian, then somehow, they start acknowledging me, as if I've suddenly transformed from a ghost to an actual person. My once translucent skin now visible to the naked eye.

I know people see what they only want to see. I can't help but wonder what they see in me when they look at me: a runaway, a misfit, a coward, an outsider, a loser, or a friend of Sebastian—and any friend of Sebastian is cool.

By the time noon arrives, I've lost my appetite. My stomach's in slip knots and it's like all of a sudden I've developed the symptoms of a fat person. I'm sweating a lot, mostly in areas that can't be seen. I'm panting. My chest is heavy. I feel lethargic.

I don't want to be here.

After lunch, I bump into Elle and she confirms that she's going to the vigil tonight. She says she's going to talk Donna into going with her. Like me, she doesn't want to go either but it'll look bad if we don't go.

At night, I put on something different for the vigil. The same black car that's been stalking me all day long follows me to the vigil. I can see two men inside. Both of them are wearing black suits. They got FBI written all over them. I'm sure they were ordered to keep an eye on me for a while, make sure I behave like a good girl and do what I'm supposed to do—that sort of thing.

I'll play the part.

For now.

They're having the vigil in Central Agatha's courtyard. Each one of my classmates, as well as their families and friends—basically, nearly the entire town of Agatha—shows up at the vigil, loaded with their candles and posters and flowers and printed out MyCircle pictures. Local as well as mainstream news channels have come as well. Reporters interviewing classmates. I try to disguise myself among the crowd but somehow one sprightly reporter manages to track me down.

Before I can blend into the crowd, the reporter is shoving a microphone in my face and asking me questions about my teammates. She wants me to express my feelings in front of the millions and millions of people watching. I'm like a dumb animal caught licking its ass. She keeps asking me questions. I compose myself and say whatever they want to hear: "They will be missed." I say some other boring stuff, but by the time I make it to the candles, I don't remember what I said.

I answer each one of the reporter's annoying little questions with short bursts, hoping my lack of thoroughness will send her far away. It works. Nobody wants to watch a lame girl struggling to find the words. People want excitement and violence.

I mimic the other grievers and check my phone.

What do you know? A new hashtag is trending over social media: #RIPBLACKBEARS.

Police haven't exactly confirmed that the members of the junior varsity lacrosse team are dead, and yet the Internet has already labeled them dead. I mean Akea has gone days without a single chirp or MyCircle post. So, clearly, she must be dead, right?

Even if we were dead, how in the world are we supposed to "rest in peace" when you have people—as in all these posters and commenters plugged into the Internet world—keep talking about us. Chirping R.I.P. isn't a way of paying one's respects. It undermines the foundation of humanity. It's man filtered through the machine. It's artificial. Stale. Lazy. It's not the least sincere. RIP? What does that even mean now? For one to rest in peace? Has the Internet taken away that luxury? I mean, if you really want to pay your respects to the dead, here's a way: Leave them the hell alone! They're dead!

And Sebastian Abernathy: what a freaking joke? The same goes for that witch, Shauna Egger, and her little puppy she drags around with her, Go-Blow-Yourself Brandon—GBYB for short. I can't believe they've shown up to the vigil. Apparently, it was Brandon's idea to come. Deep down inside I know he still feels some sort of regret for what he did to me, but one could never tell by the way he acts in front of people.

He's goofing off again, making rude comments like "Why is everybody so quiet?"

I swear some people don't even have a bone of compassion in them. Some people just don't get it. Brandon and Shauna have no right being here, especially Shauna. Shauna couldn't stand my ass when I was alive. So, why in the hell would she care about me in death? It's as if she's here to celebrate our deaths, like it's one big, happy party! It makes me so mad! I just want to explode—

"—Judith," some freshman kid standing next to me is calling out my name.

I turn to the kid. It's Kevin and he's looking down at my arm. He looks worried. It's not until I follow his eyes that I realize my elbow has popped out of joint. A momentary wave of panic rushes through my body, causing me to freak out for a second. Relief settles in once I straighten out my arm.

He looks disgusted. He should be.

"You okay?" Kevin says, dragging from a cigarette. "Your arm. . . "

I just want to put out that cigarette on his eyeball.

"Judith—"

"Why can't you just leave me alone, *Kevin*?" I say. "I wish everyone would just leave me alone."

I push the kid aside and leave the vigil, even angrier than before I showed up.

I don't belong here.

Days start to blur into one another. It snows one day. We get about seven inches, give or take. It's total panic since most of the nearby stores had already cleared out after what happened in Benjamin Creek; and then, after Four Lakes, a lot of people thought the end of the world was near. I guess most people had to make due with only milk and white bread. We end up missing three days of school. Months pass. I get lost in the routine of doing absolutely nothing. I feel as if I'm retired—but retired from what?

It's not until one afternoon I wake up wandering through a field of daisies with thousands of monarch butterflies flying around me that I realize what happened back at Four Lakes.

The very next morning, the idea hits me out of the blue while I'm eating cereal and watching the cartoon, *Tiger-nauts.* The rustling sound of my dad turning the pages of the daily newspaper—that unavoidable background noise. I swear my dad is the last person on earth who still reads the paper. Maybe there are others out there like my dad, clinging to old pastimes. People like my dad is the reason newspapers still exist—he even gives *The Herald* contributions, like that one guy from the paper who's always asking for money to save print. But when all of the dads from this time period go away, what will happen to the newspaper? Will it just exist in the digital realm? Why would anyone get his or her news from the Internet when all of it is simply phony and consumed by false narratives? There might be some facts on there, but really, most of it is just bullshit or rumors, word of mouth. Nobody takes the Internet seriously. I mean, seriously?

After my dad's finished with the paper, I dig it out from the basket next to the couch and take it to my room before school starts. I flip to the OBITUARY section in the back and look over the names of people who just died. It could work. After all, who's going to be looking for someone who's already dead?

I take a detour through the woods behind my neighborhood and walk through the cemetery before school starts. The realization that my plan may evidently *not* work comes over me like a cold breeze—I mean, I've thought of this sort of thing many times before. The person has to be someone who can't afford a proper burial. The family would have to have little to no money, no funeral home to put embalming fluid in the body. This idea won't work! I think people have to be embalmed before they can be put in the ground. It's the law, ain't it? I keep my mind open for other options.

It's like nothing ever happen. That fool, Sebastian, is back to ignoring me. I even combed my hair before First Period and put on some makeup, but he can't even bring himself to look at me. He's made a new friend. Diana's now a part of Sebastian's posse. She's had a complete makeover from top to bottom. She's rocking a new pixie cut. From now on, she wants to be known as Dylan. Sebastian never hung out with Dylan when he was a she. For all I know, Sebastian ignored Diana just as much as me. And now they're like butt buddies. I can never win. I'm back to being a nobody.

At lunch, another much better idea suddenly comes to me as I watch Brandon secretly hold his phone underneath the table and take photos of Shauna while she's eating lunch directly across from him. He starts texting someone; then, seconds later, three of his friends seated next to him at the same table brandish their phones from their pockets, look down at their phones, and bust out laughing. I don't feel the least amount of sympathy for Shauna for the entire Internet now knowing what color underwear she's wearing underneath her skirt. I mean, it's Brandon. Why is she even sitting at the same table as him? She's sitting just two feet away from him, and yet she doesn't have a clue as to what he's doing to her or what effect it'll have on her in the future. Did he do those kinds of things to me when we were together? How many other photos of me does he have stored in that phone of his?

Of all people, I should know that whatever's posted on the Internet stays on the Internet. Even if you make your most desperate attempt to erase it from existence, it's there like a mustard stain that will never go away.

It's there.

Forever.

After Brandon's finished eating, I follow him to the trashcan where he dumps his bag full of scraps as well as his coke can in the trash.

I follow right behind him. I dump my trash as well.

As he turns around and walks the other way, I reach down in the trashcan and pull out Brandon's trash and stuff it in my bookbag while nobody's looking.

Acquire Brandon's DNA. Check. Next are the internal workings of Brandon's phone. I wait for my moment as he's strolling to Third Period. He's so busy texting that he doesn't even know where he's going. What a fool? I bump into him, making sure to concentrate most of the impact on the same hand that he's texting.

He stumbles backward as the phone drops to the floor.

"Watch where you're going!" shouts Brandon as he frantically searches for his phone that's already in my hand.

"Sorry," I say as I hold out his phone.

He snatches the phone away from my hand and looks for any scratch marks. He doesn't say anything to me, and I don't expect him to say anything either, only underneath his voice when he walks away. He's got no spine.

"Nice shoes," I say before he turns the other way and point at the pair of black and red high-tops.

He shakes his head and keeps on walking and texting at the same time.

It's like stealing candy from an ant.

Since the sub covering for Mr. Mebane, Mrs. Whatever, let us out super early, I have ten minutes to kill before heading to Fourth Period. So, I stop by the library and grab a computer in the back. A couple of students are scrambling to complete last-minute homework by sharing answers and so forth—it's rather pathetic. So, I don't have to worry about them paying any attention to me. Which works out in my favor. One of the few great features of being a ghost at school; however, the drawbacks outweigh the rewards. I pull up Brandon's PhotoBag page and scroll through his most recent posts. I'm surprised that he hasn't posted the photo that he took in the lunchroom—that one photo of Shauna Egger: Previously on, "What Shauna's wearing underneath her skirt?"—but I'm sure he's working his way to it, possibly adding a filter or effects from one of his many photo apps or even coming up with a MIME with captions like "It's getting hot in *here*—here spelled her" or something perverted like that. I scroll through dozens of photos until I come across this shaky video taken last Friday night. In the video, Brandon takes a massive hit from a blunt and holds the smoke in his cheeks, both ballooned outward like a puffer fish. He puts his lips against the empty chamber of a handgun and blows a mouthful of smoke through the end of the barrel. One of his friends—Jamal, I think it is—sucks in the smoke with a deep inhale, then, seconds later, causing him to violently cough. Others are laughing at his reaction. I lean close to the computer's speaker and hear the sound of a horn in the background. The video shakes as Brandon pulls the phone away from his face. The dimly lit room gradually comes into light. Before the video stops, I get a closer look at the surroundings, the interior, walls covered in slabs of wood. The walls appear to have no dry wall. It appears as if they're hanging out inside the room of an unfinished house. I put on a pair of greasy headphones and watch the video again. I listen closer to that horn in the background and I realize it's a train. I read comments beside the video.

One commenter, SQUIRRELLYCAT4EVER, posts a comment: "Chilling at the house."

I scroll through other photos, more photos with Brandon and his friends hanging out at this so-called "house."

It's almost as if they're rubbing it in people's face.

It's like an invitation, really.

The stage is set. The house. Which happens to be one of the houses from a new development, Hawk's Ridge, which is right next to the train tracks that run through the heart of Agatha. So far, there are only a handful of houses that have already been built. Five houses are currently in development. Three already have frames. Two are enclosed. One looks as if the builder ran out of money halfway through building the house. It's pretty easy to find "the house." All I have to do is follow the beer cans and cigarette butts.

Next day at school I ask Brandon what size shoe he wears. He shrugs me off and tells me to get lost and then he follows with the name, Darky. My name's Judith, I want to tell him, but I stay in character—I kind of like that name, Darky; nobody's ever called me that name before. I tell Brandon that I want to get Abe a pair of shoes for his birthday but I don't want to get caught rummaging through his shoes. He looks as if he wears the same size as you. Brandon rolls his eyes and looks at me as if I'm nuts. He thinks I'm joking or there's a joke in admitting the size of his shoe to me. He's so insecure about himself that he can't even answer a simple question. He tells me to go in Abe's room whenever he's not there and find out for myself—I mean, duh! I tell Brandon that my brother is one of those people who never leaves his room. He's always guarding his stuff. This is, by far, the most Brandon and I have talked. I feel almost bad for what's about to happen to him in the next forty-eight hours. All Brandon has to do is remain insecure, expect an upcoming punch line, and continue to act like himself and ignore me as much as he adores me. Finally, Brandon caves in and tells me his shoe-size. He wears a size eight. Really? I thought it would be bigger, especially with a guy having a big mouth. You know what they say about guys with small feet. Or, is it small hands?

Shauna's shoe size is much easier to obtain. I wait until she's in gym class and sneak into her locker.

Turns out we both have the same shoe size.

Fun fact: I actually own the exact same pair. Her shoes are much newer, though, and the tread isn't as badly worn down as mine.

I grab a palmful of her hair from the comb in her purse just to make it sell.

After school, I track down Jamal's friend, a sophomore named Key. I ask Key if he can hook me up with some weed—only a dime. He knows a guy who knows a guy who can only sell an eighth. I only have two hundred dollars to my name and all of it has been the leftover savings from the past three birthdays—twenty from the aunt, twenty here and there from other relatives and fifty or so from the parents every year, depends on my behavior or grades that year. If all of my math is correct, both Brandon and Shauna's shoes combine will cost exactly a hundred and eighty-seventy dollars—Shauna's shoes costing the most. I end up grabbing a twenty from my mother while she's handling supper. All the leftover change will go to disposable shoe covers, which should only cost a couple of dollars, and a box of painter's plastic that I'll buy a the home improvement store.

Before I do all of my shopping, I meet up with Key's dealer, L.J. The transaction goes smoothly. I still can't believe how easy it is to buy drugs around here. It's like paying for gas.

Later that afternoon, I stop at the shoe store, Hot Kicks, and a skinny pale kid sells me two pairs of shoes, one for "Abe," and another pair for myself. The name on the kid's nametag reads Joshua, but he goes by Josh. I introduce myself to him. I give him my last name that way he'll give me his. Josh's incredibly shy and somewhat reserved, but I squeeze a last name out of him. We talk about his part-time job for a while, what it's like touching people's feet all day long. He works till closing, but he says it's not too bad of a job. He's saving up money on the side for a brand new car. He doesn't own a car. Apparently, Josh lives within walking distance. He recently moved here from Spartacus. I later look up Joshua Lamb on the Internet and come across his social media pages. He only has a handful of followers and most of them look like spambots.

Lastly, I check Josh's active PhotoBag page where he posts more personal photos of himself. What he's currently reading. He appears to be into graphic novels or comic books—I can't tell which is which these days. In the last year, he has traveled overseas. He takes a lot of his photos from the inside of trains. The bullet train in China. A rickety train in India. He posts photos of the different people he's met in his travels. Mountainous landscapes. Ancient temples and ruined cities. Sunsets. Photos of indigenous street food, charred meat on a stick, crickets and snails and all sorts of crispy bugs. It appears as if he does most of his traveling alone. He's perfect.

I wait until both of my parents are asleep before doing a test run. I stop at the house. Good thing Brandon or any of his friends aren't getting stoned inside, otherwise all of this planning would've been for nothing. They've left a trail, though. DNA everywhere. I put on disposable shoe covers and plastic gloves and clean up the best I can.

Tomorrow, I plan my getaway.

I spend the next day planning my every move. I make color-coded stickies of each task. Yellow stickies are cautious tasks: making sure they're no cameras near Hot Kicks; then stealing Abe's car keys while he's playing video games; making sure to line the trunk with painter's plastic—this one is the most important part. If a single drop of blood should somehow wind up inside the trunk, then the whole thing is a bust. The green stickies represent future tasks: go about Josh's daily schedule, if it really comes down to that, so simply enough, don't draw any unwanted attention to myself; and finally, use that hard-earned money that Josh has been saving up to buy one ticket to Tokyo, Japan. The red sticky: Make sure to steal my dad's gun.

My mother's usually out by nine, but she doesn't crash until thirty minutes after. Hot Kicks closes at ten. I'm pushing my luck if I'm not on the road by fifteen till and the thought of aborting crosses my mind several times. Everything is already set. I run into the risk of Brandon and his sicko friends showing up at the house tomorrow night. Tonight *is* the night.

I decide to go ahead with the plan. I sneak into my parents' bedroom before I gather everything that I need for tonight. I start with the red sticky and grab the Beretta from my dad's closet. My mother stirs in the bed as I'm closing the lockbox. She's been known to wake up in the middle of the night. The wine usually knocks my mother out as soon as she hits the recliner; but, every now and then, she'll wake up once the wine has worn off and lie in bed and watch crime shows until the sun rises. No need to worry about my dad. He's out of it downstairs. Even an elephant couldn't wake him. I give my dad a poke on the shoulder just to be sure. He mumbles something in his sleep, then he gets back to snoring over the sounds of his nightly Westerns. Tonight's choice: *A Fistful of Dollars.* Seems like everything he watches on TV stars Clint Eastwood or someone who looks just like Clint Eastwood.

I head back to my room and grab the weed, then the cigar and sock that I grabbed earlier from Abe's sock drawer. I find a spare to his car, so I don't have to worry about picking the car keys from his pockets while he's slaying zombie overlords. If only my parents knew how *bad* he can really be. He's great at disguising himself. Whenever he goes out, he always takes a bottle of cologne and Visine. If only my parents knew the truth about their own son.

I grab the curling iron from my bathroom—it's the closest thing I own that resembles a you-know-what. I place it inside the side pouch of my bookbag.

Lastly, I grab the last two things from the kitchen: a knife and a couple of zip ties. The zip ties just in case Josh decides to try something on me before the show begins.

I arrive at Hot Kicks as soon as they're about to close. I park in a shadowy area several feet from his route; I keep my head down; and through the corner of my eye, I watch him messing around the shoe store—putting back boxes of shoes, arranging the shoes on display cases, sweeping the floors—before he finally says his goodbyes to a co-worker. I take out the skeleton mask that I wore trick or treatin' on a Halloween when I was around nine years old. I can't believe it still fits. I remember all the other girls dressed up as witches or fairies or princesses that year and I went as something scary. Imagine that: an innocent little girl wearing the scariest and most demonic and hideous mask—sunken eyes sockets, pointy cheek bones—and my oily ponytail hanging out the back of the rubbery mask. I even made a piece of what was supposed to be human flesh from scratch. I cut off a strip of raw chuck steak from the fridge and implant strands of my own hair inside the steak with a needle, then dowse the steak with red floor coloring and corn syrup and chewed on it from the corner of my mouth all night long. Too much? Probably so, now that I look back at how I was, but it really freaked the kids out, even some of the parents.

I duck in the bushes and wait for Josh to round the corner of the strip mall. Sure enough, he falls for the bait I planted underneath the floodlight. He stops, takes a knee as if he's in a huddle, and picks up the graphic novel from the sidewalk.

Before he stands upright, I creep up behind him and pistol-whip him in the back of the head.

Just like in all those DIY videos I watched, I aim right for the top of the neck. The blow has to be at the right spot; otherwise it can result in paralysis or even worse, death.

Josh staggers forward, throwing out his arm. He attempts to reach around, but his arm goes weightless.

Once he blacks out, I quickly check the back of his head. I run my gloved fingers across the red spot on the back of his head. I pull my fingers away. No blood, only a knot about the size of a gumball. He'll live.

---

I can't imagine what was going through Josh's mind when his eyes rolled back, the doubling image of Death Himself standing over him.

---

After a short yet nerve-racking drive, I arrive at the house in Hawk's Ridge without hearing a single peep from Josh.

Before I tend to Josh, I stage the room to make it look like Brandon and Shauna were both here together and of course, it wouldn't be a party without the main star of the film, yours truly. First, I start by taking the new shoes that I bought at Hot Kicks and cover the bottom of each shoe with a layer of mud. I put on "Brandon's shoes" first and walk up the stairs. I map out the struggle, lots of skid marks—basically, pretending I'm wrestling around with another person even though it's just me. I look so silly, but it's all for special effects.

I walk back downstairs and do the same with the other pair of shoes, "Shauna's shoes." I feel almost bad for getting them all dirty. I walk up the stairs. I mostly hang around the area of the soon-to-be murder. Shauna doesn't get her hands dirty per se, but I do put her at the scene of the crime.

Next, I remove the shoes, stick them in my bookbag, and put on the disposable shoe covers yet again—good thing that I brought an entire box.

Then, I pull out the lunch bag from my bookbag of props and crumble the Ziploc bag speckled with tiny globs of peanut butter and grape jelly and place it on the floor. I remove the semi-crushed coke can with Brandon's greasy fingerprints and place it on the floor, as well.

Lastly, I pull out the handful of Shauna's hair that I collected from her comb the other day and randomly scatter several strands of hair around the scene. I wedge one hair underneath the splinter of a piece of warped plywood.

I light up a blunt with the fireplace lighter and take a couple of hits before I grab Josh from the trunk. I'll take two hits and I'm already feeling pretty buzzed. I blow a couple of hits through the barrel of my dad's Berretta. The weed will help lessen the soon-to-be pain. I'm also guessing that the forensic people can tell whether or not the gun was used as paraphernalia to get stoned before it was fired. I'm guessing that these overly schooled investigators have all sorts of neat ways of collecting evidence. I'm guessing.

Once every piece of evidence is in its proper place, I check on Josh downstairs. I put on my mask. I don't want him to see my face because after I swap bodies, I want Josh's mind to be free and open. If he sees my face, it could possibly affect the way he handles the situation. So, I remain in character. I put on my death stare, gun ready. I open the trunk, only to find Josh wide-awake. His eyes are jacked open as if he just got an electrical shock. He has red marks along his wrist from where he possibly tried to free himself. I check the wound yet again. He squirms and pulls his head away from me. I pull back on the hammer of the Berretta. Place the barrel just inches away from his forehead. Show him I'm not playing around.

"Make a sound and you're dead," I tell him. "Nod if you understand."

He can barely bring himself to nod.

I run my fingers across the backside of his head.

I feel the same knot, a little bigger and rounder than before, but no blood. I put away the superglue, then remove his shoes, and stick them both in a plastic grocery bag. Then, I slip on disposable shoe covers over his socks.

I tell Josh to get out of the trunk, slowly.

He follows my demands and makes his way into the house.

After I zip tie Josh's already tied wrists to the 2 x 4 running vertically from the floor to the ceiling, I slide the pair of plastic gloves in his pockets.

"Why are you doing this to me—"

"—What'd I tell you about making a sound?"

"Please," he pleads. "Whatever it is you're about to do, please don't do it."

"I wish it were that easy."

I stand behind Josh so that he can't see my face. I remove the mask and place it over his face, the holes for the eyes facing the other way so he can't see what's about to happen next. I don't want him to see the horror.

"Please don't," he says frantically.

"Shut up," I tell him.

He shuts up.

I promised myself that I wouldn't give any speeches or put any unwanted ideas in his head before I killed myself.

Soon, his head will be my head. I will know every single thought racing inside his head.

I peel back the mask to his nose so he can breathe. I cram Abe's sock into his mouth and tape his mouth shut.

Finally, I stick the edge of the knife into the plywood next to him—loose enough for him to wiggle the blade free when the time comes. After Judith is dead, I'll eventually find the knife next to my leg, then I'll be able to cut my way through the zip ties.

I don't want it to happen this way—I really don't—but it's the only way. It certainly isn't the prettiest way to go out, but that's life. Life isn't a fairy tale like your mother read to you when you were a child—that I've learned. Those who tell you differently haven't been living in the real world. I have to do what I have to do in order to survive because life is violent, physically, emotionally—and it certainly isn't the most pleasant way for someone to go out either, but who does anyway. Everybody dies. It's a fact. It's, by far, the only fact we know to be true. The body dies. It's nature. The body gets old. It withers. It fades. Then, eventually, it dies. Nobody goes out peacefully or the way they want. They don't get to pick how they die. Those who do are the lucky ones. Sure, Judith's parents will be upset. The few people who knew her or talked to her or gave her the time to listen to her will miss her. I'm not so sure if her mother will ever get over her death. Alcohol has a way of momentarily covering up old wounds, but in the end, there's only so much it can do before it starts to destroy a person. Abe will go about his life like he always does. He's strong. I know his sister's death will make him a much brighter and stronger individual. Her dad will be okay. He'll have to do some explaining as to how his registered firearm ended up at the scene of a crime; but once investigators collect all the evidence, his name will be cleared. He's a fighter like all of those rugged cardboard cowboys in those movies he watches. He'll carry on, as he's been doing. One day, when all of this has passed, he will ride off into that red sunset with a pure heart. Last but certainly not least, Brandon Eugene but certainly not least, Brandon Eugene Milton, a young man who had his entire future ahead of him, and his partner in crime, Shauna Egger, a Queen of all royal bitches, may or may not be convicted with the rape and murder of Judith Ilderton. So far, the evidence is persuasive enough for a conviction, but I guess that will be in the hands of a jury. More than likely, they'll go to jail for who knows how long. If the system does its job as it's supposed to do, all of this will be a simple reminder for them to think twice before insulting an individual who may be different from them.

No matter what, this life will rage on and continue to create and destroy.

As for me, I have another journey that awaits me.

Another story.

One life ends.

Another begins.

Ringing in my ears. I wake up with a massive erection in my pants. Something about the smell of gunpowder makes me as hard as a jackhammer—*Is that a movie quote?*

I try to move from my seated position, but my hands have been tied together.

Out of desperation, I bend back my right hand and come across an object in the floor. I feel the handle along my skin, the steel, the sharpness of the blade. It takes me a couple of minutes to figure out what has happened, but once everything falls into place, I understand what I have to do.

I rub the zip ties along the sharpness of the knife until I'm no longer stationary. I do the same with the other zip ties and cut through the zip ties until both of my hands are free. I remove the mask from my face, then the sock from my mouth.

A young woman—maybe sixteen years old—is lying on the floor feet away from me. Her blue jeans are wrapped around her ankles. She's not moving. She doesn't appear as if she's breathing. The first thing that comes through my mind is that she's drunk. Possibly had one way too many. She was popping a squat, as most teenagers tend to do whenever there's not a toilet nearby, then she passed out. The side of her face is familiar. I think I knew her or know her or at least maybe did so in another life. The dream is as hazy as a dream after you wake up, but the fragments of something terrible happening still remain relevant. I remember. *This girl.* She was in my dreams. Crying. She was about to do something to herself, something that was going to be talked about for days or even weeks. Next thing I heard was groaning.

I stand to my feet. The world starts shaking.

A sudden rush of blood causes me to stagger, but I manage to stand without falling over.

I touch the backside of my head and run my fingers over a knot and it's like this button of pain. I must've fallen.

I ignore my pain and call out to the young woman to see if she's awake but she's not responding to my voice. She's not doing anything. I conclude, as I take two steps closer, she's dead. The gun on floor is still smoking. A curling iron to the left of the body isn't plugged in or anything, but it appears as if it was used for something. It's just there. Which is strange. Her underwear is down by her ankles, as well. Parts of inner thighs appear spotty-red. I examine the body. She was shot in the chest. A puddle of blood has already formed underneath her body. A stream of blood bubbles from the corners of her mouth and nostrils. The sight of the body causes me to get sick. I try to hold it in but I can feel the vomit making its hasty climb. I grab the first thing I can find—a bookbag—and throw up into the bookbag.

Once I've pulled myself together, I get a better look at her face, the cuts and bruises, then all the strangle marks around her neck. I pick up the phone on the floor—Judith's phone. The name suddenly comes to me as soon as I slide open her phone. I know her. Her name is Judith Ilderton. She was a good person, although misunderstood. A lot of people went out of their way to judge her when they should've been taking a step back and looking at themselves in the mirror. I know what she wants me to do—or at least, wanted me to do.

I start taking pictures of her. All angles. She wanted me to capture what was done to her. The horror. The unspeakable crime. I pull up her messages and send the graphic pictures to both Brandon and Shauna's phone. But they won't get these. Not yet at least. They don't know, but the pictures will be hidden inside their phones with some racy comments to boot, mainly regarding Judith's current state.

I swipe my thumb across the screen of the phone.

The text messages appear on the screen:

Brandon to Judith: *Sup, Judy. Let's get together at 'the house' tonight.*
Judith responds to Brandon's text: *Sounds good. I'll bring my father's gun.*
Brandon to Judith: *Shauna said she was dying to tag along. Cool?*
Judith to Brandon: *Very cool.*

I put a yellow smiley face emoji at the end. That's what the kids are doing nowadays.

I wipe my prints from the phone and place it back on the floor.

As I'm about to leave, I realize that I'm missing the last important steps. I reach in my pocket and pull out a pair of plastic gloves. I put them on.

I grab the gun—the second *red* sticky, remember?

Let's say our two perps weren't born yesterday, and they still have a few brain cells swimming upstairs. If they were here, that'd be the first thing they'd grab: the gun used to kill Judith. The cops can't charge a suspect without finding the weapon used to kill the victim. I place the gun in my pocket. I pick up the curling iron from the floor and stuff it inside the nearly ruined bookbag.

Once I wrap up the frame job, I meticulously collect every little thing that would put me at the scene. There aren't many things, except for cut zip ties, the plastic lining in the trunk of Judith's brother's car, which can be thrown away in a dumpster down the street.

Now, the most crucial step: I pick up Judith's phone again and use Judith's finger to dial three numbers into the phone. I place the phone in her palm with the screen facing downward. That way her killer never noticed Judith had dialed the police while she was being attacked.

Finally, I grab the bag of shoes from the garage and I leave like I was there.

Agatha is a small enough town to get where you need to by just walking. The town would make a perfect hub for electric cars. The most driving you would do is maybe ten miles tops. Then, you're in the next town. I stop at Brandon's house before the sun rises. I clean every inch of the gun with my shirt, then plant the gun in an old flowerpot on the porch: I place it where Brandon would never find it; however, any average cop could find it if he or she looked hard enough.

The next day, I clear out all of the money in my savings account and buy a ticket to Tokyo, Japan. I manage to find a seat on a plane. It's a middle seat, but I'm not complaining. The flight leaves Charlotte at three o'clock in the afternoon.

So, I buy a train ticket and take the train to Charlotte. It's only a couple of hours, but I don't mind riding trains.

I love them, actually.

Right about now, the homicide department has sent their best man to the crime scene at Hawk's Ridge: a hotshot detective with a credible track record. Seasoned. Well respected. The type of detective who solves crimes in his sleep.

A talky man placing his carry-on in the storage bin above the seats starts complaining about the boarding process and the attitude the cute stewardess was showing him. He takes a seat next to me and lets out a lippy sigh of relief. I can smell the cheap beer on his breath. The gel in his hair. He retreats back into his phone.

The woman with the window seat to the left of me watches maintenance workers below on the airport apron. The laptop is sleeping on her lap. She appears deep in thought. I wonder what she's thinking about—family, friends, a lover?

When the detective arrives at Hawk's Ridge, the first thing he'll see is a gold Chevy Cavalier parked in the garage.

That's the first thing he'll see, the way it's parked, backed in—*Was she planning for a quick getaway?*

The detective will make his way into the house and follow the work lights, pass investigators hard at work, dusting fingerprints, marking and collecting each piece of evidence, taking pictures of shoeprints along the floor. He'll then make his way upstairs where he'll find a young woman named Judith Ilderton, not just another body to him but a new case. Soon, he'll come to know everything about Judith and learn that she was once a daughter, a sister, and a friend. She was a young woman who carried herself way beyond her years. The sight of Judith won't be easy. Never is for any detective. Each case is personal. Like his own child. This one is personal. If he has to, he'll walk the edge of the earth searching for Judith's killer, not because it's just his job, but because he's an instrument of justice. He'll mentally play out the scene in his head: the game—perhaps *Spin the Gun*, a new game that's grown in popularity among teenagers—was being played, night started out fun, two people involved, he'll conclude, getting high and then getting the munchies and somewhere in the purple haze something went terribly, *terribly* wrong, one of the two suspects forced his way onto Judith—there were two of them and each one was rough with her—one thing lead to another and before

Judith realized, she was being taken advantage of; she didn't like it; she was a fighter; it was in her blood; that was what she did, she fought, but a struggle occurred and Judith desperately tried her best to defend herself but the suspect or suspects were too much for her; then a glimmer of hope rose from the wet darkness as she gained control over a gun, she popped off three rounds but each one missed her target—one bullet in the framing of the wall, another one, the detective discovers, in the ceiling—then somewhere in the struggle, one of the suspects got the gun, shot Judith point blank in the chest. Later, when all the evidence is collected, the detective will wonder why Judith brought her father's gun to the house. He'll check Brandon's social media pages, see what Brandon's been up these days, what he's been posting or chirping—he'll come to find out that Brandon has done a very bad thing.

One question may arise: why did Brandon not bring his own gun?

Maybe his stepfather caught him with the gun, took it away from him, never gave it back. All the dedicated detective has to do is look through the text messages. He will. And when the detective does, he'll only have one question left for Brandon: Why Judith?

The woman next to me continues to stare out the window. The man, on the other hand, directs his attention toward me. He sharpens his eyes, studying me. He appears disturbingly interested in me, but I'm not the least turned off by the way he's looking at me. I'm—more or less—intrigued by how rattled he is by my presence.

"You okay over there, guy?" he asks.

He's got a slight New York accent. I can tell he was born with it, but spending time in the South had shaved off some of the edge.

"Yeah," I say shortly. I keep my answer to the point. "I'm ok," I say to the man.

He looks as if he's waiting for a more in-depth response. I cut through the silence and ask the man, "Are you okay?"

He's stunned by the remark, left without any words.

I glance at the woman sitting in the window seat to the left of me. She turns her ear toward me as if she's trying to get a better listen. I have an audience now.

"Yeah," the man answers with a spike in tone. "You know how it goes, you know with these second-rate services. You can never win, am I right?" The man looks me over and lets out another sigh. "So, where you headed?"

"Tokyo," I say.

Surprised by my response, his eyes widened.

"Really?"

"I have a layover in Dallas, then Los Angeles."

"Don't you hate that?" he asks but doesn't expect a response from me.

"And you?"

He pauses, then finally answers: "Dallas." He readjusts himself in the seat. "I swear every time I go I can't wait to leave."

With the back of his head pressed against the headrest, he asks me, "So, Tokyo, huh? Business or pleasure?"

"A little bit of both," I say.

Again, he's staring at me as if he's waiting for a more in-depth response, same with the woman sitting to the left, her chin curling upward, eyes narrowing. I leave both the man and the woman hanging in suspense by letting them figure out my story from the little details that I have shared. I let them fill in the gaps for themselves. I let them make up their own story about me.

www.ingramcontent.com/pod-product-compliance
Lightning Source LLC
Chambersburg PA
CBHW030929020726
47498CB00001B/169

*9780997645330*